Praises for *Tain...*

"A fantastic story...I love it! Just to make sure, I reread *Tainted Justice*... the ending is so satisfying. New kind of book...a must-read for thriller lovers"

-Whitney Miller

"I am finding your book very interesting. I keep turning the pages (scrolling down, in this case) because I want to know what is going to happen next... you have a winner!"

-Bonnie Heidema

"...good story about reality, the way the world is going."

-Maddie Wingett

"Great premise for a book...It reflects problems people are definitely talking and thinking about."

-Laura Austin

"The first chapter certainly did jolt me at the end! ...wonderful tension there, and had me hooked once I saw Brian put the revolver in his pocket. Very well done! ... promising a great story"

-Annemarie Kline

"Good story...engrossing...intriguing political manipulations...getting more involved with the story and liking it...lots of suspense"

-Shelley Dibble

"Very exciting. The author has captured the sense of depression and panic of the characters who face what they think of as economic extinction...The story is powerful."

-David Decarlo

Cover Design: Reza Mostmand

TAINTED JUSTICE

V. M. GOPAUL

UNITYWORKS

NEWMARKET, ON

Acknowledgement

I am profoundly indebted to my late uncle, Vinod Gungah, an English teacher and writer, who encouraged me to take English literature in high school. It became a dream for myself to one day write a novel. Four decades later, Carol Craig, an editor and coach, taught me how to write *Tainted Justice* from start to finish. I am grateful to Carol for making my dream come true.

A huge thanks to Mervin Ching, who as an ex-Law enforcement officer, gave me valuable insight into the working of this profession.

I am grateful to Gorav Malik for reading the manuscript and polishing it as he went over many times.

Profound thanks to Laura Linneman for her proofreading and editing work. She can be contacted at: laura.linneman@gmail.com

Many readers took the time to read the manuscript as it was being developed. I appreciated their feedback, which has made this book a better product. One of them is my wife, Gaye Gopaul, an avid thriller reader. In our house, hundreds of books are spread out everywhere--on shelves, floors and tables. Both of us love to read them.

TAINTED JUSTICE

Brian Baldwin flipped the channel on the remote as he anxiously listened for the call. For a brief moment, he watched his team, the New York Giants, as they scored. Then he turned his attention to the phone and the call he was expecting. Silence. No ringing. He went back to the remote control, once again nervously flipping through channels. Just then, the mailbox door slammed shut. In one quick motion, Brian lifted his legs from the coffee table and jumped to his feet.

When he poked his head out the front door, he dug his hand into the box to reach for the mail.

"Any good news?" asked the postman.

When Brian finished shifting through the envelopes, with head shaking, he said, "No. Damn. Nothing. How long will it take them to mail me a job offer?"

"Brian, I hope something good will happen soon."

The despair he felt inside sank even lower. An income was what he needed to fight off his creditors. Brian rocked back on his heels. "Better be soon. I am almost at the end of my road."

"Merry Christmas." The postman waved goodbye and continued his route, walking down the long walkway past the reindeer and snow angel.

Back inside the room, Brian turned his attention to a letter he received from the law office Hartman & Fried. He read it several times, each time focusing on the word "Foreclosure" at the top of the page and the date below. The tremor in his hand became more pronounced each time he read it. He dropped the letter on the table.

"How did this happen?" He wiped his moist face with his palm.

The thought of losing his 3500 square foot house with its gabled roof and gardens – a house he had worked years to earn – made his stomach roll.

He plopped down on the chair by the telephone. For a moment he stared at the floor, then dialed the bank manager's number. At the other end, the office assistant put him on hold. The earpiece played the theme song from *The Sting*. He felt stung all right. He was losing control of his life. His girlfriend walked out on him over an argument as silly as whether or not to buy milk. The limits had maxed out on all his credit cards. With two missed payments, loss of a job he loved, and a foreclosure letter in his hand, the knot in his stomach grew tighter.

The manager's voice interrupted his train of thought. For the next ten minutes Brian argued against the foreclosure. In the end, he accepted the manager's assessment of his bad credit rating, and the fact that he had run out of time to put his financial life in order. Brian hung up without saying good-bye.

He stared at the floor for several minutes, then stood. "Those bastards." Brian went to his bedroom, opened the drawer of the bedside table, pulled out his handgun, then left.

***

Jason McDeere entered Rose's Coffee Time and Rocky Delgado followed close behind him. As he expected for a typical mid-afternoon, few customers occupied the restaurant. With a nod to the waitress, Jason chose a corner where the closest customers were several tables away. Both he and Rocky plunged into the wooden chairs across from each other.

Noticing them, the waitress hurried over soon after delivering a check to one of her other customers. With a glowing smile she said, "Haven't seen you in a while. What kept you away? Coffee or my service?"

Jason attempted a faint smile. "Both are great. Just low in cash these days." At the beginning of December 2007, he had received notice his hours had been cut to part-time.

Back on the first of October 2007, Softek International, his employer, announced layoff of fifteen hundred jobs by the end of the year, shedding five hundred each month. The timing was well planned to ensure that each employee would provide the necessary knowledge transfer before leaving. Everyone knew management's dirty secret—jobs were being shipped overseas.

Even now, Jason was so angry he had trouble focusing on the menu.

He wished he could have quit on the day of the announcement. But his financial situation was bad, with no prospect of finding another job soon, so he'd stayed with only half the income. The company had wanted him to pass on the information he'd spent years learning so that someone else could take over his job. When he discovered how the CEO poured money into working vacations, catered lunches and limousines for those who were staying behind, he'd felt doubly betrayed. It was obvious the CEO was pampering those he needed while discarding the rest.

The waitress said, "Your company hasn't been good to its employees or us. My business is down."

Softek was the largest employer in the Oregon town of Corvallis where Jason and Rocky worked. "Hope our luck will change," said Jason as he pulled at his beard. He was sporting a two-week growth that hadn't quite filled in yet and it made him look like a mountain man--rebellious.

"What will it be? Coffee and cake?"

"Just coffee for me," replied Rocky.

Still trying to put on a brave face, Jason said, "Same here." After the waitress walked away, he leaned forward. "Where's Brian? Why isn't he here?" He pointed to an empty chair. "Usually he sat there during the morning coffee ritual."

"He said he felt sick," said Rocky.

"He has been using that as an excuse a lot lately." Jason tapped a finger on the tabletop. "It's been hard on him since he was let go. Depression is creeping in. He's got to pull out of it," Jason said, fear making his stomach sour.

With eyes pointing directly at his friend and eyebrows arched, Rocky said, "Situation is so unpredictable." A sheet of concern shadowed his face.

"Rocky, I worry about Brian. He's too withdrawn."

Rocky took a sip of water. "It's difficult loosing a job. Each of us is handling it differently. He'll be fine." Rocky's job had been spared the axe. He was indispensable as the team leader with the most experience. He would be the liaison between the local office and that in Mumbai, India.

"Look, Rocky," Jason said, spreading his hands palms up on the table, "Brian helped me a lot when I joined Softek. I owe him big time."

"He's looking for a job. I hear he has a prospect in California."

Jason looked around at glum faces of some of his coworkers and leaned in further. "Brian just lost his girlfriend. That's also weighing on him."

Jason couldn't help but reflect just for a moment on the friendship between him and Rocky. In 1974, almost thirty-four years ago, Jason's father, Fred, was locked up in a Salem jail, and one month into incarceration, he was found dead in his cell of an apparent cardiac arrest. Jason was too young to fully grasp the reasons for his father's punishment, but one thing became crystal clear-—everyone hated him for his father's accusation of murder. The Corvallis rumor mill spewed gossip about his parents, his older brother and even Jason. Quickly, every friend and neighbor, except Brian and Rocky, discarded his family like rotten tomatoes. Rocky stuck with Jason and defended him whenever attacks were hurled at him. His poor mom. The memory caused a chill to run through him.

The waitress approached their table, placed two coffees and two slices of freshly baked blueberry pie in front of them. "It's on the house."

Jason managed a weak smile. "It's been a while since someone has been so nice to me. You're a sweetheart."

Rocky looked down at the food with hungry eyes and bit into the pie with melting ice cream on top. "Brian is tough. He can handle it," he said through a mouthful of ice cream. After swallowing, he looked Jason in the eyes and asked, "How are you doing?"

Usually Jason presented a brave face to the world, then when he was alone retreated into his cave and wrestled with his problems until resolved. This time it was different. He felt as though he'd fallen into a deep hole and needed to tell his story. "I shouldn't have taken this job." He caressed the cup. "At the interview, they lured with promise of job security." He blew air. "A farce. I must admit working and living in Corvallis was enticing. Now, my future looks bleak. On top of all my problems, the value of my house went down by thirty percent. Thanks to this sub-prime mortgage and real estate crisis." He shook his head and looked out the window. "Last August when the market tanked I sold my shipping company stock at a loss." With tight lips, he said, "I panicked." Telling his story to someone felt like he was able to release the pressure from inside.

Rocky looked around as though embarrassed by Jason's outburst. "You look as depressed as Brian. You have to snap out of it." Leaning forward, he consoled Jason, saying, "Be positive. At least you've got your health. You can find another job." Then louder, as though trying to impart confidence, he added, "With your credentials, you could get out of this town and get a job easily. I'm sure of it."

Still looking out the window, Jason said, "Yeah, I guess."

"You look tired. You need sleep."

"It's hard to sleep. All these thoughts keep churning in my head. What Softek is doing to us is wrong." He took another sip of his coffee.

"Welcome to America. People get hired and fired all the time."

"It's the *way* they're doing it that doesn't seem right to me." Jason's voice rose high enough to attract the attention from the customer sitting the closest him.

Rocky waved his hand at Jason to lower his voice. "Cool down. You're getting hot for nothing." Rocky smoothed his thick, salt-white hair with his palm.

Jason carved a small piece of the pie and whispered so that only Rocky could hear. "They have to pay." After washing the food down with another sip, Jason continued. "I had a very good job with Microsoft. I should have never quit and gone to Softek. Now, after the company secured a government contract, it's shipping all the jobs overseas. It's not fair."

"They haven't broken any law."

He paused for a moment, calculating a response. "I don't buy that. I can sue them." His voice rose again.

Rocky dropped his fork. "You're crazy. What will you sue them for? First you would need a lawyer, and you know how much they charge."

"Look, hundreds people are in our situation. And it's hard to find a decent job in this area to support a family. These days a person's lucky to find something in fast food." Jason paused for a moment then snapped his fingers. "Class-action suit. That's what we need."

***

Brian Baldwin entered the main office of Softek where he had worked for the last three years. He marched past two security guards who were always talking to each other, but their hawkish eyes constantly scanned people going and coming from the office. Brian pressed the security pass at the scanner and a light on it changed from red to green. *It still works.* In a half circular motion he passed through the metal turnstile just wide enough for a person's body to pass through. Palms sweating, he took the elevator to the twelfth floor where the office of Clint Whitney, the chief information officer, was located. After finding an empty office, he asked Gail Crawford, the executive assistant, "Where's Clint?"

"Do you have an appointment with Mr. Whitney?" Gail calmly inquired.

"No. I want to talk to him. Right away."

"Is there anything I can do?"

"No. Where is he? I want to see him *now*!"

Gail clicked the mouse a couple of times, peeked at the computer screen and said, "He's not in the office. It's his lunch hour. Nothing is booked." ˎ

"Where is he?" Brian asked with deadly composure. "Call him."

Gail first scanned Brian's face, then the light jacket he was wearing. "What's your name?" she asked.

"Brian Baldwin."

She used her best secretary's voice. "Brian, it looks like you're angry about something. Can we talk in the room over there?"

"Damn right I'm angry," he said, fighting back the logjam of emotion in his throat. "I'm losing everything, including my job."

"You'll find a new job. Hopefully, soon."

"No, I'll find *him*." Brian walked away.

Behind him, Brian could hear Gail call Clint's cell phone and leave a message. Then she called security.

Worried now, Brian rushed to the elevator, pressed the button and waited, tapping the travertine with his toe. When the doors opened, much to Brian's surprise, Clint Whitney appeared. "I want to talk to you," Brian said.

Looking at his watch, Clint said, "Now's not a good time. Make an appointment with Gail."

His former boss pushed past him, but as he did, Brian pulled his handgun from his waistband. "Let's go in that room." He waved the gun, shoving Clint into the conference room. Then he closed the door and said, "Sit down."

Clint in normal circumstances appeared immaculately dressed, not a hair out of place. Now he seemed to have lost his composure. His jet black hair was ruffled from running a hand through it. Fear gripped his face. "Don't do anything you'll regret. What do you want?"

"You've shipped fifteen hundred jobs overseas. Who do you think you are? Do you know what you're doing?" Brian pointed the gun to Clint's chest and cocked the trigger.

Still standing, the man tried to speak, but Brian was tired of talking, tired of lies. In one smooth move, he pulled the trigger. With a loud bang, the man hurled back and fell to the floor. Then he mumbled few words between gasps. Blood oozed out of open wounds in the chest. Brian ignored the ringing in his ear caused by the blast and rushed out to the door, without stopping to check on him what had happened.

After closing the door behind him, he descended the stairs. Arriving on the ground floor, he tried to push open the exit door but it was locked. From one end of the corridor, he spotted guards talking to two police officers, but they hadn't seen him. Not yet. Careful not to move too quickly and risk notice, he turned around and walked to a closed door. He opened the door, turned off the light, walked past the mop and hid himself behind a trolley loaded with cleaning solutions, toilet paper and rags.

Brian heard heavy footsteps pass by in the hallway next to the janitor's room where he was hiding. He held his breath, feeling trapped. He dug his cell phone out of his pocket and sent a text message to Jason. *S.O.S.*

***

Later that day at 4:25 Jason McDeere passed through the front door of the building where he was about to have a consultation with a class-action attorney, an appointment shortly made after seeing Rocky earlier.

The elevator doors opened to an elegant reception area. Jason looked at the receptionist sitting at a desk next to a wall with a big gold-plated sign that said Lambert, Johnson & McQuire. "I'm here to see Mr. Johnson," he said.

She checked the appointment book. "It's Mrs. Johnson. Please have a seat. Can I get you coffee, tea or soda?"

He shook his head then sat in a wing chair next to a table with a variety of magazines stacked atop it. He felt as though he were going for a job interview, where he would have to convince someone to hire him. Would he succeed in convincing the lawyer to take this class-action suit? He peered around the lobby. A vase filled with fresh flowers stood on a semicircle table behind him. Under his feet, a Persian carpet glowed with rich colors. The law firm must be successful at what it did to afford a luxurious office and a gorgeous receptionist. A blurb on the firm's website flattered itself of going after the National Bank in a teller's case and negotiated a handsome settlement.

When he booked this appointment, he queried about the cost and was assured that the first half was complimentary for new clients. The clicking of high heels on the floor tiles disturbed his train of thought.

"My name is Irva Johnson." The lawyer extended her hand. "Mr. McDeere, pleased to meet you."

"The pleasure is all mine," he replied. He quickly sized her up. She looked elegant in the navy jacket. A sassy blonde. He had to admit she had a distinguished appearance.

They both went to a conference room with a long table surrounded by comfortable chairs and a bookshelf spanning a whole wall. Other walls were graced with rare, expensive paintings.

They sank into chairs opposite each other. Then Jason placed a folder on the table and said, "Mrs. Johnson, you've heard that Softek is laying off fifteen hundred employees?"

"Yes, I have," she said, her face set in stone.

Jason cleared his throat and leaned forward, knowing that he had to make an impact on the lawyer. He explained the situation briefly. "First, they tricked us. They hired a lot of people over a period of a year so that they could get government contracts. After showing that they had enough software engineers and had secured a contract, they fired us. They're sending our jobs offshore. It's not right. I want to file a class-action suit."

"To win a case like this is very difficult," the lawyer said, steepling her fingers.

"Mrs. Johnson, a lot of people are suffering. When the country is going through a sub-prime mortgage crisis, it's not a good time for anyone to be out of work. Companies have stopped hiring because of the credit crunch."

"First, a court will look to see if Softek did anything wrong. Second, if such action has caused pain and suffering."

"Absolutely. I am in pain and I am suffering. Now what's the next step?"

"There's no precedent for such a class-action suit."

"Maybe it's time to start one." Jason looked at her poker face, certain he had not made any headway so far. He decided to play his hand. "Morally, it's wrong. A big corporation took advantage of us. We should have our day in court."

The lawyer leaned back and eyed Jason closely. "The defendants will fight with all the ammunition they have. And they have plenty. That's the first thing to consider. After months of investigation, legal research and negotiations, which all cost time and money, let's say the defendant decides not to admit any wrongdoing and, of course, decides not to compensate. The case goes to court. Once in court, what are our chances? Very slim. We don't like to lose a case or win small. Our reputation is based on that. Also, the chance of keeping your job is almost nil. Mr. McDeere, I'm sorry," she said, starting to rise. "It's not a case we like to take."

With that, Jason was dismissed. At the elevator, he punched the wall. "Damn her!" He pounded on the elevator door with his fist. Tired of waiting, he took the stairs. As he exited the building, he threw the paper with notes scribbled during session with the attorney in the garbage.

Jason decided to walk home. Fresh air should help quell his rising fear and anger. He took to the street in a residential neighborhood of Corvallis. His body moved instinctively in the right direction but his thoughts were far away. *What to do next?* He was overtaken by an emptiness that went far beyond anything his lunch of coffee and warm pie could fill. His empty stomach growled with a piercing ache. As he mechanically walked the sidewalk, with head lowered, he recalled everything that once was a part of his life, but all that had disappeared now. His wife and his children had left him, and his job was coming to an end.

Depressed by the many turns in his life, he found this new disappointment hard to bear, hard to shake off. He could no longer muster the will to fight. He wished there was a switch in his brain that could turn off all the thoughts churning in there. Looking up to the sky, he counted the rooftops he passed. Then he stopped, faced each front door. It happened to be that he was next to Brian's house where reindeer ornaments stood on the snow-covered lawn. Steam was rising from his breath.

As he continued walking, it occurred to Jason that he hadn't thought of buying presents for his children, despite the fact that Christmas was only a few days away. He was consumed with too many problems. *Who was he kidding?* He didn't have the money to buy presents, unless he went into further debt.

He stopped walking. He lifted both hands over his lips and nose to blow air but it wasn't enough to remove the chill. With a sigh, he calculated the chances of getting his job back. He could plead with his boss. It was worth a try. He changed his direction and headed towards Softek.

Frustrated, he trudged through the commercial district past the supermarket, where he noticed a crowd in front of an electronic store. It was odd to see a group of twenty or more, each absorbed by a TV screen. As he moved closer, more people crossed the road to join the gathering. *What could it be?* Perhaps a terrorist attack, he thought. Jason strained to catch a glimpse but there was no room between heads to see without being rude. As the crowd was repositioning for a better view, he was looking for an opening. Suddenly, a tall man moved and Jason squeezed in. His heart stopped. The caption on the screen read: Seven dead in a mass murder at Softek.

And on the top left corner of the screen was a picture of Brian.

2

Jason McDeere moved away from the crowd and headed in the direction of the Softek building, picking up the pace as he went. He heard his cell phone ring and dug it from his pocket. Gail Crawford, the executive assistant of Clint Whitney.

"Why did Brian kill Clint Whitney?" she sobbed, leaving out the perfunctory greeting. Jason refused to absorb Gail's plea. "What did you say?" He cupped one ear with the palm and tuned out traffic noise.

"Clint is dead." The sobbing continued. "I don't know who else."

"Where is Brian?"

"He is in the building... somewhere."

He pressed his temple hard. "I don't know, sorry... really don't know, but I'll find out. I'll call you."

Still running, Jason folded his cell phone and looked around for a taxi. As one pulled up beside him, he hopped in the back seat. "Take me to Softek, fast," he told the taxi driver who merely nodded.

Breaking news interrupted the radio program. The announcer reported that a disgruntled worker was in the Softek building. "He is considered armed and dangerous. Allegedly, he has killed one senior employee and plans to kill more." The report stopped after announcing that police officers, special emergency units and ambulances had surrounded the building.

Jason wanted to get to the scene as fast as he could, but as usual the traffic was in a noon-hour crawl. He hoped and prayed that he could get there soon and prevent any more casualties, especially Brian's. They had known each other for a long time and Jason didn't want to see his friend waste away his life. Like many of his colleagues, Jason included, Brian was going through a difficult time. There was no need to lose more lives over it. He turned his attention to the radio to get more developing news, but the station was reporting the weather forecast. As the traffic came to a halt, he dialed Brian's cell phone, but got an off signal. A red flag indicated a message from Brian. It read, "Call."

When he reached the Softek building, several police cars with flashing lights blocked the parking lot entrance. The traffic ahead gave way to an ambulance with deafening sirens leaving the scene. He handed a ten-dollar bill, borrowed earlier from Rocky, to the driver. "Drop me off here."

He hurried toward the main entrance where another ambulance was parked with the back doors open. As he got closer, the attendants rolled a stretcher past him with a body lying on it, covered from head to toe. A shockwave erupted inside him. He hoped it would not be his friend. He could not wait. He inched closer and asked, "Who is the person?" The paramedics ignored Jason, rolled the body into the vehicle, closed the doors and headed to the front.

***

Two days later, friends, family members and a few strangers silently filed into the Mack-Giffin Funeral Home in black suits or dresses, their heads lowered. Jason McDeere arrived an hour before the service. There were about a dozen cars in the parking lot with many empty spots. Across the street, the media circus was getting ready for action. They were lined up along the street and on people's lawns in a motorcade of vehicles and tents. Reporters and technicians were moving around testing equipment in and around CNN vans with different types of antennas on their roofs. Fox News staff was doing the same many yards away. In between these two media heavyweights were the local TV stations. A reporter from Corvallis Gazette Times, seated in from seat of a Ford Taurus, was busy typing something on a laptop. The neighborhood looked like a foreign invasion had hit.

Jason passed the media frenzy and entered the reception hall where several of Brian's co-workers, parents and friends, were all milling around. He walked up to the parents to convey his condolences. The father had a blank look, as though unable to explain why he should be at his son's funeral. The mother seemed so overwhelmed with sadness she simply couldn't talk. Jolene, Brian's ex-girlfriend, was sitting by herself in a loveseat, appearing terribly shaken. Her red eyes showed she hadn't stopped pouring tears since she heard the news.

Jason sat next to Jolene and said, "I'm so sorry. I wanted to talk to Brian on Monday. I got busy." Jason looked at her with compassion as she tried to stop sobbing, a river of tears rolling down her cheeks.

"I loved him so much." She squeezed her thin, pointed nose with a napkin. A summer tan had long faded, leaving white skin, contrasted with a black dress on a thin body.

He put his arm around her shoulder. "When I saw him on TV, I wanted to get to Softek as fast I could. I feel so bad that I didn't get there in time."

"After Brian lost his job, he was concerned about losing his house. The longer it went on, the more depressed he became." She stopped to wipe additional tears. "One day he told me he was worried. He saw bank repo signs going up in front of houses on his street."

Jason identified with Brian's despair. In a low, subdued voice, he said, "I'm worried who will be next." He looked around the room at co-workers huddled in groups of three and four. More mourners had filled the room, which looked bright to compensate the mood of the occasion. Fresh, colorful flowers perfectly arranged graced several tables.

"On Monday Brian said he felt like he was ready to break. He was very stressed out. He yelled at me. I thought he was going to hit –"

"Was he on medication?"

"Yes, but he was never violent. He had been seeing his doctor about his depression." She paused for a moment. "The doctor put him on anti-depressants. His mood was getting better, but last Sunday something happened. He wasn't talking much and looked pale and worried."

"About what?" Jason probed.

"About finding a job. He had missed payments on his house. He was counting on an offer coming in soon."

A friend approached Jolene and gave her a long hug. Jason took that as his cue to leave them. More unfamiliar people entered but Rocky was missing. Jason understood how divided the town had become and Rocky had to protect his job. Being at the funeral might give the wrong impression. Jason moved to a group of workers and listened. "The media is going wild. Did you see the headlines? They're calling Brian all kinds of names. Crazy, psychopath, schizophrenic! Can you believe that? One paper goes as far as saying he shouldn't have been hired by Softek."

The service was about to start. Jason saw the signal ushering them to the Chapel. After everyone took a seat, the minister reminded them not to jump to any judgment. He urged everyone to let the Lord be the final judge. Brian hadn't grown up in a religious family and had only been to church a few times. To him celebrating Christmas once a year was enough religious activity.

The minister, a few friends and relatives shared thoughtful memories of Brian's life. Then the service was over. Jason was one of the pall bearers. Holding the casket, he murmured thanks to Brian for his help. "I'm sorry I wasn't there for you, bud," he whispered, choking back tears.

When the casket was in the hearse, Jason headed to his car to go to the cemetery. He'd started his engine when he heard a knock and rolled down the window to find a dark-haired woman with wide brown eyes staring down at him.

"My name is Shallen Xu. I'm from the *Post*. Can I talk to you?"

"*Washington Post*?" Jason gave his best disinterested look.

"Yeah." She raised her voice to compensate for the engine noise.

"No." He reached for the window button.

"Not now. Tomorrow," she pleaded.

"Not to the media." He shook his head.

"It wouldn't be more than half an hour."

"You people have already smeared Brian's name. You want to do more damage?"

"No. I have a different angle." She handed him her business card.

Slow and loud, he repeated, "I'm not interested."

"In case you change your mind. Call me on my cell phone. I'm staying at one of the hotels in town." She moved the card closer. After a short pause, he took the card and drove off to the cemetery to stand out in the cold with the other mourners.

The casket slowly descended into Brian's final resting place. The mourners threw flowers as their final farewell. Jason looked around at the sad and teary faces. No one could bring Brian back. This was final. The suffering was too difficult to bear. It reminded him of when he was ten years old and his father's casket had been interred in a gravesite at the opposite corner of the cemetery. Then, the loss he'd suffered was from the injustice directed to his family from all sides—the police investigation, the judicial system, the jail security. He was much older now, but his feelings were the same about Brian's death. Something had to be done to prevent another tragedy from occurring.

***

Three hours later, Jason McDeere headed home, well aware of the emptiness inside him from the loss of a friend. One picture he could not discard from his mind, the reporter's face from Washington Post appearing through his car window. *Could she be of any help?* A slight guilt shrouded his heart for brushing her off when she pleaded for an interview. He rationalized it was to protect Brian's reputation from being further muddied by the media. In the desperate situation he was in, perhaps she could help in finding justice.

When the car turned into the driveway and stopped, he pulled Shallen Xu's card and said her name loud. Jason punched number on the cell phone and made an appointment to see her the next day.

***

At 9.00 a.m. Jason McDeere entered the hotel restaurant. After a quick scan of the place he spotted a woman with a radiant smile at the corner table. Jason walked toward Shallen Xu whose dark hair hung just above her shoulders. What was a woman like her doing working as a journalist? She should be somewhere in Paris modeling for a fashion designer, taking a walk on the runway instead of chasing stories across a continent. He sat across from her.

"Thank you so much for coming." Her smile continued as she extended a handshake.

Jason rehearsed what he had to tell the reporter many time over. "As I said on the phone, I want to defend Brian's name and not let anyone smear his honor. He deserves fairness like anyone else. That's the only reason I came." He waved away any notion that he would talk about anything else.

"What do you mean?" The reporter gave him a puzzled look while reaching for a notepad from her purse.

"The local media has been merciless. They're printing gossip and accusations. It's hard to take." He looked away, the memory still fresh from seeing the casket lying in a hole. Brian's death hadn't sunk in yet. He refused to digest all the facts. *Maybe Brian did not kill anyone.*

The place was busy with groups of two or three at each of the tables. The waitress approached the table holding a coffee pot. She looked at Jason, and poured him a cup of coffee in response to his nod. Without a word, she signaled for Jason's order. Then she turned her attention to Shallen. "Ma'am?" She poured her a cup. Both of them ordered the daily special. The waitress turned and walked away.

Once she was gone Shallen scribbled something. "Tell me about Brian

Baldwin."

"He was a nice guy. He helped me get a job at Softek International two years ago. He was a senior system analyst, very smart and hard working. When I began the job, he helped me get started. Gave me documentation of the systems and passwords for the databases and so on. That's unusual in my business." He looked at her and took a sip of coffee.

"How so?" She was still immersed in her notebook.

"Job security. Everyone is watching his back. Afraid his job will be given to a junior. Not sharing knowledge means protecting your territory. Animal instinct, you know."

She nodded.

"At work and outside of work we hung out a lot. He's not a violent person, though everyone owns a gun in this town. It's like planting an American flag in the front lawn. It's the American way."

Shallen Xu frowned. "When he went on this rampage, was he still working at Softek?"

He didn't like the word rampage.

Just then, the waitress came with two plates in her left hand and the coffee jug in her right. She first poured more coffee, and after putting the pot down she placed the plates of egg and toast on the table. She turned around and left without saying a word.

"He's been out of work since October. He missed a few mortgage payments. His house went into foreclosure. But the real issue is why American jobs are going overseas." Jason fiddled with his fork. "Brian was pushed to disaster. I fully understand why he was depressed because I'm going through a similar situation. Many of my fellow workers are in the same sinking boat. I'm afraid someone else will reach boiling point like Brian."

"Are you blaming management?"

"Absolutely. And politicians too." He forked a piece of scrambled egg.

She paused from her writing, washed down a bite of toast with coffee. "What can politicians do?"

"A lot. Softek totally relies on government contracts. Such contracts should oblige Softek to give US government jobs to US citizens and not send them overseas. I want to see Senator Quest about it. It has to stop," he said, raising his voice.

Still chewing, Shallen looked as though she was mentally revising what she had just written. "Senator Quest? When will you be seeing him?"

"I'll call his office later today. It's hard to get an appointment with politicians except during election. Wish me luck."

With a smile she said, "Anything else?"

"Yes. I saw a law office about filing a class-action suit."

"What happened?" She leveled her eyes at him.

"It didn't go well." He shook his head.

"What was your assessment of the lawyer?"

"She's after money."

"What are *you* after?" Shallen asked.

He paused, peering thoughtfully at her. "Justice. And what are *you* after? Small town story? From the *Washington Post*. Perhaps you've traveled across a continent. You must be looking for something special."

"Do you really want to know?" Her eyebrows arched.

"Of course, you're talking about a friend of mine." He turned his face away from her until he could compose himself, then turned back.

"You have to keep a secret." She gave him a serious look.

Jason's head motioned forward. "Now it's getting interesting. Tell me."

"You can't mention it to anyone."

"I promise," Jason said.

"Not even to your wife."

"Separated."

"Ahh. Sorry. I think the murders were a setup."

"What do you mean?" Eyes wide and ears perfectly tuned to what she had to say, he bent forward.

"Someone, or a group, had enough control to make these deaths happen."

Jason set his coffee cup down. "What proof do you have?"

"None so far."

"How can you say that? This is speculation." Jason moved closer to the reporter and waved his hands in the air.

"Yes. But similar incidences have happened in Florida, Nebraska and Texas."

"Are they all related?" Jason inquired.

"I don't know. It's worth investigating. It may be that Brian was set up to commit this act." Shallen scanned the room as if checking no one was listening to her.

"Mafia? Or drug cartels?" Jason whispered.

She gave a smile and shook her head. "No, nothing like that. I don't know exactly who. We're still investigating. Two common threads in all four of them though. They are outsourcing and an ex-employee committed the crime."

He frowned.

"All four incidents may be linked somehow."

"Brian was set up to do this?"

The reporter said, "I'm still investigating. I'll let you know if I find out more information."

***

Jason McDeere brought up the Google web page on his laptop. He typed the words "Senator Quest" in the search field and clicked on the "I'm Feeling Lucky" button. The doorbell rang. He walked over, opened the front door and beamed a smile at his two children, Sarah and Keenan, who walked past him into the house. The smile faded as he turned to his estranged wife, Kara. Absorbed in researching the senator, he had totally forgotten that his kids were coming for the afternoon. Time had slipped away from him as he juggled his thoughts: Brian, the murders, not being able to reach him at a crucial time, and of course lowering the casket in the grave – all those thoughts had been churning in his mind. Taking action, any action, had helped to release the pressure mounting in Jason's body, mind and soul. He was still taken aback by what Shallen had said, but with his kids here, he had no time to think about it now. He would have to put his search on the back burner until he could get Kara to leave.

Jason looked at his watch. "It's one. What time will you be back?"

She shrugged. "I don't know. Why are you so nosy?"

"Kara, I'm not nosy. I just want to know how to plan my afternoon."

She came closer to Jason to check that the children were out of hearing distance. "What are you getting the kids for Christmas?"

He wished she hadn't asked. He was tired of her nagging. "I haven't decided, yet."

"When will you decide—Christmas Eve?" she said, sarcasm lacing her words. "Never mind. I'll be back around four." She turned around and left.

He watched her receding back. She still looked as attractive as she had at their first meeting. "Okay. Don't be late."

On his way back to his laptop on the kitchen table, he stopped at the family room where Sarah and Keenan had already removed their winter jackets and placed them in the closet. Keenan was settling down with his Super Nintendo and Sarah was curled up on the couch with a novel. "Hey, guys. I've got treats." Both jumped with joy and followed their father to the kitchen counter. Each took a chocolate bar and returned to their activities.

Jason peered at his Google search result. He dialed the numbers on his cell phone and listened to the Season's Greetings message from the Senator's office. What happened to Merry Christmas? Jason wasn't religious but a confirmed traditionalist. He said, "My name is Jason McDeere. I want to make an appointment with Senator Quest."

The executive assistant said, "One moment, sir. Let me check the calendar." After a short silence, she was back. "December 28. Ahh. 3:30 p.m."

"Can it be sooner?" he pleaded.

"The Senator arrived from Washington yesterday. His schedule is booked."

"It's urgent. Can't you squeeze me in earlier?"

She fired a quick and firm response. "The Senator is very busy."

"I understand it's the Christmas Season. Could you tell the Senator that I'm calling from Corvallis? I'm an employee at Softek." After she noted his name and cell number, he wished her a Merry Christmas and hung up.

He stood up, walked to the window, and looked out at his backyard. It was filled with brown maple leaves and a few patches of snow. He calculated how much money he had. He couldn't miss one single mortgage payment if he wanted to keep his house. He liked his home and hoped to one day reunite his family in a place filled with fond memories. With his paycheck reduced to half, there was no slack left.

Still looking at the window, he heard footsteps approaching from behind him. "Dad, I'm bored. Can we play Uno?"

He turned and caressed his son's cheek. "That's a good idea." He had to off load his mind of the financial problems. Besides, he hadn't seen his kids in a week. It was too long. Last week had been filled with emotional turmoil. He needed to spend time with his kids.

He closed his laptop and pushed it to one end of the table. All three settled around the other end. Sarah dealt the cards. He brought the cards closer to his chest then peered at his cell phone when it started to ring. Still holding the cards in his left hand, he reached for the cell phone and pressed the green button. It was the senator's office. He placed the cards on the table. The voice at the other end said, "Could you be here at three this afternoon?"

Three? He couldn't refuse this offer. He'd have to wait for days to see the senator. He looked at the kids and thought of how Kara would react. She'd be ticked, but what else could he do? "Yes," Jason said. After hanging up, he ran his fingers through his hair. Then he returned to the game. Everyone was silent, their eyes focused on their hands. In successive order, Sarah and Keenan put a few cards on the table and picked up a few.

"Dad, your turn," said Sarah.

"Yeah," said Jason, his thoughts returned to the game. He was torn between being with his kids and having to leave soon. After the first round was over, he said, "Okay, kids, it was lot of fun. Unfortunately, I have to leave for an important meeting."

"But, Dad, we just got here." Sarah groaned.

"Yeah." Keenan scowled.

"I have no choice. One more game till your mom comes." Now for the really tough critic. Kara. He picked up the phone. He dreaded this call. After a brief pause and a deep breath, he punched a few numbers on his cell and Kara answered. He tapped the table with his fingers. "Where are you?" he said when she picked up.

"In a dressing room."

"Naked?"

"No!"

"Are you buying a dress, again?" He grimaced and continued tapping the table.

"Yes, for the Christmas party."

"You bought a dress a few months ago." He raised his eyebrows.

"Why are you calling?" said Kara, her voice tense.

"Ahh, I have a problem."

"You always have a problem. Tell me something new."

Jason ignored Kara's usual sarcasm. "I have to leave immediately to see Senator Quest."

"The Senator?"

"Yeah." He looked out the window.

"Why? You're not exactly his chief of staff. What's the urgency?"

Her words irritated him but he resisted a verbal sparring. "I want to see him about the layoffs at Softek. See if he could get the CEO to rehire us."

A pause. Kara said, "I'll be there at three."

"No. I have to be in Salem at three." He looked at his watch. "You have to come now, please."

"I have to try on this dress and go to the bank."

"Look, I can't miss this appointment. I may never get another one. Pick up the kids now and when I return I'll take them for the weekend. Then you can continue shopping or banking or whatever. I promise. Please?"

To his relief, she finally gave in.

***

Jason McDeere got in his car and, fifteen minutes later, the tires were squealing on the I-5 ramp heading north to Salem. He revved up to the speed limit and followed the taillights ahead of him. In the other direction, drivers were leaving Salem to start an early weekend before Christmas. His mind shifted back and forth between finding the money to buy presents for his children and what to say to the Senator. Jason needed to do a better job persuading the Senator than he had the lawyer. He pounded the steering wheel, recalling how disappointed and upset he was at his failure to convince the lawyer to take his case.

He watched the speedometer as it inched up over the speed limit. He didn't want to wind up in a traffic trap. The cops were like vultures, ready to snap a victim to meet their quotas, and this was a good time of year to collect more money for government coffers. Jason slowed down; he couldn't afford to get a speeding ticket.

Why had a busy politician given him the time of day? The Senator must be reading the headline news of the killing in Corvallis that had spread statewide and nationwide.

Jason's eyes caught the 253 sign. He exited the freeway and continued until he was on Mission St. SE. He took a quick look at the directions on the passenger seat, and then made a right turn. After a few traffic lights, he found the building that housed the Senator's office.

He walked through the door into the reception area after exiting the elevator. The walls were filled with Senator Quest's pictures: one when he was a boy scout, another as a football player, a few with Republican presidents and many with his family. Jason walked over to the receptionist who greeted him with a sweet voice. A Happy Holidays decoration was pasted to the wall behind her.

After introducing himself he said, "I was just wondering why Senator Quest wanted to see me on such short notice?" He looked at her perfect white teeth and her perfect smile. She was thirty-something with natural blonde hair dropping straight down to her shoulders. She was pretty. He read her name tag: Julia Svenborg.

"Just be happy you got an appointment. Others have to wait." The real smile was still holding.

"I am. You may have heard the Senator mention something?"

"I didn't hear anything." She switched to a plastic smile.

"I understand."

"Even if I did, I wouldn't tell you." She reached for a ringing phone that came at the right time to avoid his probing questions, so he took a seat.

Jason impatiently tapped his foot. He had seen the Senator a few times at campaign rallies shaking hands and kissing babies for photo-ops. Jason didn't get involved in politics too much, but he took his civic duty seriously. He studied the characters of the candidates, sorted out the qualities that would help Oregon and America. He never deviated from his principles, regardless of pressure.

Now, as he looked up, a man with a six-six frame and no fat stood in front of him. Jason jumped to his feet and shook Senator Quest's hand. The Senator gave Jason a friendly welcome with a broad smile and ushered him into his office. After he closed the door the Senator gestured toward a red leather wing back chair. Jason sat on the sofa instead. "I don't plan to take much of your time. It's about what's happening in Corvallis. It's horrible."

The Senator crossed his legs with his freshly shined shoes pointing towards Jason. He rubbed his chin and said, "Jason, I'm following the situation closely. I agree it's a tragedy. Corvallis is such a nice place. This must be devastating to its citizens."

Jason nodded. "The whole town is suffering."

The Senator was soft spoken and always took his time to answer. "In what way?"

"This tragedy could have been prevented."

After a reflective moment, the politician said, "How so?"

Jason leaned forward. He jabbed the air with his index finger as he said, "The main problem is outsourcing."

"Outsourcing is definitely a hot potato and politicians avoid dealing with it. CNN makes a big issue about it during every six o'clock news hour – not that CNN can, or has the capacity to, fix anything in America. They're more concerned about the ratings. As a senator I know you're well aware of the emotional, trade and internal implications of outsourcing."

The Senator poked his chin and grimaced. A moment of silence fell in the air as if he was recalibrating a response. "Currently, on the senate floor, there's a debate going on about this issue."

Jason knew that if debates went on long enough, the issue could disappear. It gave the media a reason to forget about one issue and move on to the next. He understood the game. "Outsourcing must be stopped."

"That would be difficult."

"If not, Americans become the losers," Jason snapped back.

The Senator turned to the window and back to Jason. He was slow and careful in his responses. "We think we're on an island by ourselves. That's not the case. We depend on other countries and others depend on us. Gradually, nations are becoming very interdependent. Globalization is taking place, which we cannot prevent. We also believe in capitalism. Companies have freedoms. In some ways we'll gain and in some ways we'll lose."

He felt a slight irritation as he didn't need a lecture on globalization. It was robbing Americans of their livelihoods. He leaned back against the sofa. "Softek employees are losing their homes. In this climate of national mortgage crisis, banks, with a snap of their fingers, are ready to foreclose. They give a homeowner no time to ask questions. In Corvallis, we're facing a double crisis. Senator, we need your help."

The Senator nodded. "I know. Owning a home is part of the American dream." The Senator looked relieved for the change of subject. His hand was resting on the arm of the chair. Then he straightened his tie. "We're working with the President and the congress to formulate a rescue plan. It will give homeowners in distress a helping hand. It will stop foreclosures dead in their tracks. This is a strong bill that will put a 90-day moratorium on bank repos."

Jason disdained the thought of losing his house. "That would help a lot."

"You work at Softek?"

Jason rubbed his forehead, easing a tension caused by the gloom-doom talk. "Only part-time for now. Soon to receive a layoff slip."

The Senator leaned forward. "What do you do there?"

"A senior software analyst. With good pay, a handsome benefit package and a promise for life-time employment." He felt a sharp pang of anger in his guts.

The Senator pulled back into his seat as if to absorb Jason's frustration. "Do you have anything lined up?"

"In my area of expertise it's difficult."

"I know. We're working hard in Salem and the surrounding areas to appear so attractive that, hopefully, some of the Silicon Valley's companies will move here."

"The real problem is that these jobs are going overseas. Politicians need to do something about it."

"We have legislation to encourage companies to be good corporate citizens, but we can't force them to stay."

"I understand that you are limited in what you can do, but Softek is a government contractor."

"I'm on the Finance Committee." The Senator stood up and walked to his desk, which was clear except for his business cards and a family picture with the dog. From a drawer he pulled out chocolates and offered one to Jason, who accepted. Then he sat in the wing back chair. "Softek does work outside security classification and, as such, it doesn't require that the workers be US citizens or undergo security checks."

"If something's not done, I'm afraid someone else will lose it, like Brian."

"That would be an even greater shame." The Senator stood, hands on hips. Frowning, he walked over to his desk. "A real shame." He picked up his business cards, returned to his seat and placed the cards in front of him. "Jason, would you be interested in a job?"

Jason was taken aback. "S-sure, Senator," he stammered.

The Senator went to his desk, punched numbers on his phone and talked for a few minutes, asking David to hire Jason. After hanging up, he went back to the wing chair. "I have good news. That was a senior manager at Layton Industries in Mountain

View, California, not too far from the Google office. They're always looking for good people." He took one of his cards from a stand on the table. On the back he scribbled a name and a phone number. "David Cohen at Layton Industries. They put together contracts for the Pentagon. You'll have a job for life. Plus, as a Silicon Valley company, it pays a competitive salary. Also, David mentioned that airfare and hotel expenses will all be paid when you go there for an interview."

Bedazzled by the offer, Jason wished the Senator a hearty Merry Christmas and headed for his car. In ten minutes he was on I-5 driving south to Corvallis. As the tension slowly dissipated, he kept saying, "Damn it, damn it, damn it." With every word yelled, he hit the steering wheel with his hand. At least his financial burden would be lighter, but he would be away from his children. He comforted himself with the thought that he could fly home twice a week. A little distance from Kara wouldn't be a bad idea. There had been quite a few arguments in the last several months. They had been sweating over the small stuff too much. Hopefully time apart would clear some bad emotions and the love between them could rekindle. "Hopefully" being the operative word.

Then a suspicion deepened. *Why did the senator find him a job so quickly?*

3

One fall evening in 2007, after saying goodbye to his aides, Richard Quest closed his office door, walked to his desk, pulled a thick report on the Iraq War from his briefcase, and sank in the chair. With his feet perched on the desk, he began to read. But soon his mind drifted from the report back to his first day in the US Senate.

Richard Quest was sworn in as a US senator on January 7, 2001, six months after his father, himself a US Republican senator, announced his retirement from politics following a severe stroke. Richard's first entry into politics, after being elected to the Oregon State Senate, came in 1992. His peers quickly noticed and admired his leadership qualities, moving him in relatively short time to the position of Minority Leader and then President of the State Senate. Richard smiled as he recalled that time in his life. It was well known among players of the senate political arena that being the son of Adam Quest had given the young Republican politician a boost in Oregon when his father had decided to move to the national scene.

Richard looked at the photograph of him in his football jersey. He knew how to play politics better than being quarterback on the bookshelf. He loved sports and his family, but his passion for winning elections and being a lawmaker outweighed anything else. At the dinner table, as his growing body was being fed, his young mind was absorbing wisdom from politics dished out by his father's life experience. He was groomed in the strategies needed to serve his state and country. Richard still remembered his father telling him "the sky is the limit." He was taught more is better— the American way—and soon followed in his father's footsteps. For decades, the recognition of the Quest family had steadily risen, reaching higher and higher plateaus in the minds of Oregonians.

Once in Washington, Senator Quest soon adjusted to the halls of Capitol Hill, where he came across many familiar faces from his father's tenure. Before stepping into his office for the first time, he knew well how the machinery of senate politics worked. Therefore, he quickly worked on a "wish-list." He avoided the committee on Aging, Indian Affairs, and Ethics, and made sure he was in the powerful Finance Committee. All freshmen came to Capitol Hill with a list. To survive the political game played in Washington, they had to. The seniors picked first; the leftovers went to the junior senators, based on Party Conference Rules. It took Senator Quest a while, as competition was fierce, but he got on the Finance, Appropriations and Armed Services Committees. *That's where the money is.*

As election campaigns rolled forward, his debt kept mounting higher and higher – into the millions. However, he knew once in Washington, with his cunning and maneuvering, the war chest would be replenished by donations flowing in from individuals and corporations who would take their fill through pork-barrel projects. Richard chuckled. It was too simple. Campaigns in America had become so expensive that a senator's monthly salary couldn't cover the cost of one minute of airtime. Milking the government cow was an acceptable practice. How did it work? It was by approving nonsense US government projects. The money from these funds went indirectly to him for his work in the government or ended up as political contributions to his campaign fund.

Senator Quest clamped his forehead with the fingers and tried to read a few more sentences of the report now lying on top of the desk. It was too hard. He leaned back and rubbed his temples, feeling a headache coming on. It was a busy and long day with meetings and phone calls. The White House staff had discussed every angle of the report, each one emphasizing that the Democrats would milk the failing strategies of the Iraq war. The Republicans couldn't let that happen.

Quest stood up and stretched, then removed his glasses and twirled them. According to party polls, the tide of American opinion was turning against the war plan. He was up for re-election in 2008. As he looked around his plush office with its Berber carpeting, bookshelves lining the wall and a large teak desk that he'd had shipped from China, his thoughts drifted to the presidential campaign. The primaries were in full swing. He picked up The *Washington Post* from his desk and squinted. One headline suggested a cost of one billion for combined Republican and Democrat candidate spending before the 2008 presidential election reached its end. Elections were costlier than they were decades ago. As he laid the paper down he recalled his father's campaigns. They were founded squarely on good ideas and the sweat of party workers. Now it had become complicated with polls, consultants, and advertising. Winning elections was not in the hands of politicians. Instead it had become a game of political professionals who earned too much and had nothing to lose. His 2008 re-election would be very costly, he thought. Just then his head began to throb intensely.

He hired Roger Hunt as consultant shortly after a strategy meeting in the summer of 2006, organized by the powerful and influential Majority Leader, Thomas Rodriguez, a Republican from Florida. Only ten senators were invited, eight of whom were senior members. Richard was one of the two juniors. He had arrived at the mansion at eight in the morning for a day-long "Pulse of the Nation" brainstorming session. This secret meeting of top Republicans only happened twice a year. Five consultants gave their reports of polling, media and opposition research. Every presentation was done using a laptop connected to a 90-inch plasma flat screen hanging on a wall. PowerPoint slides were intermingled with web pages. The more tech savvy the reports, the more the senators were impressed. Just before lunch break, the last item piqued everyone's attention: scandal about the Democrats. The more dirt was thrown at their opponents, the more the room thundered with applause. At the end of this session, the senators looked happy and satisfied by the consultants' good work.

During the lunch break, the politicians were well fed on salad, chicken, sliced roasted beef, scallops, shrimp, fruits and desserts. All smelled decadently delicious. With a coffee cup in hand, Senator Quest motioned Roger Hunt, a well-known consultant, to the library. After closing the door of this octagon shaped room, he offered Hunt a seat in one of the wing backed chairs. Then the Senator sat on a brown, shiny leather chair opposite him. Behind the Senator, covering most of the wall, hung a large picture of Emmanuel Rodriguez.

"The presentation was fantastic, Roger," said the Senator furrowing his forehead.

Nodding, Hunt said, "Thanks. We have an uphill battle till November 2008."

"That's what I wanted to talk to you about." He looked directly at Hunt, hoping for a brilliant answer from the Yale-trained political consultant. "I want you on my team."

Hunt deftly sidestepped the offer saying, "I'm worried. Now, in 2006, many Republicans are getting complacent."

The Senator waved the idea away. "I won't accept euphoria. At least take comfort in an economy that is doing well. Unemployment is the lowest in decades. We can definitely take credit for that. So what's your worry?" The Senator combed his hair with his fingers. He stood up and walked to the window facing a deep backyard. He waited then turned to face Hunt.

"Senator, it's all about the economy. Most of the time, candidates get elected

Lisa Ward   p 158
Joe Snyder   p 162
Trench coat   p 163
Jeff Dowell   p 170, 173
Fay Whitney   p 179
Linda Sims   p 182
James Polawski   p 184
Jerry Whitney   p 195, 196 ***
Amanda   p 201
Stefanie Pastore   p 230
Roger White   p 230   CEO of Layton
Susan Delaney   p 270

INDEX

1. Brian Baldwin — P1, 5, 6,* 33*
2. Jason McDeere — P2, 9, 34, 36, 39, 43, 45, 166,*** 183
3. Softer — P1, 34, 42,* 53
4. Clint Whitney — P5
5. Shallen Xu — P14, 17,* 40, 49, 89#
6. Senator Quest (Richard) — P18, 19, 22, 24,* 26, 41,** 79,*** 162
7. Sarah + Keenan — P18
8. Kara — P18, 59
9. David Cohen — P25, 36,
10. Layton Industries — P25, 36, 37, 62, 63, 72
11. Roger Hunt — P27, 28, 41, 43, 52,* 125,*** 134***
12. Thomas Rodriguez — P28
13. Martha — P31
    Muktar Gamble — P31, 34   CEO of Softer
    Corvallis, Oregon — P40
    Mr. Johnson — P45
    Guy Volpa — P52, 124
    Rose's coffee time — P2, 54
    Rocky — P2, 55
    Indira Gupta — P68, 70, 167***
    Khalid — P76, 78
    Don Zimmerman — P76
    Jasmine — P77
    Terrance — P84
    John Mead — P86
    Barbara — P86, 87
    Senator Giovani — P89
    Paul Schubert — P119
    Tom Martin — P137
    Carl Grove — P141

or rejected based on the economy." Hunt wore a professorial expression. "When Americans have money in their pocket, they're happy."

"How is that a problem?"

Hunt turned to him as if he were one of his students. "Don't you see? The Republicans are euphoric because of the economy. As an analyst I watch the weekly economic index more than the polls. The downturn has already started. It will plunge America in a recession by the end of 2008. There is a bubble forming in the real estate market. It will burst soon, like it does in any section of our economy. But if they don't realize the danger ahead, the Republican Party could be in for a big fall. And *that's* a problem," said Hunt.

Quest looked up to the ceiling. He said softly, "And the war in Iraq isn't going well." Caressing his chin, he walked back to the chair and sank into it. "The President can always pull a few more tricks out of his hat." He placed the cup on the table after taking a sip.

"Like what? He's running out of them." Roger shook his head.

"Homeland Security can raise the terrorist attack alarm to code red a few times."

Roger waved his hand as if that was a given. "And then what?"

"Then the Americans will be on our side, instead of following those bastards, the Democrats." The Senator smiled.

"The mood is definitely changing. Americans are very patriotic and our party has counted on that. But they're getting smarter." Hunt crossed his leg as if he was enjoying his lecture to a US senator.

"Are you sure they're getting smarter?"

"Of course, I'm sure."

"How serious are you about helping the Republican Party?" The Senator leaned forward.

"Very serious. I ran my data through my predictor program. It shows that there is a good chance that the Republicans will lose both houses in the next election."

"What predictor program?"

"It's software I developed."

"No one has heard of it?" Hunt always had a trick up his sleeve.

"Only very few people know about it. Now you're one of them."

The Senator slammed a fist onto the table. "We can't lose both houses. That can't happen."

"Hate to tell you. I've been right eight out of ten times." His broad smile spread wider. He stretched and made himself more comfortable in the chair.

The Senator scowled at Hunt. He was arrogant and smart. Quest didn't care about the first but he needed the latter quality. He had interviewed two other consultants, but none matched his prowess. Hunt focused on a state and wrestled with the Democrats until he snatched the position from his opponent. He was the tiger of the jungle, always powerful, and cunning enough to bring down his prey, afterwards preening with satisfaction. "Tell me, Roger, how would you handle Oregon in the next election?"

"What are the issues?" he came back quickly.

"In Oregon, the economy has a chronic economic illness, unlike the rest of the country. I'm trying to persuade Silicon Valley companies to move there. It's a challenge as our educational system doesn't produce enough technical professionals. I'm working with the governor. I have shown up with him at a few public meetings. Attending is risky though. He's a Democrat and always brings up gay and lesbian rights, or he undermines my pro-life agenda."

Hunt shook his head. "It's a problem. It will be an uphill battle. I love a good challenge though, Senator."

"To win, I will have to throw dirt at the other guy. Of course, it will mean a lot of money." The Senator took a sip of the coffee and looked at the floor-to-ceiling bookcase made of Chinese teak and loaded with books, old and new.

"Do you have strong corporate sponsors?"

"Yes. Two at the moment."

"My analysis shows you will need about ten," said Hunt.

"That's hard. I can't get more projects approved. Mid-term election is this November. No one wants to do anything stupid to lose control of the senate."

"Get more projects," he insisted.

"It's difficult. The senior senators have put a moratorium on any new endeavors. " The Senator purposely left no room for flexibility.

"I know, Senator. Then we'll have to work with two."

"Yes, but like you said, it won't be enough." He fought down a wave of depression. "Any ideas?"

Hunt placed his hands palms up, as though he were an open book. "Senator, are you trying to hire me?"

"Only if you can win this one!"

"I have a sure-win idea," Hunt said with confidence. "I'll tell you about it once I'm on the payroll."

That fateful meeting took place over a year ago. Since then Hunt had proved to be the tiger that he was called by some.

Back to his office work, Quest leaned back on the swivel chair. Just then, the phone rang. It was Martha, the Senator's wife. "Honey, what time will you be home?"

Quest looked at his watch. "Just finishing reading up a report on the Iraq war. I'll leave in ten." He shoved papers in his leather briefcase, signed off at his computer for security reasons and left his office.

***

The limo drove through Capitol Street, turned left on Marion, then right on Cottage and stopped at the prestigious Martin building. Richard Quest got out of the vehicle with his gym bag thanked the driver and the limo drove off. The Senator greeted the security guard as he opened the door, then swiped his membership card, pushed the turnstile and entered the lounge area of the gym. A right turn into a corridor led to the locker room. He entered one of the change rooms, closed the door behind him and, after changing his clothing, he came out. As he approached one of the mirrors, he adjusted the front of his baseball cap lower, looked at his blue jeans, then pulled up the scarf around his neck to cover his ears and chin. Finally, he zipped up his winter coat. After securing his gym bag in one of the lockers, he left through the fire exit door at the back of the building.

With a quick look to his right and to his left, he walked until he reached Wilson Park. As expected, he located Muhtar Gamble, founder and CEO of Softek International, seated on a bench by himself. Walking up the lane, the Senator glanced to an area filled with slides, swings and other children's play things, but not a soul was using them. Beyond were a few seniors getting some fresh air in the afternoon sun, but the distance made their faces indistinguishable.

Walking towards him, still many yards away, was Gamble, who could easily fit in with those seniors enjoying the open air. He wore a woolen winter hat, a thick scarf around his neck and a heavy coat. Just the man's eyes, nose and lips were visible. Quest took a seat at one end of the bench, and Gamble sat at the other end, leaving two feet between them. "Sorry to ask you here in such a hurry," Quest said. "We have to make it quick. We can't be here for too long."

Muhtar nodded with his vision fixed ahead at the play area. He held a coffee cup with both gloved hands as if trying to keep them warm. "Where is Roger?"

Roger Hunt always dealt with Muhtar. This meeting was an exception. "He couldn't come. He had to be with his family. Christmas, you know. I happen to be in Salem. I was shocked when I heard about the shooting at Softek." He shook his head.

Muhtar's head bowed, another silence followed. "I was shocked, too. I was having lunch when I got a call from Gail, Clint's executive assistant." He took a deep breath and Quest watched the vapor billow from his mouth. "Clint and I were close. We grew up together. The news hit me like a tsunami, unexpected. After two calls to Gail, I decided to go back to the office." Muhtar's eyelids vibrated like butterfly wings as though trying to prevent the tears from rolling down his cheeks.

"How did this murderer get in the building? His security card should have been cancelled." Quest rubbed both hands vigorously.

"I called the CEO of the security company that handles security passes at Softek," Muhtar said. He took a sip of coffee. "She told me that Brian's access to the building was never cancelled as it should have been when his job was terminated almost three months ago. The CEO explained that it fell through the cracks when the security guards were changing shifts. Each thought the other had disabled Brian's card. In the end, no one disabled it. I'll cancel the security contract with this firm. We are signing a new contract with another company."

The Senator turned his head towards the man, who appeared terribly shaken. Then he turned his eyes back to the seniors, to a woman walking a dog on a leash. Quest tracked her movements, and sighed with relief when she turned into the lane leading to the entrance of the park. He did not want anyone noticing his presence. "Suspend the layoffs!" he growled.

Muhtar nodded. "Yes. Roger called me about it."

"This is a severe blow. I could lose an election over this. We have a disaster on our hands. Damage control is needed." The Senator knew what he was talking about. He had been there and done that many times over the course of his career. The worst was when a rookie reporter, looking for fame, accused his father of having a mistress. A terrible storm followed that lasted for months. The crisis was diffused by leaking new information. "First thing is to restrict information flow to the media. They will come sniffing around. No interviews. Not a word to a reporter."

"I understand."

"Did you talk to the psychiatrist?"

"I talked to the psychiatrist." Muhtar had regained his composure.

"Is he on our payroll?" The Senator looked at the bare trees, at a jogger being followed by a German Sheppard.

"Yes. He told me about Brian's depression but he didn't consider it to be serious. According to him, the high dosage of anti-depressant should have made him a happy-go-lucky person," said Muhtar.

Quest did not buy the explanation. "Doctors are a bunch of idiots."

"Then he looked at the report from the coroner's office and found an unknown substance in Brian's body."

"What was it?" Quest straightened his back, still looking ahead of him.

"He doesn't know."

"Every profession has an escape clause. Doctors say, 'We don't know' and politicians say, 'No comment.' This situation can potentially cause a lot of problems for me. How are the other ex-employees doing?" the Senator asked, suddenly feeling antsy. He stood up and started to walk. Muhtar followed him and they continued on in silence for a few moments. The Senator pulled the collar up around his neck as joggers and their dogs passed them by. They continued walking until the next bench, where they promptly sat. "Where were we? Yes. Ex-employees."

"So far, so good. The psychiatrist is looking at every patient very carefully. He wants to see each of them again. Soon."

"Jason McDeere came to see me the other day. I offered him a job at Layton. What do you know about him?"

"I've seen him a few times. I can't say I know him personally," said Muhtar.

"He's a smart fellow. A software professional. He was asking a lot of questions. He's going for an interview tomorrow."

"With Cohen?" asked Muhtar. "Is he going to take the job?"

"He's hungry. He's on half salary. Right now he's barely keeping up with his mortgage payment. I told David to put a lot of money on the table."

"Anything I should do?"

Nothing should get in his way, the Senator thought. He blurted out, "Find out everything you can about him. Bug his house if you have to, and put a private eye on him. Also ask the investigator to check the chemical in Brian's autopsy report."

Over the past decades, Muhtar Gamble had been a regular contributor to the Quest campaign funds of both father and son. In the last US election, Richard Quest promised to bring employment to Oregon and, through his help, Softek signed an armed services contract of two hundred million. Muhtar was a hard-core Republican.

Quest imagined Softek as a sinking ship. He had to cash in while goods were available. "I need 5 million to be transferred from Softek-Mumbai to my Swiss account through the Cayman Islands. The election campaign will get kick started soon."

"What route?"

"Roger will be in touch. This is our last meeting. Merry Christmas!" He stood up and without a glance at Muhtar, or a handshake, he walked away.

***

As the taxi slowed down, Jason McDeere checked his piece of paper and said, "It's here." After paying the fare and thanking the driver, he got out of the car and entered the doors of a building the front of which had Layton Industries written in huge letters. He looked at his watch. He was ten minutes early for his job interview with David Cohen, the Information Technology manager. As instructed, he reported at the security counter. He walked past two security guards and spoke to one of the duty officers at the counter. After checking Jason's name on a sheet of paper, the officer advised him of a security briefing, to which he agreed without hesitation. Two officers who introduced themselves as Henry and Sylvia immediately escorted Jason to a small room.

All three sat around a table. Henry said, "As part of our security procedures, I'll ask you a few questions. We will be recording." He looked up to a camera attached to a wall close to the ceiling with the lens pointed at them. "Any objection?"

Every word came out in a monotone, as though the officer had said it hundreds of times. Jason looked at the man's round face and bald head, then with a shrug said, "No."

Henry pressed a button on a remote control, leaned forward and started talking to the microphone on the table. "My name is Henry. This is Sylvia. Mr. McDeere, where were you born?" His eyes were fixed on the paper, his hand holding a pen as though ready to write.

"Jacksonville, Florida," said Jason.

After writing a tick, Henry said, "Have you served in the US Armed Forces?"

"No."

"Have you traveled or been a resident of Iran, Libya, or North Korea?"

"No," said Jason.

"Have you ever been convicted in a court of law on felony, fraud, extortion or bribery charges?"

"No. How detailed is this questioning going to be?" Jason cleared his throat.

"Not too detailed, sir. We are almost done," he said in an agreeable manner, apparently not meant to offend his listener.

"Whatever you hear or see cannot be discussed with anyone after you leave this building."

Jason nodded.

Henry forwarded a sheet. "Do you mind signing this confidentiality agreement?"

Jason read the document from top to bottom. It was a similar agreement to ones he'd had to sign at previous jobs, only usually it happened *after* getting the job, not before. He wrote his name at the blank spot and signed at the bottom of the page. Then he handed it over to Henry.

"Those are all the questions, Mr. McDeere. Thank you for your co-operation. Once you are in this building, taking pictures is not allowed." This process was starting to annoy Jason but he resisted acting on his feelings.

They left the room and Jason was asked to take a seat next to the security counter in the lobby. After about ten minutes, Henry appeared behind the counter. Jason stood up and walked towards him.

Henry said, "Mr. Cohen will be here shortly."

Jason placed his briefcase on the floor next to a black leather bench and took a seat. He looked around. All the guards and officers wore ties and cheap navy blue suits. His was black, newer and a lot more expensive. Normally, for techie jobs, the dress code was anything goes, except shorts and t-shirts. This place was different.

A man appeared in front of him in blue shirt and pants with sharp pleats and greeted Jason with a vigorous handshake. "I am David Cohen, pleased to meet you." He signed something at the security counter and then the officer handed him a visitor's badge which he passed on to Jason.

Together they walked past the elevators and turned left. They were followed by another security guard. This place was more secure than most federal penitentiaries, Jason thought. Both entered room 1A. The guard remained at the door. In the middle was a large table with a telephone on it, surrounded by a dozen chairs. They sat across from each other.

"Thanks for coming here on such short notice. We needed someone last month." Cohen placed a folder on the table. "How was the flight?"

"Fine." Jason pulled a pad and pen out of his briefcase.

"First, I'll tell you what we do here. We have many divisions. We're a subcontractor for the Department of Defense. That's what we do. Nothing else. Sorry about the security formality. "

"I survived."

"You'll be working in the Cruise Guidance Systems division. CGS for short. This is divided into many groups, one being DMDS."

"What is DMDS for?" asked Jason.

"Sorry. Don't let me do all the talking. Feel free to interrupt me. It stands for Data Management and Decision Support."

"Is this a database project?" Jason made a note.

"Kind of. In a nutshell, the area blocks are scanned by satellites as needed. Then it is dumped into a storage area through a satellite link. Afterwards, we load the data from files into one of the many databases through a process called ETL."

"Is ETL for extract, transform and load process?" Jason placed his hand on the armrest and tried to look attentive.

"Yes."

"I have worked with that and I'm very familiar with the process." Jason nodded while rubbing his palms together. *What is an area block?* This question could wait.

"After the transformation, the data is loaded into another database."

"How fast is the link transfer rate?"

"I can't tell you much about it now. Once you join us, you will be offered information. I'll give you a hint though. It is super fast. Faster than you can imagine."

"I see." Jason pulled back slightly in the chair. *He sure isn't saying much.*

"After the transformation, the load process refreshes the data warehouse. It gives us the best data to use."

"What database do you use? Oracle?"

"No. It's proprietary. And I can't tell you much now. Information will be given on a need-to-know basis."

"How about the hardware?"

"Again, all I can say is that the computers are super, super fast. Each uses array CPU technology, capable of crunching billions of arithmetic calculations in seconds."

"Wow. Impressive." Jason's excitement returned.

Cohen continued. "After that our data analysts check the data and decide how refined and useful it is. Whether it meets our standards."

"What *is* this data?"

"The surface of the world is divided into what is called interest blocks. Also called area blocks. Simply put, the earth is divided into thousand square mile areas. Each area has an identification tag. Each is scanned by US defense satellites to find the characteristics of the terrain. Does this make sense?"

He had a vague idea of the concept and could deepen his knowledge later. "A little bit." He relaxed slightly.

"These steps happen many times until the top grade of data is achieved. Then it is loaded into a simulation cruise missile to check the path. That's all I can say."

"What will my position be?"

"Looking at your resume. I think you will fit well in a data analyst position."

"Can you elaborate?"

"Yes. Your job will be to ensure the missiles are loaded with the highest quality of data."

"I will need training." These processes and technologies were more complex than he was used to. It didn't worry him though. He was a fast learner.

"You will be in training for six months. Shadowing another analyst."

"Sorry. Can I visit the washroom? Had a lot coffee on the plane." Jason was trying to hide the fidgeting.

"Sure." Cohen got up, walked to the door and opened it.

Jason followed close behind. The security guard was still standing by the door.

Cohen said, "The gentleman will show you the washroom."

They walked down the hall, made one right turn and there it was. The officer followed Jason into the bathroom as he did his business and washed his hands. Together they walked back to the meeting room; neither spoke a word. Jason didn't dare as the guard's stone face didn't invite any conversation. A prickle of anxiety edged up his spine.

When Jason closed the door behind him, David Cohen was scribbling something on the resume.

"Where were we? You will be involved in all the steps," Cohen continued.

"It sounds interesting and challenging," said Jason. The security started to bother him. If he'd had another job offer, or his financial situation was stable, he wouldn't have put up with all the security crap.

"Very good." Cohen looked satisfied.

"Security seems very tight."

"Yes. You will get used to it after a short time. Our employees are very satisfied. Our salaries are competitive. We have lots of bonuses, like free food any time within the campus area. Good medical coverage and so on."

"When will I be needed?"

"First, there is a security check process. Sorry. It takes about a week. Based on the first check DoD may decide to go for an international check. That could take another two weeks." After clearing his throat, Cohen looked down at the paperwork then up at Jason's eyes. "But we need you here right away. I don't know if I can speed up the security check. I have tried; it never works. There are so many layers of bureaucracy and at each level the process moves slower than molasses. You know government employees like to take extended coffee breaks and lunches, and they'll use any excuse to leave work early. It does take longer than it should."

"Does this mean I get the job?" Jason said.

"If you want it."

"Yes, I want it. Do you have any questions for me?"

"Let me see." David Cohen looked at the resume. "You have the work experience we are looking for. By the way, I forgot to mention you get free gym membership, signing bonus and moving expenses."

As Cohen assembled his papers, Jason put his pad and pencil in the briefcase. Then Jason, Cohen and the security guard walked back to the security counter. After returning the visitors badge, Jason stepped outside to take in a good dose of fresh air. As he waited to catch a taxi to the airport, he knew he should be feeling good about this job but he wasn't. It was the easiest job interview in the world. In his experience, it usually took weeks or months, going through three to four interviews and through many people. He felt relieved of his financial burden. And the technology at Layton was the best. He liked challenges and new processes or technology. He would be on the learning curve for a long time. Yet, he felt uneasy. He couldn't pinpoint what it was with accuracy. Maybe it was just happening faster than he'd expected. Everything would be fine, once he moved into the job and was more settled . . . he hoped.

4

At precisely five to 10:00 in the morning Roger Hunt unlocked the door and entered his private home office. In his left hand he carried a wiretap detector, which he waved up and down near the top corners, walls and floors, and then placed it on the desk. The light remained off. With that done he fired up his laptop. After it came up, he pulled a Blackberry from his belt, moved it closer to the light of the laptop and started the smart phone's security program. After punching in numbers and a password, he lifted the Blackberry closer to his right ear and waited for an answer to the ringing.

"Good morning, Roger," said David Cohen at the other end.

"Top of the morning to you, too." The Monday morning meeting had been slated on their calendars for a long time. It happened regardless of where they were in the world. In his line of work, security was not only required but reached a level that neared fanaticism. Therefore he always took extra measures to avoid anyone listening to his conversations, especially of a business nature. He depended a lot on this smart phone. Roger had written a special security software for his Blackberry with extra encryption to achieve a secure line.

He stood up, holding the Blackberry close to his ear, and proceeded. "Today we have some very urgent matters to discuss."

"Shoot," said David with a tone that let Roger know he was ready to receive.

"The *Post* ran an article this morning. It mentions the shooting at Softek and raises some interesting concerns. It points out that the Corvallis incident may be related to three others: Florida, Nebraska. Ahh, what's the third? Texas." He started to pace in the dark twenty by twenty room.

"Did you know about these shootings in these states? Now in Oregon. Is there a connection?"

"Yes, but I didn't think it was significant enough to follow up. Now I have a good reason to pursue it." Roger stopped in the middle of the room, his face pointed at the ceiling.

"Anything to do with Softek?"

"Don't know, yet." Roger switched the phone from his left ear to his right.

"The shooting in Corvallis looks like the job of a lonely, disgruntled person."

"Maybe not." He pressed his forehead with his fingers.

"What do you mean?" said David.

"The article also mentions Jason McDeere, whom you saw yesterday." He returned to the chair and slowly curled his body in it.

"What did it say?"

"Jason is a good friend of Brian, the killer. Did you hear me?" Roger raised his voice.

"I'm listening."

"And he also wants to start a class-action suit against Softek." He pressed his forehead. The thought of a lawsuit gave him a headache.

"Does the Senator know about it?" said David.

"Yes. I just spoke with him. He told me to put enough hurdles in front of Jason to make his life painful and unlivable." Roger sat on the edge of his desk, the glow of the laptop giving everything an eerie blue incandescence.

"Why?"

"We want to prevent him from launching a class-action suit." Roger moved the laptop cursor around, as if looking for something.

"No one can prevent him from starting one, if he really wants to," David said, his voice firm.

"He certainly can. But I will make his life so miserable that he'll be sorry if he does. And you know I have the power to do it. He'll soon realize that it isn't worth it." Roger started the Outlook program to check his mail.

"I don't understand. Why so much trouble?" said David.

"Already, a bitch from the *Post* is snooping around in the small town of Corvallis. I don't like having that snake around my neck."

"Ok, Roger. No need to get worked up about it. I know you can handle it," said David.

Roger knew that tone – it was meant to calm him when he got upset, as he was now.

"Next. With a class-action suit, hungry lawyers will be all over Softek like hyenas smelling dead meat. You understand?"

"You're a lawyer. You know your breed," said David.

"Know them too well." After graduating from Yale, Roger Hunt worked in the DA's office as a prosecutor for a while until he got bored. He also learned as a young lawyer that power was his first love, and money came a close second. He wanted an ocean to swim in to catch bigger fish. Washington, the source of power and money, was the place for him to be. Being a political consultant with a genius IQ would fit well among Republicans.

"Yes. We have to be careful," admitted David.

Roger leaned forward to continue his lecture, knowing full well that his solo audience was getting his point. "2008 is election year. The Battle of the Titans will start. The senator's campaign needs funds. Loads of them. We're counting on Softek's contribution. If the company is tied up in a court battle, the contribution will disappear."

"So I shouldn't give Jason the job?"

"Give him the job. Of course. We want him in our net where we can control him." His voice spiked again and he stood. He inhales a deep breath to calm himself down. Tension always made his blood pressure rise.

"I understand."

A pause followed. "With the job, give him more perks. Then he'll have no reason to go anywhere else." Roger sat back down and ran his finger across the desktop. No dust. He ran a tight ship in every aspect of his life. Head stuck in the wheeling and dealings of Washington, he was well versed in the knowledge that to win control was the name of the game

"I did that. And he will take the job. He looks hungry," David said, confidence lacing his words.

"Send him to Alaska. It will be difficult to start a class-action suit from there."

"I can't." Roger could hear the trepidation in David's voice, as though afraid to upset Roger further.

"Why?"

"I needed someone here last month." Was that actually a whine in the man's voice?

"Last month? Why?" Roger tapped his fingers impatiently on the desktop.

"The Defense Department upgrade project for the missile guidance system has to be completed soon. I'll need Jason to meet the deadline. I can't miss it," David pleaded, obviously hoping Roger would change his mind.

"The Senator needs funds for his upcoming campaign. We need millions from

Softek. We don't want a piss-ant like Jason spoiling our plans."

"Ok," David said, submissive when push came to shove.

"That means raising the surveillance on him to code red. As in red hot."

"Who is taking care of surveillance?" David said.

"I'm in charge of that." Roger made certain he left no room for argument. He stood, tiring of the cat and mouse game.

"How about the renewal of our contracts?" David said.

Roger paused for effect. "There will be an enormous increase in funding for the Department of Defense. The Pentagon wants to pour more into the cruise missile system. Nothing to worry about. Your contract is safe." Roger glanced at Yahoo! Finance web page listing all the companies whose stocks he owned.

Roger Hunt smiled when he heard the sigh of relief in the other man's voice. Although he would never tell David this, he owned a hundred thousand shares of Layton Industries – by proxy. Roger's part of the bargain was to supply contracts to Layton at regular interval such that the companies showed good profit every quarter. For the last three years Layton's stock price had steadily climbed. *No sir,* he thought as he brought up Layton's stock price on his computer. *The contract will be safe with me.*

***

Jason McDeere turned off the TV and placed the remote on the coffee table in front of him. After removing his Rolex watch--the hands were ticking towards ten in the morning--he placed it on the table. Next he went to the bedroom, pulled open a drawer in his night stand, and retrieved his wedding ring. Then he returned to the couch and gently dropped the ring next to the watch. It was decision time. Over the last few days the worry about how to afford Christmas gifts for his children had been churning in his mind. Waiting was no longer an option as it was already Christmas Eve. Having no extra cash to spare and the credit cards maxed out, the only choice left for him was to sell his jewelry. He had just finished watching an Oliver Jewelry advertisement on TV, where the owner was waving dollar bills in his hand to entice cash-strapped viewers to sell their sentimental possessions. Jason wasn't into ornaments, and found guys with necklaces, finger rings and earrings repulsive. He had only two pieces of jewelry. He decided to keep the wedding ring, just in case his relationship with Kara would one day magically improve…a remote hope.

Next thing he knew he was on the freeway driving to Oliver's place in Salem.

He never thought he would sink so low. He turned the volume of the radio way up, hoping to drown out the disappointment that surfaced from inside him. The happy, sometimes nostalgic emotions, evoked by old Christmas songs battled with his anger at not being a good father. He felt a slight consolation though. The price of gold had shot up above a thousand dollars, and he would get a good price for his watch.

Once there, he saw a human-size picture of Oliver pasted on the window; he was dressed in jeans, leather shoes, and a wide-rim hat that showed his Texas origins. As he walked through the door, the client bell rang. The store was packed. On one side, sales people hobnobbed with clients and, in between, all kinds of jewelry and ornaments lay in cases. The place made his eyes pop. The haggling and the exchange of gold and silver for cash made it seem like a Moroccan street market. After watching Oliver's gold rush for ten minutes, he finally found an opportunity to make the exchange. Jason wasn't in a mood to bargain. He just took the offer and got out of the pawn shop with cash in his pocket. A bitter moment. The Rolex watch was a birthday present from his father. Sitting in the car, engine already started, he couldn't muster enough energy to drive out of the parking spot. Upon seeing his wrist devoid of the Rolex, sadness overwhelmed his heart and mind. He rested his forehead on the center of the steering wheel, forcing back a sob. He was powerless. It took an eternity to regain his composure. A good cry was what he needed. *I'll get the Rolex back.* He put the car in motion.

He drove to the mall. As expected the area was jammed with people doing last minute shopping. Those entering were empty-handed and others coming out were loaded with plastic bags filled with purchases. With so many people in the mall – in the stores, restaurants, parking lots and corridors – Jason wanted to spend as little time as possible in the shopping center. He decided what to get for Sarah. At fifteen she had become fashion conscious. One of her window-shopping indulgences was to go from one fashion store to another trying on clothes, pretending to be a model. Jason entered the first store he saw and bought her a dress.

For Keenan it was easy too. He went to CJ Games and got Xbox's Wireless Wheel, which looked like a steering wheel. While he was there, he bought him some games for the Xbox.

He returned to his car as fast as he could. Holding his keys in his hand, he stared outside, just to catch his breath. The parking was packed to full capacity with cars. Like ants on a mission shoppers moved from their cars to the mall and back. Then it hit him.

Kara!

Not to buy a present for her would be a blunder that would be difficult for her to forgive and forget. He dug bills out of his pocket. He had enough to buy her a small gift. He kept looking at the remaining money, calculating how much it would take to buy an appropriate gift that would be enough to appease her, but not so much that it would leave him penniless. *That's the last thing I need right now.*

An idea brought a smile to his face. It was a brilliant idea, actually. He went back to the mall and entered a jewelry store. After talking with the sales lady for a good twenty minutes, and looking at necklaces and earrings, he made the final decision that would fit his budget. When they were dating about two decades ago, while romancing and exchanging life stories, Kara told him how she wanted a small heart necklace and matching earrings, but her parents wouldn't buy them for her because she was grounded for misbehavior. Jason bought them, hoping to score a few points. Could this gesture put a little shine on their broken marriage, he wondered? *A slim chance, very slim.*

***

When Jason McDeere got out of the car after pulling into the driveway, he noticed Mr. Johnson, the next door neighbor, rushing towards him. Usually, he enjoyed this social time with the 70-year-old retiree, to whom Jason had a fatherly respect. Jason's father would have been the same age, had he been alive. When it came to local news Mr. Johnson was a lot more interesting than Google. He was always up-to-date on the latest gossip – who was moving in and who was moving out of the area. His mind was a storehouse of the good, the bad and the ugly of Corvallis trivia. As a former car salesman, he loved to talk.

"Jason, are you having problems with your furnace?"

"No, Mr. Johnson, why?" He shook his head, feeling immediately suspicious.

"I saw these two fellows pull in your driveway." He yanked his woolen hat lower to protect his ears from a swift wind.

"What fellows?" Jason said.

"Two white guys in their thirties, I suppose."

"Who were they?"

"From the natural gas company."

"The gas company?"

"Did you make a service call?" Mr. Johnson said, trying to be helpful.

"No. I did *not* make a call." He opened the back door of his Jetta.

"Problem?" Mr. Johnson rearranged the scarf around his neck to avoid a cold gust of wind.

"No heating problem that I know of." Jason reached for the colorfully wrapped boxes with matching ribbons and bows. He turned back towards Mr. Johnson after placing the gift boxes on the car roof.

"How do you know they were from the utility company?" Jason had gone past suspicion. The uneasy feeling had become a dull pain in his stomach.

"They pulled up in a truck with Embridge Gas Distribution written on the side."

"Did they go in?"

"One stayed in the van and the other went inside the house." Jason couldn't understand what his neighbor was telling him. Why would a service person for the gas company enter his house without his permission, and how did they get in? The door was locked. The uneasy feeling grew. He wasn't scared, rather puzzled and concerned.

"Have you seen them before?"

"The van, but not these two technicians."

"How long was the one inside?" Jason asked.

Mr. Johnson put a finger to his lip and tapped as he thought. He looked at his old wristwatch. "Oh, let me see. Maybe an hour."

"What time did the man enter?" Jason asked, his anxiety mounting.

"I'd say shortly after you left. I was waiting for a call from my daughter. So it must have been about twenty minutes after you drove away. Where did you go?"

"To Salem, to buy Christmas gifts for the kids and Kara."

"How are they?" said Mr. Johnson in a neighborly way.

"They're fine," he said impatiently. "The servicemen – what were they wearing?"

"Just normal uniforms. Ahh … yeah, they had something attached to their ears. You know, I see young kids wearing them. Not hearing aids. Bit bigger. You know what I mean."

"Must be earphones. For a cell phone, maybe." The puzzled look on the older man's face intensified. His nose and ears turned slightly red as the sun and wind hit them.

"What did you buy?" Mr. Johnson asked, once again turning the conversation back to Jason's shopping trip, always fishing for information for his next listener.

"Just a few simple things. Couldn't afford anything big," Jason said. The elderly man was never shy about asking personal or probing questions. But Jason didn't mind. In some ways he invited curiosity about his life. Besides, Mr. Johnson gave him the fatherly concern that he so desperately missed.

"Have you found a job yet?"

"Maybe. I have one that looks promising. In Mountain View, California."

"Are you selling and moving?"

"I'm not sure. I'd love to chat with you, Mr. Johnson, but I have to go in and check on my house."

"Let me know if you find anything."

"How did the gas technician get in?"

"The side door."

"Hmm. The side door. What else did you see?"

"Nothing much." A pause. "Yes, he was carrying a tool box and something in a plastic bag, but I couldn't tell you what."

"Thanks for the info. Let me know if you see anything else."

"Have a great Christmas. We should go for lunch next week."

"Sure." Jason started to walk away then turned back. "When did they leave?" Jason said.

The old man looked at his watch again. "About fifteen to twenty minutes ago."

"Very strange. I never made a service request. I'll go inside and have a look around." Jason walked away from his neighbor, but a thought kept hammering away at him. *Who are they?*

At the door, he carefully inspected the frame and the lock, but couldn't find any sign of forced entry. He dug into his pocket to fetch his keys and diligently inserted one into the gold plated lock. He was careful not to handle the door unless absolutely necessary. He didn't want his fingerprints planted over those of the intruder. He pushed the door open with the tip of the key, then entered the kitchen. He feared seeing pots, pans, chairs and tables all turned upside down, but there were no signs of any disturbance.

One thing was clear to him—someone had parked a van in his driveway in broad daylight and entered his house. And it was not petty theft. Jason walked through the dining room, family room and library, and still saw no visible disturbance. He trusted Mr. Johnson's sound mind. The man wouldn't make up anything, especially something as important as this.

Someone had been definitely in his house, perhaps looking for something. He climbed two flights of stairs to the second floor. The drawers of his bedroom were closed as he expected. Everything was in place in both the bathrooms and the bedrooms. He went down to the basement and entered the furnace room. It was humming, the pilot light still burning. Then he went to his office on the first floor where his laptop looked untouched. He examined every object on the table. The mug, paper, pencil, and pen – all were exactly as he'd left them. The chairs and the fixtures were positioned identically to the way they'd been when he'd left the house this morning. He sighed with relief that no physical damage had been done, yet he felt anger that his privacy had been violated.

He took a seat on his swivel chair, his elbow perched on the armrest and his fingers squeezing his lower lip. *Who were they?* The thought kept ringing in his mind. He began a methodical analysis of the situation. IRS agents? The freelance consulting that had earned him a few thousand dollars that he hadn't declared on his income tax? The IRS was too powerful an entity to enter his house secretly. They would simply wave a warrant and demand to search a house. FBI or local police investigators? Once inside, they would have turned everything upside down and leave a big mess behind. Perhaps related to the Softek incident. Nothing was taken as far he could tell. Who else?

He grabbed a stack of business cards from the desk in front of him and picked one. He went outside the house and walked about a block down the street. He called Kara; he needed to talk to her. Though she moved to her own place after the separation, half of the house still belonged to her. No answer. He left a message about seeing her later. Then he called some friends but they had nothing unusual to report.

Finally, he punched in numbers on his cell phone as he read them from the business card. Shallen.

After he'd introduced himself, Shallen cheerfully said, "Good to hear from you. What's up?"

Her response reminded him of their first meeting in the restaurant on the day after Brian's funeral. He regretted that he was unable to reciprocate with a cordial response to her. He was still in emotional turmoil from the news that someone had entered his home without his permission.

He paced the sidewalk, scarcely noticing the bare trees lining the street. "Did you write an article about the Softek incident?"

"Yes. An article appeared this morning. Early edition," Shallen said.

"Shouldn't I have been informed?"

"I'm sorry I didn't call you." She sounded truly apologetic.

"What's in it?"

"Everything we talked about. The shooting, outsourcing, and a class-action suit by ex-employees of Softek. That's all."

"Shouldn't you have called me?" he insisted, ducking his head against the wind.

"It was clear that I am from the *Post*. I wrote what you told me," she said, still sounding quite congenial. "I thought everything was on the record. Get a copy of the *Post* and have a look."

"I will."

The wind howled in the silence that stretched between them. "You sound worried," she said at last, breaking the silence. "What is it?"

"A couple of guys, masquerading as furnace technicians, entered my house." Worry lodged firmly in his mind.

"And you didn't call them?" said Shallen.

"No. And I checked inside the house. Found no intrusion whatsoever. What do you think their purpose was?"

"Wiretapping." Shallen gave it to him straight without a hint of hesitation.

"Wiretapping?" Jason murmured.

"I'll be in Corvallis in the new year. I want to explore the story further. I would like to talk to you." Shallen said.

He needed to trust someone. "Okay," he said. "By the way ... Merry Christmas. See you soon."

***

With presents in one hand, Jason McDeere pressed the doorbell with the other. Within moments Kara craned her head through the front door of her house. "Kids, your dad is here," she called. Then to Jason she said, "Come in."

Jason handed the presents over to Kara, hoping that he would get an invitation for Christmas Day. Sarah and Keenan came rushing to him. He gave each of them kisses and hugs.

"How was the interview?"

"It went very well. I got the job." He closed the door behind him.

"So quick!" Kara walked to the decorated pine tree in the foyer to pile the kid's presents on top of the others.

"That's the scary part." He gave a fake laugh and placed Kara's present on the foyer table.

"What do you mean?" Her words were filled with curiosity.

"Who gets a job in one interview?"

"Where is it?" said Kara

"Layton Industries in Mountain View, California"

"What do they do?"

"It's a US Defense Department subcontractor. A strange place. Their security is worse than Leavenworth."

"Are you taking it?" she asked. Jason watched as the kids ran back to what they were doing before.

"What are my options? None!" he said, furrowing his brow.

"I agree. You're in a deep financial hole." The words hit him like a two by four in the midsection. His money decisions had always been the cause of conflict in his marriage. "The faster you get out, the better."

"You don't have to rub it in." Although he agreed, her nagging never helped.

"Face the truth, Jason," Kara hissed.

"When I move to Mountain View, what are we going to do with the house?" He wanted a change of subject.

"We have to discuss it, but not now."

"When? It has to be soon." He was tired of the way she always put problems off. Then he got the blame when things went wrong.

She paused. "How about the day after Christmas?"

"Okay." He looked at the door and it reminded him of the break-in. "Did you order furnace service for the house?"

"Me. No. Why would I do that?" She gave him a where-is-this-going look.

"Apparently two guys went into the house this afternoon," Jason said.

"Where were you?" Kara looked at the reflection of her hairdo in the door glass.

"In Salem. Buying presents. Mr. Johnson saw them go in and out. I checked inside and found no sign of an intruder."

"Maybe the bank is after you." Sarcasm laced her words.

"Banks don't do that. You should know. You work at one." Jason took a deep breath to ease the pain in his stomach.

"All joking aside, it is worrisome." She looked a bit perturbed.

He was reaching for the door. "What are you doing for Christmas Day?"

"Going to my parents' place," Kara said.

"Why not have it at your place?"

"Because they invited us."

"What are you doing?" Kara said as if to be polite.

"Don't know yet. Stay at home, fill out security forms for the job, I guess."

"Join us then," said Kara.

"No. Your parents didn't invite me. I don't want to crash the party."

"They wouldn't mind."

"Christmas dinner with your father would be as bad as an IRS audit. I want to enjoy my turkey dinner and not be grilled by your father. Have a Merry Christmas." He left after hugs and kisses for the children, none for Kara. Once outside, he opened the door of the car and sank in the seat, still holding the key. He sat motionless. *How can she go to her parent's place?* In the seventeen years that he had known her, fifteen years since Sarah's birth and eleven years since Keenan's birth, this was the first time he would be spending Christmas without any of them.

***

Roget Hunt unlocked the door, entered his sanctuary and waved the black rectangular block in the air close to every surface in the room. When the bug check was over, he leaned towards the window, lifted one of the leaves of the blind to peek outside. The red sun barely touched the ocean's horizon, casting a glow on the shiny surface below. Just above it, clouds scuttled by the fiery celestial ball while on the beach a few people walked the shimmering sand of this beautiful, natural setting.

Roger had purchased this 10 million dollar property for its pricey and prestigious Del Mar, California neighborhood, and more importantly for the privacy it gave him. As a political consultant he had the right skills to get all the money he wanted or needed. He knew no one was watching him. How could they? Since he bought this place, no one except him had entered this room. A private man with many secrets, Roger had a sure way to protect his asset and prestige as a high profile consultant.

Roger sank into the chair, switched on a small table lamp and activated the Blackberry security program. After signing on, he punched in a number and waited for a response. "Good afternoon, Guy, its Roger."

"What's up?" the man at the other end responded.

"To start, I'll be handling all the security for Jason McDeere from here on out."

"Okay, boss," said Guy Volpa, an ex-FBI agent who transformed from being a government employee to freelance security consultant for high-profile personalities.

When Guy called him boss, it put a smile on his face, turning any anger he might feel to instant pleasure. "How did the bugging go? Were you able to get inside McDeere's house?" He fired up his laptop.

"As planned," Volpa said in his usual confident manner.

"Did you use wireless?" With a few clicks on the Internet browser, a list of all the stocks Roger owned dropped down on the screen, the movement of prices revealed in a green "up" arrow or a red "down" arrow.

"Yes. I used the latest technology."

"Will it work the way we want?" Rogers wanted to make sure Volpa was ahead of the enemy.

"Guaranteed, sir. I used equipment developed by ex-Nokia employees and in an obscure town in Germany. Very expensive, though."

"Good." The response brought Roger more warm feelings.

"Each wireless receptor transmits voice and pictures to a neighboring antenna positioned in a secret location, which in turn sends all the information we need to our control center."

"Did you check it out?" Roger lifted his free hand to release his tension.

"Absolutely. He talked to his neighbor about my two guys going in his house. He checked though every room of the entire house. He sat in the chair of his home office, picked up a business card and walked out of the house."

"What does that mean?" Roger leapt to his feet, not liking what he'd heard.

"I don't know."

"Where did he go?"

"He walked down the street."

"Volpa, you lost his trail." Roger's anger sprang back with a vengeance.

"That's all I can do for now," Volpa argued.

"Where was his car?" Roger demanded.

"In the driveway," said Volpa.

"He walked. Why did he do that?"

"I don't know."

"Volpa, I pay good money to know everything about a suspect. He walked down the road to make a phone call. And you didn't catch it."

"Boss, you have to understand that we had only a few hours notice to do this job."

"This Jason guy wants to start a class-action suit against one of our companies. This is serious. I want to make sure it doesn't happen." Roger was boiling inside. "What is your next move?" he yelled.

"We took care of the front, back and inside of the house. Next is his cell phone and car." Volpa explained.

"I expect a much better job. I want him in my net."

After hanging up, his attention switched back to his laptop screen. His eyes popped wide open at the red arrow beside Softek International, with prices plunging a whopping thirty percent. Scouring the business news, he noticed a Wall Street analyst had bad-mouthed Softek, citing outsourcing as the possible cause of the killing of the CIO. The analyst also mentioned the early edition *Post* article, recommending investors sell the stock, based on the fear of an ex-employee's class-action suit. He couldn't let that happen.

5

Jason McDeere arrived at Rose's Coffee Time a few minutes before noon. Moments after he picked a seat in a secluded corner, "Happy" Molly came by to pour a cup of coffee. Every customer got a Molly smile, rain or shine, no discrimination. As he watched her receding back, he thought she must be making good tips on her figure and charming personality. After sniffing the aroma and taking a few sips of freshly brewed coffee, he glanced at his empty wrist. He missed his gold watch. With lips tightened, he suppressed a nostalgic memory then turned his head to the clock hanging on the wall behind the cash register. It was already several minutes past noon.

Kara was late. Again.

He grimaced in frustration and glanced around the half empty place. For many years his grandmother had drilled into Jason the importance of being early for all appointments. His family often laughed at the thought of her being early for her own funeral.

Another glance at the entrance gave him little comfort. Kara was nowhere in sight. He huffed a sigh and then swallowed more coffee while reminding himself that there was no need to get worked up. Patience was not his strongest virtue but he gave himself points for trying. Just as he was about to give up on her, he saw her emerge from a car in front of the restaurant. Though she was ten minutes late, he forced himself to be cheerful and not to mention her tardiness. That would be suicidal. She would walk out without any resolution. He was determined they would discuss what to do about the house and end the meeting in an amicable fashion as smoothly as possible . . . he hoped. Over the years they had grown apart, never seeing eye-to-eye on anything. They could be looking at the same sky, yet disagree about what they were seeing. A crack between them had been growing wider with time.

Kara's face appeared in the frame of the front door. In hurried pace, she continued to Jason. "I drove the kids to my parents' place," Kara said with a hint of apology, as she lowered herself into a wooden chair across from him and then dropped her rather large handbag on the chair next to her. She breathed a sigh of relief.

"Good, you made it," Jason said with a fake smile, determined to hide his true feelings.

Molly approached them with a pair of menus, dropped one in front of each of them and poured coffee for both. She penciled their orders and walked over to the next customer.

"It has been a busy day, so far." She scanned the restaurant.

"How did Sarah and Keenan like their presents?" Jason said, filled with a mixture of impatience and eagerness. Witnessing their reactions would have been so much better than hearing about it afterward.

"Sarah wore the dress right away. She went nuts about the color. Good choice. Kept checking her dress in the mirror all day. It was a perfect selection. Keenan went wild. " Kara's face radiated for the first time since she'd arrived.

"Oh, I wish I'd been there." Jason beamed too, imagining his children tearing off the wrapping paper, surprise written on their faces. He felt proud to be a father. Restoring his family life must rank higher in time to come.

"What did you do?" Kara said, the radiance dimming. Kara glanced at the dessert section of the menu just as the waitress reappeared to take their order. Then she snapped up the menus and left.

"Rocky called. He thought I would get sick of filling out security forms all day, so his cure was to have me join his family. Turkey-induced happiness. I couldn't refuse his offer." He looked around, only to notice tables and chairs filled with mostly seniors. *Seniors' specials day at Rose's?* There had always been a lot of seniors in Corvallis.

An awkward silence passed between them as they sipped their coffee. "Guess what?" Kara said, breaking the standoff. "Aunt Mary and Uncle Joe showed up. They almost missed their connection in Chicago. Major snowstorm, thanks to a Canadian cold blast."

"We can blame the Canadians for everything. They're not listening." Jason reciprocated Kara's smile.

"Thanks for the necklace and earrings. You didn't have to do that. But it was thoughtful." Kara gave a nod of approval.

"Didn't you get anything for me?" Jason blurted out, suddenly realizing the blunder he'd just committed.

In the silence that followed she touched her handbag, as if she didn't know how to answer him. "I didn't have time."

"What's the real reason?" Jason knew he was treading risky waters.

"I didn't want to give you any ideas."

"What ideas?" Jason's probe was calculated.

Slowly and precisely, like an accomplished chess player, Kara made her move. "Let's not go there. Let's talk about the house."

Molly appeared with quiche for her and a club sandwich for him.

Jason made two triangular sandwiches disappear in a hurry, easing the hunger pangs, while Kara gingerly sliced the quiche into small pieces. Every time she placed the fork on the plate, she touched her lips with her napkin.

He broke the silence. "I want to hang on to the house."

"Can't do that." Jason had ignored Kara's many past objections, yet now he had no choice but to acknowledge them.

"Why? Father missing in action? That's not me." He massaged the muscle between his shoulder and neck to lessen the mounting tension.

"By taking a job in Silicon Valley, you *will* be missing in action. You don't need a house." She sat back in the chair.

"The kids love the house. They miss their bedrooms." Jason used the emotion card to win ground. It was always difficult to argue with Kara's lawyer-like mind. Winning was her goal in any conversation.

"They'll get used to it," Kara fired back.

"I'm hoping we can get together. Live as a family again."

"My hope has evaporated. You haven't done anything to rescue the relationship."

"You can't blame me for everything."

She threw down her napkin. "We could have settled our score through therapy. Instead of talking, you run for your cave and solve problems by yourself. Hello. There are two of us."

"Shrinks are for weaklings."

"Weaklings. Strength is not exactly oozing out of you. Relationships make people change. It's a must. You're the immoveable rock of Gibraltar." Kara wrapped her hair around her ear.

"Exaggeration gets you nowhere. It's your trademark. You beat Fox News hands down. I have changed. I like--no *love*--your cooking," he said, tongue in cheek, then took a sip to wash down the sandwich. He knew the conversation could get sidetracked into unpleasant territory. He moved his head and shoulder to ease the tension.

"This is no time to be funny." Kara groaned.

"Seriously. We can't sell the house." Jason watched two more seniors walk in to take the next table. *There must be a seniors' convention in the neighborhood.*

"Who says we can't," Kara said, her voice lowered.

"The housing market is spiraling into an abyss. We have negative equity right now," Jason said.

"Good reason to sell now and cut our losses. To me, the timing doesn't matter. I sell low and buy low. Paying rent is not an acceptable option for me." Kara moved her head slowly to scan the place. Some seniors were leaving.

"You've seen the foreclosure signs and auctions in town." Jason was determined to defend his territory.

"I have."

"Buyers are hiding. They're waiting for the prices to hit rock bottom. When will that happen? Who knows? It will take time," said Jason.

She threw up her hands. "I give up. As long as you keep the house, *you* pay the mortgage. Don't miss one single payment." The reconciliation made the tension on Kara's face disappear. She was busy hooking the last piece of quiche with her fork.

As Jason's eyes scanned the place, he weighed in on what he was about to say. "I can live with that! I have a job and can afford it." Jason took another deep breath to keep the tension headache under control.

"Money in your hand disappears like water through a sieve," Kara said.

"You always talk like a banker's daughter." Jason felt as though she were treating him like a child.

"Being careful with money is common sense. But you don't get it. You'll never get it. That's the truth."

Jason leaned forward with an eye on the seniors to ensure they weren't listening. He lowered his voice. "The truth is we're not selling the house at a fire sale price and I *can* afford to keep the payment going on it. You can count on that."

"Why are you whispering?" She frowned.

"I don't want them listening." He waved his hand toward an old couple at a nearby table.

"They're not eavesdropping. They're looking at their menus."

"Maybe." He shrugged, unconvinced.

Molly came by to check if everything was all right. She penciled an order of two blueberry pies, cleared the plates and disappeared. The fresh smell of warm pie, which no one can resist, filled the restaurant. It must be spiced with some special ingredient.

"Ok. We can keep the house for a while. We'll decide what to do with it later. When are you moving?"

He was not sure what she meant. "To California?"

"Yes."

"Don't know. I'm going through security checks. Just have to wait." Jason sat back and straightened his tie.

"Good you finally have a job," Kara said.

"What's that supposed to mean?"

"You haven't noticed? You've been a miserable person."

"I know. It hasn't been weeks in Paradise Beach for me, either. I've gone to hell and back, and lived to tell the story." He laid his hands out, palms up.

Molly set the pies in front of them and poured more coffee.

"Yeah. It must have been hell." Kara nodded her head in agreement.

"I got a job and yet I feel I shouldn't have it."

Kara frowned. "What do you mean? You're not thinking of turning it down?" She hit the table in frustration.

"What I mean is that hundreds of my coworkers and ex-coworkers are still going through the pain. I'm getting a good paying job. My problems are behind me. I don't know if I deserve it." He combed his thick hair with his fingers.

Kara paused for a moment of reflection then looked out the wide windows. "Over the years that I've known you, there is one quality that I find attractive. You have compassion for others."

Outside, the sun was hiding behind the clouds, still too shy to come out fully. Jason wondered where her thoughts were coming from. Empathy was out of character for her. He pressed his point harder. "I should be with them, suffer like them and not abandon them."

"They'll manage. They're adults."

"I'm betraying their loyalty. That's what it is." He pushed the blueberry pie away. Suddenly, it didn't look so good.

"You have no choice. You have to take the job." Kara emphasized "the job."

"I know." It was a foregone conclusion.

"If your conscience is bothering you, you should go after justice and fairness."

"I've never known this side of you. You're talking like a Greek philosopher."

She stabbed the berries with her fork. "After our separation, I've had a chance to think and I've sifted through the details of our lives together and separately."

"I have too." For the first time in years, he felt like they were on the same page.

To his surprise she said, "Start a class-action suit. It will sooth your nerves, make you feel better."

"I've looked into it already. It's very costly. With my salary, there's not enough money to dole out for a class-action suit. If you weren't always asking for so much, always pushing me . . ." Jason was testing her motive for the idea.

"I know," she said, once again surprising him. "But you would be helping your friends. If you don't, guilt will follow you the rest of your life."

"In Mountain View I won't have time for a class-action suit. I'll be stuck working on some missile guidance system project." He watched her eyes, fishing for the truth.

"I'll help you." Kara continued eating her pie.

Jason placed his fork on his plate. "You'll help me. Did I hear right?"

"Yes. I will." She couldn't have been any clearer.

"I know you have a lawyer's mind. Don't like to lose an argument. How can you help?"

"Right now I don't know exactly what I can do, since I've never done it before. I'll figure it out and put some time into it. But I'll tell you this, I want half of your settlement." She flashed him a smile of confidence.

"Now, you're talking like a business analyst." Jason tugged at his hair, giving serious thought to this offer.

"More like a lawyer. I like the court procedures."

"You get half of what I get. That's too much. Usually a law firm would only take 30 percent of the total settlement. Including expenses." He rubbed his chin.

"A law firm will take 30% of the global settlement," Kara said. "I mean 30 % of what the court gives you. I'm serious but you're right – it's too early to decide on my cut."

"Right. It is too early." Compensation for her efforts would only be fair. "It's a deal." He groaned.

She looked at her watch. "Oh, oh. I have to go. I'll get the check. Merry Christmas." Her grin was wide enough to cause crater-like dimples.

"Late but acceptable." He grinned widely.

"Need a ride?"

"No. I'll stay and finish my pie."

He watched her go to the cash register and out of the door. He couldn't believe what had just happened. He threw his head back and closed his eyes, relieved from head to toe. He had dreaded the outcome of this meeting. There must be a God somewhere. The meeting went well. Keeping the house where he could visit Sarah and Keenan during his home visit readied him mentally for the move.

California, here I come.

Compassion and justice. Jason didn't pretend to know what Kara had meant by that, but he felt certain he would discover her true meaning – in time. He wasn't just a tech head. He knew that the laid-off workers were treated unfairly. Once they were no longer useful to Softek, they were discarded like garbage. They were hired under the pretext of securing a government contract. Now, the government was turning a blind eye to the employees' desperation. Helping his friends, in memory of Brian, felt like the right thing to do. Jason dreamt of wearing the compassion and justice badge of honor. America could use some of these virtues . . . the world too.

Kara's eagerness to help was a mystery to him. He knew it wasn't about money as the only ones who got rich on a suit such as this were the lawyers. Whatever the reason he was sure he would come to learn the truth, in time.

***

Jason McDeere lifted the blinds in his room to let the morning sunlight in. He sank into the swivel chair in front of the desk and fired up the MacBook laptop. He had a definite purpose in mind. After the computer was up, he typed Mountain View on the Google page and a listing of maps, colleges, high schools, city departments, restaurants, and real estate came into view. He browsed some of them only to satisfy his curiosity as he would soon be moving there to live for . . . how long? Who knew? He was hoping the job would last long enough to get back on his feet financially.

The sun's rays distracted his attention as it became brighter, shining directly on him. He gazed through the window into a blue sky, thinking perhaps Mother Nature was giving him her blessing. He took a moment to reflect on the present and future. His life was turning around, though slowly like a big ship. Still, he was happy with the direction it was heading. He shifted back to the web page. Why couldn't Google read his mind? He was interested in the availability and price of accommodation rentals in Mountain View, California, but none of the selections gave him any information. With several clicks of the mouse he flipped through more Internet pages while he grunted and groaned, disappointed by Google's results. He switched to another search engine and laughed out loud at some of the flashing funny advertisements he saw. He didn't care how noisy he was. He was alone in the house.

The phone rang and it was David Cohen at the other end. He was happy to hear from his prospective employer.

"The job offer is on its way. FedEx should deliver it to you this afternoon," said David in a rather loud and firm voice.

"What's in it?" Jason was dying to know the details, especially the salary. Anything else would be bonus.

"What we discussed when you were here." David cleared his throat.

"While you're on the phone, can we go over the details?" Jason tried to sound relaxed.

"Certainly, the ninety thousand salary, medical, and three weeks vacation is all conditional upon security clearance."

"That's ten thousand more than we discussed." Jason smiled at the unexpected extra.

"Because we want you here ASAP."

"When do I start?" Jason hoped to hide his eagerness.

"Today is the twenty-seventh. I would like you to leave Corvallis on Jan 2nd."

"That would be okay with me. I'm ready." Jason was imagining David as a boss. Would Jason be willing to march to his orders? *Probably*. In previous job, on some occasions, Jason had not seen eye-to-eye with his supervisors. A mental note not to rock the boat sunk in a corner of his mind.

"I'm hoping there will be no problems." David's voice faded.

"Sorry. Didn't hear what you said." Jason was on his feet like a spring-loaded piston. He pressed the cell phone closer to his ear and his nose was almost touching the window, in an attempt to get better reception.

"Hope you will be here by the 2nd." The phone communication improved.

"What do you mean?" Jason sensed some doubt.

"The Pentagon has received all your security papers. Usually they are as slow as turtles when it comes to work. During the holiday season, they do a disappearing act and don't normally show up at the office. But we have connections. We're bribing someone with double pay to clear your application by tomorrow."

"That's a very powerful connection." As he looked outside, he palmed his thick hair.

"One more thing. I took the liberty of starting you in our Alaska office. I hope you don't mind."

"Alaska?" Jason shot back, a little louder than intended.

"Why. Is there a problem?" David's voice quivered, suggesting a hidden agenda.

"Yes." He returned to the chair and sank into it.

"We have our production launch pad installation here. We download our new or upgraded software into real missiles. No one has ever entered this place on day one. Minimum of six months. Because I need someone like you in Alaska right away, I made all kinds of unusual exceptions. The Pentagon wasn't happy about the shortcuts in your case."

"David, I understand your problem. But I can't go to Alaska." He rubbed his eyes, groaning inwardly.

"It's a very friendly work environment, like a big family. I can add another ten to the top of your salary, if it would make it easier," said David.

"I have two kids. I can't be too far away." He tapped the table with his fingertips.

"No problem. Bring your family with you. We'll pay for all your expenses including relocation, private schools, and we'll find a job for your wife on the US Navy Base. No problem." David sounded desperate, willing to hoola dance to satisfy his demands.

"The problem is that my wife and I are separated." Jason hesitated getting into his personal information, but he had no choice.

"Oh. Sorry about that. I didn't know." David sounded sincerely apologetic.

"I should have told you about it but my marital status never came up." He moved his head back and forth, hoping to release the tension around his neck.

"No problem. I'll fly you back home once a month."

"I desperately need a job. But I'd be away from my children for too long, and going to Alaska would make it very difficult. I'll have to think about it."

"Ok. But don't take too long. It's an excellent opportunity for you and your family. Once you start, a lot more benefits will come your way. I can't discuss them with you now." Jason could hear the used-car sales pitch.

"I would prefer to stay in Corvallis, but with no jobs here, Mountain View was my only alternative." He rubbed his forehead.

"Mountain View is only a development and test site. We are doing an upgrade project for the Defense Department and we need someone with your background in our real-time launch site in Alaska. I need a decision from you soon."

"I can't make a decision right now." A headache was building and he rubbed his temples.

"Let me ask you this. What will it take for you to move to Alaska? More money, more vacation time? Just tell me. I'll make it happen." David seemed desperate, as though fearful of losing him. Jason hoped it would work to his advantage.

"I'm not sure," Jason said, the headache now pounding.

They talked a few minutes longer, then hung up. He threw the cell phone on the table, slammed the laptop shut and closed the door. Then he lowered the blinds, turned off the light and flopped on the leather couch. Some powerful and destructive emotion was forming inside him. It had more force than a storm. It was more like a volcano rumbling inside his gut, causing a burning pain, with eruptions of anger coming at him in waves. Why hadn't David informed him that he might have to move to Alaska? He rubbed his temples and then put his hand over his eyes, wishing he could go to sleep and forget this day had ever happened.

Kara wouldn't even consider moving to Alaska, which would definitely make it out of the question. He would have to drive to Portland from Corvallis and then fly to

Alaska. The one-way journey could tax him a good part of a day. The travel time would be costly and wouldn't leave him much free time to spend with his children. What about the class action suit? He wouldn't be able to do anything about it. Many thoughts churned in his mind, shifting from one to the other in no logical order. He needed someone to talk to. Anybody. Even a shrink.

The rumbling in his stomach was getting louder and more painful. He jumped off the couch and descended the stairs to the kitchen. He opened the fridge door, only to find empty shelves. He checked the freezer section and discovered a month-old container of ice cream alone on the shelf. The milk in the ice cream would make the pain in his empty stomach worse. He settled for two end slices of a loaf of bread and frost bitten cheese. After eating he returned to the cave-like atmosphere of his room where he could think better.

Back on the couch, lying on his side, he was regaining some strength from the food he just ate. He grabbed the cell and turned on the light. He rubbed his eyes while scrolling down the number list on the small screen. He pressed the send button and waited. After introducing himself, he recognized the voice of Julia Svenborg, Senator Quest's executive assistant.

"Mr. McDeere. What do you need this time?" She groaned. He could have slapped her for the unfriendly response. Fortunately, she was so far away.

"I would like to speak to Senator Quest, please." The request was carefully couched in the most cordial and friendly manner he could muster. Inside him the volcano was still bleeding red-hot emotion.

"Ahh let me see. The Senator is in a meeting as we speak. Then he has a luncheon and afterward he is leaving for Washington. I don't think the Senator will have time to return your call today," she said in a slow monotone as if she had eternity.

"It's urgent…"

"It's always urgent, Mr. McDeere. How urgent can it be this time?" Julia said.

"Very urgent. The Martians will be attacking us soon," he blurted out. Then he regretted being so thoughtless. Still, this person at the other end of the line was irritating him beyond belief.

"Ha-ha-ha. I've heard many reasons to talk to the Senator, but yours beat them all," Julia said.

"Seriously, I have to discuss a very important matter. Just let him know I called."

"I will."

Five minutes later, he was back in the kitchen again. He opened the fridge door only to find the bare shelves again. He went after the ice cream. Why were they sending him to Alaska? Just then the phone rang. The Senator. Startled, he flipped it open to answer the call.

"Jason, what can I do for you?" the Senator said in a strong, friendly voice.

"I talked to David Cohen. To my surprise he is sending me to Alaska. Senator, this was not what we agreed upon. Mountain View, California is already too far to be away from my family. I can't neglect my children. Alaska is unimaginable."

"Take your family with you." The words were loaded with enthusiasm, as if it the logical thing to do.

"I can't." Jason was careful not to show sensed a frustration emerging inside him.

"It will be a good experience for them. See another part of America." The Senator was trying to sound convincing, but it wasn't working.

"I've considered that, but my children are at an age that they don't want to move. My in-laws live in town and my wife refuses to be too far from them. Health reasons."

"Jason, I can't meddle in David's business. Who and where is left up to him. He is just a contact and a nice fellow. As a Defense Department contractor, I know his company always needs people. Where he places you is up to him."

"I understand, Senator. But I can't take a job in Alaska. I would rather work in McDonalds here." He sighed. "With my credentials, I'm sure I'll find something better than a restaurant job." Jason placed the spoon in the ice cream container.

"I'll call David. Then I'll call you back." They hung up.

Jason scraped the bottom of the container while looking at the cell phone and waiting for it to ring.

The Senator called back to tell Jason that he could start his job on the 2nd of January in Mountain View. He was relieved by the news yet that uneasy feeling he'd had at the interview returned. Something wasn't right about all of this, but he just couldn't put his finger on it. He licked the spoon one last time, then, threw the container in the garbage. He was just over-thinking it. Everything would be fine. Just fine.

6

Jason McDeere shoved the Styrofoam cup in the garbage bin after a final gulp of lukewarm coffee. Instinctively giving a glance at his empty wrist, he then entered through the front door of the Layton Industries building, reporting for work on the first day. As he hoped, his arrival was on time: 8:30 AM according to the wall clock. Two of the younger security officers looked tired as if they needed another rest day post New Year's Day. The older one of the three, a woman, appeared ready for work. All were dressed in clean, crisp navy blue uniforms.

After introducing himself at the counter, Jason watched as the female officer checked a list in front of her. Then she ushered him inside the security office. He walked through the entrance near the counter and sat on a high stool, as she instructed. Jason said, "What's happening?"

"We're taking your picture and making you a security badge," she said as though the answer was obvious.

"What if I don't want my picture taken? I feel like a prisoner starting jail time." Upon speaking the words, Jason felt a release of tension.

She looked at the sheet in her hand. "Mr. McDeere. This is a procedure dictated by the Department of Defense. I didn't make it up. Believe me. You will be entering a classified building. As such, your access to anywhere in this building has to be stored, in case auditing and verification is needed." She looked straight at him.

"Without the picture –"

"Without the picture, there would be no pass. Without the pass, you cannot enter the building." Her eyes turned fierce and unbending.

Jason grimaced and said, "Ok." He couldn't win.

He straightened his upper body, looked directly into the camera lens, recalibrated his smile then waited for her cue. The flash showered him with a burst of bright light. The officer checked on the computer screen. She said, "Good" and disappeared while Jason watched the other officers attend to visitors, make phone calls, wearing serious expressions at all times. The officer returned holding a laminated badge with Jason's picture pasted to a security pass. The officer warned him, "If you lose this badge, please inform this 800 number immediately. Wait in the lobby and I'll call Mr.

Cohen to come down."

Seated on a black leather chair, Jason watched employees file in through the front door, press their security badges into the scanner, wait for the green light to come on, and pass through a narrow revolving door, one at a time. They wore business casual dress, as he expected. He had worn a dark pair of pants with fresh pleats and a blue long sleeve shirt. As he tapped his fingers on his knees, his mind examined again the motives of all the players, while feeling tension building in his stomach. Why had Cohen tried to send him to Alaska and then reversed his decision after Senator Quest's intervention? It suggested a very close working relationship between Layton Industries and the Senator. He vowed to find out, somehow. While thoughts churned endless, he fixed his eyes on the revolving door, both of these concerns fought for his attention. Just then, David Cohen slid through the narrow pathway afforded by the revolving door.

They vigorously shook hands, exchanged New Year's greetings, but David's smile didn't reach his lips. Dry as a desert rock. Maybe he needed another day of rest like the two security officers. Or, perhaps, he didn't like being trumped by the Senator, which may have caused his ego to be steamrolled.

As they walked past the elevators, David said, "On our left is our employee lounge, which you'll find very useful from time to time." It was spacious, filled with a sofa, chairs and a coffee table clustered in the corner.

"I find that the security is unusually tight. Does it have to be so rigid?" Jason wanted to clear the bad taste left from dealing with the security woman.

David turned to Jason. "Yes. It is tight. None of us like it, but we learn to live with it." As they walked, David dutifully described the dining hall and free meals served.

Jason nodded, impressed. In his twenty years of work, he'd never received a free lunch. Hunger pangs reminded him he hadn't eaten well lately. "What kinds of meals do they serve?"

David listed the local and international dishes served and then patted his potbelly. They passed a long bank of windows on their left, the dining hall on the right.

"One could gain weight in this place," Jason said.

"That's true. We'll stop at the coffee shop and get something. Then we'll talk a bit before going to the office." David pointed to the right.

They stepped to the end of the line, which moved in slow motion, until it was their turn. Jason loaded his tray with a tall coffee, one egg and bacon, one doughnut, one muffin, one cream cheese Danish and said, "That's enough for now. Thank you." The lady behind the counter frowned, which invoked a flush of embarrassment in Jason. Free food at a workplace was a fascination. Both Jason and David sought a secluded area of the coffee shop and sat down, satisfied with their plates full of delicious food.

"How can the company afford all this?" Jason took a sip of coffee and then tucked into his scrambled eggs and bacon.

"The employees have to work hard here. We need the energy." David took a bite of his muffin.

"I hope I didn't get you into trouble by calling the Senator," Jason said, politely fishing for information.

"Not at all. We need someone with your technical background here and in Alaska."

"Does the Senator normally get involved?" Jason looked straight at David's brown eyes, closely examining his response.

"No." Silence followed David's short reply, as Jason sensed that he asked a forbidden question and tried a different tactic?.

"What will I be doing here? Same as what we discussed in the interview?" Jason straightened his back and slowed the intake of food.

"Same position, but it has changed slightly. You will be working with the test team headed by Indira Gupta. Gupta is extremely smart and has been working with us for over ten years" David looked at Jason's bulging cheeks and then the plate from which the eggs, bacon and toast had disappeared within a few minutes. "She is one of our most dedicated DMDS members."

Still chewing, Jason said, "That's data management and decision support."

"That's correct," David said.

"Ok." Jason nodded.

"Our client – our only client – is the Department of Defense. They dictate to us the rules and we follow their protocols as best we can. Because we deal with sensitive and classified information regarding the defense of our country, it is important we obey the rules. If not, our client can cancel our contract at any time. In short notice, we'll all be out of a job. Therefore…" A passerby caught his attention, to which David saluted with a quick wave of his hand, "… you will be watching and not doing much for the next six months. You will be under Indira's constant and regular supervision. I hope this won't be a problem."

"Oh no, I have no problem with a woman being my superior. In fact I have lots of experience. My wife thinks she's my boss." He laughed.

David adjusted his glasses. "I meant about security."

Jason wasn't connecting with the humorless person sitting across from him. David was about ten years older and had much less hair. Jason would have lots of time to discover what made the new boss laugh, if anything.

"Security is fine, too." Jason cleared his throat, choking on the thought of security. Then he lowered his head, ready to attack the honey-glazed doughnut, but instead took a sip of coffee to wash down the greasy taste of bacon lingering in his mouth.

David pulled an envelope from his pocket and handed it to Jason. "Here's some pocket money. It's part of you relocation expense." David caressed his bald, shiny head.

This was the first time Jason had ever received money in an envelope for moving expenses. Although Jason wanted to know how much was in it, he didn't want to open it now and appear too greedy. He could wait. He would also have to come up with rent when he found an apartment.

"What is the limit for relocation expenses?" Jason took a bite of the freshly glazed doughnut.

"Ten thousand." David placed the last piece of the muffin in his mouth.

"That's generous." Jason looked around at the people leaving to start their day at Layton.

"It is. You will notice that Layton is very good to its employees. We create a family environment here. We work very hard and play together. We give our employees no reason to leave the company." David wiped his mouth and placed the napkin on the plate.

"That's good. But why?"

"Jason, our client demands that no one leaves the company before retirement, except in case of severe illness. You'll understand the reason. We work on sensitive projects for the protection of our nation. Many continue to work as consultants well after retirement." He sipped more coffee and greeted colleagues with nods as they passed.

As Jason gobbled up more food, he noticed that David was fidgeting as if ready to move on. "Thank you for hiring me."

"Jason, I look forward to your contribution to my department and Layton. We should go to the office now." David placed the cup down.

Both grabbed their trays, walked to the trash bin, where they disposed the cups and wrappings and stacked the trays. They walked back to the elevators. "It's a very secure building," Jason said.

They got off on the third floor. "Very secure. Surveillance cameras are everywhere except in washrooms." David looked straight in Jason's eyes.

"Everywhere," Jason said softly. *Free food. Hard work. Can't leave the company till death do employees and Layton part.* It felt like a prison where highly paid inmates were stuck for life without a parole hearing.

"My office is over there." David waved to the left. "The DMDS group is right here." They walked to the cubicle next to his office. "And this is Indira Gupta, the team leader." David paused while Jason and Indira shook hands. The top of her head leveled with David's and came short, by a few inches, of Jason's 6-foot frame. Her skin was dark, almost black, and she had a thin, long face, no sign of cheekbones. Her bushy hair was braided at the back, and tucked behind her ears with a straight part in the middle of her head. "Indira will introduce you to the team members and give you the lowdown on the kind of work you will be involved in." David nodded, then left.

Indira walked around introducing Jason to the employees at each cubicle. Each employee greeted Jason with a smile and a handshake. Then Jason and Indira went to the Eisenhower conference room. Indira closed the door while Jason looked around, then seated himself comfortably in one of the dozen chairs surrounding the light brown table. The walls were decorated with large colorful pictures of cruise missiles, each demonstrating a particular weapons capability. At one end of the rectangular room was a wide flat-screen TV.

"How many interviews did you have?" Indira took a seat across from Jason.

"One." Jason turned to her, interrupting his inspection of the room.

"Very unusual." She stood up and walked to the DVD player attached to the

TV.

"Why do you say that?" Jason watched Indira bend down, peering at buttons as if deciding which one to press.

Indira straightened and turned around to face Jason. "It always takes three to four interviews. One with the manager, David. One with me. One from our security group and one from HR. Your hiring is very unusual."

"I got the impression someone was urgently needed."

Indira stared at him as if he'd grown two heads. "This position needed to be filled, but it wasn't urgent by any means. We could have continued working and met our delivery deadlines without filling this position."

"It wasn't urgent? Then why the hurry?" Jason looked at Indira's thin, tall frame. He rubbed his forehead.

"You must have a very powerful person behind your application," Indira said, shaking her head.

"Senator Quest, from my state. Do you know him?"

"No. Politics have never interested me." Indira took a seat next to him.

"I went to see the Senator about layoffs and outsourcing our jobs. After discussing various issues, I told him I needed a job. He called David. I got the impression the Senator owned Layton Industries."

"I don't know much about the involvement of the Senator, except our work is mainly for the US government, but one thing you will learn quickly here is that information is protected at all levels. Every person gets a piece of information on a need-to-know basis. David wouldn't tell me anything unless it was directly related to my work." Indira took a deep breath.

"How strict is this policy?" Jason looked at the notepad in front of him.

"Very strict. You are not to discuss work with anyone except someone in our group, especially not friends and family.

"Before I forget, when you leave the office your desk must be clear . . . as in empty. Everything should be locked away. Every evening there is a security check. Any breach could result in losing your job." She reached for the machine. "I'll start with the DVD." Indira walked to the switch, turned off the light and took a seat. Both watched.

It showed a theater control room, with screens of all sizes and buttons and lights. Then missiles shot up and, after reaching certain altitude, cruised over mountains, deserted terrains, forests, oceans, and lakes. They were fired from many platforms--mobile launchers, small or big ships, and aircrafts. All travelled to their destinations in terrain-hugging flight paths to deliver pinpoint precision strike. In this DVD the targets were trees, mountains and other missile. The missing piece of the puzzle were the real targets – real situations in a real war. Jason remembered the live coverage he'd seen of war in Iraq, and felt sure these two versions looked very different.

When the DVD was over, Indira turned the light on. She pointed to a picture on the wall. "The main components are an airframe, propulsion system, guidance system and weapon payload. Our concern here is only the guidance system."

"Is it complicated?" Jason's mouth was half open, the shock he had just experienced still fresh.

"It's the brain. Very complex. No one in our department knows everything about it. Each of us know parts of it," she explained in a professorial demeanor.

"Really," Jason said softly.

"That's all for now. In the next month you will have to take four courses on building security and software security, and the other two on confidentiality."

"What kind of ammunition is in the payload?" Jason said as he combed his hair with his fingers.

"It's not our concern. Therefore, we don't ask such questions." Indira's reply was a bit stern.

"Ok. David said that you have a PhD. Which university?" Jason wondered about her age. She looked twenty something, but dark skin was good at hiding one's age, especially a female's age.

"Princeton. Everyone in the department has at least one PhD. How about you?"

"Just a bachelor in computer science. Wanted to do graduate studies, but it didn't work out. I'm a fast learner." He laughed, but Indira didn't appreciate his humor. He felt heat creeping up his spine.

"It's difficult to understand why you were hired. But you're here so we'll make the best of you." Indira's flat reaction made Jason feel like an outsider in a fish bowl of PhDs.

"You were born in the US?" Jason asked.

"In India. Came here when I was five." Indira moved the hair hanging across her forehead to the back of her ear.

"Interesting." Jason frowned, still assessing this meeting.

She looked at her watch. "I have to run to a status meeting. I'll take you to your desk." She walked him to his office. The tabletop, shining with a light brown veneer, was completely bare, except a DELL laptop.

"Thank you for your help," Jason said.

"Again, security is important. Your desk will be cleared everyday and all papers, pencils, etc. will be put in drawers and overhead shelves and locked away."

"I understand the drill." He didn't need a constant reminder. He got enough nagging from Kara. It must be the motherhood instinct.

"Your laptop also must be put away. And of course restarted everyday for updates." He rolled his eyes when he wasn't facing her, then immediately regretted it when he thought of the security cameras.

After Indira turned around and left, Jason sank into the chair in front of the desk. *What a place!* He sat motionless just staring at the office partition wall. It took him a few minutes to realize he was an employee of Layton Industries. He opened the laptop with a 15-inch screen but didn't turn it on. He looked around. With no one in sight, he dug the envelope out of his pocket, ripped one end open and counted ten hundred dollar bills. The money eased the tension building inside him since he'd first entered the front door of the building, but only slightly. It would take a lot of internal change to adjust to this new job. Would he be able to do it? Only time would tell.

* * *

Jason sank his hand in his pocket and retrieved a thin plastic card, which he inserted into the hotel door slot then watched a green light come on. He entered the room, which was big enough for a double bed, a desk, a chair, a couch, two pictures decorating the walls and lamp fixtures. He'd returned from an unsuccessful outing in search of renting an apartment, but he didn't let that bother him as it was only the first attempt since he had arrived in Mountain View. He saw a dozen apartments, large and small, in different neighborhoods, but none of them matched his liking.

After throwing his bag on the couch, he sat by the desk to take stock of the rental units he'd just visited. Looking at the sheet of paper, he rubbed his eyes, unable to focus. Since he had started his search, right after finishing work at five, he had been an unwilling participant, but he had to do it, knowing that he couldn't live in a hotel forever. His thoughts drifted to what had happened at Layton Industries on his first day of work. Why did he have only one interview? Why cash in an envelope? He would be working with Indira as her subordinate, but she gave him every inkling she did not want him on her team. In the last few weeks since Brian's death, it was slowly becoming clearer that something was up. He jumped to his feet and started pacing the length of room around the bed. He hit his forehead with the palm of his hand, frustrated. "What, what, what?" He had no choice but to find out.

Back to the desk again, he cracked open his laptop. As it was booting up, he grabbed the phone to order room service. He quickly punched in the numbers then gave his order for a sandwich, fries, salad and a coffee. Then he hung up and reached for his suitcase lying on the floor. He searched through several compartments to locate an Internet cable, one end of which he connected to the back of the computer and the other to the outlet in the wall next to the desk.

He brought up a web site to search for apartments in Mountain View and the surrounding areas. As he was browsing the results of the search, studying information on each item of the list on the screen, an alarm bell rang and a firewall popup came up. It was the sophisticated software installed on his computer to trap and stop any program seeking access to the Internet. It could catch anything, rogue programs, viruses and worms. With this popup window, on top of the apartment list demanding his immediate attention, he could do nothing but react to the choices of granting or denying access. He carefully studied what was happening. The popup window also showed the name of the program wanting access to the Internet from his computer, which piqued his curiosity.

A knock at the door made him scratch his head and jump to his feet. He opened the door to receive the food and tipped for the service. Quickly, after closing the door, he returned to the desk, and placed the tray on the floor. He didn't recognize the name of the program wanting access. To his astonishment, upon further scrutiny of every line on the screen, he could see it was spy software. The date associated with the program clearly indicated his laptop had been tampered with on the day the two gas company technicians had intruded into his house.

He stood up then, pacing back and forth in the room, and rubbing the sweat from his face. *What is going on?* The same fearful thought kept ringing in his head. The intruder software had now provided him with solid evidence that someone, or a group, were snooping around in his life. What did they want from him? His stomach growled louder as thoughts kept churning in his head, the pain intensifying in his belly. He cleared the couch, flopped onto it and started eating the sandwich to sooth his nerves. After a few bites he discarded the food, his hunger gone. He gulped down his anger and frustration with coffee.

First, he was determined to find out what the program was doing and, secondly, who was behind it. With a few clicks on the firewall window, he blocked all access to wp123.exe then moved it to a different folder such that it would never be executed automatically. He went to the Internet to download a program called Ripper to unlock the secrets buried in wp123.exe. Ripper started the disk whirring, followed by silence. By the dots moving back and forth, he knew it would take some time – seconds or even minutes. Finally, random characters splashed across the screen. It wouldn't be easy to decode the logical paths from the spy software. He stood up, paced the room many times, occasionally wiping the sweat from his brow, and then went back to the screen to discover more about the puzzling, convoluted activities it was programmed to do. After hours with his nose nearly pressed to the screen, one thing was becoming clearer.

Finally, he discovered that the spy ware was designed to capture his email transactions, any conversation while the laptop was on, take the signal from the video cam and send all the information to a website called volpaPI.com. Once more Jason went to the Internet and searched the domain name volpaPI.com, and found the name of the owner, Volpa PI, located in Prescott, Arizona. He also noted its Internet Protocol number 163.23.0.1.

He closed down his computer, feeling exhausted from the stress. But he was determined to find out who hired the private investigator. *What does someone want from me?* He switched the lights off and went to bed, depressed. Before he fell asleep on the couch, he promised to crack the door of the website wide open and discover who had broken into his computer.

* * *

Roger Hunt walked through the sliding doors of the Los Angeles International Airport into a space filled with passengers pushing dollies loaded with luggage, randomly navigating their way on the sidewalk, or occasionally bumping into each other. Most of the time it was a civilized activity, but not today. Outside, the road was lined with taxi drivers, cars from the passenger pickup zone and illegally parked cars with their engines running, the drivers ready to scoop up passengers while escaping the dirty looks of traffic authority.

Roger carried only a leather handbag as he headed to the front of the taxi line. He crawled into the back seat of the first one and, after instructing the driver as to the destination, he continued the work that was started on the plane. LA's slow traffic had a reputation worldwide for the daily air pollution it generated, but Roger didn't care; in fact he enjoyed it. The longer the journey took, the better. As the taxi crawled he was earning money. Every hour he was seated in the taxi would be billed to Senator Quest's campaign account for the strategy planning he was doing.

Normally he would strike up a conversation with the driver. No matter where he went, he constantly polled the political pulse of the nation from anyone he encountered. Taxi drivers knew a lot from eavesdropping on their passengers. Some had valuable information, even better than the pollster's measure of the political wind. Once, Roger had come across someone with a doctorate degree in geography, who, after graduation, could find no employment except driving taxi for menial pay, long hours and insults from cheap and grouchy passengers. This educated person had predicted the election results. Other drivers would say anything to please the passengers.

The traffic came to a halt. Roger looked through the window, and reflected on how to get his client re-elected in the upcoming election. He was proud of his record: thirty wins, no losses. He was regarded as the star among national political analysts. He had to protect his reputation of zero loss. Since political consultancy started in the 1930's, he held an unsurpassed record. In his three-decade-long career, he had made Republican senators and governors winners and Democrat candidates losers. He always got a good laugh, thinking about the victories he had enjoyed. He suppressed a long, loud laugh now. Instead, he grinned as the traffic started to move at its slow LA pace.

Once the warm feeling subsided, he turned to the notepad and scribbled the name Don Zimmerman. Actually *ex*-Florida Governor Don Zimmerman, a Democrat. For months Roger successfully unleashed the fury from the IRS, the investigation of the FBI, and the payback from a zealot state prosecutor until he brought down the governor's career just before the election. While Roger was in the vehicle rolling down the freeway to meet Khalid, Zimmerman was serving seven years in federal prison after the judge found him guilty of kickbacks.

Roger peered through the windshield, then furiously scribbled the strategic plan for TV, direct mail, and door-to-door activities for the Senator's campaign.

The car came to a dead stop. Roger shoved his notepad, pen, Blackberry and glasses into the briefcase. After a glance at the meter, he dug money from his pocket and handed it to the driver. Then the taxi drove off. He walked through the revolving door into the lobby of a prestigious building of the business section. He had been here before. Therefore, he passed by the information counter and waited for the elevator door to open. Roger preferred Khalid's old office in the low-rent area, where he was less likely to meet anyone he knew during his visit. Business had been good enough for Khalid to afford the more expensive rent. He knew that meeting Khalid would be dangerous for his career. However, to finance Senator Quest's campaign he had to see him. When he got off on the fifth floor, he turned right and hastily entered the door with Khalid Enterprise written in extra large letters.

As he walked into the reception room, he received a warm welcome from Jasmine, Khalid's wife. He took off his hat and sunglasses, which made him look unprofessional, and shoved them in his bag.

With a wide smile, Jasmine said, "Coffee. It is fresh for you, Mr. Hunt."

He could never refuse her Turkish coffee. "Sure." She disappeared. He scanned the room, placed his briefcase on the sofa and slowly lowered his body next to it. The office had the elegance of a Middle Eastern palace. It was huge. Khalid must be making good money these days. At the far end, there were real palm trees surrounding a pool of water, behind which the wall was decorated with camels and tents in a desert. From where he sat, the ensemble appeared to create an artificial oasis. There were carpets with bright colors and intricate patterns everywhere: on the floor and the walls; which were ornamented with jeweled framed pictures.

"How was the trip?" She placed a small cup and baklava on the table in front of Roger.

"Very good." He inhaled the fresh aroma. Jasmine's presence restored his confidence in Khalid. She was sweet and gentle. No danger could come from a person who married such a beautiful woman.

"Khalid's on the phone. He will be with you shortly." She returned to her desk and started typing something on the computer keyboard.

"I can wait." Of course he could.

The keystrokes stopped. Jasmine turned to Roger and said, "How long have you been a political consultant?"

"It seems like forever. When I was fifteen I worked for Richard Nixon."

"Really." Her brow furrowed only slightly, hinting at her forty years.

He nodded, placing the small cup on a side table after a tiny sip.

"How did you get involved with him?" she said.

"I supported him and discussed his platform with other students in high school." He took another tiny sip, rolled the black, strong liquid around his palate and let it flow, in controlled measure, down his throat. "An interesting thing happened."

She glanced at the phone lights and muttered, "Khalid's still on the phone. But you were saying?"

"A girl was strongly opposed to Nixon. During recess, we got into a heated debate. We went on arguing for awhile. She became more and more frustrated, so finally she stopped arguing and beat me up." He laughed.

She gave him a puzzled look. Roger surmised that in Arabia women never beat up men.

"I consider that as the start of my career," Roger said with a wry smile.

"Khalid is ready for you now."

The office door opened. "Ah, my friend," said Khalid. He was stocky and short with dyed black hair. He was definitely much older than his wife.

"Good to see you," Roger said.

"Come in. Bring your coffee. We'll talk. So good to see you."

He sat down across from Khalid's desk. "I was just talking to a guy who wanted to sell me ten stores. He came to America from Iraq and opened stores for Arabs, especially from Iraq. After five years he is going broke. I told him you have to think like Americans and not like Iraqis. He did not listen. Now he is going broke." He was pointing one hand towards the ceiling.

"If you buy them, how many stores will you have?" Roger placed the cup on the desk and crossed his legs.

"Ahh, it will come to one hundred and twenty-two. Not bad. Ten years ago, I had one store in LA. After this deal I will have stores in every state. Can you believe that? I love America." Khalid talked fast. His face was beaming with joy.

"Good." Roger shook his head with approval.

"What can I do for you, Mr. Hunt?" He pulled back into his chair next to a glass window with a view of the city. He touched the tie hanging on an expensive and well starched shirt.

"I need five million transferred from a company called Softek International in Mumbai to Senator Quest's campaign."

"From Mumbai."

"Any problem?" Roger asked.

"No. No. No. My name is money mule." His fat face lit up again.

"That's why I'm here."

"I have transferred money from all around the world: Columbia, Brazil, Australia, India, Pakistan and even Israel. You know I've already made three trips for you. From Australia, South Africa and Chile." His accent was strong, coming from the back of his throat.

"I know – you're the best." He shook his head.

"When do you want it?" Khalid said.

"Right away. The money is waiting for you." Roger shook his head.

"How do I get it? Cash or from a bank account?"

"Either way." He looked out the window.

"I like bank transfers. Traveling with five million isn't a joke. You know what I mean."

"I understand. It's up to you." Roger straightened his back and caressed the shiny, curves of the armrest with his palm.

"I'll do a bank transfer to my account in Dubai. Then the next day it will be in the campaign fund."

Roger paused for thought. "How much will it cost?" Except for his light breathing Roger's body stilled as he waited.

"One million." Like a pointed arrow, Khalid's eyes pierced Roger, as he waited for a reaction.

"One million is high, don't you think?" Roger flinched.

"When I get it you get the money the next day. It's not high at all. With terrorist checks at sea and at the airport, it is hell to bring money to the US. I have to be careful. Very careful." He shook his head.

"One million is too much," Roger said, testing to see how firm Khalid stood.

"This is the cost of doing business. It is a dangerous business. Lots of people are watching. If I get caught, I go to jail and lose my business."

"Why is it more now than before?" Rogers placed both feet on the floor and searched for a more comfortable position in the well-padded chair.

"The main reason is this, my friend. From India, it is safer to transfer the five million to Dubai, the financial capital of the Middle East. I have good connections there. Then it goes to the Cayman Islands, where I have a shipping business. From there it goes to the US in a cargo container. Then I distribute all five million to my stores. At this point, the money will no longer flow like a river. Drip by drip, it will be disguised as store sales so the IRS will never find out." Khalid waved both hands vigorously to emphasize his last point.

"That's high. I can't justify that to the Senator." Roger rubbed his chin.

"Mr. Hunt, it is very, very difficult in shipyards. Anywhere in America. A year ago there was only one inspector per ship load, not four." He moved four fingers towards Roger. "Before sniff dogs only knew drugs. Now they have taught them to detect people and money."

"That's the price of combating terrorist activities." Roger shifted his weight from one side to another on the chair.

"My friend. If it was possible, I would do it for less, but this is how the money is laundered properly. It takes time. And there is the risk of losing everything."

"I understand the risk, but your cut has gone up." Roger breathed harder.

"There are two factors." Khalid pointed two fingers in the air. "Number one is: You get the money right away from my bank account. It takes six months to clean the money. In the meantime, I am paying interest on the borrowed five million."

"I see." Roger understood his point but how would he explain it to the Senator?

"Second point I want to make, my friend. This one is very important. The IRS already knows about my money laundering business. How they found out, I don't know. I am very careful."

"The Democrats informed them." Roger laughed.

"They audit me every single year but I'm smarter than them. Much smarter. They are watching me. The FBI is watching me too." He grinned widely.

"How do you know?"

"My guys are always watching their backs. You know, I have my men doing all the work, so I have to pay them, but they are all reliable."

"This is confidential. Your mules shouldn't know whose money they're handling. You understand?"

"I understand. You can trust me. You know that. Or, you can wait and get the money when it is here in the US. It will take weeks or months though."

"No, I need it right away. I'm planning the campaign."

"How is the Senator's campaign going?" he asked, his accent hard to understand at times.

"It will be tough. The mood of the nation is changing. It's leaning more towards the liberals, which is disaster for me, but I've never lost an election. I don't want this one to be the first. I'll need all the money I can get to fight back."

That settled, they stood and shook hands. Roger asked Khalid to wait for the signal that the money would be ready in Mumbai.

Roger walked out of the office with a gracious goodbye to Jasmine. While waiting for the elevator, he put on his hat and sunglasses and snapped his fingers. He forgot to ask Khalid whether Jasmine was his second or third wife. Next time.

Going down, he thought about the million dollars that Khalid would be charging for money laundering. How would he ever convince Senator Quest that it was a fair price?

7

Jason McDeere exited the revolving door of the five-star hotel with his mind set; he would take public transportation to work. Normally, he would have taken a taxi. He noticed a tall, muscular man with dark sunglasses, bushy hair with a ponytail hanging just below his shoulders and an unforgettable face. Jason had seen him loitering in the hotel lobby where he was staying, or outside Layton Industry. Jason crossed the street and continued walking on the sidewalk. From the sound of footsteps behind him he could tell someone was following him, maybe five feet away. Jason didn't turn around to verify. It was better not to give his follower any attention.

After zigzagging through several streets, Jason reached a bus stop. As expected, the tall man followed him and stopped a few feet away. When the bus arrived, Jason climbed aboard with half a dozen other passengers who were on their way to work, no doubt. Once inside, he navigated through the crowded aisle towards the end. The bus crawled along Middlefield Road through the morning rush-hour traffic, punctuated by many stops, starts and turns. To maintain his balance, Jason hung on to a shiny pole. Both he and the tall man exchanged quick glances, but avoided face-to-face contact. Jason studied the man's profile. He had obviously been assigned to watch Jason's every move. Surveillance had been slapped on him a few weeks ago, he knew, but now, finally, there was no doubt in his mind: someone was after him. Analyzing the man, Jason could see his face was stone serious, robotic almost. As if he would do whatever his boss told him to do. *Is he looking for the right moment to kill me?* Jason felt a rise in body heat and panic building in his chest.

Wiping the sweat from his neck with a handkerchief, he got off at Shoreline Boulevard and Middlefield, and walked to the Layton building. As Jason went through the revolving front door, a peek outside confirmed that Stone Face had followed him from the hotel to his workplace.

He hurried past the elevators, straight to the cafeteria. After placing an order, he loaded his tray with two scrambled eggs, toast and a tall cup of coffee and sat at an isolated table. As he lifted the cup for a sip, his hand shook. He stared at the eggs but his appetite had suddenly vanished. To ease the tension in his neck, he supported his upper body with his elbow. Head down, he took several calming breaths to ease the persistent muscle ache. Sufficiently settled, he searched his bag lying on the chair next to him and removed a sheet of paper from it. Then he pushed the tray aside to make room for the sheet of paper.

Jason studied four names soon after suspecting of being followed. All four names worked in the computer network department, just one floor below his office. He remembered very well what Indira had said – not to talk to anyone except on a need-to-know basis. For the last few afternoons, when Indira left work for the day, Jason headed downstairs pretending his work computer had network problems. He was told one of the four was hired as a computer hacker.

Looking at the food service workers at the cafeteria serving a long line of hungry people, he rubbed his temples then grabbed the cup for another sip. Occasionally, he stared at the ceiling. It was decision time. He could wait no longer. Who among the four was a hacker? Who could crack the www.VolpaPI.com website? No time to waste. It must be done quickly.

Slowly and carefully he examined every name on the list. It was decision time. He pointed the pen at one name.

Gabor wasn't a friendly guy at all, which was apparent when Jason approached him. He was in his forties with a "don't-bother-me" attitude. The type with a personality perfectly molded after company policy. It would be risky to approach him for help. He crossed that one off his list.

The next one, Lance, lacked confidence. Jason wondered how he got the job. Probably, he aced all the exams by cramming the night before. *Definitely not that one.* He lacked the free spirit and deep knowledge of computers that a hacker would need. Jason crossed his name off the list.

Jason crossed a third name off the list. Her name was Audrey, a long-timer. This one had the knowledge and personality, but Jason couldn't trust her. Before giving Jason any information she asked too many questions. She acted like a detective probing a suspect. It was obvious to Jason she wouldn't willingly share anything. If she suspected any breach of policy, she was the type who would report it to David Cohen.

Jason was impressed with Terrance. He was new to the company, technically adept and willing to go the extra mile whenever there was any mishap. His face radiated delight in solving problems. His dress code, long hair and glasses gave one the distinct impression of a hacker. But could Jason trust him?

Jason picked at his scrambled eggs, put away the tray, and went up to his cubicle to plan his day. He should talk to Terrance as soon as possible, but not at the expense of losing his job. The day went by painfully slow as he waited for six o'clock to arrive, when Indira ended her workday. As always, she left on time.

At five after six, Jason went to Indira's desk to make sure it was cleared and her laptop closed. Then he descended one floor down, taking the staircase. Walking down the aisle bordered with cubicles, he saw that they were occupied. Just like at Softek, people worked a lot of overtime at Layton Industry.

He approached Terrance from behind and surreptitiously regarded his actions. Upon noticing someone close by, Terrance closed the Facebook and Hacker.com screens with two fast, successive mouse clicks. Then he turned to Jason and very calmly said, "What's up?"

Jason scanned the area and whispered, "If you're not busy right now, can we go for a coffee?"

"I need a break. Let's do it." As Terrance locked his computer, Jason read a modern Zen poem posted on the wall in front of Terrance.

'To follow the path:

Look to the master,

Follow the master,

Walk with the master,

See through the master,

Become the master.'

Five minutes later, alone in the elevator with Terrance, Jason questioned him about it. "The poem on the wall looks familiar. What is it?"

"It's a hacker's mantra. To become a master one imitates the mind-set of masters."

Alone in the elevator, Jason said, "Why the interest in hacking?"

"Long time ago, five years to be exact, I used to be a bad guy. Now I use what I know for the good guys . . . if there is such a thing. Usually I don't talk about it. I shouldn't. I could lose this job. As you know security and surveillance in this building is very tight."

"How involved were you – in hacking, I mean?"

They exited the elevators. "I did a lot of it." Terrance emphasized the past.

"Let's have dinner, before the crowd gets here."

Both grabbed a tray, fork, spoon, and knife. Jason wasn't feeling very hungry. He only had soup and toast. Terrance put four slices of pizza on his tray then they located a seat.

"I don't want to intrude, but what is a lot?"

"I learned to program when I was twelve..." Terrance glanced around. "Let's move there." They sat at a table surrounded by empty ones, then Terrance continued. "One has to be extremely careful. Why are you so interested?"

"I shouldn't put you in such an awkward position. Just wondered what one needed to know," Jason said.

Terrance held off talking a bite of the pizza. "You want to be one?" Terrance looked straight in Jason's eyes.

"I'm in a very serious situation." Jason stirred the soup with his spoon.

"How serious?" Terrance's expression held surprising compassion.

"Very serious. I need to know what technical knowledge is required to hack a website," Jason said.

Terrance frowned, as though considering how much to say. Finally, he leaned forward. "I know six different computer languages. I received all the certifications for Windows, UNIX and Linux. Also, I know how to set up Internet programs. I'm one of the designers of Hacker-howto.com"

Jason whistled. "That's impressive. By the way I saw you use Facebook. I understand from Indira that we're not supposed to visit such sites. In fact, I thought Facebook was totally blocked from Layton employees. Facebook isn't available from my office computer," he said pointedly. "How did you manage to use it?"

"Ahh..." Terrance's hesitation continued.

Jason noticed a slight change of color in Terrance's face. "I'm sorry to put you on the spot like that. I know I'm being too intrusive."

"Look—" He lowered his voice. "I'm breaking company policy. I could get fired for it." For someone who could be fired, he appeared only slightly worried. "You're not going to tell anybody?"

"No. No. I wouldn't tell anyone."

"I have a contrarian mentality. When someone says don't, I do the opposite. I'm fascinated with any challenge. I will try to break any rule." He said it as though daring Jason to report him.

"I have this problem and it looks like you're the person I need to talk to."

"Go ahead." He devoured the pizza slices as if he hadn't eaten for days.

Hesitating, Jason finally said, "Don't tell anybody."

"Trust me," Terrance slurred with a mouthful of food.

"I have to break into a website. I'll tell you more later."

Jason thought he had finally found the person he was looking for. He just hoped that Terrance wouldn't turn him in.

***

Shallen Xu dropped her handbag in the chair and fired up the computer after placing the tall Starbucks cup next to the keyboard. While Windows was coming alive with occasional sound bites, hard disk grinds, flashing icons on the desktop, all familiar sequences to her, she gulped one more mouthful of fresh coffee, followed by two more in quick succession. A couple of deep breaths released the tension that had been building inside her chest.

She had just arrived in the office after witnessing a demonstration held by Iraq war opponents in front of the White House earlier today. The procession along Pennsylvania Avenue had been made up of all colors, races and ages, including veterans, seniors, Green Peace members, mothers against war and many more. All singing, shouting, yelling. It was the interview with a sad, angry mother who gave Shallen a chill colder than a Washington winter wind upon hearing about the loss of her son on the battlefield.

Lifting her eyes to measure the computer's progress, Shallen caught Barbara's approach from the corner of her vision. Barbara, John Mead's assistant secretary, leaned over the cubicle partition that reached her chest and said, "John wants to see you."

Shallen forced a smile. "Can't it wait?" She was just getting ready to write an article for the evening edition.

"No, it can't. He wanted to see you at 10:00." Barbara nodded her head vigorously, suggesting the request was firm, emergency written all over her face.

"I was at the Iraq war demonstration." Shallen didn't need to give Barbara any reason; the woman was only an assistant, not the executive secretary. But it was good office politics to give her something to tell John. Shallen, like many reporters, often wondered about the conversations that went on between Barbara and John behind closed doors.

"I told him you were out on assignment," Barbara said.

"What does he want to talk to me about?" Shallen's smile dimmed.

"He didn't say. Just asked me to keep an eye out for you when you came in the office," Barbara said, always loyal to her boss.

"It must be important then." Shallen reached for the mouse to check her email.

"I should say so," Barbara said in a tone that conveyed she should be in his office now and not fingering the keyboard or enjoying coffee with its strong, espresso aroma.

"I'll be there shortly." Shallen took a few more sips of the coffee just to let the woman know she couldn't be cowed. Then, holding the coffee cup, notepad and pen, she headed towards John Mead's office, following Barbara many steps behind. The assistant's hips gyrated with every step forward, perfectly synchronized with each leg motion. Every bit of the fried chicken she so loved must have descended directly to her hips.

By virtue of her position as executive assistant for over twenty years, Barbara exercised undeserved power. The tension between her and reporters was notorious, as taut as a rope in a tug of war.

Shallen walked the aisle bordered by four-by-four foot reporters' cubicles, each occupying a desk with a stack of papers several inches high. Mead's office was in the corner of one end of the floor. Shallen craned her head through a crack in the doorway, and John waved her in with his phone stuck between his ear and shoulder. She sat across from him and placed the Starbucks cup at the edge of the desk, while he continued talking.

"It's Peter," he whispered to her, then pressed his mouth closer to the phone. "Peter, Shallen just came in my office. I'll call you later." After hanging up he leaned forward and cleared his throat.

"Peter Patka is in Manchester, New Hampshire, covering the primaries. Now, where are we?" He threw a quick glance at the calendar in front of him. "Today is the 7th of January, '08. Okay. New Hampshire's state primary is tomorrow." He squinted. "I want you to join Peter," he said, pointing a finger at her.

Shallen forced a smile. "I'm going to Mountain View, California in the next few days." The plan wasn't definite.

"Mountain View? What the hell is going on there?" He waved his hand and shook his head as if he was being kept in the dark about something.

"I'm following a lead on the Softek killing in Corvallis, Oregon." Shallen lifted the cup and held it up, ready to sip in case the tension started to mount.

"Who's in Mountain View?" He leaned back in his chair as if to assess the situation.

"Jason McDeere was an employee at Softek at the time of the killing. He's now working in Mountain View. I have a lead that could link Senator Quest to the killing."

John nearly jerked out of his chair. "What the hell are you talking about, Shallen?" He ran over and slammed the door shut before turning on her and lowering his voice. "What would Senator Quest have to do with a nut who went on a rampage at a company?"

"That's what I'm investigating, sir," she said, forcing herself to keep eye contact despite the anger written there.

"Keep away from him," he said, his jaw working with anger. "You touch him and we're all out of jobs. Besides, it's ludicrous to think he's behind this Softek business. You want to talk to this McDeere, you do it for the Softek story, but you leave the Senator alone. Understood?"

"Understood," she said, resentment festering in her and spilling over. "But I've already made an appointment to see Jason," she added. She knew she had lied, and the minute she saw John's face she knew it was a mistake.

A hard silence fell over the room as he rounded his desk and took a seat, steepling his hands as he stared at her, undoubtedly trying to make her flinch but she held firm. "No. No. The primaries – the US presidential election is our most pressing concern. I'm giving you a lifetime opportunity to cover the elections." He continued shaking his head until his cell rang.

John cupped his ringing cell phone. "It's my wife." He flipped open the phone and placed it to his ear. "Hi, honey." He listened. "I can't join you for lunch. I have to be in the office. There's a political storm gathering around Washington. I'm waiting for a call from a reporter. I'll call you later. Love you."

Shallen didn't want to cover the primaries. US elections would go on forever.

She would be stuck going from town to town for the rest of the year, with no chance to see Jason. And she wanted to see him, but how could she convince her boss?

When John hung up, Shallen decided to come at it from a different angle. "Exactly the same kind of killing happened in three states: Florida, Nebraska, and Texas. And now in Oregon. One common factor in all of them is that in each company where the murders occurred, outsourcing was an issue. Big layoffs in each company. Work was farmed overseas. I don't want the trail to go cold." She took a sip of her now cold coffee and grimaced.

"Shallen, what are you hoping to discover with this Jason?" His eyes narrowed, and he gave her a pointed look. He'd drawn a line, with no hint of any wavering.

"He met the Senator. Also the disgruntled employee, Brian, who did the killing, was a very good friend of Jason's. Brian killed himself."

Both of their attentions were drawn to the door as Barbara barged in without knocking. "Senator Giavani wants to talk to you. He says it's urgent." John nodded an affirmative, then Barbara walked out and closed the door behind her.

He picked up the phone, punched a flashing light and suddenly became mild mannered, his fierceness gone. All he could say was "Yes, Senator," "No, Senator," and "I understand, Senator." The conversation ended and he turned to Shallen.

"We're following a lead on Senator Giavani. The rumor is that he had an affair with a black woman and possibly fathered a child. We can't locate the child, so I called his Chief of Staff to confirm it. Didn't get an answer. I left a message for the Senator that we are going ahead with the story. It's a ruse, of course. I was hoping he'd crack, but he didn't."

It was a cat and mouse game that news media and politicians liked to play. An on-going tug of war. Shallen had been with the *Post* for five years and understood the game. She said, "Are we printing it?"

"If I do, then his candidacy in the Republican primaries will be dead. We'll take a major hit for lack of evidence. The whole Republican Party will come down on us like a sledge hammer. I'll end up losing my job. The answer is no." He emphasized the negative answer with a pointed finger at Shallen. He turned to Shallen. "Without solid proof we won't. Otherwise, the Senator will sue our pants off. I called his office hoping for any hint of truth to the story. You understand. Now you know why you're to stay away from Senator Quest. You're in way over your head, and besides, these conspiracy theories about senators have been going around for years. You should be smarter than that."

How ironic that he was talking about conspiracy theories involving Giavani, then chastising her for *her* conspiracy theory. Shallen nodded her head to suggest she agreed with her boss. She'd had enough of Senator Giavani's problem. She wanted her own problem resolved. "I really want to go to California to scoop the outsourcing angle," she said, coming at it from a different tack. "Before other papers print it. I think I have a hot lead, but I need an insider to verify the information I have."

Barbara's face appeared again through the doorway. "Jeffry wants to see you about Senator Giavani's story. He wants to know what to do with the story. Print or not."

"Tell him that I just spoke with Senator Giavani. Put it on hold. We can't go with the story yet. We need two sources of verification." Barbara turned around and closed the door behind her.

Shallen continued, "Last time I met Jason, he unquestionably linked outsourcing as the main reason for the killings at Corvallis. If the Senator played any part in this—"

John pounded a fist so hard on his desk that her coffee spilled, pouring lukewarm liquid onto her lap. "Goddamn it, Shallen, I said you're not to touch this story. Do I make myself clear, or do you need to find a new job!"

She made one final attempt. "My fear is that a local paper could print the story, and become a national hero. It will be better if we were first."

John's eyebrows lowered, followed by silence. Under ordinary circumstances he loved to wrestle with the politicians in Washington. He was known to be a shark in this business. He loved the power – loved the smell of blood. But the only blood he was smelling was hers.

"Let me make this perfectly clear. I need someone to cover the primaries."

Shallen could see she was losing the war. She held up her hands. "Okay, okay, but I think the outsourcing angle is a good one. I won't touch the Senator, but at least let me follow the outsourcing lead. That's only fair."

He scratched his head. Shallen felt a tug at the end of the line. He was hooked. All she had to do was reel him in.

"If I weave a common thread between all four – the killings in Florida, Nebraska, Texas and Oregon – then I could have a national story. It will be a feeding frenzy. Right now, the economy and the war are the main issues in the primaries. Suddenly, we can change the agenda, make outsourcing the prime issue."

He let out a long, slow sigh, obviously relieved that she had moved past any allegations about the Senator. He was throwing her a bone. "Okay. We go with it. I'll find someone else to cover the primaries."

"John, I need your help on this one." She flashed her usual radiant smile, a signature of pleading that she didn't relish, but would use if she needed to.

John leaned back followed by a long pause. "What help?"

"A Washington insider who can confirm my story . . . about outsourcing." She knew one had to earn such privilege with a badge of seniority. Her short five years with the *Post* might not be enough to buy such a request. Pushing the limit was a thrill to her, like taking a scary roller-coaster ride.

"It's too early. First, follow the lead you have. Talk to this Jason guy. See what he gives you." He continued rubbing his chin and staring at Shallen, as if he was trying to assess something.

"Okay . . . I'll talk to Jason," Shallen said, throwing a mental fist into the air. "He may have valuable information. But it's just information. Until it is verified we can't print the story. I understand."

"In the meantime, I have someone." John tapped a pen on the desk, his brows furrowed. "We call him Trench Coat, a present day Deep Throat. That's all I'll say for now. Let me know what you find. If warranted, I'll get you in to see and talk to this informant. He hates corruption in the government. He wants to keep politicians in line. But your story must stink like high heavens before he'll even consider seeing you."

"Is he good?"

"The best, but he has too many rules. Make one mistake and he'll disappear and never talk to us again. He'll only confirm information, never volunteer anything. It's important that you're careful. His answers are simple. Yes or no."

Was the Senator responsible for the deaths at Softek, yes or no?

"I understand perfectly, sir."

***

Jason McDeere stood in front of his hotel room door. He shuffled through different compartments of his bag until he dug out a tweezers and magnifying glass. Holding the magnifying glass in his right hand he placed the rim close to the edge of the door that touched the frame, peered through the thick concave glass and was happy to see a hair, one end stuck to the frame and the other to the door, both ends held firmly in place by a small piece of transparent Scotch tape. Pinching the tweezers, he gently removed the tape at only one end, leaving the rest hanging from the frame. He inserted the hotel room card, opened the door, and breathed a sigh of relief, reassuring himself again that no intruder had entered his room.

He picked up clothes from off the floor, shoved them into a gym bag, threw the bag into a closet and closed the door. He straightened the bedspread. Another scan of the room and he murmured, "Clean enough."

For a moment, he stood there. Then it dawned on him he hadn't given Terrance the room number, and he didn't want him asking the hotel clerk in case he was later questioned by his employer should they suspect they were doing something illegal. He looked at the time on his watch.

"He'll be here in five minutes!" He moaned, then quickly left the room, ran downstairs to the front of the hotel building and located a spot outside, not far from the revolving door at the entrance. He stood behind a parked bus in the driveway, hoping no one would notice him. The hotel entrance was busy with guests arriving in taxis and private cars. They would get out, pull luggage from the trunk or back seat of the vehicle. Several concierges flashed smiles, no doubt trying to earn a living.

Nonchalantly pretending to be a lost tourist, he looked at a map. Every now and then, he glanced at the entrance from the street of the circular driveway. He spotted Terrance Murdock, a skinny guy with red hair hanging down to his earlobes. His body was white as a lily as though it had never been touched by the California sun. Jason felt certain that most of the man's waking life had been spent in a room in front of a computer. As Jason looked on, Terrance turned his head sideways, as if absorbing a place he had never been before. Jason carefully calculated Terrance's pace and started to walk toward the entrance, avoiding his eyes. Terrance, with a twenty-something frame, entered one quadrant of the revolving door. Jason entered the next quadrant, right behind him. As Terrance stepped into the lobby and looked around, Jason turned to him and said, "Terrance, in two minutes, just come up to 203. Take the back entrance." Jason pointed to a set of stairs that opened off the main floor from the outside. "You'll be less likely to be seen that way." Then he speeded ahead of him.

Two minutes later, right on target, Terrance knocked on Jason's door, and Jason opened it, waving him in while holding the phone to his ear. He bent over to clear the sofa of the laptop bag and dropped it on the floor. "I'm ordering pizza. What topping would you like?"

Terrance shrugged while lowing himself into the seat. "Anything. On second thought, make it Hawaiian."

"Drink?"

"Orange Crush."

After hanging up the phone, Jason turned to Terrance and said, "Thanks for coming. It occurred to me you might not come."

"No, no. I love a good challenge. Geekhead is my middle name." He chuckled.

"Sorry about the clandestine entrance. I have to be careful." He sobered, frowning.

"In California you have to be. You never know who is watching. What with all the terrorists these days." Terrance shook his head.

"It's nothing like that."

"What then?"

Jason paced the floor, then deciding he could trust the man, halted in front of him. "Somebody or a group is after me. And I don't know who they are, but I have to find out."

"What do you have that they want?" Terrance frowned.

"I don't know. I just know two guys broke into my house, before Christmas. Then last week I find spy software on my laptop, with a direct link to a private investigator's website. What does that tell you?"

Terrance pulled a flash disk from his shirt pocket. "Let's crack this baby."

"Let's switch seats." Jason sat in the armchair.

Terrance looked at the Mac's screen, the program already running. He pressed the memory stick into the side of the laptop and tapped on keys. "It will take a minute." He turned to Jason.

"What's happening?" Jason asked.

"I'm drilling a hole into the VolpaPI.com website." Terrance laughed.

Jason glanced at the screen. "What's running?"

"In this hacker's club I belong to, we developed a program to guess user ID and passwords at the rate of a million a minute. I've cracked a lot of sites with this one. It's very powerful." He smiled, obviously proud of his talent.

"What was your best work?"

"Oh, where do I start?"

He tapped his chin for a minute, then snapped his fingers.

"I have to say when we drilled a hole in the Pentagon accounting website –" Terrance roared with laughter – "that was way too cool."

"You busted into the Pentagon? Weren't you afraid you would get caught?"

"No. Even if they did catch me, they wouldn't say anything. They would just plug the hole in their web network. It would be embarrassing to admit that they were vulnerable – especially to an underage hacker. They avoid publicity at all costs." Terrance peered at the changing characters.

"What do you do at Layton?" Jason said.

"Same as what I'm doing for you." He took his hand off the keyboard and waved at Jason.

"What do you mean?"

"To know a hacker's mind, they hired one. I work in the computer network department. I develop and run security programs to find vulnerability points in their website."

"How did they find you?"

"Last March, my friends and I bugged all the cell phones of Hollywood stars. During Oscar night, we could hear everything that the stars were saying and doing. We posted some of them in Facebook. A day later I got a call from Layton."

"Impressive." Jason grimaced with astonishment.

"Now, how did *you* find *me*?"

"I searched in the company directory under computer network then selected four from the security group. For days I watched each one of you in your department. One morning you walked into the coffee bar and I knew I had found the person I was looking for. You looked like death warmed over. The pale face, unkempt hair, t-shirt, blue jeans, glasses. A perfect geek. On the back of your t-shirt it said, 'Catch me, if you can'." Jason laughed, remembering and Terrance joined in.

Suddenly, he looked at his watch. "This program has been running for a while and it still hasn't drilled even a small hole into the program. What kind of a site is it?" Terrance leaned back in the chair, cradling his head in his hands, his eyes fixed to the ceiling, but before Jason could answer, the doorbell rang.

"Pizza delivery." Jason rushed to the door and the delivery boy handed him a box and drinks. He paid the guy and included a generous tip.

As Jason thanked the guy and shut the door, Terrance jumped off his chair and shouted, "This website isn't using Windows! That's why I can't crack it."

"Why not?" Jason placed the box on the bed and the drinks on the floor.

"We've found so many security issues in Windows. It's as bad as the Pentagon. We find them, they fix them and then we find more." Terrance grabbed a piece of pizza, the steam still rising.

"What can we do next?" Jason took a bite with one hand while holding a can of pop with the other.

He inserted new software. "The program they're using is called Bulldog. It can rip the guts out of Windows. But it's not Windows, for sure. I have to find out more information about this site." Terrance was chewing and pacing the floor. For the next few minutes they were both silent as they ate and thought.

"Of course!" Jason snapped his fingers. "I found all the registration information about the website owner. That should help."

Terrance came alive with hope. Together they looked at the printed sheet with the "ownership record for VampaPI.com" as a heading at the top. "Strange this site has no Home page," Terrance said slowly. He set his drink down and began chewing his nails.

"It gives only the IP address," Jason said. "But why the IP address and not an Internet Service Provider?"

Terrance tapped a spot on the page. "Simple. The ownership address is in Nevada. They have their own computer hidden somewhere there. This way they have complete control." Terrance walked to the laptop. "The program is still running. This is bad. This program hasn't even cracked a hairline. This is very bad." Terrance grabbed another piece of pizza and began walking while eating his pizza and drinking his soda.

"How bad is it?" Jason went to the box for another slice.

"I've never seen one like this."

"Is the firewall very thick?"

"Thick isn't the word for it. This is not a firewall; it's a concrete wall. It will need a nuclear bomb to blast this open." His laughter was laced with sarcasm.

"What do we do next?" The pizza suddenly felt like a lump of coal in Jason's stomach.

"I'll abort Bulldog. Let me download a more powerful program." Terrance downloaded the new software and they waited in silence.

Finally, Jason had to say something to break the tension. "How powerful is this one?"

"I don't know. My geekhead friends have been working on this. This is our latest. We have some new algorithms that we've discovered and we're using Assembly language rather than C language."

"You can program in Assembly? That's very impressive." Jason gave him a high five. Very few people knew how to program in Assembly language. It was the most efficient way to enhance program performance, yet the most tedious and time consuming.   "Oh yeah. It cranks the CPU into high gear and works like a giant monster with ten heads." Terrance lifted all his fingers up.

"Does it do multitasking?" Jason said.

"This program will attack the website from ten different directions, throwing a shower of fire until it becomes weak and can find an entry point."

"That's serious multitasking." Jason felt hopeful that he could peek at the treasures hidden in the belly of this site.

"The download is done. Yes." Terrance shook his fist. "I'm running it."

"Is it legal?" Jason knew that hacking could get them both fired, but he had to know who was monitoring him and why.

"No. You know about identity theft. It happens all the time. But how many have gone to jail for that? It's the embarrassment that prevents site owners from taking legal action. If you don't get caught you're fine." He didn't look worried.

Jason stared at the screen. "What is it doing?"

"It's working. There are ten bars and each is spitting dots, which means attacks are taking place. It will take some time."

"Crooks steal credit card information from websites. Do you do that?" Jason felt a measure of fear building inside him at the thought he might be hooked up with someone who was stealing ID and money.

"No. No. We just break in for fun. But we never take anything. We don't drop worms at any of the sites. We have a code of conduct. We don't break our code." Terrance pursed his lips, obviously serious about his hacker values.

"I have to find out what this site is all about, and yet at the same time I feel like I'm an intruder." Questions were churning in Jason's head.

"I wouldn't feel guilty. They're after you for something, and they've already violated your privacy."

"That's true. I could go to the authorities, but what could they do? Take a few notes on their notepad and forget about it. They have more obvious crooks to chase." Jason pressed his thumb deep into his neck, but it did nothing to ease the tension building there. He felt the pain of tight muscles.

Terrance scratched his head. "This is taking too long." He paced the carpeted floor again.

"Yes, it is taking too long. What time is it?"

"Almost midnight." Terrance glanced at his watch, which reminded Jason of his Rolex. He would need to reclaim it soon, after the next payday.

"How much longer?" Jason asked.

"Give it some more time." Terrence went to the pizza box and picked up the last small slice. He put it in his mouth, then grabbed the soda can but it was empty. "We need more food. Let's order more pizza."

"It's getting late. Let's call it a night. We both have to work and we don't want to lose our jobs," Jason said.

"Are you kidding? I want to crack this, even it takes all night. But I'll need more food. I work better when I'm eating." Terrance was still picking stuck cheese from the box.

"You already ate most of the large pizza, and you're as skinny as a match stick."

"I can eat two large pizzas, easily–especially when I'm working on a program."

"It's late. You're all wired up from the pop, but you look tired and I feel tired." Jason put the box into the garbage by the bathroom door.

"Before we call it a night, I want to make a little change to the program and run it on verbose mode." Terrence clapped his hands.

"What will that do?" Jason said.

"It will tell us exactly what is going on, instead of these moving dots on the progression bar."

"Once we start that, we'll be here all night," Jason complained. "We both need to go to bed." Frustrated, he combed his fingers through his hair.

"We have to find out what these PI's want from you. You could be in danger and you don't even know it."

This thought hit Jason hard. He *could* be in danger. "I know you want to help me, but let's talk about it tomorrow."

Finally, Terrance yawned and nodded his head in agreement, then removed the flash memory from the laptop. "Okay."

"One thing –" Jason paused until he had the other man's attention. "Don't tell anyone what we did tonight. If anyone asks, just say you came for pizza." Jason secured the other man's promise. Then he walked him to the door, watched him leave and closed the door quickly.

After he was gone, Jason lay flat on the bed, both hands spread out, his eyes fixed to the ceiling. What if he got caught and was accused of stealing private information? What if he *was* in danger? Or his family was in danger? The questions swirled around like a windstorm in his head. Whatever the answer, it couldn't be good.

8

Driving north on I-5, Jason McDeere's attention constantly jumped around, from the road in front of him to the rear view mirror to the side mirrors and back to the road. He sighted a freeway exit that would lead him to the Lancaster Mall, where he had a lunch appointment with Kara, Sarah and Keenan. Except for the house invasion, Kara had been kept in the dark. It was time to tell her all—every move of his life was under surveillance.

As he was about to turn off onto the exit ramp, he noted all the vehicles behind him. If he were being followed, which he suspected he was, it would be difficult for him to detect. His pursuers could be driving anything—bus, cars, motorcycles. He had to be vigilant but not surrender his peace of mind. He would fight with whatever he had. He also had to protect his family.

He found himself driving along Center Street. After a quick check of the mirrors, he took a turn on Lancaster Drive, and then slowed the car to a roll, all the while watching for a parking spot. Passing countless rows of vehicles, luck wasn't on his side. He positioned himself in the illegal zone, from where he could clearly see a huge "Lancaster Mall" sign hanging off a wooden beam under the entrance roof. As he watched shoppers going in and out of the mall, he breathed a sigh of relief that no one had followed him so far, not that he had noticed anyway.

At the entrance a few teenagers smoked and others playfully chased each other. After about a ten-minute wait he saw Kara, Sarah and Keenan enter the mall. He started driving until he found a legal parking spot this time. The car squeezed in between an SUV and eight-seat Caravan. Once out of the car, he sped to the Sears's loading zone. He entered the building through Sears's shipping and receiving, and, with no time to waste, he spotted a way into the store. He exited the store into the mall and walked towards the food court.

From where he stood, he had a clear view of Kara sitting by herself and occasionally scanning the area. As Jason had planned, she was positioned where he could easily identify any person around her. Beyond the seating area, a ten-person queue stood waiting at McDonalds where Keenan, who was behind a tall, fat man, craned his head toward a teenager behind the register. Sarah inched forward at the Pizza

Schmizza lineup to get her fill of her favorite food.

Jason's eyes shifted horizontally back and forth like a windshield wiper on a rainy day, analyzing every face. After five minutes of surveillance, he breathed a sigh of relief. He didn't think anyone was watching Kara or his children. But he had to be sure. He came out of hiding and took a seat in front of Kara, which startled her.

"Where have you been? I've been waiting for you for ages." She furrowed her forehead, a slight tightness in her face revealing her displeasure. He knew she always exaggerated every event. It was her who was usually late, but he didn't want to remind her. It would only start a fight.

"Sorry," he said softly. He hoped to appease her.

"I've been here –" She peeked at her watch and opened both hands – "already fifteen minutes." She grimaced and shook her head. "Why here? In a mall food court. Why not a decent restaurant? Did you see Keenan?" She turned towards the eatery. "He's getting a Big Mac, super-sized fries and a large coke. And Sarah is getting a pizza. You've sunk to a new low."

Heat climbed his neck, but he fought back the anger. "They have to eat." He paused, softening his response. "Nothing wrong with that." He expected her to be upset. He restrained himself, hoping, after the usual fit, she would calm down.

"Jason, they're both overweight. Especially Sarah."

At forty, Kara didn't look her age. She ate healthy and kept a close watch on her weight. He looked at her well-coiffed hair and blue eyes. "Kara, you always exaggerate. Sarah is not overweight. She's fifteen. At her age, girls do put on some weight and lose it later. As for Keenan, he needs food. Besides, he eats at McDonalds only a few times a year." Jason pleaded his case.

She lowered her voice. "Why did you pick *this* place?"

"This place?" He looked around.

"Yes. Why?" She turned to see how Keenan and Sarah were doing.

"It's a noisy, busy place. That's what I wanted."

"The other thing that bugged me is that when you called from California, you were so argumentative." A familiar trait. She was starting another round of confrontation.

"I don't plead guilty to anything." Anger was starting to boil inside him but it must be muffled at all cost.

"I know." Her piercing blue eyes gave him a shot of disappointment.

"This time I was yelling for a reason," he said calmly and slowly. He rubbed his chin to stifle his rising frustration.

"Reason, hey. Give me the reason." She shook her head as if he better have an exceptionally good explanation. Or else.

He glanced over his shoulder. "I'm going to tell you something that you're not going to like."

Four noisy teenagers arrived at the next table. One was yelling, two were giggling and one was talking on the cell phone.

She leaned forward. "I'm listening. Why are you whispering?"

"That's one of the reasons I wanted it here," he said just above the noise of the teenagers.

"Ok. Stop messing around. Just give it to me." She waved her hand.

"I'm under surveillance." He glanced over his shoulder again.

"Surveillance? By whom? Your employer?" Her eyes opened wide.

"Kara, I don't know. First it was the house." He shook his shoulders and rubbed his forehead.

"But you didn't find anything in the house. Maybe Mr. Johnson was hallucinating." She gave him an expression of disbelief.

"I'm definitely being followed. It's very serious. A private investigator has been hired to track my every move. My house and laptop have been bugged. A tall man with a ponytail follows me from my hotel to work and back. He is watching me twenty-four hours a day, seven days a week. They're here somewhere." He quickly checked on Sarah and Keenan, then returned to Kara.

"Who would be doing that? What do they want from you? You're not rich or famous. Were you a Russian spy in your previous life?" She laughed.

He wasn't amused. "There may be someone here watching us. Did you see anyone following you?"

"This sounds creepy." She paused and focused on the table. "Jason, don't talk like that."

He shook his head. "It is true. We're being followed. As least me, for sure."

"What did you find on your computer? I want to know if this is real." She took a few deep breaths.

"It is real, Kara. They installed spy software to record all my email, conversations and movements. At the firm, I de-installed it; then I put it back. Now, they only record meaningless things."

"What are you going to do?" Kara said. Her anger was replaced with anxiety.

"I have to find out who Volpa PI is. Why is he recording my life, frame by frame? If I can break into his website, it will open up a new world of illegal bugging. Who knows what I'll find. That would also lead me to the person who hired Volpa. I hope." Jason noticed an ache building in his stomach.

"Is it a person or a company?" The furrow on her forehead deepened.

"I wish I knew. It may be Softek or Layton Industry or the Senator."

"Not our Senator," she objected. She raised her voice. "Why would he do such a thing? He's busy in Washington. Why would he be snooping around someone like you?" She pointed to him. "From Corvallis." She twisted her lower lips, as if she was thinking of something. "Sarah mentioned just a few days ago that she noticed two guys in their thirties watching her." She waved her hand in the air. "I didn't think it was anything serious."

He paused. Then in a deep, slow voice, he said, "Everyone I've met in the last few weeks is a suspect. I can't rule out anyone."

"Sarah is coming," she whispered. "Don't tell the kids anything." She scanned the area again. "Keenan will be here soon."

"Kara, keep an eye on your back." He stared at her to make his point. "Are you getting something to eat?"

"What you just said killed my appetite."

"Mine too." Just then both kids arrived at the table. Jason joked and talked to his children, whom he hadn't seen for two weeks. After they'd finished eating, Jason and Kara found themselves alone again, by design. Sarah went to Victoria's Secret, Keenan to the GameStop and the adults continued their conversation.

"Given that Big Brother is watching me, should we go ahead with the class-action suit?" Jason said.

"Class-action. Yeah, I don't know. After what you just told me, I can't think clearly. Will they go after me and our children?" She flipped the cell phone lying on the table back and forth on the table with her fingers.

"I worry too. How far will they go to get what they want?" He scanned the area once more. He spotted someone gawking his way. After a close examination, the skinny thin man was searching for his lost family in the crowd.

"Not knowing who your enemy is – that's the scariest part." Kara lifted her eyes toward Jason.

"You were going to see a lawyer last week. How did it go?" The skinny man had found his family and was sharing his food with them.

"I talked to my father's lawyer. He recommended that I talk to Paul C. Schubert, a partner at the Salem law firm Schubert & Tottan, which I did. They are young and friendly. Not arrogant at all. In fact, I liked them. They're energetic and looking for business. He wants to talk to you," Kara said.

"Should we go ahead?" Jason said.

"You wanted to do it for Brian's sake and for justice." Her eyes appeared grave.

"Brian and justice." He would be putting his family's lives in jeopardy.

She continued fiddling with the cell phone. "Sometimes, one has to do the right thing, fight the evils of the world. If you don't do it, Brian and the others will have died in vain. Who's next?"

Jason knew exactly who would be next. And the thought was unsettling.

***

Roger Hunt arrived at the Senator's office precisely at 9:00 am, as expected, for a weekly briefing. Seated behind the desk, Senator Quest waved him in and said, "Close the door behind you. Will you?" After shuffling some papers on a mostly bare desk, he closed the folder and placed it aside. The Senator stood up to shake Roger's hand. His tall, lean frame towered over Roger. "Roger, lots to talk about." The Senator's rapid hand movements confirmed the slight impatience in his voice.

After throwing the briefcase on the floor, Roger plunged into the armchair across from the Senator's desk. He momentarily fixed on the blue eyes of the Senator, who leaned back in his swivel chair, arms resting on armrests, one leg over the other, and ready to listen. Without hesitation, Roger said, "Me too, me too." He then pulled out a file, notepad and pen. Roger fingered his pen, feeling primed for this session. The foremost thought on his mind was to ask the Senator again to make him a Deputy Chief of Staff.

"How is your predictor software working?" Quest's impatience was growing.

"Fine, fine. I use it a lot," Roger said fondly.

"We need some kind of a crystal ball. The election has been on my mind a lot lately. Primaries are underway and the whole nation is gearing up for the judgment day in November, whether we like it or not. If I don't win, I'll be looking for a new job in the New Year and you too."

"Senator, keeping the finger on the political pulse of Oregonians is my job. Turning their opinion to your side is what I get paid for. You lose, I lose too." Losing was abhorrent to him. He had a record to protect, at all cost. Roger cherished the moments when he dished out advice to his candidates. He often reminded himself and others of the Napoleon quote: "A well-reasoned and extremely circumspect defensive, should be followed by a rapid and audacious attack."

"In politics, nothing is for sure. The uncertainty keeps our ears on alert like bears in the political forest. Danger can attack us from anywhere." Quest's eyes narrowed and he tapped his fist on the desk as if to demand answers.

"It's a bit early to achieve a clear vision of success. We're ten months away from November '08." His chest swelled and he spoke slowly and firmly to show his confidence and his power.

"Roger, where are we?" The Senator's impatience continued. Not a good sign. A worried client was often one with battered confidence. As part of a winning strategy in a political candidate, charisma was number one and confidence was a close second.

"I received the results from the pollsters. Taking the public temperature on issues isn't easy. I see a move in your favor, which of course is like money in the bank."

The Senator's whole body was suddenly energized by this promising news. "Did you do an in-depth analysis? What makes voters' opinions move one way or another?" He was smiling.

"Yes. Of course we did, Senator. It was after you introduced the Farm Bill on the Senate floor and engineered maneuvers until it saw passage that it was well received by Oregonians. They see that as helping the poor – the tired farmer in Oregon and the country. We can win points by helping farmers." Roger scribbled a note to himself on the pad.

"That's good news. We're nine months away from the 2008 election. Do you have a solid strategy, plan of action and sure-fire win for me?"

"On the back of the Farmers Bill, we have to build momentum. In the coming days and weeks, I have booked interviews for you on all major networks. Also, I'll be appearing in a few talk shows myself, to further enhance your position."

"Roger, that's great. Do you have a date and time?" He glanced at his desk calendar.

"Not yet. This afternoon I'm hoping it will be finalized by the networks." Roger continued writing.

"Food prices are going up around the world. Putting more money in US farmers' hands will give them an advantage, making them feel rich around election time." The Senator laughed.

"Also, there is a green revolution taking place caused by high oil prices. We have to milk that cow, although it doesn't belong to Republican values." He was ready to do anything to win.

"What about beyond the days and months? What is our long-range forecast?" The Senator stood and walked toward the picture of his late father, as if pleading for his help.

"That's precisely what I wanted to talk to you about. I have been working on a comprehensive plan, as I have discussed the last few weeks." Roger's eyes followed the tall, well-dressed man.

The Senator turned to Roger and said, "I know you have been working on it. Why is it taking so long?" He caressed his silk tie.

Roger shifted his body in the chair and looked straight at the Senator until he caught his full attention. "This round should be better than the last election. The American electorate is changing. One can predict who will win the next election if one can read electorates' minds. In other words, I don't drown myself in research numbers; rather I draw insight from them. To me decoding how the electorate will vote is like finding nuggets of gold from a mountain of dirt. The closer we get to November, the clearer it should become." He breathed deeply, feeling an air of superiority over the Senator who came from a privileged background, everything handed him, unlike Roger who had been forced to scrabble, to use his cunning and wits to pull himself up out of poverty.

"That's your part of the equation." The Senator wrung his hands.

"In formulating the plan I came to realize something. One key element in executing a well-thought plan is resources. Management of all our human and financial assets is crucial. That can be achieved if I am here at all times." Roger picked up his Blackberry and punched something with a tiny pen.

"Roger, of course. That's not a problem. Just tell me what you want." He threw both hands into the air.

"If I were nominated as the Deputy Chief of Staff, it would give me the official authority in Capitol Hill to mange resources on your behalf."

"Ah. I see." Silence filled the air of the large office.

Roger knew not to expect immediate acceptance. The Senator would need some time to shuffle the inner circle of his office staff. He immediately changed the subject by handing him a financial report. "We have to raise more campaign funds."

"Why are the funds so low?" He took a quick glance at items descriptions and dollar amounts.

"They're not bad yet. But once the campaign shifts gear, and when we get the TV ad phase going, funds will be needed." Roger examined the Senator's face.

The Senator's attention stopped at the middle of the page and then his puzzled stare turned to Roger. "The fund from Softek. Last week you indicated Muhtar Gamble authorized his Mumbai CEO to transfer five million to our accounts. I don't see five. What happened? Is Gamble backing out of his promise? Can't happen!" Quest returned to the seat and shuffled through a stack of folders until he pulled one out.

"No. He did authorize five. The money mule took one." After clearing his throat, Roger studied the face of his client.

"One mil? Roger, that's excessive, don't you think?" Quest pulled back in the chair with the folder in his lap. A pregnant silence filled the room. Roger knew he was expecting a serious answer.

Roger stood up from the leather seat, shifted around behind the chair and then supported his body holding the back of it. "Senator, my sentiment is the same. But he wouldn't do it for less."

"You must ask him to lower it." He threw the folder on the desk.

"I did. He blames tight control at our seaport in the US, the fight on terrorism and so on."

"One mil. Just like that." He snapped his fingers.

"Senator, he explained that we were sent the money right away, from his own bank. But it would take him months before he sees it in his account. There's the cost of doing business with us, not to mention the risk. He has to be careful in how he does the money laundering. He doesn't want to get caught. It's a dangerous business. He thinks he is being followed by federal agents."

"Not too happy with that. Let's move on." The Senator glanced at his watch.

"That's all for now." Roger started gathering his stuff.

"Oh yeah. One more thing. Make sure this McDeere guy doesn't start a class-action suit. You know I have direct contact with Gamble. Through our secret liaison, Gamble, the Softek CEO, contacted me. He is saying that to get more funding from Softek, the class-action suit must be stopped. He is panicking. This bastard threatened to cut me loose. After what I've done for him and Softek."

"A class-action suit?" For a few seconds he sat motionless. "I'm not sure if McDeere will start one." He caressed his chin and continued to study the Senator's reaction.

"We can't be sure of anything."

Roger shook his head. "I checked with my surveillance people. We watch McDeere twenty-four seven. We see him when he gets up, when he goes to work, when he talks to his family. So far we haven't heard him talk about a suit. He yells a lot at his wife, or ex-wife, an unusual relationship between them, but he doesn't seem like one to start legal action. He has a good job with ample benefits. Based on the conversation with David Cohen, he should have plenty of money in his pocket."

"Is he happy there?"

"He seems to be happy at Layton, thanks to you."

"When I first saw him, he impressed me as a smart fellow. I've been in politics long enough to know that I have to watch my back. I'm suspicious of everybody. You know that."

"If I notice anything I'll let you know."

"I want you to do more."

"Make sure he doesn't start a class-action suit. When you can assure me of that I'll make you the Deputy Chief of Staff." The Senator's voice was strong and firm.

***

Jason Mcdeere unhooked his eyes from the program editor to acknowledge the presence of Indira, next to his desk. She said, "It's meeting time."

Jason peeked at the shiny Rolex, which he got back from the pawn shop. He had missed it a lot and promised never to lose it again. Jason had been in front of the computer since 7:30 am and it was almost 10:00 now. As he peeled his eyes from the screen, they burned from fatigue and he rubbed them. The pressure of overtime at Layton had been mounting daily, which had taken him away from the more urgent task of hacking into the Volpa PI website. Time was running out for him to find out who was after him. He desperately needed time off of work. How could he convince Indira that he must spend less hours at work or even dare mention it to her? The chances were slim to nothing that she'd give him time off. Everyone in the department regularly put in ten to twelve hours a day. He hoped to discover some flexibility in Indira. So far she had been unyielding.

He jumped to his feet, slapped the laptop shut and, after grabbing a pen and a notepad, he traced Indira's steps to the small conference room. Now that it was just the two of them, face to face with the door closed, Jason watched as Indira examined a printed sheet. "Jason, you have been at Layton for two weeks. It's time for a one-on-one discussion about your progress."

"We need that." Jason rubbed his eyes.

"How are you adjusting?" Indira placed the information sheet on the table and directed her attention to Jason, as though ready to absorb Jason's every word.

"With surveillance cameras everywhere in the building, I feel like I'm losing my privacy. I have to admit I'm not totally comfortable with it. I guess, like everyone else, I'll have to learn to live with it." He cleared his dry throat. Outside the building, with private investigators and the tall, Robot Man watching his every move, he was less charitable. He wanted the surveillance gone.

Indira rested both hands on the printed paper. She pushed her upper body up, while waiting to receive Jason's full attention. "Everyone has the same issue. That way we all get the same treatment. How about work?" She opened her eyes wider, her black pupils more visible. Her bright blue jacket contrasted with her dark skin and white blouse. A well-molded corporate worker. A loyal soldier ready to march to the drum of her commander.

He rubbed his eyes to soothe the pain. "In my whole IT career, I have never seen a place like Layton."

"Layton's very different from most places. It comes in different shades. What strikes you as different?"

"Employees here have only one life. Work."

"It is highly encouraged. And it has its rewards too. Here, for every overtime hour, one gets paid. This fortunately has made us all rich. Looking at your chart, you could put in a few more hours," she said with authority.

Jason leaned back in his chair and glanced at the bare walls. "I'll ramp up slowly. I'm new here. When I finish my training, I'll have a better reason to put in extra hours."

"It's ok. Even when you're on a learning curve, you can bill more than sixty hours a week. We get paid by DoD, by number of hours we bill. The more billable hours mean more revenue for the company." She cracked a smile of satisfaction.

Biting his lips, Jason stared at her eyes and then clothes, all the while digesting the words that she had just spoken. Cheat, yes, that's what she had asked her subordinate to do. He controlled the fire building inside him. A deep breath, followed by a moment of silence, calmed him enough not to blow his top.

"As you know," he said, "I'm living in a hotel. It's fine for a short while, but I'm starting to get claustrophobic in just one room. I'm suffering from cave syndrome. A bigger place would help tremendously. I've been searching for a rental in Mountain View and the surrounding area. It's taking longer than expected. On weekends, I have to go home to spend time with my family." He lowered his voice, hoping to receive sympathy from Indira.

"You can do all that and still put in a lot of overtime." She lifted her chin as though proud of having the brightest idea.

"What do you mean?" He crossed his leg and leaned forward, ready to be enlightened.

"When you're having lunch, traveling or searching for a place, just read a manual or think about a software program. Next day, at the office, you can enter that time as work time. Although you only spent ten minutes on job related tasks, you can bill for one hour."

"I didn't know that would be acceptable." In the flash of a second, he rewinded and played her reply a few times, just to make sure he'd heard correctly.

"It's totally acceptable. Many of us file sixty hours plus per week."

"What does DoD think of this practice? Don't they ask any questions?"

"So far, DoD hasn't. Maybe they never will. In the meantime, Layton Industries present an excellent financial report every quarter and stock prices always inch up." She waved her hand three times. "I encourage you to buy our stock for your 401k and you'll feel richer every quarter. With the extra money you can take your family on an exotic vacation or buy a bigger house. Or a newer car. That's how we operate."

After the meeting was over, he returned to his desk. Indira's picture of work ethics at Layton hit him like a hammer blow. His energy was so drained by how the company raked free money into their coffers that he couldn't even open his laptop. He threw the notepad on his desk and sank into the swivel office chair. He started to scribble while meditating on Indira's words. *That's how we operate.* He couldn't accept money for work not performed. To do so would be unethical and unprofessional. What if they were caught? The US government could shut Layton Industries and put everyone in the company, including him, in jail, which is exactly where he could end up by hacking into Volpa's website. As his outlook grew bleaker, thinking of spending time behind bars and receiving weekly visits from his children, his head pounded like a jackhammer.

He stood and headed down to the lobby, then walked outside. If he was lucky, the fresh air would ease the pulsating migraine pain. He walked briskly ahead, without turning back to check whether the tall, unwanted man was following him. Taking a few deep breaths, his mind cleared only slightly.

What had he gotten himself into? At Layton, it seemed, everyone milked the US government through exaggerated overtime charges. A powerful hand was allowing this fraud to happen. Who could that person be? Sweat from the midday California sun formed instantly on his brow and he swiped at it with the back of his hand. Someone with enough power to blindly rob the US government. His conscience wouldn't allow him to be part of the scandal. Justice should reign.

Then his thoughts turned to Softek, where management pushed employees to work overtime, but without extra pay. They worked in an atmosphere of fear of losing their jobs and not finding any employment in rural Corvallis. The thought caused the pain to spread from his head to every part of his body. Something must be done. But what? What? *What?*

After walking for about half an hour, he suddenly clapped his hands with a

sense of joy having found a treasure among his thoughts. He yelled, "Damn, yes, yes."
He felt like jumping for joy, but it would look silly for a 45 year old to act like a child.
His whole body was washed with a sense of relief and purpose. The search had ended.
For the last many days, he had been wracking his brain to find a good reason to file a
class-action suit against Softek. A case against his former employee would convince a
law firm to launch the suit.

And he'd just found it.

Non-payment of overtime at Softek could be a solid case for a class-action
suit. But what about the corruption at Layton? That would be something for another
day, another migraine.

9

Jason McDeere moved the armchair closer to the bed. After flopping in it, he swung his tired feet on top of the bed and continued fingering the remote, trying to drown his anxiety of being watched all the time. There was nothing interesting on TV that caught his attention.

Lately, Indira's pressure for him to put more overtime in was weighing on his mind. Then, just ten minutes earlier, after parking his rented car in the hotel parking lot, he had seen two men watching him as he exited the car and entered the front of the building. They had been doing that ever since he moved to Mountain View. Since Brian's death he had lost his freedom. It was the same as losing one's life. How long would this house arrest last? He felt like a high-paid prisoner, working for the US government.

Feet still on the bed, he checked the Rolex and tried to relax, but the pressure at the base of his head was back. It was only a few minutes to six but the six o'clock news couldn't come soon enough.

Just then, the cell phone rang and he bolted off the bed. He reached for the phone on the nightstand. It was Shallen at the other end. He shouldn't be talking to her in case someone was listening in. "I can't hear you. Bad connection," he yelled, hoping she'd get the picture that he didn't want her to say more than the initial greeting. With the remote in his left hand, he cranked the volume until the TV blared louder. Then he moved the cell phone closer to the TV. With a press of a button he ended Shallen's connection.

Then he went to the laptop, which was already on. With a few clicks of the mouse, he popped up a list of all the programs currently running on the computer. Scrolling down the list of programs, his eyes fell to the end of the list and he located the Wp123.exe, the rogue program. With a final click on the selection "End Process," the spy software was dead.

"I found a big hole in your net," he muttered. "Soon I'll know who is after me."

He grabbed his briefcase lying on the floor, searched the pockets and pulled out a deck of business cards. Shuffling through them, he found Shallen's business card.

After bringing up the Outlook program on the laptop, he typed in:

> Hi Shallen:
>
> Thanks for the phone call. I had to hang up.
> Can't say much now. Be at San Antonio Shopping
> Center, at El Camino Real and San Antonio Road
> in Mountain View, California. More precisely
> at 550 Showers Drive. Wal-Mart, clothing
> section. 7:00 pm. Thursday.
>
> Sorry for the short notice. Please be there.

The email was dispatched with the cursor positioned on the "Send" button.

Jason quickly reinstated Wp123.exe and double checked to be sure the spyware was running. Very likely someone was monitoring this program. Any interruption could give his intruders a hint that he was on to them, so he'd made the interruption brief. Now he just hoped Shallen got the message, and would meet him at the prescribed place and time.

***

After Jason Deere's workday ended, he drove to the front lot of the hotel, where he usually parked. Two men, sitting inside a parked Malibu, stared in his direction. He jumped out of his car and raced towards the hotel entrance. Arriving in the room, he turned the lights on, pulled the curtains wide, and glanced out the window, assuring himself that the two men were still in the Malibu. Then he threw the briefcase on the bed.

At the desk he disabled the spyware program again and called a taxi driver with Skype software to meet him in front of the Acer Paints building. He knew the exact location, using Google Streetview.

He walked to the front door, pushed it ajar, then stuck his head out to survey the hallway in both directions. Confirming no one was in sight, he descended one level of stairs and hurried towards a service elevator, which landed him to the ground floor. When the elevator door opened, he craned his head to look down the hallway. A hotel worker was pushing a trolley away from him. In the opposite direction, at the end of the hallway, an exit sign hung from the ceiling just above a door.

He opened another door across from the elevator leading into a janitor's storage room. An electrician's overalls hung on a peg. He quickly slid into it, then placed a blue cap he found on a small table on his head. Then he rushed back to the hallway only to discover someone approaching him. It was one of his "handlers." He turned his head towards a light fixture on the wall, pretending to examine the outlet. After a short time, he heard the elevator door ding. Once the man was inside and the elevator moving, Jason raced for the exit. Outside he inhaled a deep breath of fresh air. Hiding behind a large green garbage bin, he saw one of the two goons scanning the area and smoking a cigarette. Jason walked in the opposite direction of them, hoping to make his way around the front entrance of the building where a taxi was waiting.

Once there, he climbed in and said to the driver, "I want to go to the San Antonio Shopping Center on Showers Drive."

"Ok." The driver nodded and the car started to roll forward.

"Before we head that way, I want to make sure no one is following me."

The driver braked the car with a sudden jerk and shifted the gear to park. He turned toward Jason and stared at him with a what-the-hell look. "I'm not doing a Starsky and Hutch routine with my car," he said, sporting a deep Latino accent. "Find another cab, *amigo*."

Jason dug a bundle of money out of his pocket and pointed to the twenty-dollar notes. "I don't want to put you in any danger. All you have to do is drive away from the San Antonio Shopping Center. I'll be watching all the vehicles behind us. Then you make a u-turn, and now we're going towards the shopping center."

The driver glanced first at the money then at Jason's face. "Just last week someone was gunned down by the Mafia. I don't want to be the next victim. Also, I don't want to know what you're involved in, mister. Take a hike. Get out of my car."

"Take this." He thrust the hand filled with bills toward the driver. "Here, a hundred more. Four hundred for your trouble. If anyone's following me, I go back to the hotel and you keep the money. Or you can drop me off anywhere. I just . . . take a hike. You keep the money. You have nothing to lose."

The driver hesitated, then took the money and put the car in gear, rolling forward. As the taxi picked up speed, Jason noticed one SUV and one van through the front windshield. Then he twisted in time to spot a truck and a taxi following them. He couldn't tell if they were ordinary drivers, or if they were tailing him. He turned to the front.

After giving few directions Jason said, "Let's go to East El Camino Real."

"Are you sure? The Shopping Center is on West El Camino Real." The driver appeared disgusted.

"Just follow my instructions." Jason was hoping the driver would do this one favor for a gringo and not just drop him off in the middle of nowhere. He twisted his neck a few times to ease the tension he was feeling. If the two guys behind him noticed he had disappeared from their radar, what would they do? Jason turned to the driver. The Latino's face was scarred, his fifty-something forehead furrowed. Both hands gripped the steering wheel, as if preparing for the worst.

He grunted. "You're not from here."

"Do a quick U-turn and head west." Jason looked around. "Speed up a bit."

The driver shook his head. "I don't want to get a ticket."

"Just snake through the cars ahead. I want to see if anyone is following," Jason said, monitoring the cars on either side of him.

"What kind of a business are you in, mister? You running away from somebody?" The tension in the man's voice eased slightly.

"I'm just a family man, earning an honest living at Layton Industries here in Mountain View. But someone is after me and I don't know why. But I'll find out. So far they haven't tried to kill me. This much I know – they're watching every move I make."

As the taxi zigzagged through heavy evening traffic, Jason tracked every vehicle. Soon they passed South Shoreline Boulevard.

The driver looked at him over his shoulder. "See anyone now?"

Jason unbuckled the seat belt, and knelt on the front seat with his hands firm on the head rest. "No. I haven't seen anyone following, but I'm not taking any chances. Where are we now? Which street did we pass?"

"This is a cab," the man growled. "You have to be seated properly. I don't want to be stopped by a cop."

"Ok." Jason changed position, facing the windshield again. "Where are we?"

"North Renstorff Ave."

"Just drop me at Showers Street, next to Wal-Mart. Ok?" Jason said.

When the car made a quick right turn onto Showers Street, Jason dug out another twenty. The brakes squeaked abruptly pulling the car to a sudden stop. He handed the twenty-dollar bill to the driver. "Sorry for the trouble."

As Jason jumped out of the front seat, the driver's tense face eased slightly and he said, "Be safe." The door was barely slammed shut, when the driver gunned the car.

Customers filed in and out of Wal-Mart. Only then did he realize his mistake. He wished he had planned the meeting with Shallen in a secluded spot. Too late. He didn't want the hired thugs to detect Shallen's involvement in his life.

At the front entrance of Wal-Mart, seniors paid to flash smiles were handing out flyers. After passing a row of cashiers, he received directions to the clothing section from an assistant dressed in blue. Once past the bins of underwear and socks, the men's, children's and women's sections expanded into a sizeable area. Women's was the largest. His watch indicated five minutes to seven. He ducked behind a rack of shirts and peeked through the hangers with a clear view of the underwear bin. Where could she be? Did she get his email? Would she be able to come on such short notice? As these questions swirled in his head, a face appeared above the racks. A man's face. Jason pretended to examine sizes on the shirts while checking out the man. He didn't have a ponytail.

With a shirt in hand Jason headed for the fitting room, which was right across an aisle with a clear view of the entrance. There he noticed a woman with black hair and a heavy handbag, her back to him. *Shallen.* He looked at the shirt in his hand and wondered what to do with it. Still holding it he walked towards her, while at the same time keeping an eye on the man. He must be the Wal-Mart security guard looking for shoplifters. *Let's hope so.*

Jason dropped the shirt in one of the bins along the way, then moved past the shelves of electronic gadgets and grabbed her arm. Startled, she turned.

"Let's go outside." He tugged her arm forward, encouraging her to say nothing. Still holding her arm, they continued walking and made a few turns until the Wal-Mart entrance was visible. They exited, then went past Crescent Jewelers, Radio Shack, a dental office and Payless Shoes. They kept walking parallel to Showers until a block of stores and offices ended. "Over there." He pointed toward Norwalk Furniture.

"What's going on?" Shallen asked, once they were outside.

"Just pretend we're a couple looking for furniture." Jason peered over his shoulder to be sure no one was following him.

Shallen's lips were pursed, confusion written in her expression. After a moment of silence, she mumbled, "Looking for furniture?"

He let her arm go. They went deep inside the store, pretending to be interested in beds, tables and chairs, far from any salesperson. Once they were safely ensconced amid a grouping of living room furniture, he turned to the entrance and watched it for a few moments. He breathed a sigh of relief. It would be safe to talk to her now.

"Would you mind telling me what the hell is going on?" Shallen's tone revealed her patience was wearing thin.

His heart was beating fast and he tried to relax. Still standing, he directed his gaze at her. "I don't have a life anymore. There are eyes everywhere. Monitoring my every move, at my work, my hotel room, even on my laptop. I wouldn't be surprised if someone isn't waiting for me when we leave."

"Why? What do they want from you?" Shallen's face tensed with curiosity. She gripped the strap of the large purse that hung from her shoulder.

"I wish I knew. Ah…I need help. Right after Brian's death, someone bugged my house and computer. Remember, I called you."

"Jason, does this have to do with the article I wrote?" Shallen frowned.

"Could be. Anything is possible." He felt more confused than ever.

"Oh my God." Shallen placed her hands on her lips. "I hope I didn't cause this."

"Thank you for coming here all the way from Washington."

"I'm here for two reasons. Because of your email, but I also wanted to follow up on the shooting at Softek. I have a suspicion that Senator Quest played a part in it," Shallen said.

Jason sat down on a buttery leather couch and Shallen took a seat beside him. "It seems to me there is someone very powerful behind this. But why the Senator?"

"If he *is* involved, perhaps he wants to protect something." Shallen's black pupils grew wider and a faint smile played on her lips.

"Like what?" Jason said.

"In the article, I mentioned you were thinking about starting a class-action suit. That could be threatening to him."

"It's not logical. I know a class-action isn't a trivial thing, but would it make a Senator consider putting someone under surveillance? Or worse, to kill that person? It doesn't make sense to me." Jason realized he had raised his voice. He turned around to check if anyone was listening. The salesperson and one couple were at a distance, busy discussing decor.

"I found out that the Senator is on the Armed Services Committee. Softek has been getting defense contracts consistently for many years. I did further digging but found no contributions from the company to his campaign fund. If we had that, we'd have a direct link. Also, I found out his campaign consultant is Roger Hunt. A very shrewd man." She flashed him her best professional smile.

"This is America. Politics and business join hands and live happily ever after. It may be unethical, but not illegal."

She stood up. "What if he fears that a class-action suit will open a full-blown investigation? What if the Senator is linked somehow to the killing at Softek?" Shallen paced behind the chair.

"That's frightening."

"This is an election year. His opponent will chew him up and spit him out."

Jason suddenly realized he was in the middle of a political storm. "The surveillance is getting on my nerves. At work, my supervisor is putting pressure on me to put in more overtime. On top of all this, I'm living in a hotel room, away from my children." He felt a headache coming on. He placed his hand on his forehead and rubbed the skin hard with his fingers.

"So far I have a theory. No hard facts. We have to find out what the Senator is up to. I don't want to put you in any more danger." She looked in his eyes as though willing him to agree.

"I'm thinking of seeing a lawyer about starting a class-action suit. When I go to a lawyer's office, the men following me will report it to the Senator, if he's involved. Let's say he is. Then the Senator would try to prevent me from launching a class-action suit. If he does, I would finally know who's behind this surveillance." He continued rubbing his forehead.

"I don't have all the pieces of the puzzle," Shallen said. "But I know of many cases where politicians use their power to get what they want. Watch your back." She gave him a meaningful look. "These people could kill you."

***

At 10:00 am Jason McDeere entered the front door of Schubert & Tottan, a law firm in Salem specializing in class-action suits. Kara had recommended meeting with Paul C. Schubert, one of the partners. After closing the door behind him, Jason went directly to a young receptionist who was expecting him and, upon presenting himself, he took a seat. The reception area had four armchairs, one coffee table and a few pictures on the wall. It was modest compared to the lobby of Lambert, Johnson & McQuire with its huge gold-plated sign. Almost a month had passed since he discussed the class-action suit with tall, elegant Mrs. Irva Johnson. It seemed like yesterday. He thought of that December day, walking out of Johnson's office, disappointed by her lack of interest in pursuing his lawsuit. It was around the same time that Brian had been killed at Softek. His friend had died on that fateful day, an event that had changed Jason's life forever. Then he was free and poor. Now he was a rich prisoner. He yearned for the old days.

A young man in a gray suit appeared and introduced himself as Paul Schubert. They moved to a small meeting room and sat across from each other.

Placing a thin folder on the table that seated four, Paul said, "After I saw Kara –" He stopped to open the folder. "Ah, a week ago," he said to establish a time frame, "I checked a few facts concerning Softek. The incident was terrible, especially just before Christmas. You must know the people who were killed. Some were top managers of the company."

Jason quickly realized that the lawyer was on the side of the victims rather than Brian. "The accused killer was a close friend of mine." Jason cleared his throat, allowing a moment to let that thought sink into his listener's head.

Paul's body language suggested uneasiness. "I'm really sorry about your friend. It was tragic, but I wonder if it could have been prevented. It caused so much suffering for Corvallis residents."

"It *could* have been prevented. But you know corporate America worships profit over employee well-being," Jason said with conviction.

"I read some articles about the incident. Some blamed outsourcing. Jobs being sent overseas. What do you think?" Schubert said.

"That's exactly what happened. Brian couldn't take it. Layoffs, foreclosures, economic despair – it drove him to the brink." Jason shook his head, remembering. "I, and many of my colleagues, were in the same boat as him. Unfortunately, I didn't recognize Brian's desperation until it was too late. It could have happened to anyone. Many nights I stayed awake wishing I could have prevented him from going to the Softek building that day. I feel sad that other employees were killed. But I squarely blame Softek management. I also smell something rotten about this. I'm not sure yet, but politics may have played an important role that lead to the killing." Jason combed his hair with his fingers and tightened his lips as a deep sadness washed over him at the memory.

"Do you think Softek treated its employees unfairly?"

Unfairly? Is that what they were calling greed these days? "More than ever we need justice in this case. That's why I'm here. If I don't do anything, Brian will go down in history as a killer. No doubt he took lives of innocent people. At the same time, one has to understand the negative influences from Softek that drove decent, honest people to do something they never would have under normal circumstances." Jason felt an anger that he had never felt before. At that very moment he understood what Brian must have felt and an equally strong sense of justice.

"Jason, how many layoffs were there?" The lawyer pulled out a yellow legal pad and scribbled something onto it. He lifted the pen, pointing directly at Jason.

Jason pressed the base of his neck, the tension easing only slightly. He lifted his eyes toward the ceiling. "It started in October of last year. Every month five hundred people were laid off until the incident. In total, fifteen hundred were let go."

Shubert took more notes. "All the jobs were outsourced?" Schubert said.

"Every single one of them." Jason banged his hand on the table.

"Jason, what can we do for you?"

"I would like you to take on this case. Help me start a class-action suit."

"First we have to establish the merit of the case, based on law. Currently, there is no state or federal law preventing a company from outsourcing. Wrongful termination could be one possibility if the employer broke an employment contract or law." After the explanation, Schubert pushed away from the table, his office chair on casters, and eased his body into a more comfortable position.

"How about not paying overtime?"

Schubert straightened his back, lowered his eyes toward the paper in front of him and tightened the grip on his pen. "Can you give me more details?"

"Yes. Every weekday most of us worked over eight hours. This happened when we had project deadlines to meet. On occasion we had to show up for work on weekends."

"How often did that happen?"

"Regularly. We only had a week or two to rest between deadlines," Jason said.

"Did you ask for overtime pay?" Schubert asked.

"We talked to our managers." Jason nodded to indicate he'd done everything he could.

Paul took a moment to make more notes and then clicked his pen closed, open, closed, open. "What was the response?"

"We were told that we were lucky to have a job. The contract with the US army was at a fixed rate; therefore, Softek couldn't afford to pay overtime. In the end we lost our jobs and no overtime was ever paid." Jason felt the betrayal all over again.

"That could definitely be open for review, but first, we have to prove that they didn't pay overtime." Schubert appeared more animated now.

Jason agreed.

"Was your employment based on a salary or hourly wage?" he asked, systematically collecting information.

"Hourly."

"In other words, you worked a certain number of hours for which you didn't get paid. Is that correct?"

"Yes." Jason's shoulders sagged in relief that the attorney was moving forward.

"We'll do some research. From our findings, if we decide to proceed, we'll put Softek on notice to correct the problem on your behalf. Then we'll wait for a response. Depending on the answer, we may decide to take depositions and then ask the court to certify the case as a class-action suit."

"That's a good idea."

"Before we proceed, let me tell you the truth about class-action suits. They're exhausting." He paused. "They can cause extreme stress for the plaintiffs, the ones representing the class. A lawsuit like this is time consuming and it could drag on for years. To make it really worthwhile, some if not all Softek employees have to come on board with the case, which is difficult but not impossible to do. This will involve all current employees and former employees. It also happens that the people we have represented weren't always in favor of us bringing these people to trial because they were afraid it might bankrupt the company and they'd lose their jobs. It's our business to educate them, let them know that companies have insurance to cover these things and that it won't come out of operating costs. Of course, the Enron debacle was one of the worst class-action suits in history, because they went belly up and didn't have anything left, insurance included."

Jason listened carefully with his fingers dovetailed and resting on the table. "I know there are many hurdles to overcome. Doing nothing is an option but not a courageous one." Jason was fully aware that such an action could earn the fury of the Senator, if he was connected at all. But he had to move forward with the lawsuit, for Brian. For justice.

***

The airport limo pulled into the gravel parking lot of Julia's Diner. After handing the fare to the driver, Roger Hunt crawled out of the back seat holding a shiny brown leather briefcase. He examined the area: the buildings, the road and the landscape to confirm he was at the right place. He breathed the warmer Prescott, Arizona air so unlike the chilly air in Washington, where he was located earlier in the day. As instructed, he wasn't to go inside the diner, where the speakers blared Billy Ray Cyrus' "Achy Breaky Heart."

A decade ago he had crisscrossed Arizona during an election for governor, but this desert state had never won Roger's "Yale" heart. The difficulty lay in adjusting enough to appreciate the southwestern appearance and lifestyle. He was a born intellectual.

He wouldn't have come here, except for Senator Quest's challenge to Roger to prevent McDeere from launching a class-action suit. To fulfill his goal of becoming the Deputy Chief of Staff he had to consult Guy Volpa in person. Any other way would have been too risky.

As expected, after one minute of waiting, a Ford Lincoln with a Diamond Taxi sign saddled on the hood rolled closer to him, the sound of crunching gravel coming from the tires. Roger read the numbers 4531 in black on white. The man at the wheel lowered the window and said, "Sir, you called a taxi to Prescott Valley."

The timing of the taxi arrival, the number pasted on the vehicle and the driver's words matched the signal he'd been given. Roger nodded. He placed himself in the front seat, buckled up and slammed the door closed. Then the driver headed back to the road again and said, "Guy Volpa is waiting for you. We'll be at his office in ten minutes."

"You work for Volpa?" Roger scrutinized the white, slightly wrinkled face, bluish gray eyes, and ponytail. He looked too hippyish for that part of Arizona. His accent was not native, rather from San Francisco.

"Sort of." The driver cracked a faint smile.

"What do you mean?" Curious, Roger leaned forward, ready to swallow every word the driver uttered.

"I drive taxi in town, but I'm really Guy's eyes and ears. There are several of us doing his work. We watch out for him, tell him who is entering and leaving Prescott. You know what I mean."

Roger pretended to understand. "Have you been watching me?" He faced the windshield studying the landscape while conversing with the driver.

"Of course. Mr. Hunt, may I say something?"

"Just call me Roger."

He nodded. "Since you've been on the Airport limo, we've checked every vehicle. We made sure no one followed you to the diner." He took a quick glance at Roger and back to the road again, then swerved toward the center to avoid a tumbleweed lying close to the side of the road.

"Thanks for taking care of my safety." He relied on Volpa's diligent work.

"There's one car ahead and one behind, and they communicate with Guy every few minutes to make sure no one sees us."

"That's quite reassuring. You're not from here, are you?" Roger moved his briefcase from his lap to the floor.

"No, from Washington. Worked for Secret Services until Guy made me an offer I couldn't refuse. I was born in California," he continued, his voice relaxed.

For the next few minutes they stared silently at the road ahead. The car headed east towards Prescott Valley, according to road signs on the two-lane road that marked a dividing line in a landscape sparsely studded with cactus trees. Occasionally, in the far distance he could see cowboys on horses minding cattle. There was a steady flow of cars and buses in the opposite direction. Infrequent skulls and horns decorated hoods. Roger grimaced, happy he didn't live in this part of the US. After passing the Diamond Valley road sign, the Ford Lincoln forked to the right. The driver pointed to a stationary car and said, "He was ahead of us and stopped to signal the road is safe to pass." After another few minutes of silent travel, he slowed and turned onto another road where an old church rose in the middle of a flat desert with a mountain backdrop in the distance.

The taxi halted at the entrance of the church. The driver said, "Guy Volpa is waiting for you inside."

Roger checked the meter set at 0 dollars and said, "How much?"

"Nothing. On the house."

Roger stepped out of the front seat and slammed the door. Then the Ford Lincoln slowly rolled out of the parking lot and faded away into the dry desert. Roger absorbed the surroundings. The high altitude gave rise to healthy, dry air--a stark contrast from the dirty air in Washington and the constant noise. But he loved politics at Capitol Hill and the thrill of a competitive life. Peace and fresh air were not for him.

With the briefcase hanging from his hand, he approached a small building with an arched entrance and wooden doors. The building gave off the distinct impression of age with its century old stone walls, something he recognized immediately from his travels throughout the US. As Roger entered, he wondered why this meeting was happening in a church, in this isolated place between Prescott and Prescott Valley. A graveyard was located next to it.

Once inside the dim interior, Guy Volpa gave him a hearty welcome and a vigorous handshake. "Welcome, welcome, Mr. Hunt." Roger looked at the man's blue eyes, his hair straight back and held together in a ponytail. He looked more like a computer nerd than a security expert. But then again maybe that's what it took these days.

Roger's greeting was less ardent as he remained distracted by Volpa's business location. From where he stood ten rows of pews rolled out to the elevated spot that housed the altar where two candles emitted a dim light. Except for the two of them, the church was empty and quiet. Guy ushered him through the door, then immediately turned right and climbed two flights of stairs. The wood under their feet squeaked all the way from the bottom to the top.

On the second floor, Volpa led the way to his office then offered Roger a seat. Curiosity had him bursting at the seams. "How in the hell did you find this hole in the wall?" He scrutinized Volpa in the ten-by-ten space.

Jolted by the sound of Roger's voice, Guy didn't hesitate to defend himself. "Prescott is my town. I sniff every stranger that enters or leaves this place." He pointed to the road through the window. "I can see everything that goes on out there. None of my clients know about this place. I've made a rare exception for you."

Roger took stock of the place. "This is a unique operation compared to Capitol Hill."

Volpa paused for a moment to follow the motion of Roger's hand as he removed his cap and glasses. As if Volpa was trying to ease the tension between them, he said, "I love this place. It's safe and quiet. You're among friends here."

"For security reasons I came here to talk about Jason McDeere."

Volpa pulled back in the chair. "Okay, boss, I'm listening."

Roger poked his cheek with the tip of his sunglasses. "I saw Senator Quest yesterday. He was very concerned about this McDeere."

"What's the worry?" Volpa waved both hands and placed one leg on the other with his cowboy boot pointing sideways.

"There are many. The main one is to prevent him from launching a class-action suit against Softek."

"Why is that so important?" Guy pulled a cigar from his office desk, lit it and leaned back, taking a puff then blowing the noxious smoke above his head.

"Softek is one our biggest campaign contributors. When a company becomes tangled up in a legal case, it has to divert funds to pay lawyers and court costs. We want that money for re-election. Plus, we don't want people investigating Softek too closely and finding out that the Senator is so . . . *involved*, should we say, with the company's internal workings. What do you have on McDeere so far?" Roger straightened his body in the wooden chair and placed his hands on the armrests. In his mind he went through the reasons he stayed a winner. His clients must always be better funded than their opponents. This was one of his strategic weapons in defeating any opponent – his secret. An enormous financial advantage was required to run a brutally negative campaign.

Volpa squinted, then pointed to the computer screen beside him on the desk. "We are tracking his every move. In his hotel room. Car and cell phone. At work. Everywhere he goes and everything he does we know."

"Does he know he is under surveillance?" Roger rubbed his ample chin.

"He definitely knows." Volpa acknowledged his client's sentiment with a nod.

"Has he ever mentioned a class-action suit?"

"Let me see." Volpa adjusted his reading glasses.

"If he is thinking about it, he must have mentioned it to his wife." Roger looked at the back of the computer screen.

"He met with his estranged wife at a mall in Salem last weekend." After a few mouse clicks, he plugged in an earphone and listened.

"What did they say?" Roger leaned forward.

"They argued about eating at a mall. Geez, she bitched and bitched."

"Any mention of a class-action?" He continued poking his face with the earpiece from his glasses.

Volpa listened to the couples' conversation and lifted his head to the ceiling. His brows furrowed, as if he was focusing on what he was hearing. "Lot of background noise… ahh. Damn, they should ban teenagers from malls. They travel in rat packs. I can't hear the pair for all the screams and giggles of these girls."

"Guy, you've lost me. Why would they pick a food court?" Roger waved his hand in dismissal to show his disappointment.

"He knows what he's doing."

"What else?"

After several mouse clicks Volpa said, "Here. A visit to a lawyer's office, yesterday."

"What did they discuss?"

"Don't know, Boss."

Roger scowled, unhappy with the explanation. "Damn it, I want to know everything."

Volpa took a deep breath. "I can't do that. It's a lawyer's office…."

"Why would he go to a law office?"

"Boss, people see a lawyer for many reasons. Maybe a divorce from his wife."

"It could be."

"They're always yelling and arguing. They can't stand each other. He's not getting any sex, either. Without lovin', a man can get mighty frustrated." Volpa gave a look of satisfaction.

"Are you sure?"

"I've handled many divorce cases. This one definitely smells like one. Yelling. Living separately. She isn't planning to move in with him in California anytime soon. All the signs are there."

Roger shook his head. He wasn't buying it. Not in the slightest. "No. He's a smart guy. A software analyst. I've never dealt with one of his kind. I need you to know everything about him. I can't live in the dark this way. I have to know everything. Every word. Every email. In my job I can't afford to take chances." In his career he dealt with politicians, reporters, interviewers, hackers, Democrats, pollsters, but never had he run into a situation with a geek. This would demand a unique strategy.

"No problem. I'll put more men on his tail. I'll find out what was said in that law office. In my business, I get juicy information from women. Women love to gossip. If Jason's wife knows about the lawsuit, sooner or later, she'll squawk to a friend, parent or somebody. I'll bug his wife's house. If I have to, I'll bug the mother and friends too. I'm confident she'll talk." He seemed determined to go to any lengths to satisfy a client.

Roger gave a nod of agreement. "One more thing. I'm thinking many steps ahead. What if I want to get rid of him?"

Volpa sliced his neck with his finger. "As in dead?"

"Yes."

Volpa pointed his finger to the floor. "I don't do that kind of work, Roger. There's a church downstairs. I don't want to damage my Karma, you know?"

"I see. Then keep what I just said confidential."

"Of course, Boss."

Roger looked at his watch. "I should get going. I have a plane to catch."

"Too bad you're in a rush. We could have done some golfing."

"Another time."

"Can I get someone to drive you to Phoenix?"

On the way to the airport Roger pondered the situation. He was worried that Jason's surveillance wasn't tight enough. Some of Jason's activities weren't being captured by Volpa. This was new territory for Roger. So far he had a dream career with a handsome income, prestige and connections. He didn't want the benefits he'd fought so hard for to evaporate. It could if he wasn't careful. His strategist mind must change gear and eliminate the enemy. This time the enemy wasn't a politician, irate group or tenacious media. It was a nerd. He didn't understand the mind of an IT person. He must do something different. But what? He had been blamed by media for using savage tactics. Winning was his prime goal. Well, he planned to win this time. *No IT geek is going to get in my way.*

10

As Jason McDeere drove along Campus Way in Corvallis, his thoughts turned to the closing hours of the weekend, which were disappearing fast. Before coming home from California, he had arranged to have his son, Keenan, for the weekend while Sarah would have a one-on-one bonding with her mother. But, like a typical teen, Keenan hadn't wanted to attend the da Vinci Days with his mother, sister, and father, preferring instead to stay with his friends. Jason turned his thoughts back to his suspicion that he was being followed.

Another glance at the rear view mirror raised his suspicions a few notches higher. Maybe he was just being paranoid. He decided to verify his misgivings. He made a sharp right on 35th Street, left on Jefferson Way, left again on 30th Street and finally right on Campus Way traveling in the same direction as before. He scrutinized the car in the mirror again. Yes, the hired thugs were behind him. He continued on until he reached the Lower Campus.

Jason eased into a crowded parking lot on the Oregon State University campus. It was an unusual sight for the quiet, intellectual university to draw so much attention. Children, old people, teenagers and parents were there for the da Vinci Days, for which the locals were very proud. Organizers promoted it as the most unique event in the US, the world, even the universe. The street buzzed with excitement.

As he was about to lock the front door of his car, he scanned the area and spotted a Grand Caravan pulling in slowly between a car and an SUV two lots away. The two men, a different pair than those from Mountain View in a Malibu, had been following him since he arrived in Corvallis late Friday. He noticed the blue van a few times but ignored it. Other worries kept him occupied. As long as they didn't threaten him or his family, he could ignore their snooping around. If there were any sign of danger, it could get ugly.

He looked at the Rolex. The hands were ticking towards two in the afternoon. He was on time to meet Kara and Sarah, who were supposed to meet him at this year's fair. Jason was excited to tell her about his exchange with the lawyer just the day before. He headed straight towards the da Vinci Days banner hanging in front of the entrance to the building.

He entered the exhibition area. The whole place was filled with booths for art, science or technology, each booth surrounded by children with wide eyes gawking at mysterious objects. The Lower Campus was converted into a festival center with food courts, beer and an entertainment stage. The higher-learning arena had a more party-like atmosphere than the Fall Farmer's Festival. The works of Leonardo da Vinci – the scientist, the animal lover, the painter, the inventor, and the artist – were everywhere. What would the great 16th century Italian inventor have thought of this event in his name? Perhaps, he'd simply laugh. Or maybe he would have been overwhelmed with gratefulness to be remembered after leaving this world so many years ago. Who wouldn't?

Jason wondered where he could find Kara and Sarah in a place teeming with people. He paused for a moment and turned 360 degrees, trying to locate his wife and daughter among the many faces. Bingo! At a distance, he saw Kara nursing a cup of coffee, one leg tightly crossed over the other as she looked down, deep in thought. He walked toward her only to receive a lukewarm acknowledgement.

For a moment, Jason studied her mood. Maybe she was worn out from weekend activities. "Why aren't you over there –" he nodded toward the booths – "instead of here?"

Kara shrugged her shoulders. "It's too crowded. Besides, I'm tired."

"What happened?" Jason said.

"I didn't sleep well." Kara dangled one leg and looked toward the booths.

Jason could relate. Still, knowing her, she would survive another weekend. Women seemed to be more resilient than men in that respect. "What's on your mind?"

"Things," she said.

The monotone answer gave him a hint she didn't want to talk about what was bothering her. "Where's Sarah?"

"Out there somewhere." She waved a hand in the direction of the exhibitions.

"Why aren't you with her?" Jason said.

"She didn't want me to follow her. That's OK. I needed a break." Kara raised her eyes toward Jason.

"Teens her age don't want to be seen with parents. She'll get over it in a few years," Jason said with acceptance. He lost his father at age ten and his mother was always busy working, cooking or cleaning. He didn't quite understand the teenage generation not wanting to be with parents. Maybe parents gave too much of their lives to their children.

"Keenan isn't with you, either?" She didn't seem too concerned, just curious.

"No. He decided to go to his friend's place to play video games." He turned around at the explosive claps of the excited audience.

"He never gets enough of that. Didn't you take him to an arcade this morning?"

"Oh. Yeah." He paused, remembering. "It was a lot of fun. We played air hockey…"

"Did you get him lunch?" Her motherly instinct had kicked in.

"We went out."

"I hope not McDonalds." She gave him a stern look.

He knew well what would meet her consent. "No. Quiznos."

"Good." Approval seeped into her tone.

"Before you go back to California, could you please bring Keenan to my place." Kara was always on top of family scheduling. Her financial, analyst mind always kept account of who was where.

"Of course. I saw the lawyer yesterday," he said, no longer able to contain his excitement.

"How did it go?" Her face was empty of emotion.

"The meeting was more hopeful than with Mrs. Johnson. With Paul Schubert it was entirely different. Young, impressive guy. He's interested in launching a class-action suit on the basis of non-payment of overtime. The executives at Softek were thieves, coercing and threatening employees to give over forty hours without paying overtime. He was cautious about the outcome, but he showed real interest." He gave a broad smile.

"Good." She sipped the coffee.

"I don't see you beaming with excitement," Jason said.

"It's your case. There's nothing in it for me."

"As we agreed, you will get a percentage if we win."

"If *you* win." She paused to emphasize the uncertainty. "And how long will it take? It could drag on for years. I don't see Softek feeling sorry for Brian or you, or opening their war chest to give you a handful of money. Remember, some of their top management was killed. Unfortunate for everyone." She got up, tossed the final sip between her glossy lips and looked around for a waste bin.

"Ok." Jason blew out a short puff of air, feeling betrayed by her lack of enthusiasm.

"I want to talk about something else." She took a seat and pulled the cuff of her denim pants down.

"What?" He felt a sinking feeling in the pit of his stomach. He pinched his lower lip and looked around. The noise around him continued, including a band that played classical music. Visitors were constantly flowing in and out of the main entrance. He turned back to receive her answer.

"Divorce." Her determination was as clear as the sun outside.

The sinking feeling in his stomach had turned into a hot flame. There was no need to blow up as often as he did. Anger and arguing never brought them closer. He took a deep breath to compose himself. She had raised the specter of divorce many times over the years but he had resisted the idea. "I don't want to throw away our marriage and our family life."

She pushed her hair behind her ear. "Jason, I understand. But the reality is it isn't working. Our relationship has been broken for many years. We can take some comfort from the fact that we've tried and it didn't work for the two of us."

A long silence fell between them. Just then he saw the two men who had been following him hiding among the crowd. Probably they were trying to eavesdrop on his conversation. He faced Kara again. "The timing isn't right. I'm under a lot of stress."

"The timing will never be right. We just have to bite the bullet and get out of it while we're still speaking. Why prolong the pain? I can't live with an uncertain relationship. I have to think about my future."

"Maybe things will settle down in a while," Jason said.

"You don't live in Corvallis anymore. I'll be seeing less and less of you. We are drifting apart. Let's face it."

He examined her carefully. Her hair was neatly coiffed with blond streaks running through her hair. Her fingernails were well manicured and her makeup was artfully applied. She looked too good for a Sunday. "Are you seeing someone?"

"No." She hesitated, and an awkward silence followed. "Yes. Ah... maybe."

"No, yes, maybe. What the hell is it?"

"There is someone at work. It seems we have a mutual attraction," she said.

"Are you dating?"

"No. But we have gone out for lunch, not just the two of us, but in a group. We've hit it off."

"Office romance. Do you know what they say about those?"

"What? Give me your sarcastic one liner."

He nodded. "Office romances are bad for your career."

"Who says?" Kara said.

"Did you read the code of conduct at work?" Jason countered.

"No, not lately."

"Read it again."

"What for?"

"First, it is frowned upon," Jason said.

"What do you know?" Kara waved her fingers. "Don't change the subject."

"What do I know? If it doesn't work out, everyone will hear about it," Jason said, feeling the anger rise up his neck and face.

The loudspeaker blared at the audience. A science nerd was preparing to talk about some discovery in the beginning of the twentieth century that had saved humanity from hunger.

After the announcement was over Kara said, "I'm serious about the divorce."

Both watched Sarah approach.

After a hug to her father, Sarah asked, "What are you two talking about?"

Kara replied, "Stuff."

"Talking about stuff? You sound like my teenage friends." Sarah gave both a suspicious glare. "Ah! You've been talking about divorce again. I can tell." There was a silence. "You two make me sick." Sara's face changed color. "I hate you!" She dashed off.

Both Jason and Kara said, "Honey, honey, honey" and followed her as she headed toward the car. Jason threw Kara a furious glance. Why today, of all days, did she have to bring up divorce? Again.

***

Roger Hunt lifted his shoulders, straightened his back and pointed his face directly at the camera. The cameraman motioned a countdown from three. When all his fingers were closed, the host read the script scrolling down the screen. "We are back to Election Room 2008. My host is Republican political analyst Roger Hunt, a well-known political consultant. We'll talk to him about the Farmers Bill that was just signed by the President. With prices of a barrel of oil and fertilizer going up, as well as food shortages, our farmers throughout this country have been screaming for help. My question to you, Mr. Hunt, why so late? Why wasn't anything done six months earlier?"

Roger forced a tense smile on his face while directing his attention to the camera. "Marcia, thanks for having me on your show. Our farmers need help. They will get a substantial $10 billion in immediate funding so we can feed hungry mouths around the world." He turned to the thirty-something host and said with a deliberate seriousness seeping into his tone, "We love our farmers and we are committed to protecting them. Especially from farmers in Brazil, India and China, in overseas markets. This bill was introduced by Senator Quest."

"For our viewers, you work for Senator Quest." Marcia nodded at Roger. She was known throughout the country for asking her guests probing questions, making them accountable, thus earning her a large audience.

"Yes, I do and I am proud of being on Senator Quest's re-election campaign team."

"Roger, farmers and ranchers across the country are struggling from disasters such as flooding and drought. Why doesn't this bill address that?" Her seriousness hadn't quavered one iota.

"Senator Quest wants our American farmers and ranchers to receive relief, which is badly needed. But the Democrats don't want that to happen. Senator Quest will continue to work hard to provide more disaster relief funding for our farmers and ranchers who badly need it. This is a serious situation our country is facing." With another opportunity to attack his opponent a slight measure of pride seeped into his tone.

"I want to go to another important subject. The *Post* accuses Senator Quest of not being transparent about campaign contributions. How do you respond to that, sir?" Eyes wide and brows raised, Marcia exhaled a breath of confidence into her accusation.

Roger paused to assess the blow to him and to Senator Quest. He scrutinized her well-coiffed hair. Then in his mind he twisted her neck until she screamed for mercy. That's what she deserved for setting this trap. Damnit, he had heard nothing of the *Post* article until now. He struggled for the right response. He had received many blows before and this one was not a knockout. Slowly, and without a hint of hesitation, he said, "Senator Quest is very serious about disclosing all contributions to his fund. We won't hide anything." He hoped it would work, buy him some time.

"But this article goes on to say that contributions were made by foreigners who do not hold US citizenship."

She knew more than she should. Ignorance was a better game than fighting back like an angry idiot. So, with innocence wrapped in his tone, he said, "I am unaware of such a practice." It was a lie. In fact he engineered such illegal fundraising.

The host shot him another look of determination as she showed him her "I'll-wrestle-you-down" smile. "The *Post* alleges that small campaign contributions—which, according to the Federal Election Commission, the names of donors need not be publicized--were bundled into one big check through a US citizen. These contributors were Iraqi citizens—not US citizens--who are not allowed to participate in US political funding."

Anger rose in the pit of his stomach as his thoughts turned to who could have leaked this information. He ran through many names. Who could it be? Who had broken into his fortress? He was obsessed with security.

But Roger had become a damn good actor over his many years, and he wasn't about to show any weakness now. Without letting his emotion show, he looked straight at the camera and said, "I can't comment on that."

The host, proud of her journalistic duty, said, "We'll leave it at that."

His anger had reached a boiling point but again he applied self-control. The crew appeared and started fingering wires from around his neck. As the listening devices were being unhooked, Roger couldn't resist firing back. Hands waving in the air, he said, "Marcia, that wasn't fair. You didn't warn me about your allegations. I was caught empty-handed."

"Is it true?" she said. Then her attention shifted to the commercial about to end.

Roger said, "I don't know." Another lie. Cowed by such a devastating blow, he lifted his briefcase from the floor and headed out with his head lowered. He had never felt so humiliated in his whole life. How would he explain this to the Senator? How would he manage the damage control?

Driving down the Washington arteries, he reached the executive secretary via cell phone. "Tell Senator Quest I need to see him. Now!"

***

Roger Hunt walked into the reception area a few minutes early and sat waiting for the Senator who was supposed to arrive any moment from a meeting. Julia Svenborg, the beautiful executive assistant, was busy on the computer and answering phone calls. Usually, Roger would have flirted with her. This time he read notes, nursing his wounds and pretending nothing serious had happened earlier that day. His eyes flip-flopped between the door and the note.

At the sight of the tall, slim senator, he jumped to his feet. Usual greetings were ignored. Hurriedly, he stuffed papers into his expensive briefcase and followed the Senator towards his office door. Once inside, the Senator dropped a slim briefcase on a small table with only two chairs then turned to face Roger who was just closing the door behind him.

The Senator screamed, "What the hell is going on?" The veins of his neck popped out.

The jolt of the thunderous voice, a definite seven on the Richter scale, surprised Roger. With a steady calm, practiced over many years, he said, "I have to find out where the breach is. Whoever did this will be punished severely."

The Senator punched a bunch of buttons and said, "Julia, hold all my calls." Then he turned to Roger. "We have a serious problem to fix. I feel like I'm in a leaking ship and if a patch isn't found immediately, my political career will sink to the bottom of the ocean."

Roger held onto the back of the chair with both hands after placing his briefcase on it.

The Senator peeled off his expensive suit jacket and hung it on a hook next to the American flag that almost reached the ceiling.

Roger said, "I read the *Post* article as soon as I could get my hands on it."

"What did it say?" The Senator leaned forward.

"Exactly what the CNN show host said. Bundled contributions. I don't know how it got leaked." Roger was apologetic but determined to find out.

"There are too many questions. Who wrote that article?" Senator threw both hands in the air.

"Shallen Xu." Roger waited for the Senator's reaction.

"Same woman. Who is she? What is she after? Can we just buy her off?" Senator Quest's face changed color and he continued pacing behind his desk.

"I checked her out." Roger maintained his serenity.

"What did you find?"

"A lot. She was born in the US, but her grandparents escaped China after the revolution and moved here in 1921. She has been with the *Post* for five years. Before that she worked for small newspapers around the country. I found everything about her life but nothing that can harm us." Roger studied the mood of his listener.

"First she traveled from Washington to Corvallis after the Softek shooting and wrote an article. Now, another article with an accusation. She thinks there is connection between the two." The Senator paced slowly towards the wall adorned with pictures of his achievements.

"I think the two are isolated. No connection," Roger said with certainty, hoping that the Senator would buy it.

"Are you sure?"

"Can't be absolutely sure." Roger shrugged his shoulders.

The Senator looked at his watch. "I wish Tom was here." He paused. "Shit, he's tied up for another fifteen minutes at a White House meeting."

Roger despised Tom Martin, the Chief of Staff. It was well known in the inner circle of the Senator's office that Tom had been opposed to Roger's promotion to become the Deputy Chief of Staff.

The Senator stood within three feet of Roger as he leaned against the chair. He flashed angry eyes at Roger. "Who leaked the information is our main concern. You're in charge of it. What happened?"

"Senator, there are only five people who handled incoming money, expenses and general accounting of the funds. Access to the database is audited and I check it to find out if security has been tampered with."

"Roger, we have to do damage control." Roger knew that when the boss mentioned his name, he was in trouble.

Roger was ready with an action plan. "I'll get a list of every contribution from a non-US citizen and return the money."

The Senator pulled the swivel chair over and sank into it. "That's the easy part.

What about the media?"

Roger straightened his shoulders, walked around the chair and sat in it after displacing his briefcase onto the floor. He felt confident that he had thought through the problem at hand enough to satisfy his client. "Yes, media. We'll stay low. No media appearances for a while until this storm blows over."

"That won't be enough. I'll still be getting calls. Lots of them." With a light push the Senator rolled himself back and folded one leg over the other.

"The standard answer should be that we are going through our list and checking for inappropriate donations. If we find any, the money will be immediately returned."

"It sounds reasonable for now. But every news source in the country will unleash their hound dogs after me. Taking money from non US citizens was a bad idea to start with." The Senator's face muscles eased only slightly.

Roger continued his strategic plan with confidence as he had weathered such storms many times over his career. "We have to compose a press release. Then let the Press Secretary make a brief appearance and issue reports that are on our side. I'll make sure everything is scripted and choreographed. No liberal media will be allowed at that meeting. Also we can blame the whole debacle on an inexperienced campaign worker. That will go over well. We can even pay for someone to admit wrongdoing. Once Americans see an innocent girl crying, their hearts will melt and they'll be only too happy to forgive you," Roger said.

"Roger, this better work. If not, you can kiss the Chief of Staff job goodbye." The Senator's tone and stern expression suggested the man had sensed danger.

"Think of it like bases loaded and the pitcher has just unleashed a fastball to end the inning." Roger's adrenalin was flowing.

The Senator paused, fear written into his expression. He scrutinized Roger carefully but his thoughts seemed to be in some distant place. He jumped to his feet and started pacing back and forth while Roger patiently waited.

"What next?" the Senator said.

Roger shook his head in utter puzzlement. "Senator, what do you mean?"

"Roger, they found out about the bundled contribution. What else might they find? Where is our exposure? What are our risks?" The Senator was standing near the flag his head slanted towards Roger.

"I'll go over security and then I'll brief you soon."

"No. That's not what I'm talking about. I'm talking about our organization, Best for Oregon. How protected is it?" The Senator's voice rose in volume.

Roger shook his head, not sure where he was going with this. "What do you mean?"

"During election year, it's customary to take a shot at the Federal Election Campaign Act. Politicians, analysts, academics, watchdogs, media and critics have taken swings at this act in the hope, at least outwardly it seems, of improving transparency and making US a more democratic country." The Senator walked back to his desk, which was filled with heaps of paper and a computer terminal.

Roger knew it was lecture time. It was best not to interrupt. He nodded and said, "Yes, yes."

The Senator pointed the index finger. "At the heart of it all is the need to receive fund contributions from the rich to influence politicians. Campaign finance reform only made political contributions excessively complicated and have created more scrutiny by everybody." The Senator held his hands out, palms up.

Roger, who had been named a genius political analyst according to reports in many of the major journals, had thought through this issue and had come up with an idea. According to the Political Action Committee, more commonly known as PAC, private groups could form an organization to influence the outcome of an election. He had formed Best for Oregon (BFO). BFO's fund could be spent on TV ads or door-to-door campaigns, on any issue under the sun such as solar energy, farm bills, denying homosexuals rights, protecting rights of unborn children, giving money to veterans, pro-tax legislation, or against taxes. Each activity was designed to benefit Senator Quest in the public opinion polls. Officially, no relationship existed between Senator Quest and BFO. Unofficially they were as close as pants and underwear. It worked very well. Millions of dollars came from Softek, through Kalid Enterprise and then it was deposited in the BFO account. BFO was Roger's brilliant idea of keeping money flowing without leaving any trace of its sources.

"Our secret is safe." Roger got up and made eye-to-eye contact with the Senator.

"If they find that Softek's getting contracts through my influence and Softek is outsourcing, I'm screwed. We cannot let media get a hold of that information. I could end up in jail."

Roger knew the Senator was right, and keeping the lid on things wasn't going to be easy. "What do you want me to do?"

"We have to protect my connections to Best. Everything that can be done must be done to keep the relationship hidden. I mean everything."

"How about keeping close eye on the reporter from the *Post*?"

Roger wasn't quite sure how far the Senator was willing to go with this. "You mean surveillance?"

"Yes." He gave a definitive nod of his head.

"Bugging her office won't be easy. We're talking the *Washington Post*. It's guarded like a king's palace. I could try other areas."

"Also, we have to be very careful." The Senator stopped pacing. "We don't want this to be another Watergate."

11

As Roger Hunt entered the restaurant, he saw Carl Grove, the genius Republican strategist, clasping his coffee cup with both hands. He was known by his friends as the architect of election campaigns and as an arrogant ass by his enemies. He cracked a smile of welcome. Roger had scheduled this meeting at the Washington International Dulles Airport eatery.

Roger peeled off his raincoat, then threw it over a chair and sank into the one closest to Carl. He was booked on the United Airline flight 83 directly to Los Angeles. Then he would drive to his San Diego beach home, which he considered to be his command center.

Over the last few days in Washington, Roger had been weathering a category three political hurricane, propelled by the leak about foreign contributions to Senator Quest's campaign, publicly announced to the world by CNN. Finding who in his inner circle of workers leaked such information would come later. The most pressing concern was damage control. He wanted to go over tactical moves with Carl who was ten years older and had won many presidential, governorship and senatorial political battles and proudly wore many badges of distinction.

Seconds after he planted himself in the chair, Roger vigorously shook his head. "Carl, thanks for coming. Where do I begin?" Carl was bald like Roger. They could easily be mistaken for twins, were it not for Carl's gray well-trimmed beard and Roger's clean shave.

"Is it that bad?" Carl said, his words friendly and comforting.

"Everything is crumbling around me. First there was a leak about contributions by foreign nationals, which I haven't had time to investigate."

"But you knew foreigners were making contributions, right?" Carl's tone was more inquisitive than judgmental as if he wanted to know the extent to which Roger was aware of every detail of operations. Carl always reminded Roger of the first rule: the amount of money in the campaign fund determined winners from losers. The second was to maintain control of everything. Nothing must be left to chance.

"Oh yeah, yeah," he admitted, fully aware. "Security was supposed to be tight, but…" Roger opened both palms on the table and looked down, reflecting what went wrong.

"Continue." Carl listened, collecting information to properly assess the situation.

"After the TV interview I immediately talked with the Senator about our moves. I did the usual press release, promised the world that I would look into it without admitting to anything, of course. I even had a young pretty woman in her early twenties, pretend to cry and to admit wrongdoing. Then bang. It hit me like a hurricane."

"Media and Democrats?" The words were laced with disgust. Carl's lips tightened after taking a sip of coffee.

Roger watched the waiter fill the cup and move to the next customer. He said, "They wanted to milk it for all it is worth. Yesterday our poll results came in. There was a ten percent drop in Senator Quest's approval rating." He placed an emphasis on the last word and shook his head again, disgusted by the turn of events.

"What does the Senator think?"

"He was furious. Still is." Roger paused. "I thought he was going to fire me right there. Where do I go from here, Carl?"

"In a situation like this I always remind myself and others that politics is about war, not democracy. Then I quote Napoleon: 'A well-reasoned and extremely circumspect defensive move should be followed by a rapid and audacious attack.'"

Roger nodded, knowing full well about the strategic maneuvers of the great French warrior. With reluctant acceptance, he said, "It's war." Roger felt comforted by the words of the man who had taught Roger the skills of fighting political wars. "What next?"

"You can add more to your defense and then go on a fierce attack." Carl talked like a general.

"Fix the information leak?" Roger asked.

"More than that. Use the media to your benefit." Carl raised his voice to compensate for the loud talk from a Chinese group that was passing by, all wearing dark suits with handbags hanging from their shoulders.

"Hmm. I have used it to the fullest. I don't see any more room to maneuver," Roger said.

"Oh, yes." Carl gently placed the cup in the saucer. "There is. Get another

Republican strategist to fight for you." Although his face appeared relaxed, his words were cloaked with gravity.

Roger looked at Carl's Hawaiian shirt spotted with yellow flowers. For a moment Roger wasn't sure what the man was talking about, though he had a way of making anything he said sound like wise counsel. After a brief hesitation, Roger said, "Who would be better than you?" Roger rubbed his chin then pointed his gaze at Carl. "But, you're going on vacation."

"Yes."

"Where are you going?"

"The Caymans. I have a beach house there. It looks like Fox News can't get enough of me. They insisted upon setting up a live link from there. All I have to do is take an hour from my relaxation time and participate in my daily political commentary, and I get paid while taking vacation."

"If I was the managing director of Fox News, I would do anything – pay your way to the moon to have you on their show everyday. You have widened their viewer audience and they make good money from you. They can afford it. Do they pay you well?"

"Very well." He turned his face away suggesting a hint of reluctance in exposing his earnings for being on Fox News. However, a smile of satisfaction suggested a handsome income.

Roger straightened his back, pushing his chest forward. "Can you talk about the Farmer's Bill that the President just signed? Something positive that might help the President? "

"That's what I was thinking. But I'll go a step further." Carl's gaze shifted to a couple who had just entered the restaurant, their faces filled with confusion. Wrong place. They turned around, walked away pulling their luggage on rollers.

"I'm listening," Roger said.

"I'll talk about the Senator's charity work, his proposed bill to increase the compensation men and women coming home from the Iraqi war will receive, especially financial help for families whose loved ones are killed in the war. Also to those who are injured in this war. In US politics, being on the right side of a war helps."

"Thanks! That should help move the next poll result up for sure." Roger offered his mentor a broad smile.

"I can also talk about the late Senator Quest, the Senator's father, who was a war hero." He emptied his cup.

Roger felt more relaxed. "That should be a good defense. An excellent strategy. But what about the offense?"

"The Senator receives help from PACs, right?" Carl spoke the words as though it was a matter of course.

Roger said, "Yes, of course. The most notable one is called Best for Oregon."

"Ok. Spend millions through this organization to attack the ideas of the Democratic candidate in Oregon. I mean attack. Use all the ammo you have. Make sure the opposition is blown away, the body scattered everywhere."

Just then Roger's Blackberry vibrated. He pulled the phone from the holster attached to his belt. After a peek at the screen, he said, "Sorry. I have to take this call."

He stood with the phone pressed to his ear and walked through the door of the restaurant into a long hallway where passengers were rushing towards the gate to catch their flights. Roger said, "Hi, Volpa, what's up?"

"Good morning, boss. I have some news. I thought I should call you."

Roger leaned on a wall, surveying the area. Many travelers walked the hallway focused on pulling their carry-on with one hand and holding their ticket with the other. He felt comfortable that no one could be listening to what he was saying. "What have you got?"

"For sure McDeere's wife is filing for divorce," Volpa said with satisfaction.

"How did you find that out?" Roger yawned. This piece of information wasn't terribly interesting to him.

"I bugged the wife's purse."

"What else?" Roger was looking for something more valuable.

"Her friends too."

"That's good. You better have more than bugging purses. It's five in the morning where you are. You didn't call me just for that," Roger growled, angry that Volpa had disturbed his conversation with Carl.

"No. There's one more thing. McDeere is starting a class-action suit." Excitement filled Volpa's voice. "The pair was yelling at each other at some fair they attended in Corvallis, Oregon. He told her about the class-action suit and she told him she wanted a divorce."

"Good work," Roger said. "I have to go now. Someone is waiting for me." Roger hung up then walked to restaurant and sank in his seat. He stared at Carl for a long moment.

"I can see by your face it wasn't a good call," Carl said.

"Damn." Roger shook his head. "I don't believe it. McDeere is starting a class-action suit against Softek."

"Class-actions happen all the time in this country. That's not original."

"This one would be deadly for my career," Roger said.

"Is Softek a big contributor to Quest's fund?"

"One of them. Without it, we would run out of 2008 campaign funds." Roger rubbed his chin. His eyes turned away from Carl, thinking of the mess he was about to get into. He swiftly scanned through the events that had led to this situation. Was it possible to have taken a different route to avoid falling into this abyss?

Carl broke the silence. "Is it that serious? Contributions are legal. Did you go over the limit?"

"The limit on the books is fine. But it's what isn't there that could be potentially dangerous." Roger was intentionally vague, hoping that Carl would understand.

"Just find another contributor. The internet is a good venue. It's going to be a major source of money for presidential candidates. As a matter of fact, for all candidates."

"The class-action will invite scrutiny from the media, Democrats, etc. The *Washington Post* has already been scratching the surface. The Senator is worried that he could be linked to illegal activities, which could bring an end to his career." Roger blinked a few times and furrowed his brow.

"What activity?" Carl's eyes opened wide.

"If they find that Softek's getting contracts through Quest's influence, and Softek is outsourcing, we're screwed. We cannot let media get a hold of that information." Roger rubbed his bald head.

After a moment of reflection, Carl lifted his eyes. Roger watched as the man scanned the hectic restaurant. Some air travelers were busy eating a quick breakfast and others were leisurely waiting. Carl returned his gaze to Roger and said, "This is very risky. My advice is to get rid of this McDeere. Plant marijuana on him – get him arrested."

Roger lost his appetite and pushed away from the table. He couldn't go that far.

Carl rested his chin in his cupped hand. "This is war, Roger, and we can't take prisoners. Send him to jail and let him rot there."

"Any other ideas?" Roger asked, no longer hungry.

Carl leaned forward, with a palm covering his lips and said, "Waste him."

Roger slowly absorbed what he had just heard and glanced from side to side. "Waste him?"

Their heads were inches apart. "Yeah. It has to be strategic."

Roger pulled back. This was beyond his job description.

Carl's eyes shifted from corner to corner to ensure no one was listening. "It's the only way."

"It's too risky. Also I would have to run this by David Cohen, our contact at Layton Industries, and the Senator."

"Just make it look like a car accident." Carl slurred the words while scratching his cheek.

"Any other option?" Roger knew that killing someone carried a lot of risk unless it was absolutely clean, and the act could in no way be traced to him or the client. Although he was certain it had been done many times over the years, it had only been hinted at. This was all too real.

"Or get him arrested for drug possession," Carl said, "if you're afraid to kill him."

Roger grimaced, considering all the options and calculating risk versus benefit of each path. "What if he isn't convicted?"

"You make sure he is and that he rots in jail without parole."

"He is definitely posing a threat to the Senator's re-election campaign and my career. But if I do anything, I have to be careful to the extreme in any path I choose. I don't know how far Cohen and the Senator will go with this idea."

"You have no choice but to get rid of him, whichever way you go. That's your best offense." Carl's expression was emphatic.

***

It was almost 2:00 PM when Jason McDeere clamped his forehead with two fingers and pressed his temples hard enough to ease the pain that had been building for hours. The pain didn't surprise him as lately it had been his unwanted companion, day or night. With strained eyes, he watched the progress bar on his computer creep forward indicating the program was crunching numbers at maximum CPU power. Already half an hour had elapsed since he started this job of uploading 300 MB of terrain mapping information into the missile simulator database. He had come to work early, very early. At 1:00 AM. Before he decided to show up so early at the office, he had tossed and turned for hours thinking about his marriage and its imminent breakup. With every passing day, his family life was inching towards it's end point. The latest blow occurred when he had received a call from Kara asking him the mailing address where she could send the divorce papers.

Jason was certain that neither loyalty nor dedication had induced him to show up for work at such an awful hour. It was the regular paycheck that kept him at Layton Industries. His joy for work had been dying a thousand deaths. Occupying his mind with the missile project was less painful than seeing his family life sink to the bottom of the ocean. It seemed it had passed the line of no return and there was nothing he could do to rescue it.

On the first day of work, precisely twenty-three days ago, his assignment was to be part of the upgrade project of BGM-109 Tomahawk. He was also repeatedly reminded he was only to read the piles of manuals on missile guidance systems and watch his colleagues do the work while clocking a 60-hour week. For six months he wasn't to run any program, just watch others do it.

But just a week ago the project plan changed. The deadline was slipping away and everyone in the department was going crazy. Extra help was needed to catch up. Requested by Indira Gupta, the team leader and approved by David Cohen, the general manager, Jason was moved from watching to hands-on and assigned the task of loading terrain data of a missile path into the simulator.

Jason pulled his chair forward to catch the computer clock precisely as it struck two. At that time his program's progress bar would cross the halfway mark of scrubbing and loading data. David Cohen's sudden and unexpected appearance beside him gave him a jolt. He lifted his tired eyes to acknowledge the other man's presence next to the cubicle desk. Indira stood behind him holding a note with her left hand and nervously twirling a pen with the other hand. She hung on David's every word, her face filled with anxiety.

"Jason, sorry to disturb you. Can we talk to you?" His voice was professionally polite but grave. He cleared his throat. "In my office."

Jason examined both faces for clues. Maybe he was getting fired. Not a bad idea but economically ruinous. "I am in the middle of loading mapping data. Can it wait?"

"I'm afraid not." David words suggested urgency.

After picking up a pen and pad from the desk, he said, "Let's go."

David took the lead, closely followed by Indira. All three entered the ten-by-twelve foot office, then David closed the door and said, "Take a seat." He sank into his swivel chair, facing Indira and Jason across the desk covered with piles of paper and a computer monitor at one end.

Indira said, "How is the loading of the data into the simulator going?"

"Had a few problems during the data cleansing process, which is expected." He gave Indira a matter-of-fact shrug. "Also the size is huge. I needed extra storage."

Indira paused for a moment. With her finger on her chin, she asked, "ETC?"

Jason levered his head towards the ceiling, visualizing the software progress bar, and after running quick calculations in his head he said, "Estimated time of completion . . . ahh." He rubbed the back of his head. "By five this afternoon."

"It's later than I was hoping for, but that will do." Indira always drove her co-workers hard. She tilted her head closer to Jason and said, "Your eyes are red. What time did you come in?"

"Very early. One in the morning." Jason suppressed the sadness he was feeling. He was touched that she asked. Could this urgent meeting be about the database? He directed his attention toward David who rolled his chair closer to them by using the fingers grips at the edge of the desk to power himself forward.

After reading a sheet of paper lying between his palms, David said, "I'm looking at your weekly report. It's approaching sixty hours." He gave Jason a scowl. "It's below the group average."

Jason felt anger boiling inside him. "Damn it. I'm trying. I've only been here over three weeks. I don't like clocking hours into the payroll system just for the sake of it. I'm hoping to ramp it up." His eyes shifted to observe Dave and Indira's reactions. Since he'd started this job, it seemed he couldn't give enough time. He had always insisted that he didn't want to compromise his honesty and integrity. Like a pressure cooker, the tension between him and others in his group had been steadily mounting.

"As you know, the missile upgrade project is running behind. We are at a crucial phase. We need more time from you. Especially on weekends."

His body shot up like a rocket and now on his feet, he walked around the chair, held onto the back of it. He lowered his vision, making eye contact with David. He said, "Weekends are sacred for me."

David tightened his lips, pushed the chair away from the desk just a few inches, and leaned back, ready to lock horns. "What do you mean?"

Jason shifted his weight to his left foot. With both hands up in the air, he said, "I have to see my children." He shook his head in disgust.

"I'm a family man too. But we need you. I'm asking for extra time from every single person. This includes Indira and myself. It is crucial. We have to deliver this project to the DoD on time. If not, all hell will break loose. Any delay will spiral to the top. The CEO of the company. There is a chance – I mean a good chance – we could lose this contract and others in the future. Our future depends on it. We won't let it happen."

Indira signaled her turn for a contribution with a raised hand. Both men looked at her. "To meet the deadline of our deliverables, a lot of work needs to be done. And I mean a lot." She wrote something on her notepad. She had the habit of always making notes.

"Indira, I understand the urgency of the project. Emailing my picture to my family will help but not enough." He gave a dry laugh. "It is also important that I see my daughter and son in person. They are going through a difficult time--"

"Jason, the logical step is to bring them here. You're working. And they are there." David's voice went up a notch in volume. "As I have mentioned before, bring them here. The company will pay all the expenses, give your wife a job and even pay for your children's private schooling."

"David, all that sounds generous, but in my case it wouldn't work." Jason shook his head.

"What's holding you back?" Indira asked. She was a devoted supporter of David.

Mouth open, Jason looked toward the ceiling, his eyes watery. Quickly, he pinched his nose to prevent tears from falling. "My wife and I have been separated and will be going through a divorce." He took a moment to compose himself, rocking his body sideways on his feet. "Soon."

"Sorry to hear that. In that case you don't need to go to Corvallis every weekend."

"My daughter is finding this family breakup very difficult to handle. Naturally, she needs me."

"Meeting the deadline is extremely important. If you can't contribute more, we'll have to find someone else. It is crucial."

Everyone had their problem to resolve. David seemed firm in his position. Jason was looking for a compromise. "How about I go back for the next few weekends?"

David stood up, walked to the corner and turned around to face Jason. "Any other reason we can't have you on weekends?"

Jason played his card to the fullest. "Yeah, as a matter of fact there is. I'm also starting a class-action suit against my previous employer, Softek. It will take some time to get it going."

"A class-action suit? Why?"

"Our jobs were wrongfully taken away and given to foreigners." Jason stood his ground.

David's eyes went wide. "Jason, that sounds like a good step, a way to heal a wound, but it has many disadvantages. It is costly, time consuming and if... and that's a big if . . . the judge rules in your favor, you will only see a few cents on the dollar. Your plate is full. You don't need any more distractions."

"I have to find justice for Brian, my friend, who became a victim of outsourcing."

"It is your choice, but I must warn you it may jeopardize your employment here. Senator Quest won't like it." David continued pacing.

"How is the Senator involved?" Jason examined the reactions on both faces.

"Softek's survival, like Layton, is based on DoD contracts. Like every politician, Senator Quest wants to help businesses in his state. This isn't unusual."

"Does Softek make political contributions to the Senator's campaign fund?" In his mind Jason drew a connection between Softek International, Layton Industries and

Senator Quest. He recalled the Senator's agitation during their first meeting, when Jason had mentioned a class-action suit.

David shook his head as if he was hiding something. "I wouldn't know."

"How about Layton? Does it make contributions?"

"I'm sure it does," David said defensively. After a pause, he added, "Most corporations give to political funds. But if they have, I am sure it would be within the bounds of regulations. Layton wouldn't do anything unlawful."

Jason turned to Indira to study her reaction. She was quiet, giving him a what-the-hell-are-you-talking-about expression. Jason said, "What was the amount?"

"I'm not privy to such information."

"It seems you have a close relationship with the Senator." His probing question was meant to annoy David in an attempt to make him angry enough to reveal something of interest.

"Not close, but I would strongly discourage you from starting the lawsuit. Otherwise, DoD will pressure us to cease your employment here."

"I would be fired? I was told Layton never fires its employees," Jason said, baiting him.

"In normal circumstances, yes. This is a good, secure job. There is plenty of opportunity for you to earn lots of money. As for your family, I can approve cost of family counseling, traveling expenses between here and Corvallis."

"The suit isn't about money. It's about justice. But I will definitely consider your offer." Jason absorbed David's every word, analyzing his tone for any hidden meaning. Losing this job would be as perilous as jumping off a cliff without a parachute.

"Noble as it sounds, there are some serious ramifications to consider." David's face continued to display the seriousness of his proposal.

"What would you suggest?" Jason asked for advice only to appease his boss.

"Before you take any action, take a hard, deep look at security, finance, family, and career. One wrong move and you could sink in quicksand. Do you really want that?" David's tone changed from suggestion to appeal.

"My security has been snatched away from me." Jason felt a queasy feeling, acid burning his stomach.

"What do you mean?"

He was barely able to contain his emotion. As calm as possible, he said, "I am being watched all the time. Did you know I'm under surveillance?"

"I don't know anything about it." David's body language suggested it was a lie.

"Maybe I'm being paranoid for nothing."

"I think you are. The best thing for everyone concerned would be to drop the class-action suit." He placed special emphasis on the words "everyone concerned."

After Jason had excused himself from the office, he wondered what David meant by "everyone concerned"? He had a strong sense that David was trying to protect someone. But who? The Senator would have the most to lose, if he was involved in something he shouldn't be.

***

Jason McDeere waited at the fifth floor elevator, watching the glass door that led to the offices where he was to meet Terrance at any moment. When Jason sighted Terrance, who lifted his credential card towards the black security box to unlock the door, Jason sighed with relief. Upon seeing a green light appear and a faint click, Terrance walked through the door towards Jason, who pressed the down button of the elevator. While both stood waiting for the elevator door to open, a few coworkers arrived at the glass door and lifted the access card to the security box one at time. Jason leaned toward Terrance and whispered, "Let's take the stairs." Jason led the way to an exit sign hanging from the ceiling near the door. He took a peek down the stairwell to ensure no one was in sight, turned to Terrance and said, "I have an urgent matter to discuss with you. Privately."

As they quietly descended the concrete steps, Terrance said, "Let's go outside. I could use some fresh air. I have already been inside this building for twelve hours and the day isn't over yet." He shook his head, sucked air through his nose and finger, then combed his hair around his ears.

Jason said, "Can't. I'm under surveillance. I am being watched all the time. Inside and out."

Terrance slowed and aimed a serious look at Jason. "Man, you are in deep shit."

"You bet I am. Being seen with me could jeopardize your life."

"Ahh...I don't care." An aura of truthfulness radiated from his new friend.

"But I do!" Jason stopped for a short moment, glanced down the stairwell and then continued his descent.

"Ok. Let's go to the janitor's washroom." He glanced at his wristwatch.

Jason turned to him and said, "The bathroom? Why."

"It's the only place where we can't be watched." Terrance adjusted his glasses. "I know an empty one."

Jason pushed the door and walked onto the ground floor. "Go ahead. I'll follow you." Jason slowed enough to stay a few steps behind Terrance. Going past the cafeteria and coffee bar, they paced a long hallway. At the end, the post office counter was visible. Ten feet before reaching it they turned right onto stairs that led down one level, and they were again in another hallway. Still pretending to be coincidently heading in the same direction, yet not together, Jason felt a sense of camaraderie with Terrance, which reminded him of Brian and Rocky. He missed the coffee breaks, the no nonsense talks and friendly arguments. In female terminology it would have been called human bonding. A strong degree of gratitude enveloped him towards this hacker who was willing to risk his life for him.

This part of the building, usually occupied by maintenance crews, wasn't busy this early in the evening. The lighting was dim, the carpets were dirty brown and the walls were covered with green wallpaper. After walking past a service elevator, they entered the washroom. The place had three urinals, two taps, and two toilet stalls. A quick examination confirmed they were the only two there. Jason turned to Terrance, "Should we lock the door?"

Terrance approached the door, and after a quick check said, "No. I don't think we can. Let's take a pee. What do you want to discuss in this stinky place?" He laughed.

Jason unzipped his pants. "My whole life stinks."

"When I'm down, I do 'despair analysis,'" Terrance said in his typical philosophical manner.

"What the hell is that?" Jason turned his face to the right.

"When I'm depressed, I ask, how bad is it? Am I homeless, thirsty, hungry, sick and dying? If not, I'm not down and out. I figure I will survive the trial and difficulty I'm going through." Terrance elevated his head towards the ceiling.

"Is that Zen philosophy?" Jason said.

"No, no. It's my own survival strategy," Terrance said.

"The way my life is going I'll be down and out soon." Jason glanced at the door, hoping no one would barge in.

"What are you talking about? You have a job with a decent salary," Terrance said.

"According to David Cohen, I'll lose it all if I don't obey his orders. That's the reason for this meeting." Dry laughter came from Terrance's direction.

"Let's talk business," said Terrance.

"I want to get information from the accounting database – of companies that make payments to Layton." Jason cleared his throat. "Is it safe for me to do that?"

Terrance devoted his full attention to the question. "Only if you have access to the right network segment."

"My investigation tells me that the missile simulation database and accounting database are on the same network segment."

"Which project are you working on?" Terrance zipped up his pants and walked to the tap.

"BGM-109 Tomahawk," Jason answered with dampened enthusiasm.

"Aren't you supposed to read manuals and watch others work for the first six months? How did that happened? Did you bribe or threatened someone?" Terrance pumped the soap container with his thumb.

"Just luck. Management is behind on their deadline and they need a rescue plan. I'm part of it." Jason's laugh was laced with sarcasm as he walked away from the urinal and motioned to the tap.

"Interesting!" Terrance was still fiddling with the soap container.

"Let's assume I crack into the database. What can I do to go unnoticed?"

"Let me see." Terrance was silent for few seconds as he ran water over his hands. "First, let's look at the risk. Every transaction, access and privilege is monitored and audited. If there's any breach an alert will go out to your team leader and an incident report will be generated. The next morning, the culprit is called to a breakfast meeting with the VP of the department. The reprimand is so harsh that you wish you were dead. You won't be fired but it will go into your employment file." He grimaced, suggesting it would be an unpleasant experience for anybody.

"I know it's risky. But I have to do it." With a sigh Jason released the tension he'd been holding. "As long as I have some energy left in me, I'll go down fighting. Your help is my lifeline . . . if there is one." Jason took a close look at his tired face in the mirror in front of him.

"You're not down and out yet. I'll watch your back." Terrance raised a wet thumb in the air.

"Thanks, man. That gives me a big boost of confidence." Jason nodded to emphasize his sincerity.

"To get into the database, of course, you will need the user ID and password." Terrance closed the tap and searched for a paper towel.

"I don't have that yet, but I'll try to find it." Jason looked at his weary eyes in the mirror. Dark circles ringed them.

"You only have a narrow passage of time to get into it, and I mean very narrow," said Terrance then stopped as footsteps approached.

Jason's head snapped up as both he and Terrance turned towards the squeaky door. A man in his late forties with navy pants, wearing a khaki shirt marked with Abe Janitorial, walked in and headed to the urinal. Jason glanced back toward the running water.

Jason had to do something. Quickly he thought to change the subject. "Oh, that's so funny. Then what happened? Did you get another date with her?" Jason laughed loud.

"I called her back and begged until she agreed to another date," said Terrance, catching on.

"Oh my God, you begged. How was your ego afterwards?"

"Totally bruised. I put a frozen bag of peas on my head to get rid of the headache." Terrance gave a fake laugh and smile, as if he was pleased to be going along with the pretense.

"How did the date go?"

Terrance turned to Jason again. "Before seeing her, I had a makeover. I got the idea from one of the reality shows. Changed from a geek to Fabio, the model. Shaved. Wrapped my long hair around my ears. Tight black shirt. Got rid of the glasses. Dress pants, the works."

"Was she impressed?" Jason closed the tap, pulled a sheet from the paper towel dispenser and looked at the janitor whose nose was pointed to the wall as though focused on a spot.

"Totally, but there's more. During all the time I was with her I didn't say a word about computers. Can you believe it? Painful." Terrance looked amused.

"What did you talk about?"

"Social stuff. Like gender equality and sharing housework between couples."

"Awesome." Jason felt impatient and wished the janitor would leave the place soon, letting the discussion continue.

"At the end I blew it."

"What happened?" Jason said.

"I tried to impress her with my cooking skills. I told her about a pot chicken recipe. It consisted of chicken, Soya sauce, garlic, onion, linseed oil in a pot, which I cooked in the oven at 500 degrees." Terrance shook the water off his hands.

"I didn't know you were a cook."

"I'm not." Terrance walked to the paper dispenser. "She was surprised when I said linseed oil."

"You blew it for sure. That's for polishing furniture."

"I really meant to say sesame seed oil," said Terrance.

"You blew it. How did it end?" Jason shook his head.

"Amazingly well. When we parted she told me that being a geek is in. Can you believe that?"

The janitor washed his hands and left.

Once he was gone, Jason turned to Terrance. "Where were we? What is this narrow passage?"

Terrance paused to reflect on the answer. He rubbed his chin as if buying time. "At 2:00 AM all the systems including network and databases start to go down for backup. The network goes first, followed by databases. There is a window of opportunity when the network goes down and you can access the database."

"How long is this window?" Jason felt a surge of energy.

"About two minutes." Terrance lifted two fingers in the air.

"It may not be enough." Jason grimaced.

"With databases you can do a lot in two minutes."

"But what if something goes wrong and I need more time?"

Terrance tapped his lips, thinking. "Tell me when you're about to do it and I can lengthen the time."

"Sounds good. But I have to prepare for it for days. The plan must be impeccable. I have to think of all the risks before any attempt is made."

"By the way. I was curious about you being fired. No one gets fired in this company." Terrance threw a paper towel in the waste bin.

"That's what I thought. According to David Cohen, in serious circumstances, Layton will kick an undesirable out of the building without a moment's notice."

Jason frowned. That's all he needed.

"I've also heard that troublesome people curiously get sick or die." Terrance continued pacing back and forth then stopped upon seeing Jason's face. Backtracking he added, "Just company gossip."

"Let's get out of here," Jason said.

12

Shallen Xu crawled into the passenger seat of the Toyota Prius. Lisa Ward rolled the hybrid car, its engine noise almost nonexistent, out of the *Washington Post* parking lot into the heavy mid-morning traffic of Washington DC. Ward, a senior investigative reporter at the *Post* who won the 2007 Pulitzer Prize for probing into oil companies' excessive influence on lawmakers, proudly drove the perfect white vehicle. Together they headed to a journalistic conference, the cost of which was placed on company expense, an event that only came rarely but was a welcome break from a stressful reporter's life. As Lisa drove, Shallen listened to the top of the hour news pouring out of the AM radio.

That day the sunlight showed up in full force, making the White House stand out brighter among barren trees. As they drove by the US presidential office with its gleaming top, Shallen turned to the right to take in the view of the beautiful landscape but the discussion that took place earlier stuck to her mind like a crab to a rock. John Mead, the Editor-in-chief, Ward and Shallen had huddled together in his office for a morning briefing. Mead shot another warning at Shallen that she would be covering the primaries fulltime soon, which she had managed to dodge for weeks. This travel time, she hoped, would give her a chance to lay bare her soul to Lisa Ward, to get her opinion on something that had been weighing heavily on her.

But for now, both observed silence, especially after the heady discussion they'd had with Mead. Shallen was running out of patience. She wanted to break the silence, but hesitated only to lend Ward the time and focus while she was about to make a left turn onto busy Pennsylvania Avenue. After the turn was complete and the car adjusted to the right lane, Shallen raised her voice to compensate for the radio.

"Lisa, John is hell bent on making me cover the primaries." She hooked her jet-black hair around her ear with a finger. "I would like to finish the Softek killing and outsourcing investigation, if I could."

Ward gazed arrow straight through the windshield. A tense expression hinted at a delayed response as she searched for an appropriate answer. "I understand both viewpoints, yours and John's, but there's an overriding issue."

Shallen understood Ward's position. She was a careful listener, a characteristic highly admired by many. She had to play the office politics correctly, Shallen knew; after all she was a senior staff member. Gossiping about the big boss was unwise in the news business or any business. "Overriding issue. Ahh. What could that be? Can you share it with me?"

Ward was forthcoming. "Definitely. It's not a secret that more reporters are needed to cover 2008 politics. We just don't have enough people to go around."

"How about hiring more staff?" Shallen said as they passed 6th Street NW and Pennsylvania Avenue. The John Marshall Park on the left stole her interest.

"Management wishes it was that easy." Ward grimaced and glanced in the rear view mirror. As Shallen only knew too well, sometimes when traffic was dense, drivers became too aggressive.

Shallen's curiosity piqued. "What's the problem? There are always fresh graduates. Someone from a small town newspaper would love an opportunity at the *Post*." Shallen examined Ward's face, decoding every movement for possible clues about the inner workings of the *Washington Post*.

"The question is readership." Ward gave Shallen a hellava serious look.

"Readership? I got the impression from the subscription department that it was on the rise."

"The subscription department never knows what's going on. They're like sleepy drivers in charge of a moving train. When it comes to readership, there are two kinds. One is the traditional one: those who have their newspaper delivered at the door and read it while eating breakfast. Slowly that part of the business is drying up as people discover the ease of the Internet. At the same time the ads revenue is coming down. We are trying to build on the second, which is the Internet type. But it will take time. Therefore, during this transition period, the revenue will be restrained." Ward checked the side mirrors.

"How long will it take?"

"Who knows?" she said, shrugging as she checked her rearview mirror and changed lanes. "But some reporting must happen, when one is covering the election. John is under tremendous pressure. He has to justify everybody's paycheck to his superior."

Ward reached for the CD compartment, and clawed the cover open to grab two chocolate bars stuffed with coconut while most of her attention was clearly on the traffic ahead. She offered one to Shallen, who reluctantly accepted it. To refuse a host's offer of food was considered impolite as part of an obscure Chinese tradition, which had been drilled into her for her entire life.

Shallen perched the bar on top of her purse resting on her lap. "I understand. All I want is more time to investigate the outsourcing and perhaps link Senator Quest's involvement. I have already spent a lot of time on it. My preliminary research shows that there may be some connection. How deep? I don't know, but I want to find out. Perhaps it's more serious. Perhaps the Senator is getting kickbacks from Softek. Huge sums. Who knows?"

"Who knows?" Ward shook her head in full agreement while chewing.

"Look at your own case. You were determined to learn the connection between oil companies and lawmakers when it came to passing or not passing a bill on climate change. It won you a Pulitzer prize."

"It sure did." Ward cracked a smile of satisfaction.

Shallen was fishing for an emotional connection. "I'm looking for the same break."

Ward's eyes sparkled. "For months I interviewed and researched with no substantial results. In addition to suffering from frustrations, I was also the target of ridicule and threats." She paused to pass a dangerously slow Oldsmobile, driven by a senior citizen. "Then one day my break came when I least expected it. A high-ranking Senator gave me the nugget of information that I was searching for."

Shallen pressed her lower lip. She felt a slight pain in her stomach, more from stress than from a lack of breakfast. "For me, I'm looking for something more."

"What do you mean?"

She hesitated as thoughts swirled in her head. Guilt wrapped around her. "I have to face my conscience."

"It's the injustice of society, abuse of power that drives us to put ourselves in risky situations. As a result some reporters have lost their jobs, get killed, go to jail."

"Mine is more personal," Shallen said.

"I'm listening."

"One day, early evening, Brian called me. He warned me that something was going to happen if things didn't turn around." She cleared her throat.

"Who is Brian?" Ward's eyes widened.

"He's the one who lost it and went on a killing rampage at Softek."

"When did he call?" Ward said.

"In November."

"In November. You were busy then with that sniper trial. I remember," Ward said.

"I figured that it was just an employee venting steam." After a moment's pause to regain her strength, she cleared her throat again. She looked at Ward for some sign of sympathy. In a lower voice she continued. "He called the night before the verdict of the sniper trial was to be announced. That trial took the Washington by storm. Everyone was busy. I meant to follow up on the lead." She waved her hand. "I didn't forget about it. But deadline after deadline kept piling on until I heard about the shooting at Softek and Brian's death." She blinked to avoid her eyes filling with tears.

Ward turned to Shallen for a long moment and returned her eyes to the road ahead, but in that moment Shallen could see she had connected with this hard-edged woman.

"We are reporters not lawmakers, not law enforcement officers, not social workers."

Shallen bit her lower lip while looking at the road that kept running past her on the side of the car. "I don't know if I could have done anything to prevent it. I've kept it to myself until now."

"It's hard on you I can tell. As I recall, you did go there right after you heard about it." Ward's face muscles tightened. Her hand hovered over her well-coiffed hair then returned to the steering wheel.

Slowly Shallen said, "Yes, I did."

"How was it?" Ward lowered the radio volume.

"I was there only one day after the incident happened. As I expected, the wounds on both sides – Brian's and the victims – were still raw and emotions ran deep."

"Did you find anything?"

"On that trip I talked to Jason, Brian's friend. At first he was reluctant to talk me. When he did talk to me, he was angry about outsourcing and losing his friend. We've been in touch since then."

"That's good. Maybe he has something that could nail the Senator if he is guilty of anything."

"He got the job with a Pentagon contractor through the Senator. And now he is under surveillance, which makes me extremely suspicious."

"Under surveillance. That sounds serious."

"It stinks. That's my reason for getting back on the case. I don't want the trail to go cold," Shallen said.

"Before going back, there are a few options to consider. Did you do your research here in Washington?" Ward paused as traffic was emptying in many directions when Pennsylvania Ave. ended. The Prius picked up speed on Constitution Ave NE. Ward continued, "Did you talk to Joe?"

"Joe Snyder, our Capitol Hill senior correspondent?" Shallen clarified.

"Yes," Ward said.

"I had a long discussion with Joe--"

"As always, he is an excellent source of information. How about our political analysts? Our informants?"

"Yes, I talked to all of them. And, accidentally I found out that non-US citizens were making contributions to Senator Quest's campaign fund. I ran an article on it. I had to make some contribution to the *Post's* revenue." She laughed loud.

"That was a good one. It was picked up by other media, including CNN's Marcia Degiromo. Anything else you discovered?"

Shallen turned on the heater. "Softek is getting DoD contracts and Senator Quest is the Chairman of the powerful Armed Services Committee."

"That shouldn't raise anyone's suspicious. It happens all the time. They will scratch each others back as long as it's not illegal."

"Did you find any kickback?" Ward was apparently trying to cover all angles.

"No. I checked the Senator's website for campaign finance records, which was updated regularly."

"The FEC?"

"Federal Election Commission. Yes. And I verified the numbers with what was posted at the Senator's website. Nothing unusual." She blew air towards the windshield.

Ward was processing every piece of information. "Nothing."

"I have some suspicions. Why does no one want to talk about this relationship between Softek and the Senator? And Jason is under surveillance. Why? By whom?" She chopped the air with her hand.

"Have you talked to Jason?"

"Yes. He thinks that his class-action suit has raised someone's concern. Someone who has a lot to lose." She took a deep breath.

"Have you raised the question with our top informant, Trench Coat?"

"He gave me a nod. That's all. Then he said to be careful."

"Something smells rotten. There's a dead body somewhere." Ward's face muscles tightened, pushing her eyebrows up.

"I want to pursue it…this time for Jason. He's in danger."

"If you want to get serious you have to travel to Corvallis and interview a lot of people including the Softek management, Softek ex-employees, Softek employees, and politicians in Corvallis and Salem."

The mission was clear. "That's what I have to do. But do you think anyone will talk?" asked Shallen.

With an assured voice Ward said, "There's always someone with an axe to grind. You have to keep looking until you find that person. It won't be easy. The key is finding the right person."

Shallen understood the challenges facing her. "Corvallis is a small place, with a tight-knit community. Will anyone talk to a stranger?"

For several blocks silence prevailed. Suddenly Ward came out of deep thought and said, "Did you say Jason is starting a class-action suit?"

"Yes," Shallen said.

She paused. "Ask, Jason to delay the class-action suit."

"I don't know if it's possible. Why?" She shook her head wondering what it had to do with her own investigation.

"With the launch of a class-action suit, it will attract a lot of media attention. Like a flock of wild dogs, everyone, small town or national, will be looking for a piece of meat. From management, politicians, employees and ex-employees. You want to be there and talk to these people first before the media circus starts."

"I see--"

"It means Jason can launch it after you get your prime cut." Ward gave Shallen a wise look.

"I'll try. It would be difficult, if not impossible to get in touch with him."

"Shallen, before you embark on this, there are a few things to consider."

"Yeah, like what?"

"It will take stamina. It's a stressful job and you have to be more than one hundred percent sure you want to go through with this, before you blow the whistle."

"That's what they taught me in my journalism courses."

"And, there are consequences."

"Consequences." Shallen gave a dry laugh. "I expect there will be. I'll be dealing with a very powerful politician."

***

Jason McDeere stroked the Rolex which read 1:25 AM, slapped closed his laptop on his desk, then motioned towards the elevator that would take him to a place sarcastically known as the dungeon situated three floors below ground. After fingering the button of the elevator panel, he waved a hand close to a black security box, triggering a green LED light, then the descent. Exiting into a hallway, Emmanuel, the security guard, awakened by closing elevator doors, greeted him. "Jason, good morning, I have a joke for you."

Jason didn't have a minute to spare. "Can't. In a hurry. Go back to sleep."

Jason could have used a joke to ease the tension he felt. To supplement his income, Emmanuel had taken a second job as a part-time caregiver at a senior's nursing home. To entertain the often bored or ailing occupants, he told them senior's jokes, which they always looked forward to, and laughed loud even though some of the jokes lacked humor. The roar of laughter kept coming, though the broken English sometimes messed up the timing of the stories. Emmanuel shared his life with Jason because he was a good listener, or at least that's what he told Jason. The real reason was to improve his English.

After navigating the hallway with a few turns, Jason faced a metal door with a knob and buttons, to which he punched a code causing a soft click, clearing the passage. This time it was Hank, another security guard with a neck as strong as a utility pole, beefy arm muscles and eyes keen enough to trace any movement around him, who was sitting in front of a video monitor and a computer screen on a small desk. He was fully awake at this awful hour. Hank checked the list hanging on the computer screen and, with a look of approval, said, "One thirty." He never smiled or talked excessively.

Jason moved past Hank to a door with a sign that read "Tomahawk Missile Simulation. Only Authorized Personnel Permitted," which he entered. The room was kept cooler than outside to absorb the heat generated by various equipment. The place was secured with one-yard thick concrete cement walls and a ceiling that was of the same strength. It would take a major bomb blast to suffer any serious damage. The room was empty except for a desk with three chairs, three computer screens, a large 50-inch flat screen monitor hanging on one wall and cruise missile pictures on other walls.

Jason had been planning and waiting for this moment for days. Earlier, around 8:00 PM, while eating pizza, he fell asleep from exhaustion. Although he had full energy it was nervous energy. He clamped his forehead to squeeze out the tension in his head. With an analytical mind, he calculated the risk and reward of this personal mission. After weighing both sides he decided it was worth going ahead. Had he covered every aspect of the plan? He hoped.

 With a toss he dropped the notebook and pen on the desk next to the keyboard. As he sank into a chair, his vision moved towards the surveillance cameras, which were continuously sweeping the room, suspended from the ceiling above and beyond the large flat-screen monitor. Who was watching him? Who knew?

He typed his username and password to start the scheduled task, which was to load the terrain data into the simulator and test the proper execution of the missile flight at 1:30 AM. The place would have been perfectly quiet except for a slight hissing sound seeping from the air vents. After twenty minutes of data loading, a message flashed on the screen to indicate the job was completed. He then typed a few commands on the keyboard to launch a fiery missile from a mobile launcher placed outside Las Vegas city limits. The visual images generated by the computer were amazingly realistic, precisely showing the irregularity of the terrain over which this missile traveled. Mountains, trees, valleys, hills, rivers, deserts. It reminded him of the times he went to the arcade to play video games with Keenan. It had been almost two weeks since he'd last seen his children. He missed them. His heart ached to see them. He thought about the divorce papers he was supposed to receive but they hadn't arrived yet. The family breakup. Slowly he was coming to realize that his kids would be better off with their mother rather than him. Since he'd last heard from Kara about the divorce procedures the anger had subsided but the sadness remained.

He turned his attention back to the simulation. The missile would normally fly over Los Angeles and beyond into the ocean. Instead, this time it deviated from the calculated path and flew over San Francisco and crashed into the ocean. It was planned that way. Just a simulation. He checked his watch. In a few minutes it would soon be 2:00 AM. Jason plugged a flash memory into the computer and brought up the program to search for "Quest" on Layton Industries' accounting database. He reviewed it carefully again. He reminded himself that he had only fifteen minutes to perform this task. He was hoping it would take a lot less time, counting on the power of the super fast computers.

At 1:55 AM, he got a last warning on the screen that the computer network was going down for backup and all users were to logout immediately, which he did. Within seconds he was able to connect to the database, bypassing the network, as instructed by Terrance. He was in. He ran the program to search the database for the word QUEST. It was going. He could tell the heavy CPU usage that was taking place. He had only ten minutes. Slowly he assembled his notebook, scribbled some words, and kept busy for the camera's sake.

After seven minutes when the search for Quest in the database was over, the file where the result was supposed to go read zero kilobytes. What happened? Did he make a mistake in the way he conducted the search? Or was there no trace of Senator Quest in the database? Quickly, he changed the program to search all payables over $1000.00 for the last ten years. He had only three minutes before the database went down. The search was going; he could tell. After two minutes it aborted. A warning flashed on the screen that said "Out of Storage Space." The program generated a file this time, but Jason didn't know what was inside. Quickly he loaded the file into his external disk so he could take it with him. He must know what happened. He was frantic. Quickly he tapped the keys with his fingers, his eyes constantly searching for clues. Before the database went down, he had to know if Senator Quest had been transferring funds. It seemed like there were millions of payables for the last ten years and it had blown the storage capacity.

The phone rang. He jumped. At the second ring, he froze. He stood still, unable to move a muscle. Never in his life, had he experienced anything so frightening. On the third ring, the paralysis lifted. Should he answer? It rang again. *I better take it.* It was Indira at the other end. *Oh, no!* Why was she calling at this time? What did she know?

In a coarse voice she said, "Is this Jason?"

He took a deep breath and tried to sound as composed as possible. The energy drained out his toes. "Yes. Why are you calling so early?"

"My phone woke me up. The text message said that one of the computers was running out of disk space. It alerted me of an impending crash."

In a slow and calm voice he said, "The terrain data that I was loading was larger than I expected. It blew the storage capacity. Nothing to worry about. It's taken care of." He was lying. Telling the truth would have been like jumping from the highest point of the Grand Canyon without the safety of a parachute.

"Did it cause any damage?" she asked with concern.

"No, no. No need to worry. Everything is fine. You should go back to sleep. I'm so sorry it caused a break in your sleep."

After he hung up, Jason returned to the screen. The database had already gone down. There was nothing he could do to evaluate any damage and fix it.

***

Indira Gupta entered the office cubicle at 7:30 AM. She dropped her rather heavy bag onto the floor next to the chair on rollers, where she seated herself after placing the coffee and muffin next to the keyboard. The database incident that had rudely awakened her at an unforgivable hour had been churning in her mind since she hung up the phone after talking to Jason.

Soon after logging in, she poked around in the computer, checking databases, logs, messages, files and networks hoping to get a better understanding of what exactly happened. It wasn't totally unexpected. Weird things did happen at weird hours. Computer failure didn't care whose sleep might be disturbed.

That morning, as some employees filed into their offices, they would be greeted with red color email in their mailboxes regarding the alert. Red indicated high priority that needed immediate attention. She knew all hell was about to break loose. When things were running smoothly, no one paid attention. When something went wrong, everyone knew and suddenly she became the wise one to offer advice or point fingers. Office politics.

As her scrutiny progressed, the phone rang with the display showing David Cohen's incoming call, which didn't surprise her. The call arrived just a few minutes after eight as indicated at the bottom right-hand corner of the screen. She had to answer it.

"Meet me at my office," he said, then hung up. His tone sounded more like an order than a request.

She jumped to her feet, glanced around the desk deciding what to take with her. The coffee and muffin hadn't been touched since they were placed on the desk. She left her cubicle, hurrying towards David's office holding a notebook and pen.

When she passed through the door, he motioned his hand. "Have a seat." His tone was laced with anger and his eyes were filled with intensity, both of which she had never seen before. Was it about the early morning storage incident or could it be something else? *I'll find out soon.*

Seated, she politely waited while David read something on the screen. "What the hell happened this morning?" David banged his fist on the desk.

She jolted. Her head turned to confirm the door was closed, thus preventing anyone from listening to this tense conversation. How embarrassing to be scolded by a boss. After a short reflection on the proper response, trying to maintain her professional composure, Indira said, "Around two in the morning, I got a cell alert message. It showed storage level had reached a critical point of eighty percent. It showed that someone in the simulation lab was connected to the system. I called and Jason answered. He told me that he was uploading data." Another short pause. She shrugged her shoulders to suggest there was no real issue. "And he ran out of space. He assured me everything was fine. Then we hung up."

David didn't seem to believe her. "Was he alone?"

Where was he going with this line of questioning? Being alone in the simulation room had never been a problem. "Yes."

"Did you check?"

"Check what?"

"Verify Jason's story. Maybe he was attempting to do something other than what he was supposed to be doing." David rolled his chair closer to the desk so that he faced her directly.

As she studied his face she felt her own face flush with heat. She was trying to hide the uneasiness that had started to build inside her. "Yes. The computers, network, messages, log files, databases--"

"Uploading data. Was Jason doing something else, eh? Something he wasn't supposed to be doing?" said David.

"What do you mean? He was given the task to load data and the log shows that." Indira bit her lower lip.

"Because he is new here, it's not a good idea for Jason to be working by himself and at that hour." David shook his head with disappointment.

"The work needed to be done before this morning. He also wanted to put extra hours in to top his sixty-hour limit. I accepted his offer."

"He's new. It wasn't a good decision."

He was pushing the wrong emotional buttons. She was totally puzzled by his reaction and accusation. "David, all of us are alone at odd hours. I didn't think it was an unusual request and he didn't breach any security policy."

"It's a security issue. It is very serious. I want to know if he was in any other database where he wasn't supposed to be."

She thought he was being unreasonable. Perhaps he was scared of something. "I checked the logs and I didn't find any trace of that."

He got up, walked to the corner of the room and turned around. "Did it show that the loading of terrain caused the failure?"

"No."

He ran his fingers over the top of his balding head. He breathed harder with frustration. "Why not? We track everything. Every move, especially in sim labs." His voice was loud enough to make his neck veins stand out.

She crossed her legs then glanced at her notebook to check something she had scribbled there. Sometimes it was hard to read her own handwriting. "Yes, we do. But the storage issue happened just before the databases were to shut down for backup. After the backup, when the databases came back up, it did some cleanup and we fixed the storage issue. I checked and didn't see anything unusual."

For a moment he seemed absorbed, his head raised toward the ceiling and his fingers pressing his forehead. "I think he was up to something."

Indira shook her head, trying to understand his suspicion. "From all the logs I read this morning he didn't do anything wrong or breach security."

"How sure are you that he wasn't in any restricted area?"

"David, from what I can see, he was not."

"Get Bill Simms to look at it. With his brilliant mind and extensive experience in network and database security, he will find something, if Jason has done anything wrong. Bill will find it. I'm sure of that."

She scribbled on the notepad. "Okay."

"Would you say that we have a security hole?"

"What do you mean?"

"When the network and databases came alive, there shouldn't have been any cleanup and fixes happening automatically. Someone should examine the problem and take action as needed. The fact that it was done automatically means there's a hole that needs to be plugged. I thought you had taken care of that."

"I have to investigate that further," she admitted. "So far, nothing suggests that there is a loophole."

"We'll leave it at that. I have two other things. Suspend Jason from the project for a while." David returned to the chair. Determination was written all over his face.

"No," Indira objected. "We really need him to finish and deliver the Tomahawk upgrade project on time. Without him we'll miss the deadline and possibly lose future Pentagon contracts."

"I can't take any risk with Jason. I want him in the penalty box. I need to find out what he is up to."

Why punish someone for the sake of punishing, she wondered? "If anything. So far his hands are not stained. Before accusing him of misconduct, we have to see if Jason has done anything wrong."

"Okay. I admit we need more investigative work done. This is what the security department would want. Certainly that's what Jeff Dowell would want done too. Once security and the Pentagon read this incident report, they will call Jeff. They will go straight to the top, the CEO," said David.

"When are you meeting Jeff Dowell?"

"The time isn't confirmed. Very likely it will be a luncheon meeting. Today."

"At the executive suite."

David's attention was distracted by something on the screen. He moved the mouse and poked the keyboard. Then he returned to Indira. "Yes, on the executive floor. Not looking forward to it. It will be torture more than a luncheon."

It would be another tense morning. "I'll get a report ready for the lunch meeting."

Indira walked out of David's office perplexed. Why was he so suspicious of Jason? And why was Jason hired with only one interview? The few weeks he had been with Layton Industries he had been juggling many things – his divorce, being away from his family, pressure of putting in long hours and coping with the stress of a new job. Jason needed more sympathy and less threats from management.

***

It was shortly after 6:00 pm when Jason McDeere entered the hotel room. It was an unusual day as he finished his shift at 3 am and, after some rest on the couch in the staff lounge, he was back at his desk by 9:00 am. His entire body was aching of tired muscles. The headache was not diminishing at all. But he wasn't paying as much attention to his fatigue as he was eager to browse the file containing Layton Industry's accounts payable, hoping to find any unusual transactions.

After placing the box of sushi dinner on the desk, he unloaded the leather bag off his shoulder and set it next to the laptop. Seated on the edge of the bed, he removed his shoes and threw them closer to the door as he couldn't muster enough muscle power to place them neatly by the door like he usually did. The floor was covered with printouts, laundry, wires, suitcase, and books, which he admitted to having been neglectful of late.

He sank into the seat and fired up his laptop, which started with flashing lights and spinning disk. As the computer came alive, he leaned forward, more to his right, to open the plastic container loaded with California rolls, sashimi, dragon rolls and Miso soup. His eyes caught something out of place. A newspaper clipping was tucked under a lamp base. His eyes immediately recognized it to be a foreign object--something he couldn't recall placing there. Why would he? He hadn't bought or read a newspaper in months. As he leaned closer to the desk top, he recognized a face on the paper. It looked familiar. It was a thumbnail picture of a younger lawyer who he had met just ten days ago. He moved the dinner aside, held the article with both hands only inches from his nose, and studied every word. He rose to his feet like a loaded spring. The headline read "Lawyer Killed in his Office." According to the report it was Paul C. Schubert, a partner of the law firm Schubert & Tottan who was killed during an apparent robbery gone bad. The office was ransacked. The killer was at large and the police had no clue who did it or why. Not a single trace of fingerprints was left behind. The lawyer's wrist and jugular veins had bled until he died.

Jason read it three times. With each pass the tremor in his hand became more pronounced. He crumpled the clipping, and throwing it to a far wall, he murmured, "How did this happen? Why me?"

He turned to the door and wondered who could have left this article in his room. He knew they weren't robbers. He walked over to the window, parted the curtains with his finger to take a peek outside. Volpa's goons were not in sight.

Frightened, he walked over and plopped down on the bed. With his back flat on the bed, hands spread out, eyes shut, and heart consumed with an inner cry for help, he cascaded into a fitful sleep.

-13-

David Cohen stepped out of the elevator onto a marble floor leading to the executive suite at the top level of the twelve-story building. Only the privileged of Layton ever benefited from this luxury of which some of the perks included fine dining, banquet, spa, TV room, and theater. This floor exuded the glamour of a five star hotel, used for meetings, celebration or just relaxation.

Cohen sank into a leather sofa, which was part of a cluster composed of lamps, tables, wing chairs, sofas, and a real Persian carpet, forming an elegant ensemble. With a sideway twist of his neck, Cohen released the nervous tension that had been building over the past few days. A quick glance at the tweed jacket he was wearing over a blue shirt, freshly ironed black dress pants, and well-polished shoes ensured him his attire matched the occasion. A Gravol pill he'd swallowed only ten minutes ago finally kicked in and he felt a sweeping relaxation of the muscles throughout his body. A few shots of whiskey would have been preferable, but alcohol was forbidden at Layton. He nodded and waved to top management arriving in groups of two, three and occasionally four as they passed by.

At exactly 12:15 David jumped to his feet when Jeff Dowell, CEO of Layton Industries, suddenly towered next to him. David came a few inches short of the chief's thin six-foot frame. As they carried on a trivial conversation, they eased into the Ronald Reagan Room, and were promptly welcomed by Roosevelt, their waiter. They sat in leather chairs facing each other, while Roosevelt took their cocktail orders. The Reagan Room could easily accommodate ten guests, and was the CEO's private dining place. On that day it was just the two of them.

A few minutes later, Roosevelt hovered over them with a tray, placing a tropical punch on the coaster in front of Dowell and a Perrier for David. David's stomach was feeling vulnerable. Mineral water seemed safe. Any specialty drink could mess up his stomach, making him nauseous, which had started after meeting with Indira earlier. Roosevelt obediently disappeared and the talk moved from trivialities, to a more serious nature.

"Two incident reports in two months. Hell. What is going on, David?" Dowell said. The admiral in him, from his years of naval service, clearly came across as though he were running a fleet rather than a company.

David understood the ramifications of what the CEO was saying and apologized profusely. Then he attacked his drink. Anything to carve out a moment of peace. Taking a washroom break was not an option at this meeting with the CEO. "This one came out of nowhere." After another swallow, he held the crystal glass. Then he eyed the crab mushroom hor d'oeuvres lying in front of him. Too risky.

Jeff held off taking a sip. "David, they are always unforeseen." He straightened his back, his silver hair combed neatly over his scalp and his face red with irritation. He said, "Problems appear from nowhere, it seems. But you have to be vigilant. Your department has to be on the ball all the time. That's what the navy teaches us: you can't let your guard down. One mistake –" he snapped his fingers – "and poof, gone." With a self-satisfied smile he sipped his tropical punch.

"I hear you." David cupped the glass as the tiny bubbles floated up towards the rim of his Perrier, which held a slice of lime. Jeff's past navy experience stayed with him even though he had retired ten years ago and founded Layton Industries. Contracting for the Pentagon had been a lucrative business, only possible with the help of friends in Washington.

"What went wrong this time?"

"What went wrong?" The brief pause gave him time to configure his response. He should say what was needed and no more. "While uploading terrain data into the Tomahawk simulator, Jason McDeere tripped a security alarm."

Jeff looked around the room clearly in deep thought. David followed his eyes. The room was decorated with expensive paintings, favorite pictures of US presidents and brass wall lamps. A chandelier hung just above them. "Jason McDeere," the CEO said with another snap of his fingers. "That name spells trouble, David."

"I should have never hired him."

The CEO caressed his wristwatch with a finger. "Why don't we get a table and order lunch," he said. Then he stood, and David quickly followed. They headed to a table, close to the windows, set with silver cutlery, cloth napkins, and crystal glasses, all surrounding a flower bouquet in the middle. "This is a double whammy. That McDeere is more trouble than he's worth."

David absorbed the view in front of him, at the Shoreline Amphitheatre and a clear expanse of green beyond that, leading to the golf course and lake waterfront.

As they found a seat, Roosevelt appeared asking if they needed any more drinks. "No. We're ready for the next course," Jeff said, winking at the waiter.

Once they placed their orders, David watched the waiter's disappearing back then said, "Our security department is going bananas. They are concerned about what else was going on when the alert happened. They have asked me and others in the department to launch a formal investigation."

"They're monkeys alright. It's their job to raise hell." Dowell cracked a smile and shook his head. "They should be asking questions and get to the bottom of the issue. Maybe they'll find something, maybe not."

David grimaced his displeasure. "I don't like the threats they're making."

They talked for another fifteen minutes when Roosevelt appeared with a tray loaded with steaming food. The New York Sirloin peppered steak with Cajun sauce and buttered glazed fresh vegetables went to the chief, along with a scoop of garlic mashed potatoes and sautéed onions. David had grilled Pacific salmon with rice and vegetables. The smell of grilled food and herbs made his mouth water despite his tender stomach. Roosevelt was the best. He was from New Orleans, where Dowell was born and raised. David had learned through the grapevine that Jeff had brought a chef from home because he didn't want to miss "mama's" cooking. No one could cook like his mother, but Roosevelt was close enough for his satisfaction, according to those in the know. The chef with gray hair and honey-colored skin disappeared again.

With the fork and knife in his hand, Dowell appeared ready to attack the food. At the last minute he turned to David instead. "I'm more concerned about Washington than our security department. Do our contacts at Pentagon know about the breach in security?"

"Yes. They get notices the same way and the same time as we get them." Just the thought gave him an uneasy feeling in his spine. The Pentagon was the devil he had to live with, but it made him none too happy.

"We can't ignore them. They're our clients." Dowell forked a piece of rare meat and swung it into his mouth. The deep breath he took and his slow jaw movements indicated he was savoring every hit to his taste buds. "Have they contacted you yet?"

"Not yet. They don't rush into anything. They will be in touch with us by the end of the day. I'm sure of it. They always are."

"This Jason – he worries me. How the hell did he get into my company?" He dropped the knife and fork on the plate and reached for the napkin on his lap.

"Through Senator Quest."

"Yes, I remember. Don't know what the Senator was thinking. Now we have a serious case on our hands. A hot potato."

David waited until the other man was done chewing. Then he rested both arms on his armrest, wondering what Layton had gotten themselves into. "Without mentioning the Senator, I strongly urged McDeere to give up the class-action suit and focus on his work."

"Yes, I was apprised of the suit." The metallic clatter of the cutlery seemed louder as the conversation stopped for a moment. After another sip of his cocktail, Dowell said, "Once, we were stationed in Guam for a special maneuver exercise. There was a young punk who had just joined the Navy. He thought he was a big shot. The kind with a huge ego. He came from California. I never liked recruits from California. Too liberal for me. Communists." The CEO rubbed his lips with a napkin, shifted his position in the chair, and adjusted his tie, suggesting to David that he was in for a long afternoon of bragging about the man's Navy days. Clearing his throat, Dowell said, "This smart ass was causing a lot of trouble. He was influencing others with his piss-poor ways. Mind you he knew the rules very well. Always pushing the regulations to the limit. Always border-line insubordination. We couldn't get rid of him. I told the captain to throw him off the deck into shark-infested waters. I was just joking. The captain wasn't. Looked as if it was an accident. He was in the water fighting for his life until the water around him turned red. The crew threw a rope ladder down and pulled him up onto the deck. After that he was straight as an arrow. Obeyed every order."

David was fixated on the story. "We don't need to throw him to the sharks, yet. I'm working on something."

"But this security incident is a cause for great concern. If we don't--"

"I agree"

"In Washington, we have a lame-duck president. The Democrats are holding the reins in Congress. The halls of Capitol Hill are full of hyenas hungry for dead meat."

"I understand someone is waiting to snatch Pentagon contracts away from us. While talking to Roger Hunt the other day, he emphasized his concerns."

"What concerns?"

David looked down at the plate with its big chunk of salmon. His appetite had long disappeared. "About protecting our interests."

"The only one who can protect us is Senator Quest. He has the power to fend off any attackers. I know there are many who would love to have our Pentagon contracts."

It was a good opportunity to remind the boss of the contributions he had made. "We did over two hundred million dollars of government business last year."

Dowell shook his head in agreement. "I know, but talking to Quest is a problem. Every time I call him, the Senator wants money, big money."

"Last month we gave him a million," said David.

"He wants a million and a half more."

David was always on top of the revenue side of the company. "I checked with accounting. It looks like after the delivery of the Tomahawk upgrade projects we should get a fat check. We have money in our bank account, which is enough for payroll and other payables for a few months."

"But payment from Tomahawk is weeks away. If I call him today, he'll want money today. Are we on schedule for delivery?"

"The last time I checked, we were. Nothing is for sure. Something can go wrong just days before delivery." This was an opportunity for redemption. "I needed Jason's help to avoid slippage in the schedule."

Dowell tapped a finger on his glass. "Ok. I'll take care of the Senator. He can't push me too hard. After all, it's illegal pay. And you have to handle Jason with extreme care. Any more messy situations would be unacceptable."

"I'll try."

"Try hard. The Senator is becoming a risk for us."

"Do we have all our eggs in one basket?"

"Yes, and it's not a good strategy. If he doesn't get elected, it will be a disaster for us. Washington is a jungle of lobbyists and interest groups, each fighting for something. Launching grenades at each other. They are worse than the hyenas, lions, baboons and other strange creatures from Africa. If he isn't re-elected, we may even have to suck up to a Democratic Senator. I don't like that thought. But give me a war, I'll fight it."

After lunch was over, David Cohen went to his office, shut the door and sank into his chair. He made notes of all the points made by the CEO. But one thing made him extremely uneasy. The story of the marine attacked by a shark. Was it real? Did he make up the story? He was known for spiking a story.

***

The waiter at Salbasgeon Suites restaurant suspended a half-full coffee in front of Shallen Xu to which she gave a nod. This was her second cup of the morning, a sure sign that the tension of this assignment was eating her up inside. When tense, her body craved a caffeine jolt. And always the first one gave way to the next. When relaxed she drank green tea, preferred by her grandmother who also drilled the idea into family members as a way of keeping with the Chinese tradition in a foreign land.

When the waiter moved to the next customer, with head lowered, she continued to scribble on a notepad. She fingered the cell phone to check if it was switched on, a nervous habit. Upon arriving in Corvallis the day before, she immediately rang, and left messages with, people of interest from a list compiled with Jason's help.

After pushing the half full breakfast plate away, she drained the cup for more caffeine energy, shoved the notepad, pen, credit card slips and cell phone in the rather large handbag and headed towards the parking lot in search of her rental car. She set her bag on the hood of the rental car, and began her hunt for the keys, moving from one compartment to the next. After almost a minute of having gone through all the pockets, a SUV pulled into the next lot. As she continued digging, she wondered if she really needed such a huge bag for all her things—brushes, makeup, wallet, credit card slips, notepads, pens, cell phone—enough paraphernalia to survive for days. Fortunately the SUV passengers, who were dressed in business attire, didn't gawk at her and left for their conference without noticing her, or at least it seemed that way.

After climbing into the car, she used the key to start the engine. Then she lifted her head for a final check of her makeup, hair, lipstick and blush in the rear view mirror. Now she was ready to roll. Still on NW 9th Street, the female, robotic voice of the GPS lady warned of the approach of NE Circle Blvd where she was supposed to take a right turn. She liked all these gadgets despite the fact that they cost the *Post* a pretty penny. She hoped such expenses would go unnoticed.

Moving along Circle Blvd, the Softek International building caught her attention. She made another right into the parking lot and drove around until she spotted a strategic place to park. It gave her a clear view of the entrance, yet it wasn't far from the reserved parking area, most of which was taken up with executives' cars. She pulled a folder from her bag and placed it on the passenger seat. She sifted through pictures and notes. The list was made up of the CEO, every one killed on that tragic day and names of a few other people that Jason had sent to Shallen in a hurry. On top of the picture of Muhtar Gamble, founder and CEO of Softek International, she put the list of names. Shallen was hoping that he would just appear at the front door, so she could jump out of her car and talk to him about the killing. She had left a message with his assistant the day before. No call back yet. Her eyes fixed on the front of the building, where a few latecomers filed in for work. She sat there for about five minutes, when a door swung open and a man wearing a dark suit and carrying a briefcase appeared. Like a big cat ready to pounce, she made a thorough examination of his face but the distance prevented her from detecting any distinguishable features. With her left hand she reached for the handbag ready to unlock and push the door open at the same time. When the man moved about five steps towards her, she relaxed. It wasn't Muhtar Gamble or anyone else on the list.

Shallen punched Gamble's number on the cell phone. After a couple of rings, a cheerful female voice answered.

"Good morning. I'm Shallen Xu from the *Post*. I left a message for Mr. Gamble. I haven't heard from him. Did he get my message?" Shallen said.

"Ms. Xu, Mr. Gamble received your message."

Shallen listened carefully. "Any idea when I can expect to hear from him?"

"No. He is a very busy man."

Shallen realized the woman's short answers were suddenly turning unfriendly. "Is he in today?"

"Yes, but he's very busy."

She didn't seem to be in a mood to help. "Just let him know I called again."

They hung up. She punched in Faye Whitney's number, the wife of Clint that Brian gunned down at Softek. She had answered Shallen's call yesterday, but she couldn't talk and she promised to call her back. Traveling on west Circle Blvd the radio gave the 12 o'clock headline news. No major catastrophe that she was aware of. The news reporter announced US anger at Iran over the country's pursuit of nuclear technology, followed by more deaths in Iraq, an earthquake in China and northeastern states blanketed by freezing rain. Shallen turned right onto Highland Drive, following GPS instructions. The traffic was light in this town of Corvallis which lauded some fifty thousand inhabitants, much better than Washington streets any time of the day.

The cell phone came alive with a tune. Who could that be? Faye Whitney, Gamble, or Rocky. Talking to any one of the people on her list would make this trip worthwhile. So far the trip had not been fruitful. She looked in the rear view mirror to ensure no one was kissing her rental car's bumper. With her handset pressed to her right ear, she slowed the car to a stop on the side of the road. She wanted to give this call her full attention. It was Barbara, John Mead's assistant secretary at the other end. Barbara. The one who loved fried chicken. *Why is she calling now?* Bad omen. She was like a back pain that never went away. Guilt came over her for entertaining such negative thoughts. After a quick memory search she recalled a few of Barbara's positive qualities that made Shallen feel slightly better.

"John was wondering when you would be back from the 'bridge to nowhere'."

Calm, calm, calm was her mantra. "Bridge to nowhere. What do you mean by that?"

"Many of us in the office are wondering what you're doing there." Barbara always delivered her words as they popped into her mind, without any filter.

Shallen's patience was running thin. "Just you. Not many."

"Let me put it another way. This is just a wild goose chase." The words were laced with sarcasm.

A blast of wind caused by a passing transport truck shook the car. The truck had come dangerously close. She eased her foot off the brake pedal, moving the car slowly to the right half a foot away from the moving traffic. She needed to make this call short. "Let's cut to the chase. Why did you call?"

"John wants your butt over here. When are you planning to return?"

The way the investigation was going, she needed lots of wiggle room. No commitment. "I don't know. When the job is done."

"Make it quick."

Barbara's words irritated her. It was like rubbing sandpaper on her soft skin. "What's the hurry?"

"Some important news is about to break."

Shallen looked into her side mirror, feeling safe from traffic behind her but not from Barbara. "What is it? Don't tell me it's another bank robbery or sniper."

"Bigger. A senator is being investigated for . . . let's say an interesting behavior in an airport washroom."

Shallen hung up after giving a vague answer. She really didn't need this call right now. Again she checked her makeup, lipstick, cheek color, and hair, an impulse she had whenever she was nervous and tense, as she was after terminating the conversation with Barbara. All was in place. Then she put the rental car in gear.

After being on the road for a half a mile she turned right onto Anjni Circle, a middle-class neighborhood that had one or two cars in each of the driveways with the occasional bike and tricycle. She spotted the house with white brick, in front of which were a Buick and a Ford pickup truck. Shallen rang the doorbell and watched the street. It was a quiet neighborhood. A car slowly passed by.

An older woman opened the door. "Can I help you?" she said, her voice loaded with suspicion.

"Mrs. Whitney?" After a nod from her, Shallen said, "My name is Shallen. I'm with the *Washington Post*. May I speak with you?"

"*Washington Post*, you said?"

"Yes, I won't take too much of your time." Shallen cracked a faint smile.

"Is this regarding my husband's death?" Her suspicion continued.

"Yes."

Her face turned almost lifeless. A deep sadness was clearly visible. "I don't think so."

"I promise I won't take too long."

"You people from the newspaper and the TV have been harassing me since the shooting."

Shallen nodded to suggest the woman's anger was understandable. "I have reason to believe your husband's death could have been avoided."

"What difference does it make now? He's gone. I'm left alone without him. I miss him so much. It has caused so much suffering. It's hard to explain. All I do day in and day out is cry." Her eyes were swelling with tears and her voice turned baby-soft.

"It's important I talk to you." Shallen was pleading.

"No. You people have been rude. You have no idea what I've been going through. Besides, nothing can bring my Clint back."

Shallen stepped forward on the front porch. "Did he say anything to you?"

"Please go. Leave now. People are watching. I can't talk to you any longer."

"I'm staying at the Salbasgeon Suites. Here is my card. You can call the number on the back."

She hesitated but took it. "Don't count on it."

Once back in her car Shallen made notes. So far the day hadn't gone well. First, the uncooperative executive secretary, followed by Barbara's sarcasm and now a fearful widow thought people were watching her.

After ten minutes of driving, Shallen parked in the library parking lot. Entering the front door, and then standing at the desk she said, "I would like to talk to Linda Sims." The librarian went to the back office while Shallen looked around. In one section a few seniors were pouring over newspapers. In another area a couple of mothers were having a heart-to-heart conversation while the children were reading books.

A woman in her mid forties appeared. "How can I help you?"

"I'm Shallen from the *Washington Post*. Can I ask you a few questions?"

"Sure, follow me."

They walked to a round table in a secluded area. Once they were both seated, Shallen dug out a notepad and pen from her large handbag.

"My name is Linda Sims. I've given interviews with newspapers many times. Once, a reporter from the *New York Times* was here during our da Vinci Days. She printed a nice article. She mentioned my name in the article, which was flattering. Are you here for our famous Winter Carnival?"

"No. I want to talk about the Softek incident back in December."

Her face lit up as though suggesting she would be open to an interview. "Ah, the mass murder. It was very sad. Things like that don't happen in Corvallis. Five in one day. It was too much to bear."

Shallen had read many articles but it wasn't clear what exactly happened. "Five people were killed. Do we know who killed whom?"

Linda placed her hands, her fingers intertwined, onto the shiny table. "It's controversial. Some people say Brian killed all five. Others say he shot three. The police killed Brian. A woman employee died. Some think she suffered a fatal wound to her head caused by police bullets in the crossfire. There's an ongoing investigation. So far it's not clear."

"What do you think of outsourcing?"

"Oh, you have a good American accent. Were you born here? We have many Chinese students in Corvallis. I see them all the time at the library. I get along with them."

"Outsourcing?"

"In Corvallis no one likes it. The university and Softek are our two biggest employers. When Softek started layoffs back in October many were wondering what was going on. Jobs were going oversees. People were angry. But everything was hidden. No one would openly admit to what was going on."

"Do you know why?"

"People have some ideas. I must tell you that I'm on the Community Recreation Committee. To give Corvallis national exposure, it would be nice if you could to do an article on the Winter Festival. It's unique like the da Vinci Days."

Shallen groaned inwardly. It was obvious by this conversation that Linda didn't want to talk about the incident. Shallen banged her open hand on the table. "Is anyone interested in knowing what really happened? Why jobs were going overseas?"

After an awkward pause, Linda said, "I'm sure many are. But it's better not to talk about it."

"What do you mean?"

Linda peered around, then lowered her voice. "There is a power beyond any one of us."

Shallen pushed harder to get something out of her. "Off the record. Can you talk?" She put her pen down.

"People are afraid of losing their jobs. There are no new jobs around here. One wrong move could mean a loss of pay, a loss of one's house or even a loss of life."

"Can you be more specific? Who is this person in power?"

"It's better left alone. I would rather talk about the winter festival."

"Maybe some other time. I want to talk about Softek. I think Senator Quest is getting a kickback from them. The only way Softek can funnel money into his campaign is to ship jobs overseas where cost of labor is a lot cheaper. What do you think?"

Linda moved closer then looked Shallen in the eye. She looked around to make sure no one was listening to their conversation. "I don't know what goes on between the Senator and Softek behind closed doors. From what I see there is something ugly going on. You are an outsider. It's for you to find out."

"It's very hard because no one wants to talk about it. There is a dark cloud over this city. People are afraid. It reminds me of a cowboy movie where a rich farmer committed a crime. When a federal agent goes to this town to investigate, everyone shuns him. The whole place is gripped in fear. The barber, the banker, and the bartender all kept a secret fearing severe punishment would follow if they talked to the agent."

"You get the picture."

"I think you have said a lot."

After leaving the library Shallen went back to the Softek parking lot. While in the car she watched the front door and at the same time calculated how to salvage a rotten day. On the cell phone contact list she searched for James Polawski, Jason McDeere's new alias. Keeping her fingers crossed, she sent him a text message requesting information about Rocky's car.

It was four-thirty and employees started to stream out of the building. After ten minutes, she received a response. Rocky drove a red Honda Civic. She searched the parking lot. Around 5:00 pm, the crowd coming out of the front door grew thicker and it became harder to distinguish faces. Holding up a picture of Rocky, she verified every face. Finally, she spotted him as he walked directly to the red car. She started the engine and followed him.

The sunlight had almost faded and she had to rely on street lights. She shut the radio and GPS system down. She needed her full concentration. She had to maintain a visual of the car. She hugged the Honda with her rental, tracking its every move. It turned right on Highland. So far so good. Approaching a major intersection, the left signal started to flash. She was hoping not to lose him. She adjusted to the left lane and waited for a green light. She was on Walnut Blvd., another busy artery. She was still close to his bumper. What if he noticed her? He pulled into Timberhill Shopping Center, then headed directly to WinCo Foods. When both cars stopped, she turned off the engine and jumped out of the car.

"Rocky?"

He was locking the door. He stared at her and said, "Yes?"

"I'm a friend of Jason. Can I talk to you for a moment?"

"Jason. Is he ok?"

"Not really," she said. "I'm from the *Washington Post*. I am investigating the Softek shooting."

He was silent for a long while, as though thinking hard about his response. His face turned stone dry. "Sorry I can't," he said with a definite edge to his voice. He walked away.

She followed him. "It's important that I talk to you."

"Don't follow me," he yelled in anger.

"Please, Rocky."

He didn't answer and picked up the pace. Shallen stood there watching him run away. She breathed hard with disappointment, shaking her head, wondering what to do next.

-14-

It was around 6:00 pm when Jason McDeere parked the rented car in its usual spot at the hotel parking lot. When he stepped out he noticed that three goons were walking towards him. This was a different pattern. Their usual routine was to park far enough away to maintain visibility without compromising their identities, and usually there were just the two. Then they would watch Jason leave or enter the hotel.

As they approached, Jason's knees felt weak. *Run.* Where could he go? They would wrestle him down and hurt him. Maybe even kill him as they did to the lawyer. A quick stock of the parking lot, where cars, buses, and pedestrians were flowing in and out, made it clear that he could easily attract attention from onlookers if needed. They wouldn't be that stupid to attack him in full sight of everyone.

The two regulars were in their late twenties, wearing shades, T-shirts tight enough to make their chest and arm muscles appear like thick cords, and denim pants. Jason looked at the older man's blue eyes, at his hair that hung straight back and was held together in a ponytail. Jason froze, his mouth half open, his arm resting on the top of the door. Several scenarios were running through his mind. All terrifying.
The new person in the group said, "Jason McDeere." He spoke slowly with a deep, serious voice, like that of an FBI agent.

Jason's mind went blank and nothing would come out of his mouth. Nothing. Finally, he forced out the word "Yes."

"Can you come with us?" he said, the two men at his side.

"What's your name?"

"It doesn't matter," the man said.

"You know my name. I would like to know yours, so I know who I'm talking to."

"Guy," he said in an impatient tone.

Jason wished he could be in control of the situation. "Where do you want to go?"

"A place we can talk," Guy said.

Where he was standing was safer than anywhere else. They were no doubt professional killers. Hopefully, they wouldn't do anything stupid, except Guy had already made a mistake by giving his name. If that really was his name. Jason cleared his throat. "Right here is fine with me." He tried to keep cool, but his heart was beating fast. He drank in more oxygen to defuse the panic attack that seemed to be just around the corner. *Not now.*

"Jason. Can I call you Jason?" After receiving a nod of acceptance, the older gentleman said, "How about there?" He pointed to a spot near his van.

What if they bagged him while no one was around, threw him in the van and drove away? No one would know. Jason scratched his head then pointed towards the hotel. "How about the restaurant?"

Guy shook his head. "Too noisy," he said firmly.

"I'll pay." Jason cracked a nervous smile.

The younger ones stood there listening with crossed arms that revealed bulging muscles. They looked strong enough to start a fight with a bull and win. The oldest one said, "Here is fine."

"Let's hear it." Jason feigned a strength he didn't feel.

"You know my men have been following you for weeks," Guy said, his confidence obvious.

"I know. But why? What have I done to you?"

"We want to keep an eye on you."

Suddenly his body's weakness disappeared, replaced with a pent-up anger, giving Jason the raw energy he needed. "Keep an eye on me. Like hell. I'm not a criminal here. I'm an honest person making an honest living. What's the problem?"

"There is only one problem."

"Who do you work for?" Jason asked, anger making his voice grow louder.

"Right now that's unimportant."

A bus pulled out. All four pairs of eyes tracked it as it went by them. "What *is* important?"

Guy rubbed his chin. "Good question. We want you to stop the class-action suit."

"That's all? That would be too simple."

"Just behave yourself," he said as if in warning. "Earn a living. Take care of your family. Go visit your daughter and son more often. I know you haven't seen them for a few weeks. You miss them."

"You know a lot about me and my children. What don't you know about me?"

"We know enough to do our job. What do you say about the class-action suit? Jason, do we have a deal?" Guy said.

"Who are you protecting? Definitely Softek. But I think there's someone else. Someone big. Who?"

"We don't need to get into that."

"How about Senator Quest?" he said, cautiously.

The older man ignored the question. "Do we have a deal or not?"

Jason took a long moment to reply. The younger thugs walked away a few steps, giving him room to breathe. "In this deal what do I get? For one, a good night sleep, knowing that these two muscle men won't burst into my room and kill me. But what else?"

"As I said, we won't bother you. You'll get your freedom back."

How much do they know? Jason wondered how he could foil their surveillance plans. Maybe he could get a new name, a new cell phone. Then with sinking clarity, he remembered sending a text message to Shallen accepting her request to delay the suit. He wondered if they had intercepted the message, and if so why approach him now if he had already agreed to the delay? Probably because they wanted him to do more than delay it. They wanted him to drop it altogether.

"What if I don't go along with your plan?"

"It would be best to do as we say. Best for you *and* for your family."

"You want a snap decision. I can't." Jason shook his head.

The man paced back and forth. "You have to decide now." He spoke in short, firm tones, suggesting no room for a delay.

"This is a serious matter. I need time."

"Why? All you have to do is forget the suit. Simple."

Jason wanted to know how far off he could put him. "Simple for you. For me I'll have to abandon my principles. What if I don't want to?"

Guy pulled out a couple of pictures. "Recognize these?"

They were pictures of Sarah and Keenan in the schoolyard. "You are a low human being! You know that?" Jason bit his lip, realizing that these men meant business.

"Don't pursue it." The man stood firm.

Jason held up his hands. "Ok. Don't touch them. I give up."

"One more thing, once you decide not to pursuit the class-action, which I strongly suggest you do, you have to make a public announcement, like through a newspaper."

"Just get out of here." He slammed the car door and walked towards the hotel entrance.

"Don't call the police," Guy called after him.

***

On Friday, at precisely 7:45, Shallen walked out of the Salbasgeon Suites through the back entrance into a lot housing garbage bins and worker's vehicles. As hoped, she saw a taxi with the engine still running, the sight of which gave her a huge sigh of relief. She hopped into the back seat and handed the driver a paper with an address on it. After a brief glance at it, he engaged the gear setting the vehicle in motion. This was the third day since Shallen had arrived in Corvallis.

"I'm in a hurry," she told the driver. "Can you go fast?"

After a nod, he pressed the gas pedal harder. "You're not from here." He looked at her through the rearview mirror.

The traffic on 9th Street was heavy with early morning vehicles. "I'm a journalist from the *Washington Post*." She glanced nervously at the vehicles on both sides of the taxi. So far she felt safe that no one was following her. She was sure that she had been followed yesterday. Last night, before going to her room, she slipped a twenty-dollar bill into one of the concierges' hand and asked him to have a taxi waiting for her in the morning.

"There's a scientific convention at Salbasgeon Suites. Are you here for that?" the driver asked, breaking into her reverie.

"No." She continued monitoring the passengers in the cars around the taxi. She wasn't in a chatty mood. When she looked in the rearview mirror she noticed his eyes sparkled as if he was looking for an opportunity to ask for a date. She avoided eye contact with the driver.

"I didn't think so." He looked at the address again. "You're going to Rocky Delgado's place. I know the dude."

Shallen lifted her head, suddenly interested. "Rocky--"

The clean-shaven driver eased his thirty-something body over, and looked into the rearview mirror to get a better view of her. "I worked at Softek, heard of that?"

She perked up. "Yes. I'm investigating the shootings."

"What have you found so far?"

"Just a hunch. Nothing to hang my hat on. It's extremely difficult to get anyone to talk about it, but I'm hoping Rocky will cooperate. Were you let go like so many others?" She reached for a notepad, a reporter's instinctive reaction, but refrained from picking it up. Instead she recorded every word mentally.

"Yes." The car snaked through the traffic ahead. "Back in October. In the first round." She focused on the cars around her on the road.

"How was it for you?" She moved forward and raised her voice to compensate for the engine noise of a nearby motorcycle.

"Terrible. For two months I couldn't find any work in this county. Just before Christmas I took this job, driving a taxi."

On second thought, she got her notepad out. "I get a sense that Senator Quest is involved. What do you think?"

"He runs Softek. It's a well-known fact that the Senator gets a handsome kickback. Everyone accepts it as politics as usual. No one will do anything about it. He's very powerful."

She nodded. Already Jason was under surveillance. And Corvallis was surrounded by a fortress of silence. "That's what politicians do. I need proof. Could you help me?"

The driver made a quick right turn. "This company is secretive. You need an insider. Rocky is a good start. Someone who handles money. Rocky and I are techies, not in the money circle. The CEO, CFO and top management—those are the ones you need to talk to. I hope you can nail the Senator. The politicians use our money and then they look after themselves first." With those final words he banged the steering wheel.

Shallen felt a knot in her stomach. Was it the lack of breakfast? Or restless sleep? Maybe both. Just then her stomach growled. She looked at the driver, but fortunately he was paying attention to the traffic ahead.

After a left turn on Hemlock Ave., the car slowed until it turned onto Bryant Street. Shallen waved her hand for him to stop when she saw a red Honda in the drive. After handing a twenty-dollar bill and a card to the driver she said, "If you can help let me know."

"Sure will. We have to fight for justice." He looked at her one last time through the rearview mirror. "I kept an eye on the vehicles behind and around. No one followed us. Good luck."

He seemed like a trustworthy person. She just wished Rocky could be so open, but she knew he was going to be a tougher nut to crack and that going after him head on would only antagonize him. No, with Rocky she was going to have to surprise him. That gave her an idea.

Without wasting a second, she rushed to the Honda she'd seen sitting in the driveway and yanked open the passenger door. *Lucky it's not locked.* After planting herself in the front seat she waited for Rocky to come out of the house. How unprofessional it was for her to enter someone's car uninvited. If he called the police, she could be charged for trespassing, end up in jail. It would ruin her career. She was praying it wouldn't go in that direction, but after the way Rocky had acted when she had tried to get information from him before, she knew if she knocked on the front door he would just slam it in her face. This was her only chance to speak with him.

Vapor from her breath fogged up the windshield. It was a cold morning. Having sat there for about twenty minutes, she felt the chill in the air. She pulled up the zipper of her leather jacket enough to squeeze the scarf under it and around her neck. Cold, hungry, nervous and tired, she thought of Faye, Rocky, Linda, Barbara and the taxi driver. She also thought about all the people who didn't want to talk to her – about how the Senator's power reigned over others. It was Brian and Jason's plights that made her want to follow through, to get at the truth. Deep down, they were all victims looking for justice and compensation. It was her duty as a reporter to bring the truth to light.

Suddenly she laughed out loud at the irony of the situation. A lot was at stake. She needed to talk to Rocky, the only person who could shed some light on the situation. *Maybe.*

Just then she noticed movement through the thick fog on the other side of the windshield. Her breathing grew louder, more from nervousness than from the cold. Thoughts kept churning through her head. She had to take this chance. The worst that could happen was she would be hammered for hiding in his car and he would kick her out – she hoped.

Shallen watched Rocky open the door to his house. After locking it behind him he headed towards the car. For the final time she rehearsed what to tell him. That's what she had been doing for most of the last twenty minutes.

When the door opened, Shallen said, "Rocky, it's me, Shallen." He froze at the sound of her voice. His body bent slightly forward, and his face became pale with disbelief. He looked at her in a daze. "I have to talk to you. It's important," Shallen said. The words brought him back to his senses.

"What the hell are you doing in my car?" The terror in his eyes sent shards of worry through Shallen.

"Get in. Get in," she pleaded.

In a daze, he straightened his body enough to scan the neighborhood before sinking into the seat and slamming the door. The bag rested on his lap. "Why are you here? Do you have any idea what you're doing?"

"I want to save Jason's life. He's in danger," she said, unable to hide the desperation in her voice.

His eyes widened, spilling over with anger. "How did you get in the car?"
"It was unlocked."

"After I saw you I was so upset. I must have left the car unlocked." There was a long silence as he leaned his head down. He blew air through his mouth and rubbed his hair. Then he slammed the steering wheel with his fist. "What do you want?"

"What is happening at Softek? There's a blanket of silence. Why?"
He clenched his fists on the steering wheel. "Everything changed after the massacre. Everyone is being watched. Everyone is afraid of losing their jobs. You have to be careful yourself." Anger was spewing out of him. "Did anyone follow you?" he yelled. He turned around to scan the road, fear visible on his face.

"I was careful. No. I suspected someone was following me yesterday." She hooked a strand of hair behind her ear.

"How is Jason?" he said with hesitation.
"Since he got the job in Mountain View, he is under constant surveillance. Why? For what reason? He doesn't exactly know anything, though he suspects it has something to do with the class-action suit." She rubbed her hands to reduce the chill.

"He has a lawsuit going?" Rocky said, shaking his head in confusion.
"Yes, and it will attract attention from all sides. This may cause a lot of problems for the Senator who we think is getting a kickback from Softek. The company was forced into outsourcing so that it can finance the Senator's campaign. What do you know

about it?" She examined his face for any reaction.

"All I know is that there is silence. Yesterday, someone came from Washington to meet with Muhtar. After the meeting, we were asked not to talk to any media. That was a strict order. Anyone found guilty would be fired on the spot. Right now talking to you could jeopardize my job."

"What do you mean?"

"I have a family to feed. A roof to keep over our heads. Jobs have completely dried up. 2009 will be the financial crisis of the century. I have to be careful," he said with a grim look.

"Rocky, who was he?" She moved closer to him.

"I saw him briefly. He was short and bald. Mean looking."

She sifted through many pictures she had brought with her in her bag. He identified one. More to herself than to him she said, "That's Roger Hunt, the Senator's campaign consultant. Why would he be here?"

"On the Senator's behalf for sure," he said.

"Yes, I'm sure you're right, but I need proof. Can you help me?"

There was a long silence. "I can't talk to you. You have to go."

She scribbled something onto a paper she pulled from her bag. "I understand."

"Just yesterday, we were told not to talk to the *Washington Post*. Just yesterday. No media. Absolutely none. Especially you. The article you wrote crashed Softek stock. I could lose my job." He banged a fist on the steering wheel with every syllable he spoke.

"I just wrote an article. I didn't take any kickback. Didn't outsource any jobs overseas. I'm not the one threatening anyone, Rocky. Don't you want to know the truth?" Shallen hoped to replace his fear with sense.

"I've got to get out of here." He waved his hand.

"Be careful." Shallen jumped out of the car.

"Good luck. And watch your back," Rocky said as she closed the door. Then he roared out of the driveway and took off.

Shallen walked towards 9th Street, disappointed that Rocky wouldn't help, the one person she was counting on. She understood he had to look after his family. So far the idea of a cover-up was just an idea. Without any concrete proof, there was no chance that John Mead would allow her to print an article based on people's opinions.

Yes, she needed evidence. Someone in the company must know about the transactions of money between Softek and the Senator. How to reach that person was the challenge. It was a well-guarded secret.

She returned to the hotel room by taxi. Following a quick shower she picked up the phone to order breakfast and then fired up the laptop. After ten minutes of sifting through her emails she answered the doorbell and placed the food next to the computer. She swallowed successive mouthfuls of coffee and continued sorting through the inbox of hundreds of unread messages. An hour later, Shallen made a few phone calls to schedule the flight going back to Washington. After more email chores, making reports and packing, it was almost time to check out.

At 11:20 Shallen rolled her luggage out of the front door of the Salbasgeon Suites. She spotted the blue Ford Fusion. Her return to home base was happening earlier than planned, as John Mead ordered her not to stay any longer. As she loaded the car, she felt sad, tired and frustrated. Sad because she was leaving Corvallis empty-handed, without incriminating evidence to support a serious article. Reporters often faced challenges in their work; certainly the last three days had been a big challenge.

After a final check of all her belongings, she started the engine, headed to the airport where she would return the rental and then fly back to Washington through Los Angeles. After a quick check of the mirrors, she started to back the car, when someone yanked the passenger door open and jumped in the seat yelling, "Drive, keep driving."

Shallen slammed on the brakes, giving the intruder a "what-the-hell are you doing" stare. An alarm triggered in her head, as such an invasion had never happened to her. Her first thought was that she was being carjacked. Instinctively she threw up her arm in a defensive position. With few moments to waste, she reached out with two forefingers, and thrust them directly into the eyes of her opponent. The intruder, having sensed an attack, ducked but not before he had received one sharp nail to the corner of his left eye.

The attack made him yell in pain. "What was that for?"
"Back off, back off," she shouted. Then she coiled her left hand and prepared for another deadly Karate strike called Shuto, the front choke, which she excelled during her black belt rehearsal. But how effective would it be away from the wide space of a dojo and a friendly opponent? Seeing him in pain, she held back the next move while she examined him. He didn't seem to have a weapon.

He cupped his left eye. "My name is Jerry Whitney."

The familiarity of the name caused her to release the tension in her arms, but only slightly. "Related to Faye Whitney?"

"I am her--"

She saw the resemblance. "– son."

"I've been watching you since yesterday. I've got some information to share. What the hell were you thinking? I could have lost an eye. Damn." He continued to press the muscles around his eye. He blinked to suggest it felt better. "I had to talk to you when no one was watching." He lifted his head, his fingers pressed to his eyes but the pain seemed to be easing. "This is the best opportunity to talk to you."

"Sorry. I'm from Washington. You don't dare take a chance there." The brakes were on and the engine was running. She rubbed her forehead trying to ease the guilt she felt at having nearly killed the boy.

"Let's drive. Someone might be watching us."

Jerry twisted his neck around, searching the parking lot for any suspicious character as he gave directions. Minutes later they were in a quiet residential area, with only her car parked on the street, and a few others in their driveways. An easy place to spot a spy. "How is your eye?" she asked as the car came to a halt.

"You're a dangerous woman. What do I call you?"

She cracked a sympathetic smile to show she really was sorry. "Shallen. It's an Americanized version of Shen-Ling."

"Ok, Shallen. We can't talk for too long. So I'm gonna make this quick." He licked his lips. "My dad didn't need to die. He was the one who fought against outsourcing. He argued with those bastards, especially Muhtar Gamble. But no. They were hell bent on sending jobs overseas and laying off Americans." He blinked several times as if preventing tears from falling. "At the funeral . . ." He stopped to take a deep breath. "At the funeral, I promised my father that I would get to the bottom of this. Truth must surface. Justice must be done. Whoever did this will pay the price. My father warned them that taking jobs away from Corvallis would cause suffering. Brian should have gone directly to Gamble's office and blown his head off." He appeared to have blown off some steam and seemed calmer now.

There was a minute of silence while Shallen quickly jotted down what he was saying on her notepad. When she was finished scribbling, she dug out a recorder from the handbag. "I'll record this." After receiving a nod, she turned on the machine and Jerry repeated his thoughts. He looked about thirty-ish wearing a blue jacket and a neatly trimmed beard. Then she followed his gaze to the lawn and the green covered with patchy snow.

"What else did you want to say?"

"The next victim was my mother. She has had two strokes since then. A nervous breakdown. Softek was supposed to give her six months pay as benefit. She has only seen three. My father did everything. He managed the mortgage, banking, insurance. All the financial aspects of life. My mother had nothing to do with it. He was planning for a good retirement. That's gone now."

"Jerry, it obviously had a profound effect on you. Did your father ever mention kickbacks?" She held the recorder in the air.

"Not exactly. I have been following Muhtar Gamble since the tragedy. He and the Senator met in Salem at a park once. I was hiding behind a bush. They talked about a five million dollar transfer from Softek in Mumbai to his Swiss account."

"Swiss account." She held a finger to her lips and wondered about the flow of money. "How did it arrive in the Senator's account?"

"That I don't know. Yet. I'm from Corvallis. Born and bred here. Dad worked in the company for twenty years. I know the insiders of Softek very well. I can get any information you want."

Shallen shook her head, excitement building inside her. In the rear view mirror a car appeared. Shallen examined the car driven by a woman.

"Local resident," Jerry said.

Relieved, Shallen lifted the machine closer to his mouth.

"Just a few days ago, Roger Hunt came to town and ordered people around. He told management to make sure to keep company secrets airtight, no leaks. No contact with media. I know Jason wants to start a class-action suit, which incidentally has them worried. The Softek stock has plummeted since the massacre. They don't like what you're doing, either. I would be watching your back, if I were you."

"I've sensed the danger. The last few days have weighed heavily on my nerves. Investigative reporting has its risks," she said with a mix of purpose and worry.

"These people will do anything to get rid of a hurdle. Politicians especially. I mean anything. Be careful."

Shallen said, "I need hard facts. I need documents showing money flowing out of the company and back into the Senator's pocket."

"I'll do whatever is needed. I work for the Works Department so I can order inspections in any building in Corvallis."

After what she had gone through, the arrival of Jerry Whitney seemed surreal. Still, she felt some skepticism. "You really are deep enough into enemy territory to help? Have you thought of the risk you're taking?"

"If they find out, they will go after me. I could lose my job or they could ice me. What would my father want me to do? I've thought about this long and hard."

A pickup truck appeared around the bend. It passed them by with a senior driver. A good percentage of Corvallis's population was over fifty, Shallen knew through her research. Jerry gave her the impression of someone who was on a serious mission.

"You clearly understand the risk. Is it worth it?"

He laughed, but there was no humor in it. "The Senator surrounds himself with smart people. They're going to make mistakes sooner or later."

"I'm counting on that too."

"Shallen, I loved my dad very much. He was taken from me. Too suddenly. At first I was angry at Brian. But after some long, hard thinking, I realized that the real cause was politics. It was power and greed. I can't call my father and say let's go fishing anymore. My mother, my children and my wife miss him a lot."

Shallen listened to a man whose heart was broken. The yearning was visible in his eyes and his behavior. It was hard for her to hear the pain in his voice. After only twenty minutes of being with him, it seemed like eternity. She pointed at her watch and indicated it was time to finish this encounter. They exchanged phone numbers, with the strong hope of continuing their exchange. Then they parted. Now came the hard work. To get the documentation to convict the Senator.

15

Shallen Xu stormed out of John Mead's office, her mind so occupied by John's reaction that her knees nearly buckled. Walking down the aisle she heard her name. She turned around to find Barbara, a splash of disappointment on her face.

"I called you several times. You didn't answer me." Barbara's words were laced with sarcasm.

In fact Shallen hadn't noticed her, though normally she would have. "No, I didn't." Shallen continued her journey towards her desk after accepting a message written on a piece of paper that Barbara handed her.

The sprawling newsroom was humming with activity at this early hour. Phones rang, reporters zipped up and down the aisles, printers spit out papers, voices emerged from hidden spots, and the occasional head bobbed up and down above the cubicles. Yet Shallen's mind shut out the buzz around her as she marched on, her mind replaying John's reaction again and again.

Upon arriving at her desk, Shallen dropped the notepad and pen next to the keyboard while sinking into a chair. Her fingers instinctively reached for the mouse and, giving it few clicks, the list of Inbox items appeared. A few messages needed her immediate attention but nothing was as pressing as the concern churning in her mind. Her vision was gradually becoming blurry. It was like a storm had taken over her body and there was nothing she could do to calm the storm.

Or maybe there is.

John was crystal clear about his demands. His face red and his forehead marked with deep furrows, he had said, "Stop investigating Senator Quest or you're fired." Shallen's report about the findings in Corvallis, which she had handed to John earlier this morning, had triggered his furious reaction. She had hoped her diligent investigation, in the clear and precise article, would please him. An hour later, John called her into his office to discuss her discovery but, instead of compliments, he had lashed out at her. She was bewildered. When she probed John about why the investigation should be stopped, he said that she was needed to cover the primaries, the same thing he had been saying for the past two months. To her it didn't make sense as she was so close to linking the Senator to a corruption scandal. All she needed were a few solid leads, which she was planning to have in her hands within a day.

As she sat with her eyes pointed at the screen, her mind was busy formulating a reaction that wouldn't diminish her honor as a human being nor as a journalist, both of which she valued.

According to her watch it was shortly after ten. She shot up out of her seat, all five foot five of her, and scanned the vast room wall to wall. The cubicle next to hers was empty. Beyond, the occupants were either on the phone or their eyes were glued to the screen. Shallen vowed to be quiet and discrete, as she lowered herself into the seat. She punched numbers into the phone and cupped the mouthpiece with her hand, which was shaking violently. Upon hearing a greeting from her colleague's message machine, she said, "Lisa, it's Shallen. Please call me back, it's urgent."

Piles of paperwork covered the desk, her purse rested on the chair, and the floor of her little office space was blanketed with newspapers, magazines, books and printouts. What could she do to replace the thought of being fired with something else? She chose to go back to the Inbox. She scanned the subject matter of each email and opened only a few. Then, after typing in a brief message, she fired them out. The anger was growing inside her, rendering her nearly helpless. How could she face her family and friends? Yet if she didn't pursue the investigation, it would be a betrayal of a trust. The trust of those in her profession, Brian's trust, and Jason's trust.

The phone rang, startling her. She attended to it with her head lowered and mouthpiece covered. It was Lisa Ward at the other end. After two minutes she hung up. Lisa informed her that John Mead, who was in the Senator's pocket, obeyed his orders religiously.

She quit her job at the *Post. What to do next?*

***

Shallen Xu entered the prestigious building where professionals working in Washington, DC, lived. Upon punching a security code, a soft click unlocked the front door, through which she eased her body, but her mind was toiling over the embarrassment she had suffered miles away, earlier that day. The clock on the wall ticked to 4:00 pm. Just below the clock, the assistant clerk greeted her from behind a desk, her eyes gleaming as she gave a nod, to which Shallen could only muster a fake smile. Turning to her right, she walked around the arrangement of white leather sofas, armchairs and a coffee table, all resting on a marble floor, below a chandelier that hung from the ceiling. The necks of two younger men, along with that of the assistant, craned to follow her movements until she disappeared from the threesome's sight into the mailbox area behind the elevators. Facing the wall holding the mailboxes was the tenant lounge where paintings decorated the walls, a wide-screen plasma TV sat on a stand in front of love seats and hassocks.

When Shallen returned home, out of force of habit, she always checked her mailbox. As usual, instinct took over when she routinely unlocked the small door to grab the mail, not that she was expecting anything to arrive. Her thoughts absorbed by what had happened earlier that day, she marched to the elevator.

Her handbag hanging from her shoulder, her mail in one hand and a plastic bag with an assortment of belongings from her ex-office in the other, she rode the elevator to the sixth floor that housed her apartment. She yearned for a healthy cry. Why? Why? Why had all this happened? After she handed her resignation letter to John Mead earlier that morning, within ten minutes she'd been escorted out of the *Washington Post* office. Criminals were treated that way. Not her. The technician had locked her computer—company policy—which had to be witnessed by someone, Barbara in this case. Humiliated, Shallen Xu shoved her belongings from the desktop, in drawers and on the floor in a few quick sweeps. When it was all done, surprisingly Barbara was not happy, sarcastic or mean, as Shallen expected her to be. Rather she showed sympathy by giving her a huge hug before calling John Mead, who escorted her out of the *Washington Post* building and into the street. She wasn't given a chance to say goodbye to colleagues and friends, who would be wondering what happened. Office gossip would go wild, no doubt turning her into a devil by day's end. But she couldn't compromise her professional integrity. She had to resign.

As the elevator door opened, she felt as if she had been shredded. Her weak legs could barely hold her as she fought back the emotional storm battling inside her.

With little strength left she turned the key to unlock the door, entered and closed the door behind her. She threw the plastic bag next to the mat loaded with shoes. The growling from her stomach returned. As she squeezed the shoes off her feet, she wondered what she could take to quell the nausea, maybe mineral water, not solid food. Upon hanging the jacket in the closet, Shallen walked past the washroom into the living room, where the walls were graced with a variety of pictures and a Japanese tapestry, while the wooden floor was outfitted with modern furniture. A Buddha statue, surrounded with flowers and incense, sat in perfect serenity in one corner.

She threw the handbag on a chair and dropped the bundle of envelopes on the coffee table, out of which a sheet of paper escaped, falling to the floor. *Probably a notice from building management.*

She bent down to pick it up. A handwritten sheet? Not typed, as she had expected. As she began to read it, she wondered who had placed it in her mailbox. When her eyes reached the middle of the white sheet, her hands trembled. She realized it was no joke; the vile, threatening words were meant for her. They were so horrible, so lewd, that she stopped reading, unable to continue. She scanned down to the final line where it said *Keep your mouth shut or you're dead.*

Following these loathsome words were three pictures: A noose hanging from a tree, a hand gun, and a nylon string.

On the third time through, her breathing grew louder. She placed a hand to her head. *Oh my God, this is meant for me.* Her head felt lighter as if she was about to faint. She recalled the fate of some of the investigative reporters she'd known through the years who had been killed for uncovering the truth that some evil characters wanted hidden. No. She needed to muster her courage. She threw the sheet of paper down and sat at the edge of the chair, holding her head, her eyes fixed at her feet.

She recalled the story her father had told her many times about the fall of the Qing Dynasty in 1911, when her grandparents and their two children were rounded up by revolutionary forces and tortured. They escaped their ordeal by paying a smuggler all their family possessions to take them across the border to Thailand after an exhaustive journey. Shallen's parents had told her the story many times lest she forgets her heritage and her family's suffering.

Her cell phone rang once, twice. The third ring made her flesh crawl. Then her senses came alive. She turned to look at her handbag, wondering who was calling her. After digging the cell phone out, she held it in her palm for another ring. Should she answer it? *Yes.* She needed to know who was after her and why. She wouldn't let anyone bully her. *Courage.* The number on the screen wiped away her fear, and a sweeping relief passed over her. It was Amanda, her younger sister, at the other end.

"Shallen," Amanda said, somewhat breathless, "Aunt Sylvia's in the South Miami Hospital for food poisoning."

Shallen totally forgot about the menacing letter. Her heart sank. "How serious?"

"Very Serious. We don't know how long she'll live. You should come here as soon as you can."

Shallen's father would be totally devastated. "I'll talk to you when I get to Miami."

"Are you going directly to the hospital?" Amanda asked.

"I'll be there on the next available flight."

Shallen said goodbye and started to hang up when her sister said, "Wait! One more thing. Something very strange. I found a FedEx letter on my kitchen table when I came home today. When I opened it, it was empty."

"Who sent it?" The words fired out in loud succession.

"Who sent it?" She sounded bewildered. "What do you mean?"

"I mean, who is the sender?" Shallen tapped her toe impatiently.

"Shallen. *You* were the sender. It was your address."

"I didn't send you any package." She shook her head.

"Strange. Very strange. And I didn't put it on the kitchen table, either." The words came out slowly but with emphasis, as though trying to convince her sister.

After hanging up, Shallen connected the dots. The handwritten letter was not a coincidence. Now, they—whoever they were—had infiltrated her family. Tears rolled down her cheeks, thinking about her sick aunt and the sadness her family would suffer. She walked over to the sofa, lowered herself onto it and, with her head tucked into her chest and her feet curled up to her stomach, she cried. She stayed in the fetal position for a long while, sobbing.

In her mind's eye, two men stood in front with the eyes of two bulls. One had a cord in his hand, the other held an axe. With face muscles tight, lips slightly apart, the man with the cord inched it towards her neck. She could see herself readying her arms and legs while running deadly moves in her mind. A front snap to the ribs, chin, throat, solar plexus and pelvis would disable her opponent momentarily. The one she preferred was to the throat, resulting in a crushed throat, a smashed Adam's apple, after which the attacker would usually die, unless given immediate medical attention. When she opened her eyes, they were gone. It was only a mental exercise.

She got to her feet, breathing hard. She inhaled deeply, held her breath for ten seconds then exhaled slowly, exhausting her lungs. She could feel her muscles relax.

She repeated this ten times, until she recovered her muscle power and her mind was clear and fresh. She walked slowly to the corner, bowed her head and asked for the Great Buddha's protection. She had to be prepared mentally, spiritually and physically, to fight the enemy. But how could she, when she didn't know who the enemy was? She would find out soon.

She packed up a suitcase, small enough to be carried on the plane as carrying-on luggage. Next she changed into casual pants, shirt and jacket. She looked around the room one last time, then left her apartment and descended to the lobby. With a fake smile, she pointed a card to the door attendant and asked him to call a cab. After a short pause she added, "Ask the driver to meet me in the tenant parking area."

"Miss Xu, taxis are not allowed there. Only tenants. How about in front?" He pointed to the front door.

She didn't want to meet the cab out front in case her enemy was watching her and was planning to trap her. "Please."

"The loading dock?"

She didn't want anyone watching her leave the building. At least she was taking enough of a precaution that hopefully nothing would happen. She grimaced. "No, I need to leave from the tenant parking area." She could hear the pleading in her tone, but it couldn't be helped. Finally, he acquiesced.

"I'll let the driver know."

She left the lobby, passed through the door next to the tenant lounge into the parking area. After ten minutes, the cab came. She checked the driver's face, which appeared familiar to her. Placing the suitcase into the trunk, Shallen then slid into the back. She gave the driver directions to the Washington Dulles International Airport.

Fifteen minutes later, she stopped writing on the notepad and looked outside the window as the car exited Freeway 495 and took Reston Street. She knew the airport was only about ten minutes away.

At the airport she went to the ATM machine to withdraw cash. Next, she went to the Porter Airline counter to buy a ticket to Miami with her credit card. Then she walked over to the United Airlines counter to book a ticket to Los Angeles, which she paid for in cash, making sure the departure time was much earlier than the one for Miami.

Hiding in a duty-free shop behind shelves of chocolate and souvenirs, she examined every face in and out of the store. From this spot, United Airlines Gate 43 to Los Angeles was clearly visible. On the drive to the airport she had come to a decision. She wasn't going to Miami. It wasn't safe. Now, she just hoped and prayed her aunt would get better. She felt wrenched that she couldn't be by her bed to comfort her, but until she knew what was going on, she was endangering everyone's lives around her, including her own.

Three minutes before the departure time, she called Jason and left a message. Then she ran towards the departure gate.

***

Jason McDeere fingered the Rolex placed on the table, then whistled softly as he looked toward the hotel room door, expecting someone to walk in at any time. Returning his attention to the new Dell laptop he bought just a few days earlier, he continued searching the Internet for a picture of Guy, Ponytail Man, who had threatened him one day earlier in front of the hotel. The man didn't give his last name. Of course he wouldn't. His height, strong voice, and unwavering position all suggested he was a former law enforcement agent. Before taking this job, he was probably a detective, FBI or CIA agent.

Showing me pictures of my children . . . who the hell does he thinks he is?

Guy was the brain behind the operation while the younger thugs were the muscle power. Jason reached for the new mobile phone and pecked numbers and letters on tiny keys, then finally pressed the send button emailing another text message to Terrance requesting an explanation for his tardiness. Tense and unable to sit any longer, he shot up out of his seat like a loaded spring and walked closer to the window. Through an opening between the curtains he searched for the men who he had found loitering in the parking lot earlier. He picked up a pair of binoculars from the floor and peered through the lenses. He located a van, two people faintly visible inside. Maybe Terrance got tied up at work.

Maybe not.

He went back to the desk and continued examining the result of a Google search on the new computer, thoroughly sanitized of viruses and protected like a king's palace. He clicked on web links, looking for Guy on the Internet. Following one of the links, his eyes stopped at a picture. Amazed at what he saw, he squinted and rubbed his eyebrows, trying hard to connect the similarity between the young man on the screen and Guy, whom he had seen the day before. Printed below the picture, he read the newspaper article regarding a rash of bank frauds in Los Angeles. When he reached the name Guy Volpa and saw that he was the investigating officer for the crime, and also the FBI representative, Jason clapped his hands together. He reexamined the young officer's photograph, his full hair and thick sideburns. Just then a knock at the door stole his attention. Relieved, he raced to open the door. It was pizza delivery, not Terrance. After receiving the pizza, and handing two ten-dollar bills to the delivery man, he returned to the middle of the room. The room was filled with suitcases, dirty clothes, books, bags, and folders. He searched for a free spot. Finally, he just dropped the box on the wrinkled sheets of his unmade bed.

Frustrated, he reached for his cell phone and composed another text message. "Where the hell are you?" He pushed send.

For the next twenty minutes he dug around for more information on Volpa, when out of the corner of his eye he caught the flashing light on his cell phone, indicating an incoming message. He shifted his attention to the small screen where Terrance's number was visible.

"Got your messages. At local police station. Picked up by FBI for interrogation about a Pentagon website break-in. Know nothing about it. See you soon."

Jason read the message a few more times until the reality of the message hit him. His phone dropped to the floor as he stood up and flopped backwards onto the bed, his eyes fixed on the ceiling, his arm collapsing the pizza box. Volpa must be behind the arrest, getting the Feds to do his dirty work. The walls of his world seemed to be closing in on him. There was very little room to move or to escape. Now Terrance was unavailable. During intense interrogation, what if Terrance told the FBI about Jason hacking into Volpa's website? Very soon agents would be chasing him too. As these thoughts churned, his anxiety level shot up.

He felt a numbness growing inside, the depth of which he had never experienced before. Total exhaustion. *Something has to end. Maybe my life.* It was unbearable to continue down the same path any longer. Hope kept a human going forward. Without it, life was meaningless. Like a fast-forward movie his whole life played in his mind. His boyhood years, his parents together, his father's death, a crush on his primary school teacher, skiing with his friends, love for Kara, his children's birthdays. He longed to see his father, whom he had never stopped missing since his death. Staring at the ceiling, his breathing shallow and his air passage restricted, he realized the futility of his life. What did it mean? Was the life being sucked out of him day by day? If he did kill himself, his children would be fatherless for the rest of their lives. And Terrance would be in Volpa's clutches, helped by the Feds. He would spend the rest of his life in jail. *This is not the time to die.* There must be some courage to be squeezed out of him, but the forces of evil were too great. He snapped upright on the end of the bed, determined not to dwell on this depressing thought.

If he was going to survive this, he needed to go on the attack, uncover the Senator's illegal activities. Only then could he prevent Terrance from going to jail. With enough energy left in him to reflect on his next move, he rose.

Back on his feet, he limped to the windows, more as a matter of routine rather than for any real purpose. He scanned the parking lot. The goons were no longer visible, or maybe they were snoring inside the van, totally unaware of what was about to happen.

With any luck he could crack the website himself. But what about the FBI? *The hell with them.* He had nothing to lose. While he was still up, he should try one more time. Weakness, caused by stress and emotional exhaustion, forced him to sit once again on the edge of the bed. With his eyes still open, he felt as though he were in a trance. He found himself walking into a pitch-dark tunnel until a stone door stood in front of him. The place was totally void of light and his eyes were of no use; yet he continued walking fully aware of the walls a few feet on either side of him and a very tall ceiling above him. Without a moment's hesitation he dug a long key, which he'd always had but hadn't realized until now, from his pocket. Upon placing the key in the lock, the heavy door opened without a sound. He was impressed by the thickness of the door. He continued to walk uninhibited, then entered a room where he found the Rolex watch, which he had been looking for. As he entered another section of the cave-like room, he saw his children's playing cards. There was no fear, only extreme calm. Soon, he found himself in another part of the cave. On the table lay a Bible that belonged to his father. It occurred to him that all these articles and people that he had been yearning to see for a long time were here, in this book. He touched the Holy Book. Only then did he come out of the dream-like state, and find himself sitting at the edge of the bed. He couldn't help but feel that his father was watching over him, that this was a message of sorts.

He walked over to the old computer on the desk. It was still running spy software. After a few pecks on the keyboard, Windows Task Manager came alive showing all the programs currently running on the computer. Going down the list he assured himself the program wp123.exe, the spy program that was planted by Volpa, was active, hoping no software engineer at VolpaPI.com would detect anything unusual that was about to happen. With a program editor he brought up the spy program. It painted the screen with a string of gobbledy-goop characters. It wasn't English, or any other language. Instead, it looked like random numbers and alphabets. To him, all of this made sense as he went directly to the part that handles authentication. Just then he realized the username and password were already imbedded in the program and acted like the key to enter the website. He made some changes to the program such that instead of depositing information into VolpaPI.com, after capturing his ingoing and outgoing emails and net surfing, he would do the reverse. The program change that was taking place would take files from the websites and copy them onto his computers. It was a brilliant idea. Why hadn't he thought of it earlier?

After he had completed the changes, the old version of wp123.exe was replaced with the modified one. He waited for the results. With a few clicks, Windows Explorer came alive, through which he navigated to a folder called VolpaPI.com.Files. As Explorer refreshed this folder, a list of file names appeared. It was a thrilling sight, and he hit the desk with excitement. Soon the exuberance he'd felt was replaced by nervousness. Knowing a lot about networks and firewalls, somebody at Volpa's office would be alerted that files were being stolen. He checked the empty storage capacity on his laptop. The 285 GB of free space gave him some relief. The files were big in size, indicating lots of information of interviews, videos, etc. As files kept coming, he peeked outside, wondering how much time he had to complete the operation. It was around 7:00 pm. As he watched, a bus pulled up and tourists emptied the coached and they filed towards the hotel entrance. The front of the hotel was lit up with lamps, as a car came in through the street entrance. Others headed to their cars. The two tough guys were nowhere in sight. *Hope they're not on their way to the hotel room.*

Finally, the program stopped copying files. Carefully, Jason McDeere activated the old version of the program and he checked to ensure everything went back to the way it was before. He was hoping to have pictures, videos, conversations in the files that could be used to nail the Senator and set Terrance free, only no one could find out before he could use them. *What are the chances?* He prayed for some luck. Otherwise, he imagined that FBI agents would escort him out of the hotel in handcuffs. Just then, a cell phone distracted his train of thought.

***

At around 7:30 pm Guy Volpa planted himself in the swivel chair with his cowboy boots perched on the desk as he reviewed the surveillance material, when Lance, who dabbled in web design, web administrator, and network like a fanatical geek, appeared at the door with a frantic look on his face. Volpa lifted his head to acknowledge Lance then continued reading. After a long pause, Volpa broke the silence. "What's up?"

"Something terrible has happened!" Lance chewed his fingernails.

"What?" Volpa watched as the thin man's anxiety intensified. "Your grandmother died?" He laughed at his own joke.

Lance shook his head. "No." His silence continued. Guy studied his frozen face, his own anxiety mounting. "What the hell is it?" he demanded. "Your wife found a new lover?" Guy cracked a smile to ease the blow of his rude remark.

Lance turned to the window. Outside, darkness draped the night. "Worse." He cleared his throat. "Someone broke into the firewall of our server." He hesitated, gazing directly at Volpa.

"Cut the computer crap," Guy said, tired of the cat and mouse game. "Just give it to me in English."

"He did an outbound transfer," said Terrance.

Guy stood up and barked, "English! Damn it. I said, English. Which part don't you understand?"

Lance scratched his head. "An intruder, ahh –" he rubbed his forehead – "stole our files."

Communicating with a computer professional presented Guy with a challenge. "Intruders stole our files? What the hell are you talking about? How did it happen?" He threw the papers on the desk and walked closer to the webmaster, who was having great difficulty telling him about the disaster that had just occurred. "How could he steal our files?" He lifted both hands in the air.

"Someone broke into our website and copied files." The man's pale face lost more color, if that was possible.

"Copied files. What files?"

"All the files."

"Lance, what kinds of files?"

"All our surveillance files, interview files, videos, everything." Lance's eyes showed frustration and regret.

Guy Volpa tried to grasp the concept of such an Internet theft. "By copying, you mean they stole the files from us?" He widened his eyes and furrowed his brow. The computerized surveillance had been in operation for two years and now he was learning something impossible had occurred.

"Yes," said Lance with reluctance.

Shaking his head, his hands in the air, he said, "This is like stealing my firstborn. Unacceptable, Lance. You guys are computer geniuses. How did this happen? You know what this means . . . my business will go down the toilet. We could all end up in jail." After a short pause, he pointed a finger at Lance and growled, "You first find out know who did it. Later, I want to know how."

"I know who did it."

He narrowed his eyes, turned to the window and back to Lance. For a moment, the words didn't register. "Give it to me."

"I located the IP address. I mean the computer address that shows the file destination." He shook his head to amend his words. "Copied. Ah. Stolen."

"You know who did it? Good. But IP addresses don't make a hell of a lot of sense to me. Give me a street address."

"In Mountain View."

Guy recalled being in that place just days before. Also fresh in his memory was a terrible experience in Silicon Valley, when, during the high-tech bubble eight years ago created by so-called smart techies, Guy lost lots of money in a real estate deal. Since then he had a mental block for anything "computer." He thought it was all fun and games, but now any thought of fun and games was gone. "Mountain View. I was in Mountain View, the land of high-tech idiots. Where in Mountain View?"

"The Hilton Garden Inn."

Guy hit the wall with his fist. "Don't tell me." He shook his head vigorously. "Bastard. Jason did it. He didn't look that smart to me. How did he do it? Are you sure?"

"I'm sure it went to a computer in that hotel. Not sure exactly who."

"Go find out how he did it and plug that bloody hole," Guy screamed. He had always disliked and mistrusted computers in his business. He was an old-fashioned guy. Why had he let high-price consultants convince him a few years back to use those damn machines to modernize his operation?

When Lance was gone, Guy called Mario. After three rings he got a response. "Were you napping? Why didn't you answer me on the first ring?"

"What's up, boss?"

"Where is that Jason guy?"

"He's in the hotel room."

"Are you sure?" Guy shouted, unable to hide his desperation.

"Why? I saw him walk through the front door around six. He was walking back and forth in the room and peeking through the window with his binoculars, his shadow clear as day. We were laughing at that moron. He thinks we're idiots."

Guy didn't see any humor in Mario's response. "I don't think you'll be laughing at what I'm about to tell you. He stole all our files."

"No, no, boss, he's in his room. He couldn't steal files without us knowing." Guy heard the uncertainty and stress in the other man's voice.

"Shut up and listen to me. Listen carefully. Go to his room. Be very careful. Watch for hotel security and cameras. Surprise him with a quiet break-in. One of you grab him and pin him to the floor. Again, with very little noise. Then the other one needs to find the computer. Break his neck and leave the room with the computer." He was about to hang up when he added, "One more thing. Make it look like robbery. Be sure to turn the whole room upside down. Ransack the place. Empty all the drawers and suitcases onto the floor."

"You mean ice him?"

"Yes. He's too much trouble."

"OK."

"I'll be on the phone while you go up there. Keep it very clean. Do a professional job." He paced the room for several minutes when Lance appeared at the door again. Holding the rims of his spectacles, he adjusted his glasses on his nose and waited. Guy held the phone to his ear while blocking the receiver. With a nod he said, "What did you find?"

Swaying like a cypress tree on a windy day, Lance's words came out with difficulty. "During the file transfer, no one was monitoring the network."

"While the robbery was taking place no one was around? Where were you?"

"It was around 7:00 pm and I went out to get something to eat." He looked frightened, and very sorry.

Guy suddenly heard Mario's voice on the phone. "I'll talk to you later," he told Lance, then uncovered the receiver. "Mario, I'm listening."

"We went through the rear door, next to the garbage bins and kitchen. A while back I slipped a fifty-dollar note to get a set of keys." He laughed. "Now we're in the service elevator going up. I'm dressed like a food delivery boy holding a tray with plates and glasses of juice. Baba is wearing a janitorial outfit with a mop. I'll talk to you when I'm in the room."

"Ok, boys. Avoid contact with anyone on your way there." Usually, it was his men that did the stealing, not his target. Time was on his side, though, he hoped. Within half an hour of the break-in, he had already launched his attack dogs and would find the prized possession. As he caressed his chin, the seriousness of this theft hit him hard. What if his clients found out about the breach of security in his operation?

"Ah. Boss, are you there?"

"Yes. Where are you?"

"We're in. The guy isn't in the room, but a computer is on the desk."

"Did I hear you right? He's not there?"

"Ah-eh. Yes." Mario had lowered his voice.

"Damn. Where did he go? He must be in the hotel. Check the bathroom, under the bed and closet. Make sure he's not hiding."

"We checked. He's not in the room."

"You have to get out of there. Fast. Check if it's the right computer that has our files. It must be."

"I don't know anything about computers. Baba, do you?" There was a pause. "Boss, we never took computer classes. To us, it's like driving a plane."

"Just take the computer and get the hell out of there." Guy was puzzled at how fast Jason had disappeared without his boys knowing about it. "Don't do anything else. You should be leaving now."

"Wait! Baba is saying something. Oh. The computer is on and he can't find the switch."

"Hell with the switch. Just pull the plug and run. Don't lose the computer; it has the files. I'll send someone to pick it up from you. Also, keep an eye on Jason. He must be in the hotel somewhere."

After hanging up the phone line, he dispatched a party of twenty men, all like Mario and Baba, to hunt down Jason. He commanded them to converge on Mountain View, book the hotel as guests and comb the place until the target was located. The message he'd given to the troops was clear. Killing Jason was the main objective.

16

Jason McDeere stood by the phone booth and quickly surveyed the dimly lit, sparsely populated, San Jose street. So far there had been no one following him. Nothing. After ordering a cab and giving the company an address just two blocks away, he ran like a guided missile through the side streets, between buildings, and stopped where the cab was waiting. He slipped into the back seat. "Greyhound Bus Station," he said to the driver. "Hurry, I have only ten minutes."

"Take it easy, pal. It's only seven blocks away. You'll be there in ten."

Jason slid down the seat in such a position that his knees were sticking up above his belly and his eyes were high enough to survey the vehicles on the road.

Time and again the driver gawked at him through the rear view mirror, frowning at his odd behavior. The cabbie watched him for a few minutes more until it seemed he could wait to satisfy his curiosity no longer. "Who are you running from?" he said with a swift turn of his head toward the back seat and then to the road again.

"No one. Stomach flu." Jason was pleased with the smart remark. Upon hearing the explanation, the driver gunned the car. Jason could tell the driver wasn't satisfied with the explanation but he dared ask no more, in case it would interfere with the amount of the tip he would receive.

After seven minutes of speedy travel, the cab stopped at the terminal. Jason slipped several ten-dollar bills to the driver, which included the fare and a generous tip. Then he darted towards the ticket counter without offering a word of gratitude. The tip would have to do.

It was 9:31 am, according to the wall clock of the sparsely occupied waiting room. He purchased a ticket to Bakersfield. Then the clerk pointed her eyes toward the row of buses. "Gate 55," she said. "Leaving in one minute."

He raced to the bus, where the driver took his ticket, slammed the door of the luggage compartment and followed him into the bus. Seniors occupied the first three rows. About two dozen were scattered all over, mainly in the second half. He absorbed the details of every face as he walked past, but recognized none of them. He checked outside for any passenger rushing to catch the bus that was already in motion. Then he planted himself by a window seat in the fifth row. He lowered the front of his cap to help cover his face, then slipped on a pair of sunglasses. With a slow turn of his head toward the back, he gazed at every face again. No one he recognized. Wrong bus. Dammit! Where was Shallen? He stared out the window into the dark night as the driver navigated the bus to make a left turn on W. San Fernando Street.

When the bus picked up speed, a woman with a hat and a bright red scarf around her neck, almost hiding her face, appeared and slid into the seat next to Jason. Shallen. He breathed a sigh of relieve. Avoiding direct visual contact with her, he spoke in a voice low enough that she could hear and no one else. "Where were you?"

"In the restroom."

"When I didn't see you, I almost got off the bus."

"A man and a woman have been following me from the airport." Shallen adjusted the collar of her white raincoat as she watched the aisle.

"Following you?" He turned his head toward the window, concerned about who might be following her. "Do they know you're on this bus? One can never be too careful." Jason pressed his chin with his fingers.

"When I left the airport I think they were right behind me. I gave a cash incentive to the taxi driver to do a few u-turns at strategic locations. It was so dangerous and scary. By the time I reached the station . . . I'm not sure what happened to them." She shook her head, her face turning pale. "I'm not sure how far behind they were. Once I hopped on the bus, I went directly to the restroom."

When he turned to her, the fear on her face intensified. He recalled the brightness with which she'd greeted him in the restaurant when they first met. That person had completely disappeared. "At least you shouldn't have had to give the driver a bribe." Not with her looks.

Shallen cracked a broad smile. She pulled the hat lower on her forehead. Both of them watched as a woman approached, wobbling her way towards them. With every step she grabbed the back of each seat, rubbing Shallen's shoulder as she passed her. When she was gone, Jason conducted another passenger survey. No one was close. No one could hear.

"Why are we here?"

"I was in Corvallis last week. A challenging time, to say the least. During the first two days my investigation was going nowhere. I was facing a wall of silence--"

"Rocky. Did he help?"

"He was like a scared puppy. I've never experienced such a negative reaction to my inquiries. No one wanted to talk to me, including Rocky. I was counting on him. He made me angry, but his position makes sense now. Softek employees were forbidden to talk to reporters. He kept running away from me every time I tried to interview him. The next morning I waited for him in the car parked in his driveway, but he wanted nothing to do with me. Now I'm certain there was a conspiracy. Employees at Softek are covering for the Senator's sins." With her head down she fingered the handle of her handbag.

Jason paused to digest Shallen's words. "This conspiracy theory isn't new. But Rocky's lack of cooperation is disappointing. Did you tell him we were in danger?"

"I told him about your situation. He asked about you, but it didn't make a difference – not enough to help me in any way. So far there are facts here and there to suggest *something*. But there's nothing concrete that a newspaper or authority would deem actionable. We need witnesses, paper trails, and clear evidence of fraud."

She was talking like a reporter. Her skin regained some of its color and vigor. "Here we are traveling incognito, taking a bus trip to nowhere, running scared with no serious plan to nail this politician." The driver was negotiating a lane change so he could take the exit onto US-101 south towards Los Angeles.

At the sound of a swirling toilet, powerful enough to reach their ears, Jason turned. Out of the corner of his eyes, he tracked the woman as she made her way to her seat. He watched her back slowly recede until she slipped into the seat with the help of both hands.

"You've gathered some key information. I have too. Let's put it all together and maybe we'll have enough to give us a solid case."

She was definitely motivated. Why? *Her life isn't in any real danger. Or is it?* Pulitzer Prize perhaps? "Where should I start? I broke into Layton's database—"

"What did you find?" Shallen said.

Her voice was loud enough that it made him turn to survey the eyes behind him in case anyone was listening to their conversation. It was dark except for a few reading lamps that hung from the ceiling. In the seat across the aisle, the passenger had earphones plugged into his ears and the young man behind had his face buried in a book. The bus was in the left lane, zipping past drivers obeying the speed limit. When Jason turned his attention back to Shallen, the eagerness in her eyes matched by her broad smile made him think about his response.

Sidestepping her question, he said, "In the process I crashed the computer system. I managed to get away with a slap on the hand. Could have been a lot worse." Just then, the darkness outside gave way to headlights of vehicles in the right lane.

"Did you learn anything useful?" Shallen said, persisting in her quest for more details.

"I have millions of accounts payable transactions for the last few years. I wrote a program to summarize the data by vendors. Then I researched every vendor, found their addresses and the nature of their businesses. I found many well-known companies like HP, IBM, Microsoft. Also there were many contractors in the military like Raytheon and Boeing."

"That's very interesting." Shallen paid attention to every word, making only occasional eye contact.

"Everything checked out, except one company. This one was the most difficult. Lots of money flowed out to this enterprise. It wasn't a company registered or known in America. Guess what?" She shook her head, waiting. "Its address was in Dubai."

"What's the name?"

"Khalid Enterprise."

She leaned forward so that she could face him directly. "Jason, did you say Khalid?"

He nodded in slow motion. He paused to reflect on her reaction. "Yes. They paid millions for some missile simulation equipment. Why?"

"Hot damn." She scanned the area as though restraining herself from bursting with joy. Her voice carried just above the rumble of the engine. "Khalid Groceries have been making contributions to Quest's campaign fund here in the US."

"Are you sure? This could be the connection we've been searching for." He held his hands together tightly.

"Absolutely."

"Do you have all the records?"

"Yes."

Jason felt the need to get up and pace, but he turned to her instead. "What did you find in Corvallis?"

"I met Jerry Whitney. I almost killed the guy when he jumped into the car as I was pulling out of the hotel parking lot, leaving empty-handed. After a very brief meeting, he made my trip worthwhile. He had been following events at Softek after the massacre. He saw something incredible. Gamble and Quest had a secret meeting in a park in Salem." She was beaming.

Jason's eyebrows shot up as he searched for some kind of understanding. "Jerry Whitney?"

"Yes. Clint Whitney's son."

"Shallen, I know who he is. Why would he help you? He would be on the wrong side of the fence, don't you think?"

"Jason, he's on our side. I'm positive. Obviously, he's upset about the death of his father. The way he explained it to me, he's more troubled by the way Softek has treated his mother. The killing could have been prevented. Apparently, Clint was against outsourcing."

He paused, considering what she had said. The same lady left her seat and wobbled towards the restroom again. After she passed them by, he said, "He can help us, but can we trust him? Right now I can't rely on anybody."

"That's a good point. One has to be careful. But Jerry isn't a Softek employee. Therefore, he's an outsider. He works for the city and knows many employees and ex-employees. He's not afraid of losing his job. He sounds sincere, like someone who wants some closure for his father, his mother and the people of Corvallis."

A long silence engulfed them as each lapsed into their own thoughts. Abruptly, he turned to Shallen and said, "Now, more than ever, I'm convinced there is a paper trail from Softek to Khalid to Quest. We have a good case to print this story. I can see the *Post* headline: Senator Quest Involved in Bribery and Money Laundering."

She pressed her lips together and adjusted her hat. She shook her head. "It wouldn't be the *Post*, that's for sure."

For the first time since they'd met, Jason thought he detected a sadness overshadowing her earlier excitement. "Why not? Are you writing a book instead of an article?"

She blinked, as if trying to hide her deeper feelings. "I got fired," said Shallen. "Not exactly. I was forced to quit."

Jason hit the window with his hand. "We're getting in deeper by the hour.

Very bizarre. Dammit. Why?"

"When I returned to the office after my trip to Corvallis I presented a report, including everything I just told you, to the editor-in-chief, John Mead. He called Senator Quest to inform him of my findings."

Jason shook his head, confused. "A newspaper in bed with a politician. How corrupt is the society we live in?" He threw his head back. "I need some fresh air." He adjusted the air vent. "Any idea why he would do that?"

"Politicians and media need each other. They scratch each other's back when it's convenient. John must need something from the Senator. I don't know what." She sounded upset but straight forward.

"It looks like they want you out of the way."

"John told me in no uncertain terms that if I didn't follow his orders, I would be fired. Getting fired at this stage of my career is suicide. Word gets around in the media circle. The only choice was to quit. I was very angry so I left the office for good."

He thought hard about this strange turn of events. "Now two of us are in deep shit."

"To put it mildly."

His cell phone buzzed. It was a text message from Indira. Probably some work related problem. It read: "Go into hiding. You are in danger. They're looking for you."

The air seemed to thicken around him. He wiped his forehead, moisture dotting his brow. After showing the message to Shallen, he said, "Who could be after me – Volpa and his gang, or the FBI?"

"Who?" Shallen blinked rapidly, as though trying to catch her equilibrium after reading the message.

"I stole files from a website called VolpaPI.com. It's the company that was doing the surveillance on behalf of the Senator. By now they must have found out. Or the FBI. My friend Terrance is in custody and being questioned by the Feds."

"Where are the files?"

"In this laptop." Jason waved his hand towards a case lying on the floor. "Indira's message does one important thing for me. It connects two more points. Guy Volpa and Layton are working together. The circle of corruption is complete. Money flowing to Quest from Layton and Softek through Khalid."

The driver braked the bus for slow-moving traffic ahead. Some people craned their necks to catch the flashing lights of what looked like police cars and emergency vehicles. Others were asleep, lulled by the motion of the Greyhound. Once past the accident scene the bus picked up speed heading south on I-5 towards Los Angeles.

After ten minutes Jason broke the silence. "What next?"

"I have nowhere to go and you have to go underground."

"Shallen, you don't need to go through with this. Just return to Washington and find another job. This could be dangerous."

"They're after me too." She told him about the mail, the warning and everything that had happened since.

"They're following you, hoping it will lead to me. They want to get me."

"I want to be part of it till the end. Otherwise, it will linger in my conscience till I reach my grave."

He tilted his head closer to her. "Conscience?"

"Yes," she whispered. "Before the massacre, Brian left a voice message warning that the layoff and outsourcing at Softek could lead to a tragic situation. It was just after Thanksgiving and my schedule was loaded with commitments. I meant to follow up as soon as time permitted. Unfortunately it was too late." Shallen turned her head away from him as if fighting an onslaught of guilt.

Jason squeezed her hand. "I felt the same, following the tragedy. Day and night I agonized whether I could have saved Brian. Finally I realized I couldn't shoulder all the blame. The load was too heavy to carry. There were many others factors that contributed to the tragic outcome."

"I know. Of course most of the blame is Quest's and Softek's. It's clear that the Senator's political life and Softek's financial goals came before ordinary people's livelihoods. It's unacceptable." She said the last word with sadness, her eyes filling with tears.

"If we knew we could have prevented World War II from happening, would we have done something different?" Jason asked, rubbing her shoulder. "If we can take any consolation, most of the time we don't have that kind of foresight. We have to deal with situations as they happen. If I hadn't gone to the Senator, I wouldn't be running for my life."

"My conscience is my guide," she agreed, a tear falling.

"It's the sum total of our past experience and knowledge, which drive us on a path. Hopefully, a good path." Jason ran a finger along her cheek, brushing away the tear. "Brian has brought us together, and if he is listening, he will get us out of this mess."

"Jason, I've come this far. I need to see the end of the story." She turned towards him and for a long minute they were absorbed in each other's eyes.

Jason rubbed his thumb gently across her lips. "Shallen, why are we going to Bakersfield, California?"

She cracked a faint smile, which became wider. "I don't know. It was your idea."

At 1:34 in the morning, the bus pulled in at Bakersfield Greyhound station located on 18th Street. They traveled to LA on the next available coach.

***

At the Wyndham San Jose Airport hotel Guy Volpa looked around the table at his four top lieutenants. The command post had called this urgent meeting to snap orders to locate Jason McDeere. One of these high-ranking assistants was Guy's twin, Henry, a perfect replica except for a thick mustache. All were fifty and over in age; all were chosen for their expertise in fugitive apprehension. All had worked for FBI, CIA or some large city police force. This assembly was Guy Volpa's A-team.

The briefing started with him pounding the veneered desktop to let off some steam. Once everyone had secured a seat, Guy scanned the faces and said, "Jason must have my files. I am assuming he does. Why wouldn't he? The computer we found in his hotel room had all our files in it. We confirmed that. But no one could assure me that copies were not made. You understand what I mean." All listened attentively and nodded as Guy pounded a fist with each word he spoke.

Henry asked, "Do we know where he is?"

Guy pulled his body forward, both hands spread in front of him as he reflected on the answer he was about to give. "Yes. Ah. Maybe. A more important question is why we lost the reporter."

All four people directed their attention to the man on Guy's left, whose face turned pink. "She must have noticed us somehow. We were very careful. We followed her for quite a while. Then suddenly the crazy taxi driver started driving like a maniac. Making turns everywhere. He could have killed someone. Too bad the cops weren't around. He could have been nailed for dangerous driving."

Guy snapped. "Stop the bull. You lost her. She was going to lead us directly to him. To Jason."

All nodded, except one.

Guy placed the full weight of his six-foot frame on the balls of his feet, unable to hide his anxiety and impatience. "I'm waiting for some phone calls. Sooner or later they – if they're together – will use their credit cards or cell phones." He paced the room as four pairs of eyes tracked his movements. "I know the reporter withdrew money at a machine at Dulles Airport. That will be enough to locate them and nail these bastards. Also I have filed a charge against Jason McDeere for hacking and stealing. So California police will be on the lookout for him." He clapped his hands, hoping to receive any help he could muster.

Another dared to speak. "How did he steal the files?"

Guy fumed. What a stupid question. "I don't understand all the details. I just know he went into my office and stole all the folders, pictures, notes, videos, contracts, everything without leaving a fingerprint behind, no DNA, no forced entry. Nothing. It all happened when I was in the office. Unbelievable." He scrutinized every eye as he spoke, making sure that everyone was fully aware of the problem.

His brother asked, "What's the damage?"

"What's the damage?" Guy plunged in the chair and pounded the table. "Enormous. That's the confidential information of all my clients, including senators, governors, lawyers, doctors. Very serious. It's life or death for me. You guys have to help me. I need to know whether he has them or not. Understand?" All nodded in agreement.

One of the men asked, "Have you notified any of your clients?"

"I've informed one." Guy grimaced. "Roger Hunt, the campaign manager and consultant of Senator Quest. All he did after I told him of the incident was to spit fire at me like a ten-headed dragon."

The phone rang. Senator Quest was at the other end. Guy didn't say much but he furrowed his brow and listened to the Senator's ranting, as the man called him names. Finally, he put a stop to the insults. "Senator, things are under control. I have my best four men here. We're going over my plan to nab this criminal." The four men's smiles beamed across the room, showing pride in his leadership. One of the men got up, stretched his arms toward the ceiling and rotated his hips back and forth. Then he jabbed the air, revealing his impatience.

"Even the Feds have failed me," said the Senator in a voice loud enough to make Guy momentarily remove the phone from his ear. "A major screw up. They didn't get Jason. Only his partner in crime. His co-conspirator. What is his name? Terrance. I wanted both of them in police custody."

Guy took a deep breath, puffing up his chest. "Senator, the Feds screw up all the time."

"You screwed it up," the Senator spat. "He hacked into *your* computer." Guy's cockiness disappeared, as he switched to a defensive mode. "We have good control of the situation. He'll make a mistake. I guarantee it. I've seen this too many times. Once he does then he'll pay. With his life."

"I talked to the Director again," Volpa said, hoping to appease the Senator. "The Feds are tracking him. They have more surveillance power. I love the Patriot Act. It's a great tool. When I was with the FBI, we yearned for it. Now it's finally here—"

The Senator cut him off. "Some crucial information will come your way from the Feds. They're tracking credit card transactions, and any phone calls." The Senator seemed to have ignored Volpa's political comments. "You have to get this guy. Otherwise he could do some serious damage." The Senator's emphasis on the risk was unmistakably clear: They either found Jason, or his career was over.

***

Shortly after ten in the morning, Jason McDeere eased alongside Shallen in the line in front of the registration desk. As they slowly moved forward, Jason's eyes darted from the clerk to the front door and back. When it came their turn, Jason said, "We're looking for a room."

After a few pecks on the keyboard, the clerk monitored the computer screen and nodded slowly. "Yes. We have one." Once they were registered as Jason and Jennifer Smith, and had paid cash, they received the door card for room 322. They rushed to the elevator but slowed their pace when they saw the clerk's strange look. Jason ushered Shallen into the elevator, then stepped in beside her. As the door was closing, he could see the clerk watching them, her head cocked, as though puzzled by the cash transaction and search for a room so early in the morning.

Once inside the room, with no time to waste, Jason unloaded the laptop from the case onto a small table. When the power and the Internet wires were hooked up, he fired up the computer. While Windows was coming alive, he watched Shallen place her suitcase on the bed and search for something.

"I could use a strong, hot cup of coffee, right now," he said. "How about you?"

"Me too," Shallen said. For a long moment they gazed at each other. Then they shook their heads in tandem. "No. Too risky to go out."

Following a few keystrokes Windows Explorer readied itself to receive his commands. Browsing the folders where Volpa's files were copied onto his hard drive, he examined a long list of neatly organized names in different business categories. They were eavesdropping, countermeasures, child custody, photographs, courtroom evidence, voice-stress analysis, location of assets, insurance claims, premarital background review and clients. Before entering the client folder, he said, "I hope to find what I'm looking for." Then his eyes popped open as names of politicians and other high profile names spread into a long list. He shouted, "Yahoo!" He turned to Shallen who held a pen between her lips and a notepad in one hand.

Following a few more pecks at the keyboard, his attention went to the Quest folder. From this list he saw many names that he didn't recognize and then some that drew immediate interest such as QUEST, GAMBLE, MCDOWELL, COHEN and MCDEERE. He turned to Shallen for advice. "Shallen, there are so many files and to hear each would take a long time. What should we examine first?"

Shallen moved to the desk and together they peered at the list. "I recognize many of the names. I see senators' names, congressmen, businessmen and White House staff. He bugged everyone associated with Quest. Let's go into QUEST." She watched Jason make another selection. "Ok. Choose office." Shallen returned to writing.

The filing was well organized, each starting with a date followed by a name. He concluded that they were recordings of conversations at the Senator's office. He first listened to the ones with Svenborg, the secretary, which provided no relevant information. Next, he listened to the conversation between Senator Quest, Khalid and Hunt. What he heard sent a bolt of excitement flashing through him.

"I found something interesting. The recording between the Senator, Khalid and Hunt." They moved closer to the laptop speaker and listened. When the recording reached the end both jumped with joy, holding hands. "Who's Hunt?" asked Jason.

"Hunt. I've heard the name from Jerry," Shallen said, squinting as though scrolling through her memory banks. "Ahh. That's right. He's the political consultant for Quest's campaign. We have enough evidence to show that Quest, Hunt and Khalid were involved in a bribery scheme and money laundering. When the FBI is on this case they will add a dozen more charges."

Shallen got up and pressed her temple. With her face toward the ceiling she said, "But we're running from someone. Who?" Jason shrugged. "It could be the FBI, Volpa or the Senator. I think we could be in serious trouble. You've hacked a website. The government frowns upon that. And you have stolen material in your possession. Being here with you makes me an accomplice. Hacking is illegal."

Jason snapped his head to the left to take in Shallen's facial expression. It had turned a dull white, indicating fear. He didn't like what he'd just heard. "Terrance always said 'It's legal as long as you aren't caught doing it'." He laughed, but immediately regretted it when he saw that she stood motionless. *She can't quit on me now.* He sprang to his feet, lifted her face slightly with his hand and looked into her eyes. She was in a daze as if unaffected by his presence. "I need you. Really need you. You can write an article that we can take to the *LA Times*." She still didn't move. *Not now.* He held her arm and gave her a shake. "Wake up." He examined her frozen face again and rubbed his finger along her cheek. Then he held both of her hands. "Your hands are cold." He pressed her shoulder down until she was seated on the chair next to him.

He raided the fridge, drawers and cupboards to find instant coffee, creamer, sugar, and cookies. As he busied himself making a hot drink, his mind fought the fear of losing her.

She gripped the mug with her fingers and gulped a few mouthfuls. After eating half of a cookie, the food resuscitated her. "This is unbelievable. I never thought this would happen to me. It reminds me of what investigative journalists do, like Lisa Ward, my mentor." She took another sip. "She told me about tough choices investigative journalists often make. Like what I'm facing – risking my family's lives." She paused, tears forming, as if she were trying to reach a solid mental and emotional footing. "I wish I could talk to Lisa now."

A long silence ensued. Jason reached over and squeezed her hand. "It's going to be okay," he said, but he knew he was only offering a band-aid. He stood, paced back and force, then took a peek at the streets. "Shallen, this is too risky. We can't use our cell phones." He waved his phone in the air. "If we use this, whoever is following us can easily pinpoint our location. We could go out of this room and look for a phone, but what if someone is waiting for us in the lobby or street? We've been here for two hours. I expect someone to come busting through here any minute." He pointed at the door.

"You're right. Both are too risky." With a tight grip she held the cup close to her chest.

Once again he paced back and forth and looked out the window. He continued this routine for several minutes. Mentally he listed all the options. "I have no experience being a fugitive except for hiding from my friends when I was a teen." He turned to her. "Do you?" She shook her head. "And we can't run forever. They'll find us sooner or later. Damnit!" He hit the air with his fist.

"What if we turn everything in to the police?" Shallen said.

"We've connected all the dots. We have a complete picture now." He counted all the names they'd collected on his fingers. "Senator Quest, Softek, Layton and Volpa. If we turn ourselves in, and if the FBI and the police are in the Senator's pocket, then the Senator gets away with a much higher crime. But if not, our crime doesn't look that bad compared to his. His is huge." All along he was studying any change in her mood.

The tension in her face eased, but only slightly. "You cracked the website without any malicious intent. You were only defending yourself," Shallen said.

"They have been snooping and sniffing in my life since December. They started the surveillance, stole my privacy, prevented me from seeing my family. What about Brian and the others who died needlessly? What about those who have been laid off and are out of work? Yes, I did hack into their computers. I agree. But I didn't do any damage. And it's a small crime compared to the one the Senator has committed."

"Ok, prosecutor, you've made your case. What next?" She took a deep breath and hooked her hair around her ear.

He was trying hard not to quit. "Going to the police would be too easy. The big criminal could get away."

"How about I write an article, telling the whole story about outsourcing, bribery, etc," she said. "Then we go to the *LA Times*. Hopefully, they will publish it."

He looked at her for a long moment. "Well, partner, what are we waiting for?"

They traded places. She moved to the laptop, tapping on the keys as he stretched his tired body on the bed filled with a suitcase and other things. Facing the ceiling, with his arm covering his eyes, he forced himself to sleep—but only for a few minutes. He managed a little shuteye only to awaken with the horrible image of police storming through his door. He changed his position and watched Shallen's furious typing. The thought of having this attractive woman writing an article, while he was resting in a hotel room in LA, seemed all too surreal. *How life takes strange twists and turns?*

Shallen continued typing, her eyes fixed on the screen. "Are you watching me?"

Jason replied, "How can you tell?"

"We women have a sixth sense," she said with a smile.

Just then, there was a noise in the hall. He jumped up and ran to the door. With an ear pressed against the wood, he listened. It was the maids socializing in the hallway. Returning to the bed, he said, "Don't mention how we got the files."

"No, of course not. But the *LA Times* will want to know every detail. They will want the whole picture. Before accepting it, they would have to examine the legitimacy of the story. We have to be prepared for a lot of questioning."

After two hours of writing, and another hour of editing, the script was ready to be submitted to the newspaper. "Let's go down to make a phone call." He closed the laptop and started packing it into the case.

With a puzzled look she said, "Jason, why are you taking the laptop with you?"

"We're taking all our possessions with us. We can't leave anything behind, even if we're planning to return."

She shook her head. "I don't understand. We don't want to lug our stuff down and back here again."

"Yes we do. If Volpa's thugs are after us and watching our every move, they could enter the room as soon as we leave. We could come in and find them inside. They could ambush and kill us. I've lived with them for many weeks. They're not as smart as they think they are. We take our stuff. If we suspect they're inside the room, we run."

***

Guy Volpa gathered his team of lieutenants at the Wyndham San Jose Airport hotel again. After everyone was seated around the table he scanned the faces. Each of the men still wore a bleak expression, but slightly less than in the morning. An hour earlier he received the general location of Jason and Shallen.

He turned to his twin brother, Henry. "Are we close to nabbing those bastards?" He spread his hands on the shiny table.

"They're not in our possession . . . yet," said his brother. He shook his head but showed growing confidence. "We're getting closer. We found the location of the hotel where they've been since this morning."

All eyes turned towards Guy. "We've dispatched our men." He looked at his watch. "An hour ago. Give me more details," he said in a low but firm voice. He felt the exhaustion throughout his entire body and a pounding headache that hadn't stopped for days. This was no time to think about his physical pain. He was hoping to receive some information that would lift his spirit.

"Only a few minutes ago I received a call from head guy. They should be there within the next twenty minutes," said Henry.

"Ten of our men--in two vans--are headed to that spot. Upon their arrival, they'll surround the building and man each of the exits. They will make sure the suspects don't leave the place unnoticed. Then two of our guys will go into the hotel to locate the room they booked," said one lieutenant. "After that, we will get a call. At that point we'll decide our next move."

Guy's impatience was growing along with his tension. "Anyone dare to estimate?"

A silence yawned throughout the room.

As always, his twin was the brave one. "Within an hour they should be in our possession. Then what do we do?" he inquired.

Guy Volpa paused to calculate a response. Quickly, he ran all the options in his mind. He realized any decision was crucial. A mistake would mean sure disaster. His assistants exuded confidence, deservedly so, in Guy's mind. Volpa knew the chances of finding Jason and Shallen and nabbing them, from his own experience of tracking suspects most of his life. This one appeared to be a done deal, if no one made a stupid mistake. He ignored his twin's question for now. "We can't afford any screw-up. They left Bakersfield without our notice. How did that happened?" He pounded the table again.

Everyone stared at each other in silence. Henry dared to move. "This time we know exactly where they are. By the help of their cell phone the Feds were able to track them down and will continue to do so."

What to do with the warm bodies?

He got up and paced the room while others waited for an answer. He turned to the group. "Before making such a decision about what to do with them, I have to talk to the Senator." He grimaced. He grabbed his ponytail with his hand and slid his fingers through his hair. "We could ice them. But we have to be careful how we do it."

***

From behind the registration desk of King's Hotel, Melody Frost tracked the unusual behavior of the two men. In the small lobby with a few old sofas, chairs, tables, the two men stood at one corner and appeared to be scanning the room, studying every face for several minutes. Also they paid close attention to anyone who entered or left the front door and the elevator. Then they disappeared toward the bar and restaurant, returning to the lobby after a few minutes. These two immediately caught Melody's attention. She knew most of the regular patrons who worked in the neighborhood. Kings was built by an LA entrepreneur in 1932, just in time for the city to host the Summer Olympics. This sixty-room hotel—too small to become part of a national chain—housed in a three-story building for low-income workers of this financial district, had a family atmosphere. It was a home away from home. The wealthy went to the prestigious Millennium Baltimore Hotel, just a few blocks away on S. Olive Street. In LA anything was possible – poor and rich could occupy the same neighborhood.

The two joined the registration line. Their eyes were wide, and like a surveillance camera, their heads constantly moved back and forth. Their demeanors suggested impatience. They wore odd clothing that looked as if it had been slapped together in a hurry. One had on a crooked green tie hanging off a blue shirt under a corduroy jacket, and a pair of jeans with running shoes. The other one looked just as odd. He was wearing sunglasses indoors, and an oversized coat.

The older said, "My friend and I –" he swung his hand toward the other man – "ahh, we came to the convention and we're looking for an old friend." He gave a fake, nervous smile. "His name is Jason McDeere. Does he happen to be staying at your hotel?"

Melody was certain there were no conventions that week. After pecking at the keyboard, she replied, "No McDeere." She examined their reactions.

The younger one said, "We're also looking for another person." He showed her a picture.

"What's the name?"

He hesitated. "I think it's Johnson."

Melody knew it was a lie, that she had caught him off guard. She searched for Johnson. "No." She shook her head.

"Have you seen this person?"

She had seen him with a woman in the morning. They were in the hotel. She stared at the two men for a good while, searching for an appropriate response. She placed her finger on her lips. "Ahh…I believe I have."

"Can I have his room number?"

She nodded. "Can't. Against management policy," she lied.

"Miss, we would appreciate your help very much." He placed a hundred dollar bill on the counter.

She looked at it, calculating how much the information was worth to them. "I can get into trouble. You know that."

He dropped another hundred dollar bill on the desk. "Hope this will make it worth your while," he said with an intense look at her.

After surveying the area to ensure no one was watching, she said, "Room 322." She grabbed the money.

The pair dashed off toward the door to the stairs.

17

The secretary led the way through the hallway, followed by Jason McDeere who placed his hand on Shallen Xu's back for moral support. They went past the sprawling newsroom with desks, computers, phones and long aisles, until they reached the conference room where they expected to be greeted by *LA Times* officials.

Half an hour earlier, Jason and Shallen left the King's hotel room, took the stairs to the first floor not too far from the lobby, where they found a telephone. Shallen made the call to the *LA Times* and Jason, a foot away from her, examined every face looking for anyone suspicious. After five minutes, she hung up and appeared beaming. They headed towards the *LA Times* head office, at 202 West 1st Street, only five blocks away from the hotel where they were staying.

The secretary stopped at the door, ushered both inside with her hand, pointed to a woman then disappeared after saying, "Stefanie Pastore, our executive editor."

Following a handshake, Shallen said, "Shallen Xu." Then she turned to Jason with a relieved smile, making it clear she was glad to have him here. "Jason McDeere."

Pastore pointed at the man and woman standing next to her. "This is Roger White, managing editor, and Susan Delaney, legal."

They huddled at one end of the large table in the center of a posh room. The walls were decorated with pictures of veteran reporters of the organization, and large windows faced the street. The place was brightly lit with fluorescent lights that hung from the ceiling. As Jason fished for wires and plugs to plug in his tape recorder, the conversation began in earnest. Shallen was tired and nervous, but her smile and enthusiasm didn't reveal the trauma of the last twenty-four hours. Jason was running on raw, nervous energy. The fight for survival. This was his last chance to fight back at the evil forces.

Jason absorbed the reaction of everyone in the room. Pastore was eager, like a fisherman thrilled by a tug at the end of the line; however, she couldn't be too euphoric until she saw the size of the catch. She listened carefully to what Shallen was saying. White nodded constantly, often checking his boss' reaction. Susan, a lawyer in her late thirties, was carefully studying every word being spoken in an emotionless way, her expression blank.

At this session, Jason had a selection of audio files and he started playing the one with Quest, Hunt and Khalid in the Senator's office, which everyone wanted to hear first, the volume on high. Pastore, White and Delaney huddled together, shoulder to shoulder, ears tuned to the speaker, the sound weak. Twenty minutes later, they pushed their chairs away from the table. The air was somber after what they had heard, but White, a young reporter in his thirties couldn't hide his excitement at the fresh national scandal. Jason knew it was a reporter's dream.

Pastore, fingertips steepled and eyes pointed to the floor, paused for a minute with lips pressed tight. The others seemed to be awaiting her reaction. "This is another blow to US politics," she said. "Another month, another scandal. Last month it was a governor caught selling a senate seat when he had a chance to nominate a vacancy." She paused again while Jason and the others gave her their full attention. No one moved. "It saddens me to think how far in the mud politics have gone. Fortunately, it's our job to bring this wrong practice to the public's attention. If we don't, society will suffer. From what I've heard so far, there's only an *appearance* of scandal. We need more substance. What else do you have?"

Jason knew that media people were natural born skeptics and they needed to be convinced. He paused for a moment to scan their faces. "There are hundreds of files and we won't have time to cover all of them. There are some, like the one with the Senator and CEO of Softek negotiating a deal. In it the CEO is asked to outsource jobs to India in return for huge campaign contributions. *Huge* sums. I mean *tens of millions*. Solid evidence!"

"Softek is a Defense Department contractor," Shallen said, "that gets its business from the government, but the Senator was able to convince management to ship these jobs overseas, lay off hundreds of Americans, and pocket the money."

Pastore said, "OK. Let's hear it." After another eighteen minutes the conversation was over. "Susan, what's your thought?"

"How did you get these surveillance recordings?"

How to explain this to a lawyer? Jason paused to examine the faces around the table as the LA Times team eagerly awaited his answer. "The Senator contracted Volpa Private Investigation to start surveillance on me. They wiretapped my house, cell phone and computer. The spyware dropped on my laptop was recording every email I received or sent, MSN messaging, chat, or web browsing. I used the same spyware to go into

Volpa's website to find out where information about me was going."

"Wouldn't that be considered hacking?" Pastore asked the lawyer.

Jason shook his head. "Technically not. I didn't crack the code of a password or user account, or damage anything. Having the spyware was like having the key to a warehouse where every moment of my life was being recorded." The three from the *LA Times* shot a look at each other. An audible sigh circled the room. How well everyone received the explanation was hard to tell.

Shallen cracked a smile that grew broader, accompanied with tenderness that she directed toward Jason, which he reciprocated. "The point is not how the files were received. Rather the focus is on the Senator's unethical and illegal behavior."

Pastore got up and started pacing the room. "We still have to do due diligence."

Jason said, "I understand." Susan made notes but said nothing more.

Shallen hooked her hair around her ear again, a sign that she was under tremendous pressure. "I was on this case for months but information surrounding this scandal was guarded like a fortress. Jason is right. It was the only way. In the article that I've written, I cover many aspects of this scandal: outsourcing, campaign funding, bribery and money laundering. Khalid had a rather unique way of converting dirty money into legitimate campaign funds. All was well orchestrated, planned and executed at the Senator's office. *With his knowledge.* He knew everything that was going on."

Pastore jumped in. "Unique way. How so?"

"The payback from Softek to the Senator worked this way: The company would give Khalid, the middleman, millions to his company in Dubai. Then Khalid would bring the money to the US and put it into his own account. Khalid runs hundreds of stores across the country. Next the money is passed through the stores' accounts and then it goes to the Senator's campaign funds below the IRS radar."

"Layton Industries, where the Senator found me a job, also sends millions to Khalid. I found that out from the company database," Jason said.

Pastore pointed to the LA Times staff. "Let's read the article. We may want to hear more of the tapes. I'll talk to our own Washington sources. In two hours we'll reconvene here."

Jason made copies of the article and passed them out to Pastore, White and Delaney. Shallen and Jason were alone in the conference room for about ten minutes when trays of sandwiches, cookies and coffee arrived. Tuna, egg salad and assorted fruit had never smelled so inviting. Hungry, despite all the stress, they both attacked the food.

Jason bit down on a sandwich and sipped coffee as he watched the busy intersection of West 1st and North Spring where the light managed the heavy traffic flow and pedestrians. He continued to survey the area for the next ten minutes with special attention paid to the two men facing the LA Times building from across the street. One was holding a Styrofoam cup, taking occasional sips. But his eyes were glued to the entrance of the building. "Shallen, come here." Jason pointed towards the traffic light pole and got close enough for their shoulders to touch. "See those two guys? They've been there for a while watching this building. One stands by the pole. The other one walks back and forth between the pole and the tree."

Shallen held a half-eaten sandwich. "Who are they?"

"They look like Volpa's men. From this angle I can't see their faces." For the next hour, they watched. Finally the men disappeared.

Pastore, White and Delaney returned on time. Everyone sat down except Pastore. She paced the room. "I checked with our reporter and other contacts in Washington. My investigation points to a credible story. I say run it."

Pastore stared at White who said, "The article is well written. Run it."

Susan Delany crossed her arms. "We've heard these people talk about breaking a law, but we don't have any evidence. Do we have paper trails? Any concrete proof?"

Pastore said, "The money laundering scheme is very clever. Never heard of such a thing. What proof can you give us?"

"Plenty. Jerry Whitney, whose father was killed at Softek, promised to give us anything we need."

Jason's phone rang and he excused himself as he took the call. It was Kara at the other end. He wanted to cut the call short and call her back after the meeting, but her screaming and crying stopped him cold. "Kara, I can't understand what you just said. Slow down. What's wrong?"

"Sarah and Keenan haven't come home from school."

For a moment Jason thought he heard her wrong. "What about Sarah and Keenan?"

"I called their friends, the school, the police. No one seems to know where they are."

A cold chill ran down his back. His knees buckled and he dropped into a chair. Volpa had been showing him pictures of his children just days ago. *Volpa is playing hard ball.* "Who has taken Sarah and Keenan?"

She sobbed. "I don't know," she screamed.

He didn't want to believe this was happening to him and his children. "And you checked with all their friends and the places they hang out?"

"I called Travis and he saw Keenan leave school. I'm going out to look for them now." Kara's voice was laden with fear and despair. The crying continued.

He didn't want to say much about his next move, in case someone was listening to the conversation. "I'll find out what happened." He was puzzled at this turn of events.

After he hung up, Jason said, "My children have been kidnapped." He stood and stormed away from the table, as the others watched in shock.

He felt a hand on his shoulder and turned to find that Pastore was beside him. "You need to go to the FBI with this."

He shook his head.

"At least consider it," she said, then tapped his shoulder in sympathy and left him to mull it over on his own.

***

At 7:15 am Richard Quest entered his office in Salem, Oregon, threw his briefcase on the sofa, and plunged in the swivel chair to log in to the computer. After firing up the Internet browser he directed his attention to an *LA Times* headline and gave a deep sigh of relief. The article on the front page discussed high gas prices in California and dependency on foreign oil supply, with no mention of his name. Jason and Shallen's trek to LA had burdened his mind in the last twenty-four hours. *Why are they headed to LA?* Maybe to show the *LA Times* the files they had taken from Volpa. Next he checked CNN and the *New York Times* and skipped the *Washington Post. The Post* was on his side. No disaster so far.

Tom Martin, the Senator's Chief of Staff, entered his office through the open doorway followed by Roger Hunt, whose presence Quest acknowledged by tearing his eyes away from the computer screen and walking to the middle of the room near the sofa. The Senator had called this urgent meeting to discuss Jason and Shallen. After rushing to the door and closing it, Quest gestured with his hand for the pair to take a seat. Everyone knew the routine: the Senator took the red leather wing back chair and the other two sank in the sofas opposite each other, Martin on the right and Roger on the left. The Senator gave them both a quick glance.

"The situation is getting too serious to my liking. I called this meeting here, away from Washington, where the media circus never stops. We have to sort out this mess with Volpa, Jason and Shallen. When this briefing is finished, we lay low until those two are caught and put in jail." Both nodded.

Martin turned to Roger. "Where are they now?"

Roger rubbed his bald head, as if searching for a response. Usually he snapped answers to any query. Today he was slow and calculating. "The FBI located his active cell phone in LA, and I relayed the precise location to Volpa. On my way here, I contacted him again for an update. He traced them to a place in LA."

The Senator leaned forward with the eagerness of a hungry lion. "Roger, where in LA?"

"Not sure, close to West 1st and North Sprint Street," said Roger with difficulty.

Quest sensed Roger was not forthcoming and could feel his temperature rise. "What the hell is at 1st and Sprint Streets? This couple didn't go there for a romantic picnic."

"Senator, I checked the location on Google Earth," said Roger. "City Hall is nearby."

The Senator smacked the arm of his chair. "Roger, they're not there to get married. What else? Any TV or newspaper office?" Throwing his hands into the air, he turned to Martin and studied his reaction.

Roger blinked and his jaw muscle twitched. "Volpa sent two of his associates to that location. They searched the area for a long time, but Jason and the reporter were never sighted."

Martin pointed his finger in the air, requesting his turn to throw verbal punches at Roger. "The FBI gave Volpa, Jason and Shallen's precise location. How did they escape?" At every word he chopped the air with the edge of his palm.

Roger's eyes appeared dull. "I don't know all the details. All Volpa told me is that they weren't sighted, but he's sure to apprehend them." The fight seemed to be taken out of him.

"Before we can take any action, we need to know more," said the Senator.

In a subdued tone Roger said, "I agree. I'll call Volpa again and get an update." He left the room and closed the door behind him.

Quest rose. "I need a cup of coffee." He walked toward a door that opened to a kitchenette. He headed to the coffeemaker to which he added filtered water.

Martin stood and watched. "Senator, in my opinion Roger has messed up royally. Volpa is a liability."

The Senator pressed the button to the coffee pot and the machine gurgled awake. "This whole thing is getting messier and riskier by the hour." As the pot was filling with fresh coffee, the Senator went to the window and stared at the sky, wondering if he had reached a point of no return. He turned to Martin in an attempt to justify his choice. "Roger is a brilliant strategist. And a Republican. His resume is filled with superb achievements. I have followed his work for decades. That's why I hired him. But for me he has performed below his reputation."

Martin nodded. "He got outsmarted by this Jason, a software wise guy." The frustration on his face was unmistakably clear.

A long pause ensued as they watched the coffee drip. The Senator rubbed his face. "My only worry right now is 'what if'. What if Jason has a record of my private conversations and uses it against me? That's my worry."

"Why not fire Roger?"

The Senator said, "Not yet. Once it is confirmed that Jason has nothing, nada, then we're fine. We can't assume he doesn't have copies of the file. We have to be certain. The implications are enormous. I could lose the next election." He didn't want to think of the worst-case scenario. "Or wind up in jail."

Together they walked to the office with their cups of coffee and took a seat.

Martin said, "If he has the files and we can talk to Jason we can work out a deal so he doesn't use what he knows to harm us."

Roger entered the room. He was pale and his rapid blinking continued as if it had never stopped. The Senator watched him close the door and move towards the sofa to take a seat, both actions performed in slow motion as if deep in thought. "Volpa hasn't located them. He thinks they're still in LA."

The Senator shouted and slammed a fist on his desk. "He thinks. That's not good enough, Roger. Do you understand the implications? At this point it would be better to get more FBI agents on this case to hunt them down."

Roger shook his head. "Volpa has kidnapped Jason's children."

The Senator put the coffee cup on the table. He stood and walked towards his desk. A long silence filled the room. "This is becoming bizarre. Why did he do that?" he boomed.

Martin stood up. "He's desperate."

The Senator turned around to face the two men. "He's turning into a vicious dog. I can see the headline, 'Senator Quest involved in Kidnapping.' How will that look?"

"Not good," Roger admitted.

A flashback of the Senator's entire life flared before him. "Roger, you've done enough damage to my political career. Why did you hire this Volpa?"

"Senator, with all due respect, you helped Jason get a job. I got Volpa to see to it that Jason didn't launch a class-action suit." Roger was getting soft.

It's time to fire Roger Hunt.

***

Jason McDeere stepped into the *LA Times* delivery truck from the loading dock. Then he turned around and extended his hand to pull Shallen up from the platform into the vehicle. He also loaded a suitcase on rollers. After the driver pulled down the sliding door of the back of the truck, they sat down in the dark.

As instructed, the driver pulled out of the LA Times parking lot and drove towards a nearby car rental office where Stefanie Pastore and Roger White were waiting. Jason and Shallen sat on stacks of day-old newspapers and stayed mostly quiet for the twenty minutes of travel. After the truck stopped, the driver pulled the door open and they jumped out to greet Pastore and White who stood waiting for their arrival.

Pastore handed Jason a set of keys and pointed. "That blue car."

Jason took his Rolex watch and extended it to Pastore, which she refused to take. "I insist. It will make me feel better if you keep it until I pay the rental expense." She hesitated. Pastore had used her credit card to secure the car. Jason and Shallen didn't want to use their cards in case they could be traced. Jason's gesture was to ensure everyone standing of his honest intentions. "This is a very special watch. To me it's worth more than the cost. Keep it as a guarantee."

She waved the watch away. "I've only known you for a few hours, but I trust you." She paused to direct her full attention to Jason and Shallen. Her eyes beamed compassion and understanding. "You two are in a terrible situation. Consider what I said about going to the FBI. Also, keep me posted. Once you're in Corvallis, call me." She glanced at the parking lot where a car was being returned. Otherwise the lot wasn't busy. "Call collect from a public phone, if you have to." After giving both a hug, she pointed her gaze exclusively at Shallen. "Be safe." Apparent on Shallen's face, and no doubt his own, was an understanding of the danger that a reporter's life could bring.

"Interesting story," said White with a nod, suggesting disbelief. Despite any possible misgivings, he vigorously shook their hands. "May your path be safe!" His face was white, with a hint of a fading California tan, but his expression was that of a calm monk. His words reminded Jason of Terrance. Jason wondered about Terrance's whereabouts. He wished he could call him, but it was too risky.

They loaded into the car and headed out of the parking lot when two guys in a car caught Jason's attention as they passed. The faces were vaguely recognizable. He tracked them through each of the mirrors. The Chevy TrailBlazer spun a decisive u-turn, barely missing a pedestrian. "We're in deep shit," yelled Jason as he pounded his fist on the steering wheel. *He must get to Corvallis to save his children.* But first he had to escape these killers on his tail.

With Shallen's handbag perched on her lap and her hand frozen in mid-air, she said, "What do you mean?" Her eyes widened and her face drained of color.

Jason stomped on the gas pedal, and the vehicle rocketed forward. Fear heavy as concrete sank in his stomach and his heart raced. A car sped ever closer behind Jason, who slowed to merge with bumper-to-bumper afternoon traffic on the North Alameda Street. Jason studied the vehicle's passengers through his rearview mirror and saw a baldheaded, forty-something driver, his forehead wide and his eyes fixed on the car ahead. Driving shotgun was a much younger man, with a bushy head of hair, a long face and broad muscular cheekbones, a cell phone stuck to his ear. Jason wasn't certain, but the pair resembled the men he'd seen earlier that day from the third floor of the LA Times building. *Could they be my pursuers?* He would find out soon.

"I think we're being followed." Like a windshield wiper, his eyes shifted between the rearview mirror and the moving vehicles on the street. In a low voice,

Jason said, "Don't look back."

The passenger of the Chevy seemed to be inspecting Jason's license plate. Then he lowered his gaze. *Is he writing something down?* Jason forced his way into a three-foot space behind a bus, causing a red Mustang to swerve to avoid a collision, which evoked rage in the driver. He punished Jason with a blast to his horn and a finger in the air. *Sorry, don't have time to spare, buddy.*

The driver jumped out into the street, both hands waving in the air, as he shouted obscenities, but Jason forged ahead unobstructed. Through his rearview mirror he saw the man step forward, just as the Chevy attempted to pass, and kicked at the front bumper. Jason eyed the altercation until a van eased behind him and the Mustang fell from his view.

"How do we get to I-5?" said Jason in a panic. Shallen shook her head, clearly unfamiliar with the area. "The glove compartment should have a map."

Shallen yanked out the map and unfolded it on her lap. "Where are we?" She scanned the street corners then placed her hand on her head. Fear filled her eyes, but she seemed to be holding up with no signs of collapse. "Okay. We're heading south on Alameda." She traced the streets on the map with her index finger, fully alert. "Hurry," she said as she moved her hand across the map in frustration, finally landing on a spot. "There are two ways to I-5. North on Alameda to the Hollywood Freeway. Or go east on 1st to I-5." She fired the words at him in rapid succession.

Jason captured her every word and admired her fast calculations, but had no chance to compliment her with the car hot on their tail. He moved into the left lane between two vehicles – so did the Chevy. It confirmed his suspicions that Volpa's killers were after them. "I'm almost certain we're in danger. One more step to confirm it." Traffic noise drowned out his words. Fortunately, his software analyst mind prevailed. He needed one more piece of evidence. At the next intersection, the lights had been green for a few seconds, and a wall of cars were already in motion after having stopped in obedience to the red light. He spotted an opening. He stepped on the gas and made a u-turn, hoping to move ahead of cars, trucks, and buses headed the other direction. Tires squealing, and with the hood pointed north, the trunk swayed in response to the quick turning motion. The gyration pulled Shallen's upper body towards Jason and the map flew off her lap. But Jason couldn't take comfort in her closeness as the drivers behind protested by honking their horns. The driver of the Chevy, still stuck at the intersection, forced his way into the flow and appeared to be searching for a way to follow them.

Shallen muffled a scream as the car stabilized and raced forward. "Jason, be careful."

"I'm sure now. They're Volpa's thugs. It's a good bet one was on the phone telling his boss where we are," said Jason with trepidation. He blinked rapidly, as his heart pulsed faster.

A short silence prevailed while Jason focused on the traffic ahead. Shallen's fingers continued their march across the map while she took turns looking at the map and the street signs. "We've got to lose them as fast as we can." She pressed her finger on her lips and paused as if to reflect on the seriousness of the situation. "Right now, Volpa's army vehicles must be converging towards us. The more we zigzag through side streets the better. Take 3rd on our right. No. We just missed it. Move to the right lane. 2nd is coming up soon, hang another right."

Like a trusting child, Jason obediently followed the instructions coming from Shallen's strategic mind. The sharp turn on 3rd made the tires squeal and smoke blurred the rear view mirror as he gunned the car on a less travelled road. After a few seconds the car stabilized and he drew a long, deep breath. "What next?"

Her eyes danced along the lines of the map. "Jason, we're coming to Rose, then Hewitt. Take Hewitt, left." Her voice was loud to compensate for the outside noise but he could hear her anxiety.

As he passed an almost empty parking lot, in front of a building of some sort, a street came into view at a corner where a high-rise was still under construction. He zipped past Rose Street and within seconds saw Hewitt Street. That's when he noticed the Chevy taking a turn onto 3rd Street only one block away. From the opposite direction three cars appeared, followed by a dump truck. He calculated that the fastest way to make a left turn without spinning the car out of control was to pass between the incoming car and the dump truck behind it. There seemed to be enough room between the two. He gripped both hands on the steering wheel ready to swerve into Hewitt when Shallen screamed, "Stop."

He slammed on the brakes and the car skidded to a dead halt as the dump truck roared by. If he had made the left turn he would have hit the dump truck nearly head on. "Phew. Damn close," said Jason. Shallen's jaw dropped open as she hung on to the door handle with one hand and dashboard with the other. He revved the engine again, completing the turn onto Hewitt.

"Which is better? Getting killed by a dump truck or Volpa's men?" Her words were nonjudgmental. "Hurry. They're behind us." Her eyes were fixed on the mirror. With one hand she held onto the handle and with the other she grabbed Jason's shoulder. "We're coming to East . . . uh . . . 1st Street. Hang a right. Quick. On 1st. Ok." She turned to the back window. "The Chevy just turned onto Hewitt. They're coming fast," she yelled.

By now Jason was getting used to being an "impolite" driver. The 1st Street was under construction, reducing it to two lanes, the traffic heavy. "Will this take us to I-5?"

"Yes. But the traffic is too slow. Volpa's men could easily catch up. I'm looking for a faster way." Her fingers shook violently as she held the map. "Move to the left lane and turn left on Vignes or Center."

"Ok." Then he did something crazy. He took Center, then made a left on Docummon, leading him to Alameda where he turned right heading north towards Hollywood Freeway. He read the white and green road sign, which took him past Commercial Street. Finally, he turned left at Arcadia Street, took a right at N Los Angeles Street and then a right onto US-101.

After twenty minutes of weaving in and out of lanes, moving ahead of cars, buses, SUVs and vans while constantly reminding himself not to get into an accident, he traveled north as fast as he could on the Hollywood Freeway. "There's I-5 North."

With a quick twist of his head to check the blind spot, he eased the car into another lane and merged onto I-5. "In about thirteen hours we'll be in Corvallis. I hope." He pressed his lips together. Like a rabbit under attack, his eyes shifted among mirrors. Dusk had set in, which would make spotting the car difficult, with any luck. "It's going to be a long night and a tiring one. Better get some sleep." He squeezed Shallen's shoulder for a minute and then returned his hand to the steering wheel to focus on slowing traffic.

"How can I?" she said in anguish.

The image of the two thugs watching the *LA Times* building flashed through Jason's mind. How had the thugs located them and come close to finding them? "Shallen, our cell phone must be off. Can you check it?"

Shallen dug out the phone. After pressing buttons, she dropped it into her handbag. "Pastore gave us good advice. Going to the FBI should be one of our top priorities. They could help locate Sarah and Keenan." She shot him a tender gaze.

Placing the cell phone into the holder, he turned his attention to the road, occasionally checking the speedometer. He would have liked to speed up and reach his destination as fast as possible, but they couldn't afford a speeding ticket now.

He switched to evaluating the best strategy of seeing his children again. Yet he didn't want to do anything foolish. Who had kidnapped his children? The Senator? Why would he make such a stupid move? It must be Volpa, who had showed Jason his children's picture. To commit a felony he must be desperate, willing to take any action to keep information from being leaked. "Going to the FBI does make sense." He viewed the mirrors, keeping a close watch on the vehicles around him. "What if –" he twisted his neck to ease the tension – "the kidnapping is to make us surface from hiding? If we surface and approach the FBI, what could happen? I could be locked up, searched and charged for having stolen property in my possession. And I could end up in jail."

She shook her head. "No. We'll fight it," she said with a forceful expression.

"It's also possible that once they find me, Sarah and Keenan are returned home." He snapped his fingers. "Then just like that, Volpa and the Senator, or whoever kidnapped my children, get away with a crime." Heat flashed through his body at the thought.

"Pastore made a good point about going to the FBI," Shallen said. "I just hope she's right."

"What other option do we have?" Jason rubbed his eyes. Fatigue was making him sleepy and making it harder to see the taillights ahead.

Shallen said, "The other option is to talk to Jerry Whitney. He promised to get bank reports showing the money transfers from Softek to Khalid. Once we have that in our hands we could send them to the *LA Times*. Maybe turn state's evidence."

"We could do that first thing in the morning, when we arrive in Corvallis. In the meantime you should shut your eyes. I don't know how long I'll last. I'm running on raw energy and I'll need your help in a few hours."

They had traveled for over four hours since leaving LA, heading due north on I-5, when Jason noticed Stockton/Sacramento on a huge overhead sign. Shallen hadn't said anything for a while, her seat reclined and her eyes shut. It was time for him to trade places with Shallen, as he could barely focus on the road ahead, but he didn't want to disturb her rest. She needed it as much as he did so he pushed ahead.

***

It was ten after six, according to the dashboard clock, when Jason McDeere pinpointed exit 228 to Corvallis. He hung a left on OR-34, tired and anxious about how the day ahead would unfold. As he crossed the Willamette River into Corvallis, he was much too tired to entertain the idea of doing anything useful at this hour of the morning. He wasn't hungry but his body needed another heavy dose of caffeine to keep him awake. At first he thought of going to Rose's Coffee Time that opened at 6:30 am but erased that idea in a hurry. Since he knew Rose's owner, and Molly, the waitress, as well as some of the regular customers, word could get around that he was in town. Instead he took two lefts and a right, then parked on SW 2nd Street, close enough for a good view of the New Morning Bakery.

After hours of driving, a sense of relief flooded him, vibrating down his hands as he let go of the steering wheel. It was a crisp morning with light snow coming down on the windshield. He turned to the right and found Shallen asleep in a well-cured brown leather jacket, a red and blue scarf snaked around her neck. He stared at the falling flakes and reminded himself that it wasn't a dream. He remembered the pushy reporter from the *Post* who wanted an interview on the day of Brian's funeral, nearly two months ago. *How my world has changed.*

Jason stepped out of the car to examine the street, mostly barren of vehicles, which he expected at this hour of the morning. He noticed only two cars and a truck as far as the eye could see, and it seemed they hadn't moved in the last few minutes. At the sight of an approaching car, he slipped back into the warmth of his vehicle. He had left California with just a thin shirt. Now he regretted that decision.

A movement in the bakery stole his attention. He gently touched Shallen's shoulder to which she responded with a groan. "Where are we," she mumbled, then opened her eyes.

"We're in Corvallis. I stopped to get coffee and the world's best blueberry corn muffins and cinnamon rolls."

Her eyes shifted from the car to the street to the storefront as if assessing her surroundings. "I could use a hot drink and food," she said with a yawn.

Still fearing he was being watched, he dashed into the bakery and out within minutes, his arms loaded with food. He drove off, his attention fixed on the vehicles in front and in back of him. The coffee and cinnamon smell filled the car. Holding the coffee cup and taking occasional sips, he sought a telephone booth, where he stopped. It was getting close to seven, according to the dashboard clock.

Jason punched numbers into the public phone and, after three rings, a man answered. "Mr. Johnson," he said.

"Yes. Who is this?" the man responded, reservation wrapped in his words.

Jason knew he had to make this snappy. "This is Jason, your neighbor. I can't talk for too long. I need a favor."

"Jason, of course. Have you found Sarah and Keenan, yet? Kara came here yesterday to check if I had seen them." His words harbored a mix of delight and concern.

"Not yet. Listen. I know it's early, but could I get you to drive to Kara's parents' house and ask them to go to a parking lot across from 250 2nd Street at 8:00. Tell them I'll be there ten minutes later."

"Jason, lately my memory hasn't been too sharp. Which intersection is that?"

"Jefferson and 2nd. Also, ask them to go to Waterworks Street and 2nd first and then drive on 2nd towards Jefferson."

"Waterworks? Yes, I know where that is."

"Have you got all that?"

"I'm writing this down. But what's this all about?"

"I don't have time to explain. I need your help. Could you just do me this one favor?"

"Okay."

"One more thing. If we don't arrive at ten after eight, ask them to leave. Tell them not to wait. Just go, immediately." Jason made him repeat every detail of the instructions and hung up.

Then he went to Byron Pl., a cul-de-sac. "From here we can see every vehicle travelling on 2nd." Well aware of the plan, Shallen gave a nod of agreement. "I want to know if they've heard anything. Maybe Sarah and Keenan are home. Or maybe Kara's parents have heard something. I keep praying and hoping." He took another sip of lukewarm coffee and put the half torn muffin in his mouth.

"I hope so too. You're strong, still holding up. I would go insane if they were my children."

He would like to know more on Shallen's opinion of marriage and having children, but it would have to wait. He spotted the car. The light green Malibu carrying Kara's parents was followed by a city bus and two cars. Jason tailed them. The bus and the Malibu hung a right on Tyler Avenue and the rest of the vehicles caravanned behind them. They rolled onto 1st and then back onto 2nd Street. The Malibu slowed then turned right into a parking lot as expected. The blue car that trailed it stopped and parked. As they eased by the car Jason could see two men inside looking into the parking lot.

"Damn it! Kara's parents are being followed." He banged the steering wheel with his fist.

He drove around a few blocks until he found a spot within full view of the vehicles, but hidden from their view. At twelve after, they drove their cars out of the lot and made a right turn. The blue car trailed the Malibu. "They *are* being followed," he hissed as he watched the two cars disappear. He placed his head on the steering wheel. He felt like crying but he had to keep it together, though he didn't know how. He hadn't cried in a long time. He felt like screaming but didn't have the energy left for that either. Should he be angry? At whom? The Senator?

Shallen ran her fingers through his hair. "We'll get through this."

Head still down, barely able to speak, he mumbled, "I feel trapped."

What to do next? Both were emotionally drained to the point of exhaustion.

"There is another way," said Shallen. "Let's go find a phone." Once there, Shallen punched in Jerry Whitney's number. "Jerry, this is Shallen." She looked at the phone then at Jason. "He hung up." She dialed again. And again no one answered the call at the other end. "This is strange. Why wouldn't he answer?"

"Let's drive to Jerry's mother's place."

Within ten minutes they were on Anjni Circle. The sky was cleared of snowflakes and the sun's brightness was visible behind the clouds. Shallen pointed to a white brick house with a Buick in the driveway, and they pulled over and got out. Shallen and Jason went up to the house and rang the doorbell. When the door opened, a woman in a pink housecoat answered. The light from the woman's face quickly vanished when she looked at Shallen, disgust clear in her expression. With her eyes diverted, the old woman said, "I told you not to come here."

Shallen gave a shot at cheerful enthusiasm. "Mrs. Whitney. Sorry to bother you."

"Go away."

"We want to talk to Jerry," she pleaded. "Last week I saw him. He promised to mail documents to help catch the Senator, who is partly responsible for your husband's death."

"My Clint is gone. He's not coming back." She shook her head, her lips in a tight straight line. "We don't want to lose our peace of mind any more than we already have. I know for a fact, Jerry won't help you. Now get out of town and don't come back." Mrs. Whitney started to close the door but Shallen put her foot in the way.

"Jerry wanted to help." Mrs. Whitney pushed her foot away and slammed the door.

Jason stood motionless, filled with disbelief. Shallen waved her hand in the air. "Jerry promised."

"I believe you." Jason put his arm around her shoulder, then turned toward the street and walked to the car.

***

At four-thirty Jason McDeere dialed Senator Quest's number. After two rings he received a response. "Senator Quest's office, how may I help you?"

He recognized the voice of the executive secretary, Julia Svenborg, recalled her perfect teeth and perfect smile. "This is Jason McDeere. I want to talk to Senator Quest." She was a lot friendlier than the last time Jason saw her.

Following a pause at the other end, she said, "Mr. McDeere. Yes. The Senator is here. I'll put you through. One moment. Please wait. One moment." That's what they wanted, for him to surface from hiding.

After a minute of listening to music, he heard, "Oh hi, Jason. I'm so happy to hear from you. Where are you?" Although the Senator's tone was cheerful he didn't sound sincere.

Of course he's happy to hear from me. "Can we meet?"

"Where are you? I'm in my Salem office. Why don't you come over now? I'll wait."

"Right now? I can't. How about tomorrow?"

"Tomorrow is fine. Any time."

"Six-thirty . . . AM."

"Six-thirty? Why so early?"

"I'm an early riser."

"Sure. I'll be here, just make sure you're here too. I look forward to this meeting. It will be nice to catch up. I haven't seen you in awhile. I'll be here. Come."

I want to see you too.

-18-

Jason McDeere slid through the revolving door of the building housing Senator Quest's office, only steps behind Shallen, every muscle wound tight. Jason wondered about the outcome of the meeting. He prayed that they would be rescued by FBI agents, as planned, if anything went wrong. He felt the wires and radio transmitters taped to the skin around his mid-section. Just the day before, when Jason and Shallen approached the FBI, they had quickly hatched a sting operation. Before accepting the danger of such a task, the feds assured them they would be listening in to their conversation with the Senator at all times and if their lives were in danger the agents would storm in.

As Jason and Shallen walked into the building two security guards motioned them over and said, "Good morning. Where are you folks going?" The guards were in there thirties with muscular builds.

Jason approached them and leaned over the desk, hoping they wouldn't see the wires beneath his clothes. "To meet with Senator Quest." The guards confirmed the appointment by browsing the computer screen, and Jason signed a sheet with his name beside it, then the two of them marched towards the elevator and rode it up to the third floor. No one was in sight. Jason breathed a sigh of relief. The reception area was just as it had been prior to Christmas of the previous year. At the swoosh of the closing elevator doors, Jason looked up in time to see the Senator appear through the office door.

"I'm happy to see you." He shook Jason's hand, then turned to Shallen. "I only expected you, Jason." Quest frowned, obviously puzzled.

Jason ignored the Senator's concern. "This is Shallen Xu."

Quest ushered them into his office and closed the door behind him. The Senator gestured to his visitors to be seated on the sofa while taking the wing back chair. The Senator couldn't take his eyes off the computer case Jason placed on his lap. "Why are we meeting so early?"

Jason wiped his moist forehead. "We have several things to settle." Then he turned to Shallen looking for emotional support.

The Senator jumped to his feet and went around the chair. Resting his body on the back he said, "I understand that you hacked Volpa's website and took his surveillance files. I'm sure you're aware that hacking is illegal in this country. You could easily end up in jail. I don't know for how long. It depends on the judge, but I assume it could be years."

Legally speaking, what this US Senator had been doing was a lot worse than hacking a website, but Jason kept his thoughts to himself. To Jason's mind, it was obvious who was more guilty of a crime and who was to pay a heavy penalty. "Let's get one thing crystal clear, Senator. Volpa works for you." Jason examined the facial expressions of the two. The Senator's cheeks and forehead turned slightly red. Shallen nodded.

The Senator's eyes were fixed on the floor. "I had absolutely nothing to do with it. I never hired him. I only came to know about Volpa after the hacking was discovered." His voice turned soft as if he were pleading. "Roger Hunt, my campaign manager, soon to be ex-manager, hired him. Look, I think we can settle this. Do you have the files?"

Jason pointed to the case on his lap. "It's all here. In my laptop." His mouth was dry.

"Just give me the laptop and I'll give you ten thousand dollars for it. You can buy ten computers with it, if you wanted to."

"Ten thousand dollars for a laptop?" That was a bribe. "Very generous of you." The sarcastic words didn't seem to disturb the politician but got a sideways smile from Shallen.

Quest waved his hand at them. "Also, you have to guarantee me that you will destroy any copies you may have made. Just an insurance policy."

"It's worth a lot more than ten thousand dollars." Jason got up, bent towards the Senator, and yelled, "Where are my children? They've gone missing for two days. Where are they? I want to know. I want to know *now*." He was so angry that he wanted to punch him. *Not yet.*

"Jason, I'm very sorry about the kidnapping. Why don't you give me the files and I'll call the FBI and see that they send a search team out right away."

Politicians are so powerful. With a snap of his fingers, FBI agents are at his service.

He looked straight in the other man's eyes. "Senator. You know who did it." His voice was rock solid. "Tell me who did it? Come on. Spill it." He walked towards the door. Shallen got up to follow him. "You get no files. I'm leaving. But if we can connect the kidnapping of my children to you –" he pointed his finger at the Senator – "you can kiss your political career goodbye. We'll end up in jail together – me for hacking and you for kidnapping. How is that for destiny?"

Shallen gave a gentle push to his arm and said, "Jason, let's go. The Senator doesn't care about your children. But he does care about his reputation."

The anger in Jason's body roared back like a tidal wave. "To have my children involved was a big mistake. I love them very much."

The Senator turned to Shallen. "Who the hell are you?" The veins in his throat became visible. When she didn't answer, he turned back to Jason. "You have to believe me. Again, I had nothing to do with it. Volpa went crazy. He's like a rabid animal. It was stupid of him to do that. But I had nothing to do with the kidnapping. I'll help you find your children."

Jason's tension eased up a bit. "Senator, I think we're getting closer to a deal. I don't mind giving up my laptop, if I can have my children back. One more thing." He paused for a short moment to get the full attention of his listener. "I've reviewed many surveillance files and it's clear that there was a cozy relationship between you, and the CEO's at Softek and Layton."

The tension on the Senator's face increased. "I meet CEOs of various companies all the time. It's part of my job to find employment for the citizens of Oregon."

Jason laughed. "Shallen visited Corvallis and did some digging. Shallen, tell the Senator what you found."

She moved a few steps closer to the desk. "Jobs were outsourced from Softek overseas by the hundreds. By doing so, Softek made huge profits. I mean huge. And some went to you as a bribe. I've discovered your dirty little secret--"

"You don't have any proof of that. This is just speculation. No proof." With every word the Senator vigorously shook his head. His face turned red and his eyes filled with loathing.

"We've scrutinized Khalid Enterprise." Seized by an intense anger, the Senator moved behind his desk. "Khalid came up with a brilliant money laundering scheme and, with Softek money, made contributions to your campaign funds."

"It's not true. I'll have to verify it with my staff. I'll let you know if I find anything, but I doubt it. Listen, you want your children, right? Why are you worried about my campaign financing? Give me the laptop and I can assure you everything will be fine."

Jason opened the flap of his briefcase and pulled out a copy of the *LA Times* with a headline reading, "Senator Quest Linked to Bribery and Outsourcing Jobs" and a picture of the Senator at the top left corner. "Shallen wrote this article. We are together in this. That's why she's with me."

"Hell, you've just gone too far." He pulled the drawer of the desk open and lifted a pistol from it. With the firearm pointed at them, he said, "Don't move. No one is going to prove anything once you two are taken care of." With his left hand he slid the phone receiver to the top of the desk and punched in numbers, his eyes still fixed on Jason and Shallen. Then he brought the receiver close to his mouth. After waiting for a moment he said, "Send five security guards."

Jason's jaw dropped, eyes wide open. "Senator, you're holding a gun. What are you going to do? Kill us?"

"I hoped it wouldn't come to that."

Jason held up his hands. "Please don't do that. Put the gun down."

"I'll use it if I have to, but I better not. In twenty minutes I'm expecting visitors and it would create a mess in my office," the Senator said with a bitter laugh. He looked at his watch. "Instead I called security and they will escort you out of here."

"You won't get away with whatever you're planning," said Shallen.

The Senator walked towards them. "I haven't read this article. I can guess what's in it. Lies and allegations. You can't prove anything. No one can. Allegations don't make one guilty of anything. I'll make sure you don't talk to anyone. The two of you have already done so much damage. It's unbelievable it has reached this point."

Within minutes, the security guards stormed into the office. The Senator unloaded the laptop case from Jason's shoulder. "Get them out of here!" he ordered.

One of the officers grabbed Jason's arm and twisted it behind his back, giving it a sharp jerk, to which he yelped. "Ahh, leave me alone." His eyes shifted to Shallen. "Leave her. Don't touch her." Shallen resisted but she was out-muscled by the guards. Forming a circle, the security guards shoved Jason and Shallen into the reception area. At the elevator, they waited after pressing the button.

The door to the stairs opened and a man holding a rifle with both hands shouted, "FBI, freeze." Another one appeared right behind him. Both agents pointed their weapons directly at the security guards who didn't get a chance to reach for their guns. One said, "Drop your weapons. Now, now." Another two agents ran to the Senator's office. The sound of footsteps could be heard running up the stairs and, moments later, a dozen men passed through the door into the reception area. The guards' faces were blank with surprise. The guards quickly unholstered their guns, and dropped them to the floor. Then they raised their hands in surrender.

***

Jason McDeere followed two federal special agents, Peter Scott and Carlos Caesar, into the Crown Plaza Building, which housed the Portland FBI office. Shallen followed a few steps behind the three men. On the fourth floor of the white building, the agents picked up slips of paper that looked like messages as they passed by the front desk. Scott disappeared to get an update on Volpa's arrest after taking Jason and Shallen into an interrogation room where both sat waiting. Ten minutes later, Scott and Caesar returned with some news.

"Our detectives went to a place in Prescott, Arizona. It's the head office of Volpa's operations," said Scott. "They talked to a few guys but no sign of Volpa. According to these two, Volpa is on his way to Corvallis to get you and Ms. Xu." He pointed his hand at them. "With luck, we hope to locate him. We have an idea what kind of vehicle he's driving. That's not much to go by. But that's all we have."

At the thought of his pursuer on his tail, Jason's anxiety increased. Even the safety of a federal office didn't allay his fears. *What is Volpa up to?* Could Jason and his family get adequate protection from these law-enforcement officers? When Volpa had first waved the pictures of Sarah and Keenan at him in front of the hotel in Mountain View, he gave Jason the distinct impression that he was a man who was used to yielding to nothing, who had the tenacity of a pit bull. Jason had grown weary of Volpa monitoring his every move. It had gone on for too long. Six weeks. "If he's after us – if he's on I-5 as we were –" he turned to Shallen – "then it will be impossible to intercept him." He leaned towards Scott, whom he was facing. "At any point on the highway there are hundreds of vehicles passing by every hour. How could law enforcement ever locate him?" He sucked a mouthful of air.

"It will be difficult, but all the highway patrol officers have been alerted." Caesar's words calmed Jason, but only slightly. "These officers are trained to know what to look for. With luck, we'll be able to question him. As of now, it's not certain if Volpa knows the whereabouts of your children."

"Any idea where my children could be? Are they safe?" The mounting fear and anger forced these words through his lips, the thoughts running like a windmill through his mind.

Scott pulled a chair and sank into it, motioning others to do the same, then gave all his attention to Jason. "Those two in Prescott don't seem to have a clue. Volpa is our best bet. If he has anything to do with it, we'll make him cooperate. But as of now, we have no idea where the children are located, or their condition."

A table surrounded by six chairs, loaded with two laptops, and a recording machine filled the room. Three bare walls under rows of ceiling lights revealed aging yellow plaster. One wall had a large mirror. The officers sat facing Jason and Shallen, Caesar on the laptop, Scott doing the talking. "We need to ask you a few questions."

"Is this being recorded?" Shallen scanned the room.

Jason couldn't shake certain thoughts from his mind. *What could I have done to prevent my family from being involved? How will it all end? When will all end?*

One officer said, "Yes, we'll be recording everything that you say. Anything you say can be used in a court of law--"

"I think we need a lawyer before we give any deposition." Shallen did a visual check of Jason's reaction.

With tight lips and a slow nod, Jason said, "We want to protect our rights." He spread his hands out on the table. "I have nothing to hide. I can tell you everything I know. Am I being charged here? What are we doing?"

"Depends on the prosecutor," said Caesar.

Jason pulled the chair closer to the table, closed his eyes and sighed, then opened them once he had himself together. "Man, the last few days have been hell. Utter hell. We were chased by thugs in LA." Jason turned to Shallen with tenderness, wondering how she'd become caught up in all this turmoil, putting her life at risk. Chances are she hadn't known what she was getting involved in, but he was grateful nevertheless. "And we haven't eaten much, slept much. Right now all I want to do is to find my children."

Shallen nodded. "It's our main concern."

Scott said, "Let me get you some food." He left the room and closed the door behind him.

"We have to talk to the Federal prosecutor. She has the final word, whether to press charges, bargain with you or just use you as a witness," said Caesar. After a pause, he grimaced. "Or we could just let you go."

For Jason, walking out free of the FBI building was the most remote possibility, like surviving three consecutive lightning strikes. "We would rather talk to an attorney first." His patience was growing thin. "Could you check to see if they've found Volpa's car?" He clamped his fingers to his forehead to ease a nagging headache.

Caesar ignored him. "The prosecutor is well aware of the case. And this is a complicated one with possible kidnapping, alleged bribery and money laundering." For another ten minutes, he continued talking about his experience as a federal officer.

Scott returned carrying a tray of food and drink. Then both agents left again to consult the prosecutor and get an update on Volpa, leaving another officer in charge while they were gone. It was widely known that FBI agents could become extremely aggressive in their crime fighting tactics. These two agents were definitely a different breed, not like his friends, family, neighbors, and colleagues. The agents never revealed their thoughts, their eyes and body language always guarded. They had a role to play in protecting citizens' rights. Would he get a fair shake? It reminded him of how bungled police work had led to his father's death.

Twenty minutes later, the two agents appeared at the doorway. "Volpa has been located. He is in police custody being questioned."

What if Volpa wasn't the kidnapper? "Did he say anything about my children?"

"He's being questioned at the Sheriff's office. As we expected, he is stubborn and hasn't been too cooperative. We're aware that he's an ex-federal agent. He knows too much. We're sending two of our field agents to the station where he is being held."

Scott nodded toward the sandwiches and drink. Jason and Shallen dug into the food, their hunger making it impossible to resist the temptation. Jason said, "What did the prosecutor say?"

"We spoke with her. She says she can't decide on anything while the investigation is ongoing. All the facts are not yet clear. The story is still unfolding as we speak. She is also consulting with the US Attorney's office to find out how to proceed." He nodded after a glance at his notepad. "Oh, yeah. We're working on a search warrant of Volpa's office."

More waiting. It was getting harder to bear. Jason and Shallen couldn't talk for fear of being watched through the mirror. Then came the news that Volpa had conceded to the kidnapping. "The children are being held in a Corvallis hotel room," said the younger of the two agents. "The local police and FBI agents have already been dispatched."

Jason felt as though he could collapse. Instead he said, "Wow, thanks guys." Jason gave the agents a high five. Turning to Shallen he threw his arm around her shoulder and gave her a hug. "My children are alive." After answering a call, Caesar gave a signal to Scott and said, "We'll be back shortly." They closed the door behind them.

Another ten minutes passed before the knob turned and two more people filed in behind Scott and Caesar. The new men were much older and both men gave blank stares – probably part of their career training. Pointing first at one, then the other, Scott said, "James Finch, from Cyber division and Larry Franklin, National Security."

Finch took over with his thick southern drawl. "We got a call from Layton Industries. The company alleged that you accessed their database without authorization. According to them, you have in your possession classified Pentagon documents in computer files and you tried to flee. It's obvious since you're here and not at Layton Industries," he said. With a serious expression and a momentary pause, he continued. "The company expects you to be at the office at this moment." His face was round with balding head. Jason guessed him to be around six feet.

"Yes, I'm here. Otherwise, I would be dead. You understand?" He fought back the anger. "I'm not a criminal. The criminals are after *me*." He poked his chest.

"Son, you have unauthorized information that belongs to the Pentagon." Finch's grave stare was directed at Jason. "That's serious. That's US government classified data. Extreme concerns have been expressed. If true, according to federal laws, it would be considered a national security offense." One hand rested on his rounded belly and with the other he waved a paper. "I have a warrant to take possession of your laptop."

Jason bounced to his feet and grabbed the paper, scanning it carefully. After reading his name and the judge's signature on the warrant, he combed his hair in resignation. He felt trapped. In a FBI office no less. "Go ahead." In defeat, he nodded toward the chair holding the case.

Finch left with the laptop. Shallen sat frozen. Franklin plunged into a chair, spread forms of some sort on the table and signaled Jason to take a seat, as he answered all kinds of questions, each question repeated two or three times. What came after that was even more grueling. Nothing escaped Franklin's attention. With gray hair, a thin face, and piercing blue eyes, he drilled into Jason's life with endless questions. While battling anguish, fatigue and sleeplessness, and under the agent's constant pressure, he kept an even temper the best he could. But the food he'd eaten at a furious pace was wreaking havoc in his stomach.

Finch entered the room, closed the door, took a seat and scanned the eyes of everyone around him. An expectant hush fell over the room while he glanced at a sheet of paper. With no sign of compassion, or any other emotion, he faced Jason and charged him with three counts. The first offense was a federal crime of conspiring to attempt to access a protected computer without authorization with intent to defraud. The second was possession of unauthorized classified government information. Waving a sheet, Finch reminded him that on the first day of employment, he had signed a document prohibiting him from removing any information, on paper or electronically, outside Layton's premises. Then came the shocker. In a classic case of kicking a man when he was down, the FBI charged him with tax fraud.

After hearing every word, Jason stared at Finch, in shock. A chill ran through him, then he flinched. Slowly his mind was devoured by the anguish of what would come afterward. The depth of the consequences of these accusations became exceedingly clear, sending numbing feelings throughout his extremities. It seemed his brain froze, choking the flow of blood through his arteries. Sweat beaded across his forehead. His legs shook, which he couldn't control no matter how hard he tried. He felt sad and depressed as nausea hit him in a tidal wave of emotion.

He faced the four federal officers, one of whom threw accusations of his disloyalty to his country. They spoke with authority, confident of the US government's power. Their faces were void of understanding or compassion. He felt as though he were in the jaws of predators. Remembering all the calamities that life had heaped on him so far, this was the most devastating. Legal battles, incarceration, misery, loneliness, deprivation, all flashed through his mind. For a moment he wondered where he was. Was this real or a dream? Yes, he was being held in the USA, in an FBI office, not in some country known for rampant injustice.

Shallen, who had been quiet up to now, burst out yelling. The sound shook Jason awake. "Accusing him of being a danger to the US government is probably the most outlandish thing I've ever heard! These charges are ridiculous." With a wave toward Jason, she added, "Look at him. Does he look like a criminal? His life and his children's lives are in danger. And he came to *you* for help. Now you're pressing charges that could send him to jail for life?" Her face was turning red, and the veins at her neck, rarely visible, now popped out.

Back on his feet, Jason took a few steps towards to Shallen. Two of them against four FBI agents who were not moved a bit by Shallen's anger. Jason asked Finch to repeat the charges, after which he walked to a corner and rested his forehead on the wall. Shallen placed her hand on Jason's back while repeatedly offering him encouraging words. He turned around and walked toward the agents. "All I wanted to know is if Layton was giving money to Senator Quest illegally. That's all." He shook his head and waved his hands in the air. "In fact I found out that Layton has been illegally contributing to the Senator's campaign through Khalid, his money laundering partner. Who should be charged? Me or him?"

Jason's plea didn't move Finch. "The thing to remember is that we see in your possession files and names of top military contractors of the Pentagon. Two of those are Raytheon and Boeing, who do business with the most guarded division of the Defense Department. They are suppliers of top-secret equipments for cruise missiles. In these files, there are model numbers, quantities, etc. They were in a laptop in your possession. Very serious. After 9/11, any unauthorized access to Pentagon computers or Pentagon agencies is considered a criminal offense," Finch said in a calm and determined voice.

Shallen took over the pleading. "He's not denying that. Yes, he uploaded the files. But you have to listen to his side. He was under surveillance by a US senator and a Pentagon subcontractor. Does that tell you something?" She paused, as if reorganizing her thoughts. "What he got are accounting files. Please listen to him. How is the US government in danger? He is not a Timothy McVeigh, a terrorist or Al-Qaeda operative."

With a furrowed forehead, Finch said, "You should have come to us at that time. One more thing. I see Volpa's files in your possession, acquired through hacking, which is again an offense. I'll leave that aside for now, until Volpa decides whether to press charges."

"I admit it was a mistake. Things were happening too fast."

"And accusing him of tax fraud. Where does that come from?" Shallen weaved her hair around her ears, as if losing patience.

Caesar and Scott seemed to be watching the drama with great interest but without saying anything. Franklin finally broke his silence. "It's not in our hands. We understand your situation and you may not have intentionally done anything to the US government. But we have to press charges. It's not under our control. It's coming from the Attorney General's office. Someone very powerful and influential is orchestrating these charges. We can't go against their wishes."

"Who could that be?" Jason murmured in a low, trembling voice, remembering his pal, Terrance, who had the guts to plow through difficulties. Jason mustered the courage to keep his fight alive as long as he had breath to breathe.

Finch continued unabated. "We have search warrants for the hotel room in Mountain View and your house in Corvallis."

He turned to Shallen. "Don't tell me you are charging her."

Finch shook his head. "She has done nothing illegal."

He thought about his children. Would he rot in jail? In a low, soft voice, he said, "What's next?"

He paused to scrutinize a sheet on the table. "We can have bail hearing set for this afternoon at 4:00 pm." He got up, reached into his back pocket and approached Jason.

With one abrupt motion, Shallen wrapped herself around Jason, whose hands were being held behind his back as they handcuffed him. She held him long and hard. It was too long, and Finch's impatience grew so thin that he nudged Jason to leave. Shallen's eyes poured out tears, two continuous beads rolling down her cheeks. "Everything will be fine. I will see you in court. I promise." She sobbed and that broke Jason's heart.

***

In the parking lot of the U.S. District Court, it was thirty minutes after four when Jason McDeere and Shallen hopped into the back seat, Scott at the wheel, and Caesar got in the front seats of car, all headed toward Corvallis. The court appearance was painfully long and tedious as legal arguments were being thrown at the judge. The courtroom was almost empty. The prosecutor wanted the accused to be locked up in jail until the trial day, while the defense lawyer argued his client didn't have any previous criminal record, he was a good citizen, a family man and that he should be freed. The judge agreed to Jason's release on a $100,000 bail, on condition that he surrendered his passport.

Jason and Shallen held hands, praying and hoping for a good outcome. They still didn't know the whereabouts of Sarah and Keenan. Twenty minutes into the journey, Caesar got a call. Jason craned his head toward the passenger seat and listened carefully. He heard only a few of the officer's monosyllabic words but couldn't make sense of the conversation. He restrained himself from interrupting the man until he had all the information.

Caesar ended the call by folding the cell phone. Then he turned diagonally toward Jason. "Good news. Your children are safe. First they are going to the police station for a deposition."

"Have they been harmed?"

"No visible abuse. For what the children have gone through, according to the officer, they were in fairly good spirits."

"I don't believe it. My worst nightmare is ending. Thank God." Jason lifted his hands and face. "They're ok." He said the words more to reassure himself than the others. For a brief moment he forgot about the national security charges. Despite everything that had happened, he said, "You two are doing a great job, and the other agents, too." Jason covered his face with his hands. To him the news that his kids were safe felt like the sweetest words he had ever heard. However, the tension didn't immediately dissipate. Still, he felt as though a heavy load had just been lifted. It would take a while to get used to the fact that they were safe. Shallen was beaming, which assured him that the worst was almost over. He punched numbers into his cell phone to tell Kara the good news. Jason couldn't wait to lay his eyes on his beloved children.

***

From Circle Boulevard, Jason McDeere drove into the Softek parking lot and found a spot in the visitor section a few minutes before the ten o'clock meeting. The return to his former workplace was surreal, as he flashed back to the time when he and his co-workers were laid-off, the death of Brian and others at Softek, and his first meeting with Shallen. Many agonizing moments had flowed through the river of Jason's memory since he left Softek. Some came rushing back as he approached the front door. He choked with emotion but resisted showing it as he presented himself at the security desk.

When he had returned to Corvallis, three days ago, after gaining his release at the bail hearing with a $100,000 bond, guaranteed by Shallen's family, he had secured a meeting with the CEO, Chairman and Board of Directors of Softek. At first the Chairman wasn't receptive but, after only a few phones calls and threats, he finally consented to listen to Jason's ideas.

The last three days were well spent resting, enjoying quality time with his children, sorting out a few personal business details, and telling his side of the story to the media of how Senator Quest had used political power for personal gain. The FBI national security charges lingered in the back of his mind, where he would like them to be kept for a while. Fighting the US government would be for another day. In spite of the uncertainty of the future, to his relief, his life was slowly returning to some semblance of normalcy. Most of all, he relished showing off his newfound love, Shallen.

The picture of Senator Quest had been on the front page of every local, state and national paper. The debate started in earnest as expected. Two camps were immediately formed, one demanding his resignation and the other wanting to give him time to defend himself. Jason gave many interviews to radio, TV and newspapers. Despite the trials of the preceding days, he found he enjoyed the celebrity status and fame he had gained, which he expected wouldn't last too long. He felt like a different person.

When Jason entered the boardroom, the CEO, Chairman, and all other members were present. As he shook hands with everyone, he received a cordial smile and nod. They were all handpicked by the Senator, and none too thrilled by his presence. He felt like he was in enemy territory but he was there to make an offer that would benefit Softek, ex-employees and Corvallis, given the setback the company had suffered since the *LA Times* published the article linking the Senator to crime.

The room was large enough to contain a well-varnished table with twelve seats. It was well lit, its walls decorated with expensive artworks that collectors could only dream of owning. Jason took a seat between CEO Muhtar Gamble, and Chairman

Jim Peterson. He scanned the room, observing each of the faces. They were all pale and the men and women were well dressed in business attire.

"Jason, let's hear what you have to say," said the Chairman in a tone that lacked enthusiasm.

Jason cleared his throat. As he went through the list of items he wanted to go over, he pulled at his tie. Like laser beams, all eyes were on him. "After I left Corvallis last month, my life completely changed. I entered a war zone. I was engaged in many fights at the same time. I was fighting to survive. Fighting for my life, my children, my marriage. I was also fighting a politically corrupt system. Finally it boiled down to discovering a corruption scheme hatched by Senator Quest. Whether you support him or not, it's none of my business." He paused for a moment to clear his throat. "I'm here for a different reason." The media had launched an attack in recent days on Softek for outsourcing hundreds of jobs overseas. "How can Softek repatriate the jobs? Rehiring ex-employees would be the honorable thing to do, in my opinion." He turned to his left and to his right, gauging the leaders' reactions.

With his arm resting on his elbow, Gamble fingered his chin as everyone waited. He paused then gazed down before turning his attention back to those at the table. "That is certainly an option, but it would be difficult to do right away." He scanned the poker faces. Only the Chairman reacted with a nod.

Jason didn't want a fight, rather an amicable solution to what he had in mind. "You could start gradually, work up to re-hiring everyone."

"We can guarantee nothing until the board decides," said Gamble, giving no further assurance.

Jason needed a decision immediately. To him it seemed as if their minds were set like cement. They needed a hard blow from a sledge hammer to crack them open. "The way I see it, these jobs belong to Americans. I'm looking for a serious reply. My other option is to launch a class-action suit. And this time I have a nation behind me." The phrase "class-action suit" made all of them squirm in their seats. "I don't think that's the right way to go, and I prefer not to. But if I have to, I will."

"We can give you your job back," said Gamble.

Jason thought for a moment. "The economy is bad here in Corvallis," he said. "It's no better in the state or in the nation. People are talking about a deep recession, a possible depression. A class-action suit will put Softek deeper into financial trouble."

Another director said, "You've threatened us with a lawsuit before. What guarantee do we have that after you get what you want, you won't still sue us?"

Jason welcomed the question of his sincerity. "I'm glad you raised this issue, one that needs to be clarified. I will not break my promise. And I can put it in writing, announce it to the media or sign a legal document."

Another member at the back, said, "We can certainly consider everything you have said so far."

This group of men needed another strike of the hammer. "Going back to last December, when I was considering a lawsuit, the company stock price sank by thirty percent. With the ferocious media attack on both the Senator and Softek, regarding outsourcing, the stock has gone down by another thirty percent."

"Jason is making a good point," said Peterson. It appeared he understood where Jason was going.

Jason was looking for closure. "Do you think the board could consider my proposal and agree to it?"

The Chairman said, "That certainly can be done." He glanced around and Jason was gratified to see some nods, grimaces and hints of smiles; however, by the look of Gamble's rigid expression, it seemed he wasn't convinced.

Jason said, "When I look at neighborhoods in Oregon or California, they are littered with real estate signs and bank repos. These signs remind me of what Brian was thinking when he was about to lose his house after the layoff. I'm sorry for what he did. Should all the blame be placed on him? Or could it have been prevented? As we speak, others like Brian are living in agony of losing their homes and jobs."

With a huff of irritation, Gamble pointed his attention to Jason, signaling his impatience. Before anyone else had a chance to respond he interjected. "Softek is a business, not a charity organization."

"Does this board have a conscience? Everyone here has a job and home. How about those who don't?"

Peterson scanned the room as if he were gauging the reaction of others. "We should give it serious consideration."

Jason addressed the others at the far end, who so far hadn't indicated their thoughts. "Now that Softek doesn't have to donate anything to Quest's campaign fund – " he smiled – "it should have lots of money to spare. Don't you think?"

One director said, "That's true."

Jason scrolled through the list in his mind. He got up and leaned on the back of his chair. "Ahh. One more thing." He held his chin with his fingers. "A compensation package for the families of the victims. I met Mrs. Whitney, and she's in a desperate and scary situation. Who knows, there could be others like her."

Gamble adjusted the rim of his glasses and said, "We compensated her according to our company policy."

Jason said, "Looking beyond bottom lines and policies, and showing a little compassion could be seen as a good deed."

Peterson was listening attentively to what Jason was saying. In a friendly tone he said, "You have some good ideas." He placed the earpiece of his glasses between his lips momentarily and then waved the glasses in the air. "We'll discuss all the points that you've recommended immediately, and get back to you with a decision. We have a lot to consider."

Jason wasn't finished yet. He dropped the bomb. "One more thing. I promise it's the last one on my list. Replacing the CEO. And he should leave immediately without any golden parachute."

Gamble raised his voice. "This is ridiculous." He appealed to all the directors. "What is he doing? He wants to run this company now."

Jason said, "Something to consider. After implementing all the measures that I brought to the table, the Softek investors will be encouraged. I think the stock price will shoot up like a rocket. A good recovery will help your portfolio, if you own the stock." He assumed that they would own Softek. "You go ahead and discuss what I am asking. I'll need the Board's decision in writing, before I go to the media."

Jason left the boardroom with pleasure after his presentation. Now he just hoped the board would do the right thing.

Jason McDeere drove into the driveway of Kara's place. He was there to pick up his children and go to the movies as part of their Sunday bonding ritual. He reflected on this most bizarre happening, where two lives, unlikely to have come together in normal circumstances, had collided, sparking a series of events that altered the futures of both. He had uncovered corruption at the highest levels of US government, which took him on a path of deep despair. He shook his head at that thought.

The Senator had been indicted, after the FBI investigation was complete. The FBI case against Jason was still pending while his lawyer negotiated a deal with the Attorney General's office, whereby he would receive immunity if he could be used as a witness, should the case go to trial. *It's a long shot.* His friend Terrance was released without any charge. The Softek board of directors didn't want to sustain any more suffering, hence they agreed to all of Jason's requests.

Before getting out of the car, he also tried to remember the details of his mortgage refinance on his house, which Kara would definitely inquire about shortly after he saw her. The divorce settlement stipulated that he would give her half the amount of the current equity of his house in cash. As pieces of the divorce agreement were being settled, Jason suffered at the thought of the break-up, though on paper it had been finalized.

He pressed the doorbell and, within a moment, Kara appeared through the open doorway. "Come in," she said with a wave of her hand, expecting his visit.

The house was quiet as he stepped forward. He noticed a wooden elephant on the foyer floor. Kara always had shown good taste in home décor. Then he turned his attention to the reason he was there. "Where are the kids?"

After pressing her wristwatch with her finger she said, "They will be here any minute. My parents took them out for ice cream while I went grocery shopping."

Jason said, "You should put off buying a house, until prices stabilize. They're still going down."

She shrugged. "I'll think about it. I like to own my own house. Living in rentals makes me feel like I'm living a temporary existence. I like permanence. Did you talk to the bank?"

Jason nodded with a smile of satisfaction that he came prepared. "Yes. It's not easy getting a loan, mortgage or refinancing from a bank these days--"

"Come in to the kitchen. I'm doing dishes." She turned around and headed towards the kitchen.

He followed her. "Not like the good old days when they shoved money in peoples' pockets. With the credit freeze my bank wants to check everything. My job, credit rating, credit cards and on and on. In my case it will take some time as I'm transitioning my job from Layton Industries to Softek." He expected her to understand perfectly as she worked for a bank. He stood with his hand on the back of the chair and watched her place the dishes in the machine after rinsing them.

As Kara walked from the sink to the machine she froze. She leaned forward, her gloved hands holding two plates, her blues eyes pointed directly at Jason. "Hurry up and get the refinancing done. You know what the agreement says. I don't want you to procrastinate." She set the plates into the dishwasher.

He didn't need to be reminded. "Based on the agreement terms I have time. Hopefully, it will be done on or before the deadline," he said with as much sweetness as he could muster given the circumstance. Jason turned toward the front door, expecting to hear the sound of his children's voices any minute.

There was an awkward silence, except for the sounds of running tap water and the intermittent clicking of dishes. "People say you put the children in danger." She gave him a withering look.

Jason straightened, took a deep breath, ready to defend the accusation. "People. Who? Your parents? That's not fair."

"Jason, those guys, Volpa and the Senator, were after you. When they couldn't get you, they went after the children. You should have seen that coming – done something."

Jason gestured with open palms. "Something. Like what?"

"Just give up the lawsuit. That's what they wanted in the first place." Her voice grew louder to compensate for the noise from the tap.

Jason ignored her argument. It would have been cowardly to do nothing about the injustice. "Volpa kidnapped Sarah and Keenan. The Senator *hired* him," he said slowly. He shook his head hoping for Kara's agreement. "Both are crooks."

Standing by the sink, she closed the tap, no doubt wanting him to pay complete attention to her words. "You should have dropped the class-action suit like you were warned. But you didn't. You insisted on pursuing it – for money. Then you endangered the children's lives. Thank God, they weren't harmed. But who knows, it may have done damage that could show up in years to come."

Though he had to admit he was terrified when he'd heard that Sarah and Keenan had been kidnapped, he thought the argument was hypocritical. When she was promised part of the compensation, she had encouraged him to go ahead with the class-action suit. "Thank God there's no sign of injury, physical or emotional. I just hope it will stay that way."

She arranged the dishes in the dishwasher, placed powdered soap in the receptacles and, after pressing buttons, the machine started. "This person you brought with you. What's her name?" She raised her voice high enough to compensate for the machine noise.

"Shallen. What about her? Where are you going with this?"

"She's a lot younger than you," she said, frowning. "I'll admit she's very beautiful, but I don't think you should get into a serious relationship with anyone right now. If you ask me, you have a lot of work to do on yourself. That could take time and it isn't easy."

"Are you jealous?"

She scrubbed the sink with a sponge. "I'm not jealous. It's just that you're a bit of a chauvinist."

Jason had been accused of his gender superiority complex before. "Ok, I am. I admit it." He raised his hands. "I'll change for the sake of mankind."

"Jason, you should see a therapist. It will do you a lot of good. I know it will. I did an internal makeover on myself." She lowered her voice. "I've seen a lot of changes happening in me. After some *more* –" she emphasized the last word – "inner work with the help of my spiritual therapist, I will feel a lot more confident entering into a new relationship."

He listened carefully to Kara's advice. Ever since their marriage, they had been bickering over everything, big and small. Over time the love, understanding and tenderness of the relationship had gradually disappeared. Had he been too hard-edged, always bent on winning an argument? Had he taken enough responsibility for the children? Maybe he wasn't compassionate enough? For a long moment, he just watched as she meticulously cleaned the stove elements after tidying up the counter. Kara had always been an organized person. He took stock of his shortcomings. "It hasn't been easy for you in our relationship. And I'm sure I have hurt you in many ways along the way. I'm sorry."

"Life is a journey, a path of self-discovery. Sometimes we find out more about our strengths, other times about our weaknesses. See, you just became better aware of yourself." She cracked a faint smile despite the sheet of sadness covering her face.

Through the window facing the street, he saw a light green Malibu pulling into the driveway. "Your parents are here. I have to go." He said goodbye and walked outdoors.

In the driveway he exchanged cordial, but not too friendly, greetings with Kara's parents. After Jason had given Sarah and Keenan hugs and kisses, all three got into his car.

As Jason drove along Harrison Boulevard, he stopped for red lights at Arnold Way. He tapped the mid-section of his steering wheel as he took stock of how the kids were doing. Sarah was buried in a book as usual. A dog on the sidewalk, dragging a young boy by a leash, caught Keenan's attention. Then Jason returned to thinking about what Kara had said. But more importantly, he focused on how he felt. The spark that once existed between them, and kept the relationship alive during both sunny and rainy days, had disappeared. *It's time to move on.* When the traffic light changed to green he gunned the car.

***

Jason McDeere drove onto Circle Boulevard with Shallen in the passenger seat. Upon noticing a huge pine tree on the right, he tapped his brakes until the car came to a halt at the stop sign. Then he took a right turn on Witham Hill Drive. Going past a shelter made of four wooden poles supporting a roof, under which a bench sat empty, he went past houses with mature trees in the front yard. He knew he was getting closer to the cemetery. Jason slowed the car until it stopped at a spot covered with gravel and grass in front of a metal fence. No one was around.

After getting out of the car, he opened the backseat to pull out two floral bouquets, chosen by Shallen in a shop in Corvallis. Upon entering the gate, only five feet away from Witham Hill Drive, a row of tall pine trees blocked the view into the cemetery from the street, and another one did the same from a residential area. Jason surveyed the headstones, trying to remember where Brian's gravesite was located.

"There it is," he told Shallen, then pointed to a corner and continued walking.

Shallen, in lock step with him, held one of the bouquets. "I feel both sad and happy being here. Sad that Brian is gone and happy that he brought us together."

Jason didn't respond but agreed with her. As they walked, he reflected on the strange journey his life had taken over the past ten weeks since that tragic incident when Brian and six others were killed. He recognized the precise spot where his friend's body rested. The granite headstone marked:

Brian Jefferson Baldwin

September 12, 1963 - December 18, 2008

From His Creator he came

Unto Him he returned

Both observed a moment of silence. Jason bent down to rest the flowers on the ground next to the tombstone. Shallen blinked back a tear as she took a deep breath. Then she wiped her nose with a tissue.

Jason found the justice he was looking for. "Buddy, I miss you. After all the trouble Shallen and I had to go through, it was worth it. We got the crooks," said Jason with a trembling voice. He held Shallen's arm as they stood together in silence for many minutes. Finally, he gave her a gentle a tug, indicating it was time to move on.

Both wore jackets. Jason felt comfortable with the sun shining brightly and a gentle wind occasionally moving through the branches. He scrolled through his memory until he recalled the fatal moment. After losing his father, Jason had come with his mother and brother to this place on the yearly anniversary of his passing. For six years they had come. As the family grew older, the desire for regular visits dissipated to none.

The grave marker lay near a tree next to the property line. The stone bore his name: Fredrick John McDeere. Silently Jason read the epitaph,

NOTHING'S SO SACRED AS HONOR

AND

NOTHING SO LOYAL AS LOVE

Jason pointed to the grave where Shallen placed the flowers on his father's final resting place. She straightened and joined her hands together in front of her, her eyes fixed on the ground.

A few moments went by as they stood in silence with his gaze fixed way above the green tree tops gently swaying back and force as the wind danced around the cemetery. Then Jason lowered his gaze towards the Rolex and tracked the movement of the minute hand for a long moment until he was ready. Myriad memories flashed back and forth, a review of a whole life of grief and joy. With a soft click he loosened the gold-plated silver band. Slowly he slid the Rolex off his wrist. He touched the gold-plated ornament with his lips. Then, his heart heavy as a rock, he placed the watch on the marker over Fred's name.

He turned to Shallen. "Let's go"

With a shocked expression, she pointed to the Rolex. "What about the watch?"

In some thirty years in his possession, Jason couldn't remember going a day without wearing it . . . except for that brief time he'd had to hock it to buy Christmas presents. "It's staying here," he said with a satisfied smile. "Let's go. I'll tell you why, latter."

She stood still for a moment as if decoding his action. "Jason, tell me now. I want to hear." She weaved strands of hair around her ear and her light brown eyes opened wide, waiting to hear the mystery behind the watch.

Jason combed his hair with his fingers, his eyes on the rooftops beyond the fence. "My father died," he said, exhaling a deep breath and watching vapor rise from his mouth, "when I was twelve. It happened suddenly."

Shallen appeared to be absorbing his words with sadness. "What happened?"

"He had a heart attack." It was as if his mind and heart were passing through turbulence, resisting collapse as recollections of past trauma rushed back at him. Although his lips were slightly parted, he couldn't speak, even if he'd wanted to. Hurled upon him with the intensity of a hurricane were memories of hatred, exclusion and injustice. As though crushed by torrents from a broken dam, the memories poured in on him. Many years ago, while in his early twenties, Jason had confidently brought these negative thoughts under control, all boxed in and hidden deep in a dark corner of his psyche, never to be opened. Never. Now, in front of Shallen, they all came rushing back. He stared at the rooftops, body motionless, unaware of his surroundings as he battled the negative forces inside. It took a few long moments that seemed like an eternity to finally halt the sinking feeling. He gripped his lips tight to stifle a cry and blinked back tears. "In a jail cell...in Salem." In a low trembling voice the words finally came out in a broken stream. "I found out when I returned home from school."

As if sensing Jason's pain, she studied his face with intensity. She squeezed his shoulder. "It must have been terrifying."

With tight lips, he nodded. "When he was gone I was very angry and sad." He rubbed his eyes. "We were close. Like pals. Did everything together. He took me fishing every summer, just me, and to a drive-in once a week." The positive memories of this father lifted his spirit, but only slightly.

Her expression suggested she wanted more, that she was ready to drill down into the details. "Was he sick?" she asked, her undivided attention on his face, eyes widened and brows lifted in concern.

His heartbeat was still racing. "No. Very healthy. It just occurred unexpectedly."

"Jason, why…why was he in jail?" she said in a sympathetic tone, totally devoid of judgment.

He rubbed his chin, preparing a response, and blew out a short, low whistle. "He was found guilty of murdering Ray Barnes." He looked at Shallen's eyes, still glistening as the sunlight landed on them, which opened like a doorway into her soul. Trustworthiness sat inside her. A reassurance blew over him, lending courage for him to open himself and bear his soul. He shook his head. "He denied it…completely."

With a nod, she said, "Okay…what was the evidence against your dad? How did you feel about it?" Jason didn't mind the journalistic probing. It was a catharsis.

"All circumstantial. Fabrications." He straightened his back, pressed his neck muscles and shifted the weight of his body from one foot to the other. "We believed him, of course. Barnes, a politician and businessman, was opposed to certain land development, which wasn't viewed kindly by some organizations. Criminals. My father believed that they killed Barnes and framed him. That's the truth. I swear."

"I believe you. From my own experience, these things happen. Journalists often risk their lives to uncover injustice in the police system," said Shallen, in a soft voice, slowly. "Was there ever any connection between Barnes and your dad?"

"Politically, they were in different camps. Dad publicly criticized him a few times, which wasn't unusual." He had regained some of the energy in his voice. "Unfortunately, he happened to be in the neighborhood where Barnes was found killed in his car."

"Jason, what did his defense attorney do?"

"The lawyer put up a good fight. But Dad didn't have an alibi. The jury found him guilty and the judge put him in jail for twenty years."

"Then what happened?" Shallen's head tilted towards his and her eyebrows arched.

"One month after he went to jail, he was found dead in his cell. Of an apparent heart attack. A total shock. A big event in Corvallis. Then the *Corvallis Gazette Times* investigated the case. It found that the case was completely botched. They never looked for any other suspect, though the murder weapon was never found. The witnesses who testified seeing my father leaving the scene have since disappeared from the planet. The paper couldn't find them. The prosecutor didn't present a thread of evidence. The Gazette concluded that the gang that killed Barnes also played a role in murdering my father. There was clear evidence the cops did a shoddy job. The article came close to accusing the sheriff of being in the gangsters' pocket. You should read the newspaper article."

"Who were these gangsters?" Shallen's listened her eyes wide.

"The Morolto crime family of Chicago. The mob. After Barnes' death, the zoning was changed and construction by Aecon Development, owned by Morolto, breezed through."

"I've heard of this mob. It was taken out many years ago in a territorial war," said Shallen. "Yes, I'll read the article. How did you feel about it?"

"Losing my dad was agonizing but what happened afterwards was even worse."

A pickup truck revving its engine on Witham Hill Drive momentarily distracted her, not that she was uninterested, rather it seemed she needed time to absorb what she had heard. "I'm listening," she said softly, care wrapped in her words.

"The rumor mill spun out of control in Corvallis, branding us as the family of a murderer. Neighbors, friends and strangers suddenly distanced themselves from my mother, brother and me. At school my brother and I were constantly bullied and ostracized."

Shallen shook her head with Jason's every word as if she understood Jason's pain. "My grandfather often told us that it is the heat of the fire that turns soft iron into steel. He went through immense suffering at the hands of others."

Jason nodded.

"I have been told that the Great Being will never test you beyond your capacity," she added, taking his hand in hers. Compassion filled her complexion, graced by smile.

Sometimes he wondered if that were true. He wasn't out of the fire yet. Now he had to fight the US government's National Security charges. Setting that thought aside, for the moment, he said, "The punishment we received at school and from our neighbors crushed me. I was skipping school, staying by myself. My brother John asked me what was eating at me."

Jason had never felt such a bond with another human as he did Shallen. Words fell short, terribly short.

"How old was your brother when it happened?"

"Fourteen – three years older than me." He took another deep breath and eyed the flowers on the ground. "I asked why Dad left us and where he went. His answer was 'to be with God.' I thought God was punishing us for the things we did wrong."

"Wrong? Like what?"

"Like skipping school, smoking and using bad words. That kind of thing."

"But you know that's not true, don't you?"

He shrugged his shoulders in agreement. "Of course," he said. "As I grew older I understood an offense was committed against my family. With time I was able to shake off the explanations that John gave. But two things remained. Guilt and injustice. I felt partly to blame for his death." He could laugh about it now. "It sounds silly, but it was so ingrained in me that it was part of me. I just couldn't get rid of it until now." His whole body relaxed. With a genuine smile, he turned his gaze to a gravesite at the other end of the cemetery. "Finally, I'm free. Thanks to Brian. Brian and Rocky stayed my friends since my father died. They never quavered in their friendship to me. It was solid like a rock. Both will always be my friends."

Shallen's black hair shimmered beneath the bright sunshine. Her eyes remained wide but a bit less than before. "What about the watch?" she said with tenderness.

Jason admired her from top to bottom. The sunlight danced in her eyes. Her skin vibrated with fresh color and wisps of dark black hair gently blew as the wind passed through it. His heart was filled with pride for sharing this moment with her. *She is beautiful.* "Dad gave me the Rolex a few months before he passed away," he said, his voice slow and calm. "Last Christmas I sold it at a pawn shop and used the money to buy Sarah and Keenan gifts. After several months of working at Layton, I was able to afford to buy back the Rolex from the pawn shop, to keep his memory alive."

Her eyes were locked on his face. "Most unusual story," she said, her expression one of awe.

"Despair hit me the hardest in the hotel room in Mountain View. It was the night we met, after I broke into Volpa's website. In my darkest hour in the hotel room Dad came to me in a vision and showed me how to get into the site."

"But, why? Why leave the watch? Someone will take it."

"Giving it back to him, rather than keeping it, releases the guilt. To give something that's dearest has the greatest significance."

She wrapped him tight in her arms, her head tilted towards his. "Let's go." Tears rolled down her cheeks but she didn't bother wiping them.

They walked together in silence, except for the whisper of the wind. Just before reaching the gate, she turned to him. "I admire your courage."

Jason didn't speak. He raised his head. The wind spoke for him.

V. M. Gopaul loves fiction writing. It's his new passion.

As a software and database specialist, Gopaul wrote seven books for IT professionals. He then turned his attention to writing two books on spirituality, which paved the way for a hidden passion to emerge. When crafting and completing *Tainted Justice*, a lifelong dream of Gopaul has now become reality. He also wanted to be different; only time will tell if he is successful. One thing is for sure: everyday life struggle and triumph that all of us face come alive in this first novel. He is bent on giving his readers a satisfying experience.

As this books goes into print, Gopaul is planning to write three more thrillers. Stay tuned at http://www.vmgopaul.com

Gopaul, married and father of two children, lives in Newmarket, Ontario, Canada.

Published by FastPencil
http://www.fastpencil.com